Paris, Picasso and Me

S. F. TAYLOR

To Lynn

Best wishes

Sue

Also by S. F. Taylor

NON-FICTION TITLES

HORNSEA REMEMBERS

...the bravery of its men who lost their lives in the First World War.

THIS SQUALID LITTLE ROOM

Lawrence of Arabia's stays in Hornsea, East Yorkshire at the end of his career in the RAF.

CRUMBS ON THE CARPET

First World War poet Wilfred Owen's last year of life in Scarborough before his death in France in 1918

Fiction Titles

SHADOW CHILD

Theft and a murder in 1669 culminate in a final act of revenge over 300 years later

Paris, Picasso and Me

"The meaning of life is to find your gift. The purpose of life is
to give it away."

Pablo Ruiz Picasso

A Southfield Writers/Coffeehouse Publication

Copyright @ S.F. Taylor 2023

ISBN: 978-1-8382517-5-8

Cover design: Thom Strid

Printed in Great Britain

Acknowledgments

Thank you once again to Mandi Allen of The Coffeehouse Writer for her continual support and guidance. This has meant that the second novel was completed in a fraction of the time it took the first.

Thank you to Thom Strid for a brilliant cover design, and for his continued support and suggestions.

And finally, thank you to my beta readers:
Pamela Curtis, Tricia Clarkson, Chris Priestnall, Thom Strid and Mandi Allen

Chapter One

June 1932

Following eighty years of success and great acclaim, the Georges Petit Gallery, Paris in latter years was criticised as 'overblown' and 'ornate'.

Pablo Ruiz Picasso did not see it that way; to him it was perfect. Visits to the Matisse exhibition the year before had left him hungering for a retrospective exhibition of his own, and at fifty years of age, on 16th June 1932, he achieved exactly that.

Works from 1900, produced by a struggling Picasso newly arrived in Paris, nestled amongst others so recent that the paint had barely dried. Two hundred and twenty-five paintings, seven sculptures and six illustrated books confirmed his position as a major force of 20th-century art.

· · ·

As the grand opening approached, he knew that success was by no means assured, but the exhibition was in no doubt his own doing and it was presented to the world as *he* saw fit: full of contradiction, with little reference to sequence or style. Picasso took charge, arranging a collection that appeared random and mismatched; an exhibition where chronology flew out of the window. This was personal and works from private collections sat alongside those from dealers. On the eve of opening, he was satisfied; he'd done all that he wanted and announced, 'I will go to the movies tomorrow!'

George Fenton was one such dealer providing works, a Londoner with family connections to the Georges Petit Gallery, a man who believed that he was named after the original owner of the Gallery who knew his father well. The fine Picasso in his possession was made available for loan by request and took its allotted place. It had rarely been in public, it was too personal. Everything was personal that day.

Chapter Two

April 1998

'Go see to your Mother Olivia...she's not stopped blubbing all morning,' Dad spoke more in exasperation than any desire to get involved with his wife's crying. Never happy with extremities of emotion, he sought solace in taping up the rest of the packing boxes which was much safer ground. Liv reluctantly went upstairs and found Barbara in Bee's bedroom, gathering up the last of the clothes she'd washed the day before and spent the morning ironing.

'Look at this! Four odd socks. Your Dad's just the same. I can never do a wash without ending up with odd socks.'

Liv took the socks from her and stuffed them into an already full bag.

'It doesn't matter Mum, I'm not moving to the other end of the world...you and Dad can bring the waifs and strays when you come to visit.'

Barbara looked pained, as if she had let everyone down.

'I know that love...it's just...'

'Just nothing...think about the positives, your washing machine won't be on half as much.'

'That doesn't matter...it's...it's such a big change...it'll be so quiet round here.' Barbara rummaged up her sleeve for a hanky and blew hard.

'Mum! You've been asking for a bit of peace and quiet for as long as I can remember.'

'This is different Olivia...I'll miss that bairn...and you.' she added quickly.

'Please don't cry...you'll set me off and Bee won't understand if we're all sad. This is supposed to be a happy day remember.'

'I know...you're right...get yourself off love...but I should be helping you with the move. Today of all days.'

'Oh there'll be plenty of time for you to help out soon but you know Dad's not well enough right now and I'd rather you came when things have settled down...anyway I've got Dom and Patrick.'

'Dom's been a great help...lovely man...but you will let me know if you're short of anything won't you?'

'I will I promise...I love you Mum...you and Dad have been so good...getting me back on my feet...I wouldn't have got this far without you two.'

'Oh get away with yer before the waterworks start up again,' and Barbara's eyes filled with tears that were ready to fall once again.

'I'm going to miss you...but I am looking forward to a new start...and cooking for you in my own kitchen.'

Barbara raised an eyebrow; she wasn't too sure about the cooking part but managed a smile after giving her nose another blow.

'Where's your Dad got to now? I told him to stop fretting over those boxes.'

'I think they're all done and packed.'

Outside, a van's horn let them know that they were ready to be off. Every available space was filled with furniture and items that had either come from Barbara and Arthur's loft or been taken out of circulation on the assurance that they were surplus to their needs. The latter was debatable but accepted nevertheless. The budget was tight and Liv had reached the stage where she appreciated anything she could get.

On her part, Barbara thrived on frugality; she loved nothing more than making limited means stretch beyond their expected capacity. 'Barbs it's not wartime y'know...we're not scraping burnt bits off toast any more,' Arthur had complained more than once, but it was said only half in jest. Taking in Liv and a baby had meant tightening the purse strings at times, although the comfort and security they gave to Liv was heartfelt and genuine. The past had been turbulent enough and now there was enough of her mother in Liv for her to see what they had gone through too.

Between them, Liv and Barbara rescued many items from the charity shops in town. 'It's all good stuff in here,' her mother reassured her when the whiff of age and elderly owner-ship reached Liv's nose. But they lived on the fringes of an affluent area and it showed in quite a few decent finds they'd picked up.

Robert wasn't convinced about the move of course, but then he always managed to make everything Liv planned sound like a bad idea. He'd been happy enough knowing she and Bee were living with her parents; satisfied with the regular access he had to his daughter once the divorce was finalised; but something changed when she told him she would be moving away to be on her own with Bee.

Having survived what she hoped would be the worst of what life had to throw in her direction, Olivia Smithson found herself standing at the front of 59 South Street, chewing on a broken fingernail. She and Bee had arrived by taxi and Dom and Patrick weren't far behind in the van. Two plastic bags sat waiting at her feet while she took in the house and the enormity of the achievement. The sold sign drooped like a stumbling drunk so Liv pulled it out and lay it down on what purported to be a lawn.

'Well I've made it this far', she said as she wiped the mud off her hands, a half smile playing across her lips. It was an amazing achievement, up against innumerable odds; a long and arduous journey with pitfalls too dark to escape without some remnant of pain still trailing behind. But here she was. The words of Elton John, heard on the radio that morning rang through her head, 'I'm still standing.' The smile turned to a laugh. It had to be a good omen, didn't it?

For the first time, Liv took more notice of the garden: a far cry from the well-tended plot at the neat little semi they'd left behind, or even Robert's immaculate lawn. Here, the weeds had claimed squatters' rights and the only sign of cultivation was an occasional daffodil poking its nodding yellow head above couch grass and dandelions. 'I know exactly how you feel,' she murmured and hummed the Elton John tune as the taxi disappeared down the road. Liv picked up her bags and looked up at the impatient little girl who had already bounded up the steps to the front door. This was their house, hers and Bee's.

Beatrice Rose, otherwise known as Bee was the saving grace of a life that had struggled, like the swaying daffodils, to rise up and be seen after six years of suppression. Overcoming death and divorce, as well as the ignominy of moving back in with her parents, this small house with its overgrown garden and peeling paintwork was where a new life, and new hopes, would begin. Here was the opportunity to get back the person she had once been and reclaim the life she would choose for herself. If there was any cause for anxiety, it would be over the future of the little girl waiting at the top of the steps, the one whose patience was diminishing by the second.

The old house might have peeling paintwork, dirt-smeared windows and weeds, unlike the immaculate house next door, but it was hers. Relief and happiness washed over in waves as she embraced the moment.

Clutching an old stuffed toy in one hand and a small bag in the other, Bee jumped up and down, 'Come on, come on, come on...Mummee!' with her four-year-old's exuberance.

From the gleaming front window of the house next door, a net curtain twitched and slightly lifted, and the elderly face of Frances Fenton looked out. Curiosity had got the better of her when she'd heard the taxi door slam shut and she could finally get a look at her new neighbours. Despite Bee's demand for attention, Liv noticed the movement and gave a small wave in her direction, but at that same time the curtain dropped back into place and her face withdrew into shadows behind.

'Mummee...hurry up. I want to see my new room!'

'Coming sweetie'

A fresh spring breeze blew Bee's brown curls around her flushed cheeks, and bright blue eyes registered every bit of excitement of what she'd been promised. Tall for her age, she sported trousers that already sat above her ankles; what she lacked in bulk, she more than made up for in height. 'I've seen more fat on a sparrer's kneecap,' Grandad had said as the marks on the bedroom doorframe rose with the passing months. Bee, perplexed, made a point of looking out at the sparrows on the bird table to try and discover if they really did have kneecaps.

'Just like our Olivia at that age, Barbs.'

Any worries Liv had felt over the move evaporated; it was an adventure she told Bee and the squeals of a happy child were all she needed to hear. It amazed her how well Bee had reacted to moving away from the home she'd known for all but four months of her life, but the promise of a big bedroom, new friends and a myriad of other temptations helped pave the way.

Liv put the key into the lock and pushed at a resisting door.

'What on earth is behind this door Bee? Come on...give it a big push, you're much stronger than I am.'

They giggled and shoved at the door until it gave way. Inside, a pile of junk mail advertising pizzas, burgers, builders and taxi firms, had wedged beneath.

'Goodness Bee, they must really like us to send all this.'

The last visit had been with Barbara and Arthur when Bee was with Robert. The house had been unlived in for almost two years but the estate agent insisted that it was definitely a sound investment. All agreed that it was ideal for her needs in terms of cost, size and location, and the agent emphasised that the area was 'ripe for regeneration.' In other words, he wanted it off his books when the past two offers had been withdrawn. Olivia Smithson's basic survey ensured that she was his perfect buyer.

The house was nothing like the home they'd left that morning, but Liv was far too happy to worry about what needed doing and determined that the move would work for both of them. Envelopes and flyers were scooped up and the door closed behind them. Bee raised her nose and sniffed.

'What's that funny smell Mummy?'

'Mm...not sure about that, Bee, but don't worry, I'll soon have it smelling as sweet as grandma's...I'll open a few windows, let the fresh air in and the stinkies out.' Bee was only half listening when thoughts quickly moved to more pressing matters. Still clutching her toy and bag she announced 'I want to find my room Mummy,' and she ran up stairs that faced the front door before Liv could stop her.

'Careful up there Bee...I'll be with you in a sec.'

Liv went down the hall to the kitchen and dumped heavy bags of food on a table that had been left behind. The remains of last night's cottage pie had been packed in a large margarine tub and carrots, green beans and a bag of apples tumbled out alongside. 'That's tonight sorted,' she thought.

The kitchen was an annexe at the back of the house, an afterthought when the original had been so tiny. There was still a good-sized garden however, even though it was just as overgrown as the front. The table and chairs left behind were welcome, if worse for wear. Arthur had already announced that he would give them a lick of paint, 'Good solid pine Olivia...can't go wrong there.' And her Mother, standing behind him, cast her eyes upwards, thinking of all the other jobs he'd promised to do at home and was yet to complete.

Liv took a deep breath at the sight of the grime on the cooker and a small worm of doubt wriggled inside. Was there a reason no one else saw the potential they had? Taking on the house after only one brief viewing had been a risk, but it was one she readily took when the prospect of independence pushed aside any doubts. The final clinch had been the reduction in price. Arthur and Barbara worked out that they could afford to pay the deposit after all, and once the survey gave it the all-clear; it was too good an opportunity to miss. Despite Robert's repeated protestations of where it was, Liv was certain it was the right decision. Time after time she'd had to argue her case against his all-consuming doubts over their daughter's future welfare. It was exhausting.

Liv opened the fridge door and although empty, the smell gave the impression that the last contents must have been festering in there for some time. She made a mental list of action: open windows, clean fridge, sort kitchen,'

Make a list of what you want to do and write it down Olivia, it will help you cope; wasn't that the advice both Marion and Dom, her mainstays on the road to recovery, repeatedly advised? However, jobs were soon put on hold at the sound of a loud yell from upstairs,

'Mummee! Quick!'

More often than not, Bee's squeals came after nothing more serious than a bumped knee or lost toy, but this sounded serious. She found Bee standing over a large dead spider at the foot of a small bed beneath the window; little hands covering much of her face. Her horror however was not because it was a spider, but that it sat in a pool of water and was dead. Liv picked it up by one of its remaining legs and dropped it outside a window. Bee was not consoled.

'It's ok Bee...the spider was dead...he's gone now.'

Bee loved spiders. Ever since Grandad taught her about them from the books they read together; spiders were a fascinating subject. They loved to save them when grandma's first instinct was to suck them up the vacuum cleaner.

'Did he drown? What if there are more, Mummy? What if he had a big family? How will they manage now?'

'Bee, he was an old spider...he lived on his own. He didn't drown...his family had all gone to find homes of their own and left him in peace and quiet. He had a good life, undisturbed by noisy children running around. He was one of the lucky ones.'

'Oh...' she said and fell silent for a moment to register what she was being told. Liv's impromptu stories always held answers to life's problems. If only mine were all so easily solved, she sighed and looked around the room.

The bed frame was old, but on top sat a new mattress Dom had delivered the week before. It lay in wait with its plastic covering still intact. It had been raining that day and droplets of water remained from when it was brought in. There had been no opportunity to do a clean before the move, let alone make up a bed. Arthur's heart scare put a stop to their coming over again and Liv convinced them that the house wasn't that bad. But it was bad enough. Bee's room would be first on the list to clean although the little girl's mind was still on the spider,

'I'll do a picture of him so I can remember him...and his family.'

'That would be a lovely thing to do BeeBee but it'll have to wait until we get all your things. Come on downstairs...Uncle Dom should be here soon.'

'Mummy my room is gorgeous! It's so big...is this really all mine? A big room just for me?'

It wasn't; the plan had been to move the single bed to the smaller of the bedrooms, but Liv didn't have the heart to burst her bubble of excitement and agreed that 'yes, it could be.'

'Love it...Love it...Love it...and Wabbit does too...and we have big walls to put up *all* my paintings now. You promised Mummy...can we put them *all* up on the wall?'

She clapped her hands and danced around the room, the spider now forgotten.

At Barbara and Arthur's, Bee's paintings, limited to a framed corkboard, had long outgrown the space it offered. 'Everything in its place Olivia' was the mantra Liv had heard throughout her own childhood, and inevitably, it was passed on to an uncomprehending Bee.

From inside her coat pocket, Bee pulled out the stuffed toy she'd been carrying since leaving home and sat it on the bed. It had one eye and a torn, partially repaired ear, but had been an essential part of her life since she was four months old. Originally intended for another child, it had been rescued before it could be taken to a charity shop eight years earlier. The rabbit had pacified a crying Bee and she had never let him go since then, despite all efforts to replace it.

The toy never failed to evoke painful memories whenever Liv saw it, but she kept herself in check and the years softened them. Whatever toys were mislaid, lost or gone beyond a state of repair, Wabbit as he had been called as soon as Bee could speak a close proximity to rabbit, stayed firmly put.

Liv picked up her giggling daughter and swung her around.

'We'll make this the best room ever BeeBee.'

Chapter Three

As the cleaning began in earnest, Liv's mobile rang. Fishing it out of her pocket, she looked at the caller's name and groaned. Robert. Already. She hadn't even wanted a mobile phone, but he'd bought it for her anyway when he knew the move would happen. He wanted to be able to call any time. 'It's so I can talk to Bee and make access arrangements'. Her finger hovered briefly over reply before dismissing it. You can wait, she thought, promising herself she would get back to him later.

The call brought on a wave of agitation; like Pavlov's dog, she never failed to respond to the signals. 'Give me a chance to move in first Rob. We're supposed to be left in peace, today at least, unless it's really urgent,' and he'd agreed, so what could he possibly want? His views on the area they were about to live in had been made perfectly clear even when she insisted that it wasn't as bad as he made out; and what they missed in the so called 'nice' part of town, they more than made up for in having a home of their own, and one that offered a good sized bedroom each. What on earth could be so urgent?

Since the day she'd moved out of the home they had once shared, he'd never stopped fretting about Bee. Through her breakdown and recovery, the redeeming factor was that Bee, as well as Liv, was being well looked after by two loving parents and grandparents. Robert could not find fault there, and was even grateful for a time. He saw his daughter on a regular basis, just as they agreed: every other weekend, and holidays to be decided between them, but something changed since he heard about the move. More than once, he'd suggested he should take over full custody, 'You'll never cope on your own, Liv.' No doubt Robert would be building up a dossier of objections after he'd seen exactly where they had moved to, but 'that's his problem and not mine,' she said to her parents when Robert had told them about what he believed would be best for his daughter. Of course, Barbara and Arthur were horrified at the thought, 'He'll never manage that lass,' her father had said, 'how can he work full time and look after a little girl?' But Robert's circumstances were not the same as they had been; he now had a wife and another baby at home. Liv looked at the phone before stuffing it back into her pocket, aware that she would not have managed even that a few months ago. 'I don't care how much of a cosy nest you've got with Marsha the Magnificent, Robert. Bee stays with me'.

At the mention of Daddy and Marsha, Bee looked up from searching for more spiders

'Is Daddy coming here...with Marsha?'

'No darling...you'll see Daddy next weekend.'

Marsha the Magnificent had been so named when Liv saw how well endowed Robert's new young wife was, compared to her, but did not believe Marsha was entirely in her husband's corner on wanting Bee, despite all he said. She'd not missed the look on Marsha's face at the start of the New Year, when the move was first suggested. As she sat struggling to feed baby Eddie, she wouldn't contribute, or corroborate any of what Robert was telling her. Arthur had taken Liv to collect Bee and waited in the car that day. He preferred to leave them to sort things out for themselves and the newly resolved Liv thought she had nipped it in bud. Even so, Robert still managed to invoke the same nagging doubts of old. At one time, they would pierce through her resolve like a knife through butter, but she was gaining strength to face him. It was time to leave that merry-go-round of oppression.

'Come on Bee, let's go look out for Uncle Dom.'

Robert's call was followed by a text, a perfunctory 'Call me' but that too was ignored. 'Not. Urgent,' and she prodded delete. 'You'll see Bee soon enough at the weekend and can play happy families in your lovely home, with the baby and Marsha-the-even-more-Magnificent now she's feeding a baby.' She felt just a twinge of guilt at naming Marsha that way but not envy. Despite Robert's pleading, she would never have gone back to their old life together.

Bee, bored of waiting for Liv to put the phone away, was exploring the other rooms.

'Bee? Where have you got to? Come on...I'm going downstairs.'

Liv went back to the kitchen, in need of a hot drink. Of course, there was no kettle yet, and even if she'd managed to bring it with her, no cup to make anything in. Teabags, yes, and chocolate biscuits for Bee, but no milk either. The biscuits were a luxury maybe but definitely needed on a day like today. There would never be money left over from the tight budget for more than essentials, either now or in the foreseeable future, but the luxury of a home that boasted so many other plusses was luxury enough. Even the thought of not sleeping in a single bed was a thrill; that and not having to get a bus every time she needed something from the shops. Having a supermarket just down the road was definitely on the luxury list.

Liv's phone rang again, but this time it was Dom. As she

answered, another yell from Bee informed her that she now needed the bathroom.

'Hi Dom...everything ok?'

'Hi, my lovely...just wanted to make sure that you're in.'

'Just arrived.'

'And we are a mere two minutes away from paradise...'

'Mm...not sure about that but it's definitely an amazing space.'

'See you soon then gorgeous...get that kettle on, we're parched.'

Liv was about to tell him that the kettle was behind him in the box marked 'kitchen' when a second plaintive cry came from the bathroom,

'Mummee...no paper!'

'Gotta go Dom...Bee emergency...I'll see you soon.'

She hung up before he could say more and with relief found half a packet of tissues still in her coat pocket. Toilet rolls had not been on the list, but she smiled to herself when she remembered that the Co-op was just a five-minute walk away. It was another happy thought and with it, Robert's call was pushed out of her head.

Bee was sorted and now stared impatiently out of the front room window, hopping from one foot to the other, eyes focused on the road as cars and trucks sailed by. A disappointed sigh was given at each one that passed. Eventually, however, a battered white van pulled up and Dom jumped out of the driver's seat.

'Mummy they're here', she yelled excitedly and ran to the front door, rattling at the knob until it opened.

'Hey buzzy Bee! How are you?'

Dom whisked up a giggling Bee for one of his big-bear hugs. She put her arms around his neck and stared into his face.

'Have you got all my things Dom?...I can't wait for you to

see my new room...its all mine except I found a dead spider near the bed when we came but Mummy told me he was old and his family were ok and they've gone to live somewhere else so it's all mine now and I'm going to do a drawing of them to put on the wall...'

'Whoa...whoa...slow down poppet...let me get my breath... where is Mummy?'

Liv appeared from the kitchen with a welcoming smile and wide-open arms.

'Mummy's here...hi Dom...thank you so much for this.'

They hugged and kissed. Even though they had only seen each other an hour earlier, it was more in celebration of their arrival and the long-awaited day.

'How's it going, Liv? Your big move...everything ok in here?'

Dom's forehead glistened with sweat before he wiped it with a fresh hankie. Bee clung to his arm.

'It's perfect...well maybe not quite perfect...tiny, tiny leak coming from somewhere in the kitchen...and the décor leaves a lot to be desired...plus we've no furniture yet...but apart from that I am so happy to be here.'

'You're not on your own my lovely Liv...you know that. I can give you a hand with anything you need doing next weekend.'

'Thank you ...I love you Dominic Raywell.'

'Right, that's enough with the sentimental crap...we have furniture to unload and throats as parched as the Sahara.'

'Ah the kettle...you'll find that in one of the boxes marked kitchen and Bee and I will pop to the shop...oh you don't know how much I love to be able to say that...we'll pop to the shops for milk...which I forgot to bring. Won't be two minutes...it's just down the road, then we'll help unload.'

'Ok...we'll make a start with the kitchen boxes then...kettle and mugs.'

Dom smiled at the rumpled figure with the wild blonde hair hopelessly working its way from a loosely tied ponytail. A streak of black dirt was smeared along one of Liv's cheeks, which he gave a quick rub with his thumb.

'Thanks, Pops!'

At fifty-nine he was old enough to be her father, even if he did not look his years, but the protective side of Dom's nature meant that in loco parentis wasn't too far from the truth. In finding strength behind the vulnerability, he was her staunch support in times of need.

'Was it really necessary to climb the chimney yourself to clean it...I'm sure there are little boys you can hire by the hour to do that...or little girls...'

He swung around and looked down at Bee, now pulling at his arm to drag him away,

'...about the size of this one here I would say...'

He made to grab her and chased the shrieking Bee to her room before the disembodied voice of Patrick shouted out.

'Don't forget this van has to be back for five.'

'Hi Patrick,' Liv called back, 'we're on it.'

'Right then...back to business...I'd better get out there. Bee if you don't let me go you won't get your stuff and that spider won't get painted.'

Liv eventually succeeded in getting a coat back on to the objecting Bee with the promise of chocolate biscuits for when they got back, and both set off in search of milk and toilet rolls at the Co-op. A quick check on the money in her purse confirmed that they were ok for cash and she smiled when she realised that her Dad had slipped in a couple of extra notes.

On their way out, Liv spotted an envelope stuck halfway through the letterbox. It had no name and no stamp, just a scrawled handwritten address with the words ' to the new occupants' at the top. It didn't look like the usual junk mail so she pushed it deep into her jacket pocket to open later.

The Co-op was not too small, perhaps not as expansive as the big supermarket two miles away, but the people were friendly enough to welcome a new face and Liv took comfort in that. Bee was even given a lollipop by a kind young woman behind the counter. She wore a name badge that said Debbie and she obviously liked children.

'Well, I hope that you come and see me again little Bee. I've got a friend who's just had a baby boy, but he can't talk as well as you just yet.'

'What's his name?'

'He's called Edward.'

Liv was turned to the shelves and checking out the array of bakery items for future reference. There was a good selection.

'Right BeeBee time to go...say 'bye to Debbie.'

Payment was made and they set off back with Bee contentedly sucking on her lollipop.

'She's a nice lady. She said her friend's got a baby but he can't talk yet.'

'My, you're good at finding out more than I do.'

The afternoon became a blur of activity; furniture and boxes were unloaded and taken to the right rooms; tea and biscuits served; and furniture shifted around again when Liv couldn't make up her mind where it should go. Bee was happy in her bedroom where toys and clothes were soon allocated their own spaces. Liv marvelled at the unexpected tidiness of her daughter when she popped her head around the door and saw what she had done.

'Wow! You have been the busy Bee.'

'I hope we stay here forever Mummy but I want Grandma and Grandpa to come soon to see my room...they will love it... and Grandma won't tell me off for not putting things away.'

'I'm sure she won't sweetie...anyway, Dom and Patrick are going now if you want to come and say 'bye'.

The two men stood waiting by the door when they came

out; Bee ran to Dom and he swept her up off her feet to give her a final hug.

'Now you look after your Mummy won't you?'

'I will...but she has to look after me too you know.'

'Oh, I know that Miss Beatrice Rose.'

Dom turned to Liv as Patrick made jokes to Bee about the state of her dress.

'You take good care, Liv and I'll see you very soon...I'm just a call away if you need anything.'

'I know that Dom...someone must have been smiling down on me the day you came into my life.'

'Seems a lifetime ago now...you're a different person Liv. Don't rush things though...take it slow and it'll all fall into place...take my word for it.'

'I will.'

Liv went with them to the door.

'Supper here soon...I promise...when I've got myself sorted...and I can't thank you enough too Patrick... for everything you've done for me today. You are amazing.' Liv took his hands in hers.

'You tryin' to make me cry Liv Smithson? Save it for that novel you're workin' on...that bestseller that's gonna make you a fortune and haul your writer friends up there with you.'

'I wish...and you'll be first up there with me...you and Dom'

'Get away with ya'.'

Patrick plonked a kiss on her and Bee's cheeks before he left for the van, followed shortly by Dom.

'Don't forget what I said.' Dom called, looking back.

'I won't Pops'. she laughed.

Bee went back to the novelty of her new bedroom, already given a quick clean with the bed made up before any other room was touched.

Liv went back into the living room and looked at the

bookcase with its racks of decent-sized shelving, put together by Dom and Patrick. It had been a great find at a cheap price and almost took up the whole wall. 'No one wants furniture like this any more,' the old man from the second-hand salesroom had said, 'they're all too keen on cheap put-it-together-yourself rubbish,' and he sold it to her for a few pounds, when in reality he would have paid Liv to take it away to give him more room in the shop. She gave it a spray and dust from the collection in the cleaning box packed by Barbara. 'Well, I hope people at least still want books when I've got three novels started and another two going around in my head,' she said to herself as dust flew into the air. Several boxes of books, a lifetime's collection from childhood onwards, lay in wait for their new home, but one shelf was reserved for the hand-written journals started many years, and another lifetime, ago.

When an exhausted happy Bee had gone to bed, Liv opened the bottle of red, kindly left by Dom on the kitchen table. 'Something to celebrate your new beginning,' it said on the note alongside. She poured a glass before setting about opening boxes of books and filling the shelves.

She paused at the journal of '92, the year life had been full of hope and expectation when her belly was swollen and she had the time to think about what the future held. She wrote of hopes of what was to come, listed names, and made up stories that she would one day read to the baby and more. She stroked the cover and held it close to her chest. A photograph fell out onto the floor. Liv picked it up, smiled and kissed it as she had so many times before and read once again the words that held no clue of what was to come, what would happen in the space of six long years. She sat on the sofa and relaxed with the wine and the journal.

Chapter Four

1992

I can't believe how much weight I've put on. Even my baggy frocks are tight! At least the weather is warmer now but some days I don't know what to do to get comfy. It's taking too long. Rob is kind and caring but there are times I'm glad when he's at work. I'm suffocating under the attention. Got angry this morning and yelled at him 'I'm not ill.' and then felt really bad when he looked hurt, but it's no use trying to be subtle, he just doesn't get the message. He hovered over me in the shops like the spectre of doom this weekend when I said I needed to go into town for a few last bits and pieces. 'Liv, darling, please... we should get home now...Liv you look tired'.

It's become his mantra, 'Liv you look tired' when in fact all I'm tired of is his constant fussing. My legs ache, my back is sore, but I really don't need Rob to point out that I look like crap when all I need to do is look in the mirror. Not that I feel bad all of the time. This morning a little elbow inside me moved from one side to the other. It woke me up! Little limbs trying to find space in the tight confines of my belly. Anyway, nothing could stop me buying the most gorgeous little rabbit from the 'The Nursery Shop'. I sneaked in before Rob realised where I was going. Its ears are long and soft and it simply demanded to be picked up stroked. What else could I do? I held it to my cheek and pictured it next to our baby. I promised Rob that if we got it we could go home. So we did.

Daniel had put in an appearance on May 2, two weeks early but healthy and perfect. It was a day full of love and promise and hope. The following week, his tiny fist grabbed the little rabbit Liv had bought and Rob captured the moment now preserved in that much-kissed photograph.

Liv glanced at the diaries of later years, books that laid bare the raw emotion of what followed; writing that relived the days, weeks and months that had been buried as deep as a sunken ship in the middle of the ocean. It had never been easy, but once begun, those memories were hauled up for painful inspection. She couldn't stop and the words and tears flowed without restraint. With the emotion laid bare, there had been no going back. But not today, 'No more,' she said to herself, replacing the photograph and straightening the journals on the shelf.

'Not today.'

She turned back to the glass of wine. Daylight was fading and darkness closed in. Liv's eyes grew heavy with the burden of the past and the worry over her future, but much had been achieved that day. She took a mouthful of wine and slotted a CD into the hastily set up player. Moby filled the air and the warmth of the wine and lull of the music drew her into a happy place. Switching on a corner lamp, a warm rush of hope, more than she had felt in a very long time, settled over her and thoughts turned to Barbara and Arthur.

Turning the music low, she called the number still listed as 'home'; it would always be home as long as they were in it, and a wary Barbara always cautious of nighttime calls, answered.

'Hi Mum only me...just wanted to let you know that we're in and it's all looking good...I know, I know I'm sorry I should have called earlier but...yes...yes...I've just seen your message... the cottage pie was lovely...very welcome...all gone...of course...yes I've nearly finished unpacking the boxes...'

Half an hour later, she managed to say 'bye. She had until next week to convert the lie to something at least resembling the truth before going back to work and before Bee started her new school. Liv turned the music back up and began another list, but after two glasses of wine, found it hard to keep her eyes open and mind focused. The bottle was re-corked and put back into the kitchen where the small pool of water had appeared on the floor following an earlier shower of rain. It was soon mopped and the irresistible lure of sleep beckoned.

She looked in on Bee, sleeping soundly and curled in a

ball, clutching Wabbit, and went to her own room feeling calm and ready for the new life ahead. Liv slept a contented, dreamless sleep for the first time in many months, and Robert's call was forgotten.

Chapter Five

Barbara and Arthur had watched Liv, Bee and the van leave after much fretting and fussing, and stood on the doorstep until they were completely out of sight. The morning had been tense with: 'Have you remembered...', 'Don't forget to...', before the final 'We're not too far away are we love...', from Barbara. Arthur, busy with the boxes, thought it best to keep out of her way.

It was a solemn pair that stepped back inside the house where stark silence lay thick as an autumn fog.

Barbara did what she always did in times of stress, or happiness, or sadness, or celebration: she put the kettle on, something to keep her occupied if only while she blew her nose and Arthur couldn't see.

Arthur went into the living room and settled in a deep red moquette chair that had seen better days. It had lost most of its pile and faded to a mottled pink on the side that caught the afternoon sun. The seat had a dent that perfectly matched the shape of Arthur, and beside the chair, upon a small table, sat his daily paper and a coaster brought back from a weekend trip to Bridlington. The moquette suite had been a wedding present from Barbara's parents but was still treated with the same reverence from when it arrived brand new.

They'd been married barely a year when a baby came into their lives, much to Barbara's consternation and surprise.

'Bloody hell Barbs, are we ready for this?'

'We'd better be, there's no goin' back now.'

They had hardly got used to living under the same roof before Barbara knew with certainty what tender breasts and missed periods meant. She was twenty-four years old, still the rabbit caught in headlights as far as sex and the physical expectation of married life were concerned, but from the outset, a bemused Arthur was happy, and from then on let Barbara take charge of all things domestic. He knew that a quiet life would benefit him in the long term and the pristine suite was duly draped in antimacassars and arm covers in preparation for family life. They muddled through together as they did with everything thrown their way, but after a long and painful birth, Barbara was certain that she wanted no more babies.

Thirty-two years later, she sat on that same sofa with her tea. There was more room to spread out her knitting wools and patterns. She would absentmindedly pick the needles up while waiting for the kettle to boil. Working on squares for the Oxfam Shop, they would eventually be sewn together to make a blanket. She could list every pullover and cardigan she had knitted over the years from the leftover wool in those blankets.

'Remember the first time our Olivia left home?' she asked to the accompaniment of clacking needles.

'I do...bit of a shock to the system as I remember but still...'

'And the second time when she got that job in London,'

'Aye...that one was a bit of a relief.'

Barbara dabbed at her eyes before picking up her knitting again, needles working even more furiously.

'I know this time it's going to take some getting used to Barb.'

'It will love, but it'll be for the best...won't it?'

'Course it will...I think she's ready...they both are...it's us that aren't.'

'I'll miss that bairn...'

She gave up on the knitting when it became too blurry to see what she was doing.

Arthur, not good at the 'emotional stuff', did the next best thing.

'Tea love?' he said and started to get up for a second mug.

'No...let me do it...you sit back down...remember what the doctor said...rest, rest and more rest...for now anyway. I don't want to be calling for another ambulance.'

'I'm not dead yet, lass.'

'I know that...I'm still washing your undies.' They both tried to smile. They'd been married long enough to know when words weren't really needed to express all they felt.

'I'll miss the routines of the little'un.'

'I know...I will too Arthur, but we're going to see them next week...if you're up to it.'

'Olivia's come a long way since she came back to us with little Bee...no thanks to that Robert. I just hope he stops all that nonsense about taking our granddaughter to live with him. Last thing she needs is it all being raked up again.'

Barbara went into the kitchen and two more mugs of tea now sat on respective tables, waiting to cool.

They would have the same conversations time and again as if by repetition the end result would be more satisfactory than the last.

'She wasn't in a good place when she came, Arthur, we know that.'

'He didn't help...just made her more twitchy and nervous. He couldn't just leave her to get on with it...constant fretting and bringing it all up again. There was nothing anyone could have done...we know that. Bee needs her Dad but that little one doesn't want to be living with him full-time. Anyway, he's got Marsha now and another babe... what's he called?'

'Eddie.'

'Eddie...aye, poor little bugger.'

Silence reigned for just two more minutes as they blew and sipped their tea.

'Bee will be starting her new school next week and Olivia back at work.'

'I remember when our Olivia was still at primary school... always writing...always making up those stories...don't know where she got her imagination from...wasn't us was it, Arthur? All those hours spent in that bedroom of hers.'

Arthur stared down at his mug and chuckled.

'Not sure my imagination goes beyond what colour to paint the kitchen next.'

'And mine's what we're having for tea.'

'I found her little books the other day when I was looking for something in the loft...you know, the ones she made of those stories...her teacher was always full of praise at what she could do...way ahead of her class. If it wasn't for Savannah she'd never have gone out.'

Savannah was the alter ego, the one who brought out the other side of Liv that few had seen before. She injected the fun side of life, the music and the concerts, trips to the cinema and later dancing at the clubs where they pretended to be eighteen. In return, Savannah was glad for the help in class when she struggled to catch up with the finer points of spelling, grammar and comprehension.

'It's hard to think of the past eight years after all that... university and London...working on those newspapers...she was happy then. Where did it go wrong, eh, Barb?'

'It was that Robert...that's where it went wrong. From the minute she met him, it went downhill.'

'Stop it now...they started off well enough and you know it...you encouraged it as I remember. No, she's picking herself up at last...and we've got little Bee don't forget.'

'I know...reminds me so much of Olivia at that age.'

'I'm looking forward to seeing them at the weekend...see what she's made of that house...just wish I'd been able to help more.'

'Well, you can't...remember what the doctor said,' and Barbara, dry-eyed now, once again picked up the knitting.

Chapter Six

'What *is* she thinking of, taking Bee to that house?'

Robert threw his phone down on the table.

'They'll be fine Rob...stop fussing. Haven't we got enough problems for you to worry about without taking on Liv's?'

'Bee should be here with me...with us...where she's safe.'

'Oh, Robert...you don't think she's safe with Liv? They'll be just fine.'

'It's just...just...'

'Just what, Rob?' Marsha sighed, knowing what was coming and it was certainly nothing new; they'd been over and over the same ground too many times.

'I know Liv...she's not ready...she doesn't live in the real world...not since...'

Marsha gave another sigh.

'Rob that was...what...almost six years ago now? Please... you have to let it go. We've been through this.'

'I can't help it...she's unstable...you know what she was like...and now she's moved out to be on her own...I don't think she's ready.'

They sat like bookends on either side of the sofa; Robert

perched on the edge of his seat, head in hands, and Marsha propped up by a small mountain of cushions. She was attempting to feed four-month-old Eddie who was taking on the stress of Marsha's situation with howls of protest. On top of that, teething had come early and they all felt his pain. None of them had had much sleep the night before. Marsha put the baby to her left breast, always his favourite for some reason, and soon enough peace settled on the room once again. She was grateful for the soothing effect it had on Eddie before Robert started fretting again. Cradling and feeding the baby was normally such a pleasurable time and certainly more relaxing when it was just the two of them. Having Eddie was everything she'd hoped it would be, so why did Robert have to be the difficult one?

Motherhood came easily to Marsha. She'd longed for a baby of her own since she was a little girl, when her room had been full of baby dolls, and all the paraphernalia that went with them. For as long as she could remember, a cot, pram and array of little dolls to cuddle and love were all she needed to be happy. When she gave birth, she knew that nothing would ever match the feeling of euphoria experienced when Edward Stephen Smithson was placed into her outstretched arms. As the tears fell, all her dreams and expectations had been realised.

Of course, it wasn't Robert's first experience of fatherhood, but it might well have been. His face was etched with deep lines of stress where Marsha's round cheeks glowed with absolute bliss. Her only real concern was Robert and his endless loop of unrealistic demands.

Robert sat frowning; watching Marsha feed a now contented Eddie. Acutely aware of the baby's age; he felt every whimper, every scream; every long silence in sleep. He saw all as a portent of something more sinister than the normal stages of life in a perfectly healthy baby.

The only part of life that gave Marsha cause for concern,

was the pressure Robert put her under. It was impossible to ignore or dismiss as unreasonable. If he had his way they would be virtually living at the hospital or at the very least camping out in the waiting room of the doctor's surgery, waiting for the next cancellation. He spent hours poring over the books; so many books. There would soon be more baby books on the shelves than Marsha's romances or Robert's vast collection from the RHS. Since the day Eddie was brought home, he would read nothing but baby books and of course became an expert in matters paediatric, especially ailments.

All was quiet, apart from the contented guzzling of a hungry baby. Marsha, content with listening to the gentle sounds of Eddie feeding, ignored Robert who stared out of the window until the mood passed. After five more minutes, he looked over to his wife:

'Want some tea, love?' He relented the earlier barbed comments when he saw Marsha burping the baby.

'First sensible thing you've said for the past half hour'.

Marsha smiled, relieved that they'd moved on from the never-ending conversation that took them on a road to nowhere.

'Thank you...I'd love a tea...oh and there's a ginger cake in the cupboard that might be nice with it,' she called after his retreating figure. He wouldn't approve of that either, but her craving for something sweet was greater.

They'd been together for almost four years and Marsha, following the birth of Eddie, found a different voice inside, one that came with the newfound confidence of her role as a mother. It took her by surprise but was welcome nonetheless. It was as if Eddie gave her the strength to speak out. At one time she would have acquiesced to Robert's demands, no matter how much they went against her own. He'd always had the more persuasive argument and she'd always relented. Set against all the things she loved about him, and everything he had been through, it hadn't seemed to be too much to ask of her, but something changed when Eddie came into her life.

Marsha had watched with helpless resignation as Robert's impulse for control grew. Was it something she'd missed or had he always been that way? She couldn't recall that it had been so bad at the beginning of their relationship, or had she just been too euphoric in the first flush of love? She still felt that love but it now came with twinges of confusion and a price.

Robert turned at the door to look at the wide expanse of Marsha, still struggling with post-baby weight four months after giving birth but said nothing. He would cut her a thin slice of cake. He strode into the kitchen and filled the kettle, as Marsha mused on the day they'd first met, how kind and thoughtful he'd been to the shy and nervous new girl in the office.

Robert whistled as he made the tea and Marsha relaxed as she listened. Warm thoughts of Marsha and Eddie engulfed him, and he cut a bigger slice of the ginger cake than he'd intended.

Returning to the living room with a tray of tea and cake, he dodged the baby clutter strewn on the floor. Life since Eddie was a constant struggle to suppress his longing for the kind of order Marsha created back in the office.

Robert negotiated his way around the soft toys. There were enough to keep Eddie supplied with a new one every day for a month. When friends and colleagues at the Parks Department heard about the new arrival, they'd all been more than generous.

He opened his mouth to say something but then thought better of it and handed over the tea and cake to a very receptive Marsha.

'He's asleep at last,' she whispered, 'and we can enjoy five minutes peace.'

Robert looked into the Moses basket given to them by someone at work whose children were long past the baby stage. Hand-me-downs were more than welcome when money was tight. Marsha had already suggested that she was in no rush to get back after maternity leave and a chunk of his salary would go to supporting Bee for a long time yet. They struggled even after his recent promotion and pay rise.

Eddie snuffled contentedly as Robert stroked the soft, warm cheeks.

'Don't you dare wake him...not before I've finished this cake.'

'He is all right isn't he Marsh?'

''Course he is...nothing wrong with that baby that a good nap and a couple of teeth putting in an appearance won't put right.'

'You're always so sure, I...'

'There's nothing to worry about Rob...he's fine trust me. Stop reading all those books for goodness sake...please?'

Marsha devoured the cake and fought the longing for another piece when she looked down at her stomach. She took in a deep breath. She was always ravenous but made concessions and contented herself with a mug of sugarless, milky tea.

Robert sat by the window again, at the little table he'd surprised Marsha with not long after they'd married. She'd longed for one just like it after seeing it in an article in one of her magazines. Robert scoured around until he found something similar at the local 'Sellit and Soon'. It looked close enough to the one she wanted and didn't take too much work to make it like new.

Marsha got up and peeked at Eddie in the basket with adoring eyes; his breathing was so quiet as his little chest rose and fell in a deep contented sleep, and her heart beat just a little faster at the unconditional love she felt for him and for

Robert. This was the cumulation of all she had wanted, but did it have to come at such a price at times?

'I'll see to Eddie tonight...you look all in...you've got work tomorrow. You've done enough Rob. Leave Eddie to me.'

'Maybe...we'll see.'

Robert's sleep had become more and more erratic as they approached the four-month mark and neither of them had been getting much rest. She even thought of asking Robert to move to the spare room but decided she couldn't bear the thought of that either. Eddie still woke up at least twice in the night and she would just have to be ready. No wonder I'm always so tired, Marsha thought; Eddie she could cope with but Robert was becoming a different matter altogether.

Robert left for work the next day at eight as usual, eyes puffed and bleary. He packed the bacon sandwich Marsha had made for him when he'd said he wasn't hungry and Marsha let out a sigh of relief at his retreating figure. It had been a stressful weekend despite all efforts to the contrary. She switched off Radio Four with its endless loop of depressing news and found Radio Two, which was much more to her liking. She needed to enjoy a happier station than the one offered by James Naughtie. It might be Robert's default as he ate breakfast, but she preferred Terry Wogan whose banter always made her laugh.

The Spice Girls came on and Marsha turned up the volume, swaying and singing to 'Spice Up Your Life' as she cleared the breakfast table. Slipping back in time, she thought of Debbie and the Richmond Club in town, their favourite haunt where music like this would have got them up on the dance floor. A boy once asked her to dance to Rick Astley and said that 'Never Gonna Give You Up' had been written especially for her. They'd laughed as he grabbed her by the waist, in the days when she had one, and pulled her up to dance. She never asked his name and never saw him again after that one night of dancing, but the happy memory lingered and popped up again today. Marsha loved to dance, but nowadays it was mostly confined to the kitchen. Robert never danced.

The window above the sink looked out on to their garden where a myriad of springtime flowers bloomed and seemed to sway to the music too. The morning sun shone, raising her spirits further.

'Right, Eddie how about you and me go to the Park? Might even get an ice cream... but don't tell Daddy!'

Eddie was stuffed into his coat and strapped into the buggy, and as they walked down the path by the garden, Marsha pictured the swing and sandpit Robert had promised he would build. Eddie would love that, and in a flush of happiness, she thought how nice it would be if he had a little brother or sister to keep him company.

'I got my first wish didn't I Eddie? I got my baby and the man I loved. Why stop there?'

They ambled along to the Park and eventually, her thoughts were bothered by no more than what they would have for tea.

Chapter Seven

1992

It was a shy young woman who tapped on the door of the Parks Department office, nervous at the start of her first job after college. Robert, not used to such polite behaviour around the workspace shouted from behind piles of invoices, unanswered mail and a withered pot plant that had died over Christmas. He was still in the early flush of marriage and had forgotten to take it home.

'Stop messing around Dave...get yourself in here...you're late...it's still your turn to make the coffee...and you'd better have brought some milk'.

He wasn't in the mood for Dave's tardiness. It was their first day back after the Christmas break and all the work that had accumulated before they'd finished had somehow morphed into the pile that faced him now. The last office administrator, 'Frosty' Barker, whose name required no explanation, left in a huff at the end of November and her replacement had been slow in materialising.

The door tentatively opened and the face of Marsha Brady peeped around.

'I don't know if I'm in the right place...but I'm looking for Robert Smithson?' she said, her voice barely a whisper.

Robert peered from behind a stack of papers and journals.

'And now you've found him...just...and you are?'

'I'm Marsha...Marsha Brady...I'm your new admin assistant.'

For the first time that morning, Robert's face lit up and upon his smile, the rest of Marsha walked into the office. Her eyes grew wide at the sight of the cluttered desk and mess on the floor. Muffled in a thick brown woollen coat and knitted hat, she blinked in the bright light and smiled back. It had been snowing heavily and she stood dripping in the warmth of the office.

'Good grief it's Scott of the Antarctic!'

'Sorry...sorry, I'm making the floor wet.'

Marsha flushed. The walk from the bus had numbed her feet and fingers, but the office radiated the heat of a greenhouse.

'Don't you worry about that, it'll be a lot worse by the end of the week...I'm just pleased to see you...and don't be put off by this lot...looks worse than it is...I promise.'

The difference between 'Frosty' Barker and Marsha Brady could not have been more pronounced. Where the former was sharp angles and a pinched face, the latter was on the right side of rounded with a warm personality that shone out of a peaches and cream complexion. From that first day, they all loved her.

Within no time at all, Marsha Brady had organised the mass of unruly paperwork, filed accounts, posted invoices and diarised appointments. Most importantly, they never ran out of milk, tea or coffee. She made their morning and afternoon drinks and at the same time kept them well supplied with homemade cakes and biscuits, leaving them to do what they did best, as Marsha put it: 'get muddy and tend to the parks and gardens'. The office became a welcoming space of flowers and fragrance, cakes and order.

By the time winter rolled into spring, Marsha had made herself indispensable. She'd slipped seamlessly into her role, relishing the difference she'd made, and at night was almost reluctant to return to the little flat she rented on the edge of town. The growing feelings she harboured for Robert were kept under strict control, but at home Marsha let her imagination run free.

Once a week, on her half-day, she went out with Debbie from the Co-op. Deborah Maxwell, her best friend since schooldays, knew what she was thinking before she did herself. Debbie would view Marsha's rush of enthusiasm during her first year in post, and the subsequent saga of Robert's life, from a more tempered and less emotive stance, but nothing could change the burgeoning feelings that grew inside Marsha.

On a warm spring morning at the end of May, barely a year into their first year of marriage, Robert's wife Olivia brought Daniel into the office. She remembered the day well. A vase of black tulips sat on her desk; 'Queen of the Night' Robert said they were called. She loved the deep, rich velvet colour and had impulsively bought them from the florist on her way to work that morning.

Olivia arrived and work stopped for all to admire the new arrival who was barely four weeks old. Tightly wrapped in a white shawl and hat, bright blue eyes peered inquisitively around and found Marsha's face when she'd smiled down at him. An intense, physical surge of longing came out of that one look.

'He's gorgeous Liv...can I hold him please...just for a minute?'

'Course you can.'

Liv handed him over to Marsha's welcoming arms and she cradled him like it was the most natural thing in the world. She spoke without once taking her eyes from Daniel's face,

'I love babies...if you ever need a sitter call me won't you... any time...I don't mind.'

'You're on...although you might regret it when he doesn't sleep.'

'Oh, I would never do that.'

Liv's face glowed in the bloom of motherhood despite her lack of sleep. Coming in to the office was something she could have done without, but it was a duty call that Robert pressured her into and couldn't be put off.

Marsha lost in the pleasure of those few moments, blocked out everything else in rapt concentration on Daniel. She failed to hear the phone, or even notice when Robert rushed back into the office.

'Right, I'm ready.'

'Oh so soon?'

'Sorry, we don't have that long.'

He took the baby from Marsha without ceremony and went out with Liv for a quick lunch, leaving Marsha with an ache in her heart and a space that she knew would only be filled when she had a baby of her own.

But Marsha never did get an opportunity to babysit. Spring rolled into summer and with August turning into one of the wettest for many years, Robert wasn't happy. Jobs took longer than expected and he flitted in and out of the office at irregular hours. In turn, his long absence that month was barely noticed until after three days, Marsha knew that something was wrong.

Over her past eight months in post, she had got to know Robert's habits, his likes and dislikes, as well as the little peculiarities of his nature. He was a creature of habit, and despite her first impressions of the office, he craved order. A baby coming into his life and the vagaries of unpredictable weather had not dented his daily routine too much and he rarely failed to let Marsha know of his whereabouts in advance, but something was different.

Robert had never taken a day's sick leave in all the years he'd worked there according to Dave. Even when Daniel was born, he took less than a week off when it was their busiest time of year. Today, the weather was dull; black clouds had formed in the distance and rain threatened to fall yet again.

The day they found out the awful truth of what had happened, stuck in Marsha's memory. She recalled every detail: being annoyed she'd forgotten her umbrella, Dave popping into the office before leaving on a job,

'Mornin' Marsha my lovely...what's new?' He'd leaned into her desk in anticipation after spotting the biscuit tin.

'Morning Dave, you any idea where Robert is? Has he gone straight to a job?'

'No idea...he's not with me today...you checked the diary?'

'Of course I have, I thought he was in the office today to go through some paperwork with me.'

'He's got a baby now don't forget...probably had a bad night and running a bit late...and I know just what that's like.'

'Mm...you're probably right. There's plenty more I can be getting on with I suppose.'

Dave had reached out for the biscuit tin and Marsha slapped his hand.

'They're for later...hands off.'

'Ok...ok...I'll be back at dinner,' he mumbled through a mouth full of lemon and cream crumbs, 'don't eat them all before I get here...I know what you and Robert are like.'

The call finally came at three in the afternoon. Robert

wouldn't be in that day, or any other day over the next month. And when he did return, it wasn't the same man they saw last and the change was profound. Pale, snappy and withdrawn, no one knew what to say or do, apart from Marsha.

It was she who took on the major role of support: the listening ear and the reassuring presence when he lost track of where he was and what he should be doing. The news about baby Daniel that broke on a dark, wet afternoon ensured that neither of their lives would ever quite be the same again.

Debbie saw Marsha become more and more drawn into Robert's world.

'You're getting obsessed Marsh...it's not good for you... for either of you.'

'You don't understand Debs...his baby died...the one I held in my arms...I can't get it out of my head...what he must be going through...he needs my support...'

'Be careful there, he's still married...he has a wife to do all that. She will be...'

'I know all that...I just care about him...he's so broken I can't help it...I wish there was more I could do that's all.'

'You've done what you can but you can't keep taking in all the lame ducks you come across...remember the last time...Pete whatshisname...Stanley? He let you take on his troubles with that trollop of an ex-girlfriend Maria Westbury who said she was pregnant, then when you'd got him sorted, found out she wasn't, he waltzed off back to her.'

'He's nothing like Pete, and I wouldn't do anything more than be a good friend to Robert...there's nothing going on.'

'Really? Well make sure it stays that way...his wife might have gone for now but like I said, he's still married to her.'

Marsha would not admit to anyone, not even Debbie, that she had loved Robert from the first week she started work at the Parks Department. He'd been the one who'd made her feel the most welcome; made her a tea on that first day to thaw out her frozen hands; and dried her coat, letting it steam over the radiator. She was barely twenty years of age, but as the weeks passed, she saw him as her ideal and hoped that one day she might meet someone just like Robert for herself.

Chapter Eight

1998

Bee's first day at her new school was not the straightforward exercise Liv had in mind when they moved, and was far from the regimented routine they'd left behind.

Breakfast was the first hurdle when Bee's favourite cereal bowl, the one with Peter Rabbit, accidentally fell to the floor and broke. When Bee had finally been consoled and sat sullenly eating toast instead of cornflakes, Liv flew from room to room in search of uniform, book bag and the school shoes bought the week before. Finding two out of three, she put together a packed lunch from what was left in the fridge. Bee sullenly watched.

'Where are my grapes? Grandma always puts in grapes,' she complained.

'I know sweetie...I'll get some for tomorrow. You love bananas though don't you?'

'S'pose...and can I have the yellow cheese and not that white stuff?'

'Not today...it'll have to be cottage.'

'Yuck!'

'Look Bee we just have to make do with what we've got... please don't sulk.'

'I'm not sulking...I don't like cottage cheese that's all.'

'Ok ok...how about peanut butter then?'

'Yes!...With jam?' Bee's face lit up for the first time that morning.

'All right just for today.'

Gone were the days of a leisurely shower before work and coming downstairs in time to give Bee a kiss on the cheek before Grandpa took her to school. Gone were the days of Grandma packing lunches for both of them from a well-stocked fridge.

School shoes were the last problem and nowhere to be found. Liv struggled to squeeze Bee's feet into last summer's sandals that barely fitted her growing feet. Bee, delighted to be wearing bright yellow shoes with white daisies on the toe, was far more upset about the cereal bowl than she was about the lunch and footwear.

'I'll be more organised tomorrow Bee-Bee,' Liv promised, looking around at the unopened boxes that still sat where they'd been left by Dom and Patrick. At least their coats were in plain sight, hanging from the neat row of hooks beside the front door.

Liv took a deep breath as she waited for Bee to finish in the bathroom. The phone vibrated in her pocket. Robert. Her finger hovered over the decline button but she couldn't ignore him again and risk yet another outburst. In recent days she'd taken to ignoring his calls on occasion but the repercussions only brought a stressful confrontation, so she answered. 'Robert, what do you want? I'm just about to take Bee to school.'

Robert was already at work and about to leave on a job but was irritated by being ignored. He would be heard.

'Why haven't you called me back? I've rung three times this week. Is everything all right? I only want to know how Bee is after the move...if she's worried about being in a strange place...going to a new school...that's all. You know I still don't think you're ready for all this and I wanted to talk to her. I worry about how this is affecting her.'

'Robert stop. What do you think is going to happen to her? Children move all the time...change homes, change schools. Some have it far worse than Bee. She's all right...we're doing fine'. Exasperation accented her every word.

Robert paused, but before Liv could hang up, he finally came out with what he really wanted to say,

'You know if Bee was with me she wouldn't have needed to change schools...she wouldn't have left the area and...'

'Goodbye Robert'.

As Liv ended the call, she heard the sound of a flushing toilet and reached up for Bee's coat. If this was going to be a success, as she had every confidence that it would be, she had to make Robert stop. The phone rang again.

'What now?'

'Why did you hang up on me? Talk to me!'

His voice was louder this time.

'Robert, she's fine...please just let me get on with things in my own way. It's time we left for school...I don't want her to be late on her first day and you'll see her at the weekend. I'll tell her you said hi, but we have to go.' She stabbed at 'hang up' again before he could say anything more.

Liv took another deep breath to assuage the anger that rose from the call. She'd responded in the way she always had: with thumping heart nerves on edge and wondering if he was right after all. Only this time there was no one else around to vent her anger to, or to calm her down. She was on her own. Time for slow deep breaths as she was told: 'inhale through the nose; one, two three; exhale through the mouth, one, two, three, four, five', until calm is restored. Bee clattered down the stairs mid-breath.

'Come on Mummy we need to go...I don't want to be late.' Liv laughed at her, 'No Bee, we won't be late. Let's get your coat on.'

Bee, oblivious to Robert's call and the heated conversation, stood still as Liv fastened her buttons with trembling hands. She briefly considered the half bottle of prescription tablets sitting in the bathroom cabinet but knew it really was getting late and there was no time now. 'I can do this for another day. I can make it to three months.'

When they stepped outside Liv brooded on Robert's call and what lay behind his irrational behaviour. Was it Marsha? More likely sleep deprivation. How old was Eddie now? Three months? Four? Then it came to her; that was it; Eddie, of course, born just before Christmas he'd be reaching four months. Of course Robert would be on edge, the same way he'd been with Bee. She even thought she might feel sorry for Marsha if she was getting the same treatment, but that was her problem.

The walk to school, despite its troubled start, was pleasant. A pale morning sun filtered through budding trees lining the road. Liv squinted in the harsh bright light, but the warmth on her face was very welcome. She glanced at the window of the 'twitching curtain' next door and was sorry that she hadn't yet had the chance to introduce herself. The curtain was lifted a little higher this morning and the face behind it came clear into view. An old woman with a hand raised in acknowledgement smiled at them. Liv waved back and the woman watched her new neighbours disappear down the road before letting the curtain drop.

Frances Fenton withdrew back to the room where she

spent most of her days. At her time of life, most of her family and friends had withdrawn into history, leaving her alone to re-live their presence through photographs and memories. A young woman with a lively little girl raised her hopes that there might at least be someone new to say hello to.

She went back to her pot of tea and poured out a second into the delicate bone china cup, wondering if they would be friendly.

Liv tucked the door key into her pocket where she discovered the envelope from the week before. She opened it as they strode in the direction of the school. Inside was a print of Alice in Wonderland looking up to the Cheshire Cat in a tree and on the back, a beautiful but wavering script, read: 'Welcome to your new home, Frances Fenton (your neighbour next door).

'Look at this Bee...it's from the lady next door. Isn't that nice of her?'

Bee, almost at a run trying to keep up, took the card.

'Mummy I love that picture...it's Alice in Wonderland... can I have it for my room?'

'Course you can...I'll leave it there for you when I get back.'

They arrived at the school gates flushed and breathless. The morning bell was ringing but Liv was pleased to see that the teacher in charge was still there waiting for the last of the stragglers. Bee's new form teacher, Miss Farley, was on duty that day. They'd already met on a visit to the school before the end of last term and she'd made a good impression on Liv; kind and gentle, speaking as much to Bee as she did to her. Bee loved her already. Robert hadn't been able to get away that day and wanted to change the date but Liv was relieved when they found out it would be difficult and so took Barbara and Arthur instead. They were thrilled with Miss Farley, especially when Barbara discovered that she knew her mother.

'Hello Bee, it's lovely to see you again...are you ready to meet your classmates? I've another newcomer starting today, a little boy called Aadi.'

'Aadi? That's a strange name.'

'It's just a bit different that's all.'

'I like it.'

'Let's go meet him and all the others shall we?'

Liv let go of Bee's hand, holding back the tears, amazed at the ease with which her daughter marched off into her new school. Small and vulnerable, she confidently strode away, hand in hand with Miss Farley.

Miss Farley looked back, 'Don't worry...they're tougher than you think...tougher than us sometimes.'

'You'll let me know if there are any problems though? You've got my mobile and my work number.'

'I will.'

Liv watched until they both disappeared inside the door and only then left for home. She tried to picture what Daniel might look like now. He would have started school the previous year and in her mind's eye, she saw a curly-haired little boy hand in hand with his little sister.

The walk gave her time to think back over the years since Bee's birth and what she meant to them all, to Robert, Barbara, and Arthur. She was the treasure at the centre of their lives, a beacon at the end of a dark road, loving, cherished and loved. Of course, Robert now had Eddie too, but where did loving care stop and interference begin?

The walk there and back had taken no more than thirty minutes, which in itself was a source of relief when she had no car and buses were few. With a fifteen minutes walk to work in the opposite direction, she considered the location of their new home perfect, despite the drawbacks that Robert went at great pains to point out. Her days would be a finely tuned logistical timetable, but one eminently doable and the exercise would do her good. She thought about getting a bike.

The route home took her past several boarded-up houses, partly demolished to make way for a new development. Maybe the estate agent was right; it was an up-and-coming area, although the group of youths hanging around did little to enhance that thought. They looked no more than fourteen or fifteen, smoking and laughing. They watched her walk by and whistled in a lairy manner, emboldened by peer bravado. They should have been at school. Liv didn't let it bother her too much although she felt for her phone just in case and walked on. The boys triggered memories of London and she compared them to the gangs who'd hung around the digs that nestled in an area where every dark corner hid an unknown menace. In comparison, those boys were tame.

Back home, Liv took pleasure in a couple of hours on her own before leaving for her afternoon shift, and arrived with the intention of emptying the rest of the boxes in the living room, impossible to ignore any longer. But somehow, she didn't get quite that far.

Chapter Nine

London 1988

'Don't seem two minutes since you was packing for university.'

Barbara's pronouncements were generally punctuated with the swift passing of time and confusion over where it had gone.

Arthur looked on in bemusement and as usual left the finer points of the day's activity to his wife and daughter. The extortionate cost of moving down south was his primary concern.

'How will you be able to afford to live in London on that wage?' he'd asked more than once when Olivia finally admitted to how little she would be earning to begin with.

'I'll be all right Dad,' she promised, dismissing the thought of struggling in the euphoria of finding out she'd been accepted for the job. They'd been impressed by her degree, her writing and her enthusiastic manner at the interview. She was told she had potential, but for what they didn't elaborate. Liv didn't care, she was too happy at the prospect of leaving her hometown again, even if it was for a very junior position. It was a start and that was good enough.

Letters from Savannah always made her feel restless and inadequate, unadventurous in comparison, so she took great pleasure in announcing in her last reply,

'I'm going to London, Sav! Wish me luck.'

Savannah was starting a new project in Africa after the first had finished; still working with children, still struggling with an uphill battle to get their plight more recognition, but still enthusiastic despite the setbacks.

London began on a high although finding accommodation was not easy. The two rooms eventually found were located in the only place she could afford. The agent told her more than once that she was lucky to have two and not be sharing. He'd mastered the art of accentuating the positives of the sub-standard accommodation he was obliged to rent, but despite their failings, found little difficulty in filling them. Arthur and Barbara were unconvinced until Liv described the alternatives she'd seen. The rooms settled on were cramped, cold and draughty, and though she could just about tolerate the conditions, sharing a bathroom with four others put her on edge, especially when the lock kept breaking and the nearest thing to hand was a rickety chair to prop under the door handle. It was never mentioned in her letters home however and she took her cue from the agent at mastering the art of keeping all communication positive.

It was December when Liv moved in and at night she piled on extra clothes to stave off the cold. The heating had packed up and the landlord was slow in getting the boiler repaired no matter how often she called. It didn't help matters when

Barbara and Arthur insisted on visiting the week before Christmas.

'It'll be nice to see the lights and go round the shops,' Barbara had said. London was exotic, an exciting place she'd only been to once before. Arthur wasn't so sure and when Liv tried to put them off he silently agreed.

'Hmm, nice,' he'd replied and went back to his paper hoping that the cost of the train fare and a hotel for one night only might just be the tipping point to change her mind. It didn't, and seven days before Christmas they set off in a festive spirit that lasted until they arrived at Olivia's door. There was no hiding their disappointment both outside and in.

'Not much bigger than my pantry...are you sure this is where you want to be love?' Barbara felt guilty over encouraging the job in the first place when she saw how Olivia was living.

'I don't have any choice right now Mum...I'll find somewhere better next year. If I do well there'll be a pay rise,' she answered more in hope than expectation, trying to convince herself as well as Barbara that it would all work out in the end.

'It's still early days but I love my job Mum...and I need to be here to get better prospects for the future...for my writing. It has to be London.'

'As long as you know what you're doing.'

They had of course helped out financially where they could but none of it was ideal, and none would keep her on the road to independence, despite every effort to the contrary.

'On consideration, I think that nice job at the Council might have been better after all. I wonder if it's still going?'

'Oh, Mum...'

London proved to be a mixed blessing, but early starts to work; walking for the bus in the cold and dark, and then returning in the cold and dark, were never easy. Even so, the sanctuary of the digs, however substandard, was a relief. The rooms were above a takeaway in Bethnal Green, close to the city centre, but the area proved to be one where the crime level was far beyond anything she'd experienced before. It was intimidating.

The long nights were the worst; as she sat with thoughts darker than the blackening sky, Liv struggled to balance her lonely, estranged life against the desire to make a long-lasting impression at work. Harsh winter weeks slowly and interminably dragged by, but even as spring arrived with its budding message of hope, Liv took each uninspiring brief with an enthusiasm that didn't quite match the job or her output.

1989

London and the dream career of stellar prospects and recognition faded fast. Insidious loneliness invaded the night, circling her tiny bedroom like a snake emerging from the undergrowth, tightening its grip when she could not sleep. To go home was to admit defeat and what would be waiting there anyway? Even trying to change her accent couldn't shake off the provincial label that had already been pinned on her.

Barbara and Arthur managed only one further visit. Mortified by the cost of the cheapest hotel; the fumes and constant drone of traffic; and the strange mix of accents they couldn't understand, they did not want to repeat the experience.

'Good grief Barbs, I thought university digs were bad.'

'I couldn't stand that noise...it never stops...I'd need earplugs.'

They'd gone out for their meals after Barbara had seen the state of the kitchen Liv shared, but she couldn't get used to 'that fancy food' and what it did to her digestion.

By the summer of '89, the job of covering the Chelsea Flower Show was a spark of light amongst the dull, uninspiring interviews she'd been given. Liv awoke to a fine sunny day and had slept well. She showered early, relieved that there was sufficient hot water in the tank for once, and put on a cotton dress that both flattered her slim frame and matched the blue of her eyes. She'd found it in a sale at a boutique round the corner and bought it even though it meant creeping dangerously close to her limit at the bank. Collecting her workbag and jacket she left for the tube in an optimistic frame of mind. It was a day that would impress Barbara and Arthur when she took their twice-weekly call, not least when they found out that Princess Diana would be there too.

Robert Smithson couldn't believe his luck when he'd been chosen to take the lead on the Council's team in planning a garden for Chelsea. For over a year, it was all he had on his mind. It drove Frosty Barker to distraction as May grew ever closer and she couldn't get him to focus on anything else.

'It might be important young man but so are these invoices. They need to be done now, not next year.'

However, Frosty's opinion changed dramatically once she too discovered that Princess Diana was to be there on the opening day.

'Have you got everything you need, Robert? You know you've only to ask. You know, I think I might go myself this year.'

Miraculously, the jobs she'd nagged him about evaporated, although it still did little to soothe his fraying nerves. Before the entourage left for Chelsea, an office junior gave him a bottle of 'Rescue Remedy' to calm him after she'd been to a weekend course on the 'Power of the Flower'. He found it still in his pocket on the first day of opening and had just put a few drops on his tongue, as instructed, when a young reporter approached him, tentative and shy.

'Hello...any chance of an interview please?'

She handed him her card, which he briefly checked before returning to look at Liv. At that moment, he wasn't sure which affected him most, the Remedy or the sight of a beautiful young woman standing in front of him. The others had gone for a break and he was on his own, too nervous to leave the garden unattended.

'Olivia Renfold, reporter with The Evening Standard' and she held out her hand.

'Hi,'

He stuffed the bottle into his pocket before shaking her outstretched hand.

'Something to calm your nerves?'

'What?...No...yes...no nothing like that...not what you think anyway.'

'Wouldn't blame you if you did...must be nerve-wracking doing this, especially with Princess Di wandering around.'

'Oh no chance she'll come in my direction...she'll only be looking at the big boys...this is small fry in comparison.'

'You wouldn't think so if you heard what some of the others have said to me...sent me away pretty sharpish.'

'Really? We're not all the same you know.'

'You mean you'll talk to me...give me a quick interview?'

'Why not...there's nothing more I can do now. We're as ready as we'll ever be.'

'Can't improve on perfection, eh?'

'Absolutely...it's Robert by the way...Robert Smithson.'

Liv started to relax at the sight of a friendly face and

welcoming smile, and Robert was thankful to break the intensity of waiting to be judged.

'Join me for a coffee?' Robert produced two cups and a battered blue flask from his rucksack.

'Thank you...best offer I've had all morning.'

Whilst Liv glanced over at the garden, Robert took in a different view. The fitted, flattering dress, the expanse of white neck, and the dangling earrings in the shape of long-stemmed roses were more than appealing. He wiped the spilt coffee from his hands on the back of a mud-stained jacket before taking it off and laying it on the stone kerb. Liv was happy to take up the offer if only to relieve the pressure of tight-fitting sandals. They tried the coffee and grimaced, both agreeing that the brown sludge really was too disgusting to drink.

They chatted easily about the Show, and the work it involved, and time passed pleasantly enough; it didn't seem like work at all, more like two friends catching up.

'Sorry about the coffee...promise I'll do better next time,'

'Next time?'

He stood up and held out his hand to help her up.

'If you'll allow me to make amends?'

She gave him a quizzical look

'Perhaps...'

'Sorry...bit presumptuous.'

He shook his head. 'Ignore me, it's been a tough few days and you appearing like...like some kind of exotic flower has thrown me.'

'Is that how you see me? An exotic flower? I've never been described as that before.'

'No! No sorry...oh god, I sound like a gibbering idiot...let me start again...how about I show you round the garden, explain the philosophy behind what we are trying to project and you write it down? A bit more professional?'

'Sounds good to me...but if I'm really honest with you I

know as much about gardening as that concrete post over there...I was only sent because the reporter who should be here has gone off sick and there was no one else to do it. So if you help me sound a little less stupid on the subject than I really am, I'll let you take me for that coffee...deal?'

'Done,' he said and his face beamed pink.

Robert, eager and engaging, drew her into this other world of his, the one about which she knew nothing. He made it sound so easy, like the graceful dancer who belies the blood, sweat and tears of hours spent practising. It became a morning of unexpected joy; he even sounded familiar though they'd never met. He wasn't a Londoner anyway.

'Where are you from then?'

Once the question had been asked and the answer given, the tone of the conversation changed. Discovering they had both been born a matter of streets away was a happy revelation.

'I should have guessed from that accent,' she laughed.

'I can't say I would have guessed from yours.'

'Yes, but you don't have to make an impression in a London office every day.'

'True...hard work is it?'

'Can be when you're trying to fit in...but it's what I wanted to do so...'

'Not sure I could do that...live so far away...don't you miss home?'

'In some ways yes, but then...'

'The work is worth it I suppose?'

Just hearing the words spoken out loud, pulled Liv up short when she struggled to convince herself, let alone anyone else, exactly what she had achieved.

'Oh absolutely'

'In that case, while I'm here...perhaps we could go out for a drink one night...that is if you...I mean...I know...'

'We come from the same town. I think I can trust you for a drink'

Robert's face lit up and he blushed once more.

'Brilliant...great...I'd love to hear more about what you do'

'It's nothing glamorous I promise you that.'

Liv looked at the beautiful compact little garden Robert had created and felt a twinge of envy.

'Is this what you do back home...create gorgeous gardens?'

Robert laughed, 'I wish...no...work at home is far more mundane...this is special...a one-off.'

He wanted to add, 'just like you', but after one meeting perhaps that would be going too far. It was uncharacteristic of him to want to impress anyone as much as he wanted to impress Liv.

She looked at him and smiled. He wasn't the most handsome of men but what he lacked in looks and height, standing at no more than five foot nine, he made up for with charm and personality. Olivia missed home and Robert's accent was enough to tempt her out for one night at least. It was a thrill to meet someone who wanted to talk as much about her as he did himself and his enthusiasm for the garden was infectious enough for her to be drawn in, to want to know more. She put her notebook and pen back into her bag; numbers were exchanged and she prepared to leave. Princess Di had been no more than the briefest glimpse of the back of her head amongst a thronging crowd, but it was enough to feed to Barbara, and for her Mother to tell her friends that 'our Olivia' met with royalty in her job.

Princess Di was the last person on Liv's mind and the differences between Olivia Renfold and Robert Smithson, hardly seemed to matter in the onrush of initial attraction and interest they took in one other. They made up a satisfying whole. Each glimpsed something beyond their own experience and held open their arms to it, eager to give it free rein, to see where it went.

The following weekend, after a date that hadn't gone far enough to satisfy either of them, she experienced a happier heart for once.

Barbara and Arthur duly met Robert Smithson and Barbara embraced the man Olivia introduced. When she discovered that his parents were no longer alive and that he lived on his own, she made a point of inviting him over for meals, even when Liv was back in London. Robert even accepted a couple of times, more to get to know more about Liv than the food, although he couldn't deny how good her roast dinner was.

'Well fancy that...you have to go all the way to London to meet somebody who just lives down the road.'

'I'm surprised you don't know him Barbs...you know every bugger else.'

'No need to swear Arthur.'

At the start of their daughter's relationship, Robert had been welcomed with enthusiasm; he was personable and held down a steady job, and that was enough.

'You work in the Parks Department eh?'

'Been there since college Mr Renfold...'

'Arthur lad...it's Arthur.'

'Right...Arthur...as I was saying, I started straight after college and last year I headed the team when we entered a garden at Chelsea...where I met Liv...er...Olivia.'

Arthur warmed to him, 'I like to do a bit of gardening meself.'

'Get away Arthur, you cut the grass when I remind you it needs doin' and shove in a few bedding plants in spring.'

'Don't listen to her...she doesn't know the half of what I do out there,' Arthur whispered to Robert.

'I heard that Arthur Renfold...I know exactly what you get up to out there. When that shed door's open I can see smoke coming out...he thinks I'm daft but I know he still has the odd roll-up despite what he's been told.'

Arthur quickly changed the subject, 'So you two are an item now?'

'Dad!'

'Just askin' that's all.'

'It's nice you live just a few streets away...fancy that...you both have to go to London to find each other,' Barbara repeated more than once over the course of the evening, feeling vindicated that home was better than 'that London'.

Once they had Robert on the hook, he wasn't to be easily let go. Following the invitations to Sunday dinner, Arthur was grateful for male company; he found plenty of common ground with Robert, and on occasion, the invitations were extended to 'inspect' the shed when Olivia and her mother were safely out of the way in the kitchen.

If Liv felt any unease over the swiftness of the move towards a more permanent relationship, it became lost beneath the desire to escape London life and find something less stressful, less lonely. When a vacancy arose for her old job at the Gazette, she was welcomed back by her old boss and life once again found a stable terrain.

The wedding was a small affair with a handful of family and friends. The only thing Liv insisted on was her choice of dress: short and cream, not white; and that the ceremony should take place at the registry office in town and not the local Church.

Apart from that, they each had their role: Barbara taking great delight in the organisation and logistics; Robert taking charge of the flowers; and Arthur taking charge of the bill. It wasn't an overly expensive affair but enjoyable nevertheless. The honeymoon was nothing more than a week in Wales, where it rained for much of the time, but Robert and Olivia were happy and she had been convinced by all that she had made the right decision. They made new friends, had a reasonable social life and the Sunday dinners at Barbara and Arthur's were a regular occurrence at least twice a month.

All was well in the Renfold and Smithson households and for a brief period of time, they were content. When anyone asked how they'd met, Robert liked to say that he'd saved Liv from the unsavoury side of life in London and Liv would smile benignly and say that she let him, although there would always be a part of her that wondered what life would be like if she'd stuck at the London job just a little longer. A provincial paper would never quite match the pull of the city. While not exactly resenting what she had given up, the shine of married life dulled within a short space of time and the quirks of opposite attraction left a longing that never quite went away; not until Daniel. Olivia's announcement that she was pregnant was an unexpected light in that darkening sky.

Chapter Ten

1994

A crumpled bed lay testament to a restless night where Liv had barely slept more than a couple of hours. The sound of the letterbox and soft thud of the morning's post reached her and she got up. Bee slept on in the cot at the other side of the room. Liv had moved to the spare bed in the early hours when the baby would not be pacified and she couldn't face Robert's intolerable nagging about what was wrong.

Despite a dramatic weight loss, Liv felt abnormally heavy as she hauled on dressing gown and slippers. She rarely looked in the mirror nowadays, unless by accident, but if she had, the reflection would not resemble the same person two years earlier. Unwashed, uncombed hair framed a white face with bloodshot eyes, a face that registered little beyond the needs of her baby.

Robert had already left for work and for that she was relieved. A house without Robert meant that the knots inside her stomach were not so tight and she could breathe more easily. A note on the kitchen table said 'Call me when you can. I'm in the office today, Rob'. She screwed it up and threw it in the bin.

Liv held Bee under her arm after a breakfast of nothing more than half a cup of coffee, and picked up the pile of mail from the mat. Three today: two official looking brown envelopes and a hand written airmail letter addressed to Olivia Smithson. The first two were left on the table by the door; the third she took upstairs. Internal warnings to eat were ignored in the urgency of more pressing matters. She dressed quickly and tucked a complacent Bee tightly into her pushchair.

Outside, the cold February air bit her face although the weather was at least calmer than yesterday. The ferocious Christmas winds had eased, and frost sparkled on the garden's grass. The walk at least kept the numbing chill at bay.

Bee, cocooned in her buggy, soon fell asleep as the rhythmic motion took effect. A pale sun broke through the lacklustre sky and trees started to drip in the silent street. Grantham Park wasn't far and Liv trod her usual route with little else on her mind other than reading the airmail letter. After a year's hiatus, she had been glad to hear from Savannah again and letters started to arrive almost weekly. For this she was grateful. As her only confidant and counsellor Sav was the closest friend she had left, despite the distance in miles. Robert had never liked her of course. He disapproved of the outlandish clothing and a carefree nature that still put domesticity in the same league as oppression. Liv kept her letters hidden from him.

A brisk walk to the Park gave Liv's cheeks a healthy glow despite the thinness of her face but her feet were soaked from walking on sodden grass. The weight of making that final decision was all-consuming, leaving little room for anything else in her mind.

The Park was empty save for a lone runner in the distance,

no one to notice a young mother talking to herself on a bench. Bee still slept as Liv pulled out the envelope and read Sav's letter.

Dearest Liv

I don't know what you are expecting me to say, but here goes. (Please ignore and screw it up if it's not the right time!!!)

My best advice to you is to get out. From everything you've told me you can't stay. It's obviously not working, it's making you ill and I can't bear to think of you stuck in that house. Go stay with your parents for a while? I love those two! They will take care of you and get you back on your feet. I can't read your letters without thinking that that's not the Liv I know. God, I wish I was there with you right now.

I'm planning on coming back soon but have a few things to finish here first. Sorry this is so short but I just needed to reach out

Stay strong Liv. I'll be with you as soon as I can

Lots of love and kisses

Sav

xxxxxxxxx

Liv sat still on the bench, looking into the distance, unaware of the cold as hot tears fell down her face.

An old man with a can in his hand, staggered up to the

bench and stopped, slurring a few indecipherable words in her direction. From his pocket he produced another can and offered it to her.

'Ha' one o' these if it helps darlin'...'

Liv, barely registering his presence, stood without answering.

'Well darlin'...you have a pleasant day too...'

In a more determined mood that the one she had started out with, her mind was made up. Bee awoke and began to cry. It was almost lunchtime and she was hungry.

Once the call had been made, packing took most of the time left before Robert got home and when he did she was ready to face him.

'I'm leaving Robert...Dad's picking me up tonight.'

'What?'

'I'm leaving...I can't do this any more. It's killing me...look at us,'

'No! We'll get through it...please Liv.'

'I'm sorry...just give me time.'

Liv stood impassive as he grabbed her arm. This was the moment he'd long been dreading but when his sorrow morphed into anger it merely cemented her resolve.

Arthur arrived to collect his daughter and granddaughter after six o'clock. It was dark and the wind had whipped up again, blowing in from the north. Its razor thrust was keenly felt despite the scarf, gloves and hat that Barbara insisted he wore before he left the house.

'Don't fuss Barbs, this is bad enough as it is.'

'I know but you're not one hundred percent yet.'

'I still can't believe it's come to this...they should have stuck together...that's what you do when things get rough. It's what we always did.'

'I know but we never went through anything like this. Nobody knows how they'll react when it happens do they?'

'I guess not...but still there's another bairn to think about now.'

'Our Olivia's not in a good place...she's not coping with that baby let alone herself. We have to bring her here...surely even Robert can see that.'

Arthur set off with a heavy heart and a sense of foreboding over what might greet him at the other end. He pulled up outside the house and looked across for a minute or two before getting out of the car. Lights shone from the kitchen and hall but he couldn't see anyone inside. He tapped gently on the door and Robert let him in.

'Hello, Robert.'

Robert didn't reply but stood to one side revealing four large bags, a pushchair and a baby car seat behind. His shoulders were slumped and his head hung low. The fight to make Liv stay had been lost long ago and the rawness of emotion was etched in a puffed face and red, tear-stained eyes. Liv called from upstairs that she would be down soon.

'I don't know what to say, lad.'

'Nothing to say...she's made up her mind...here's their stuff.'

Arthur looked around uneasily before loading the car.

When it was done, Liv came downstairs, paler and even thinner than the last time he'd seen her. Arthur tried to hide his shock but stayed mute on the subject. Olivia held the baby close.

'We need the car seat fitting.'

'I'll do it.'

'Thank you, Robert.'

Arthur stood with Olivia as Robert went out.

'Are you absolutely sure this is what you want? Not too late to change your mind y'know?'

'I won't change my mind.'

Robert came back before long, announcing that it was all done and Arthur resigned to the fact that he would be taking Olivia and the baby back home.

'I'll start the car and get it warmed up before you two come out...give me a minute...it's bitter out there.'

Liv and Bee were left standing in the hall with Robert. She pulled the shawl up close and tight but didn't look up. Robert bent to kiss the warm, sweet-smelling head of his daughter.

'If you change your mind...'

'I won't. You'll see Bee...we'll sort something out.'

She didn't wait for Arthur to come back to the house and Robert, numb with pain, watched their every step from the doorway. Arthur took the baby and after much fumbling with cold fingers managed to strap her into her seat. Olivia sat at the back too.

'All ready now?'

She'd left the house without turning and sat next to Bee with eyes cast down. Arthur paused before getting in and turned to see Robert standing in the doorway.

'Just give me a minute love...I won't be long.'

Arthur closed the car door and went back to the house, ushering Robert inside.

'I'm sorry it's come to this Robert...I really am...mebbe she'll feel different after a time away...I'm sure of it...you take care lad...we'll look after them both I promise you that...'

And as an afterthought, but not certain if it was such a good idea considering Barbara's last words to him, added, 'Ring any time.'

'I don't know what to do Arthur...'

'I know lad...you just see to yourself for a bit...let things settle down...I'm not far away if you want to talk...and you'll see Beatrice...don't worry about that.'

'Why did it have to happen? What did we do?'

'It was nothing you did...stop thinking like that. No one's to blame for any of it. We need to focus on that little one right now...do what's best for her...for all of you.'

'I know.'

Robert's heart was too full to say more. Arthur gave him a quick hug; he wasn't usually the hugging sort, but it felt like the right thing to do. Robert was left watching the car disappear down the street. Eventually, he shut the door to find a small pink hat dropped on the floor and fell to his knees beside it. There would be many reminders over the long days, weeks and months ahead; a stray toy under the sofa; a dummy in the kitchen; each accusing him of not doing enough to make them stay. Robert picked up the hat and held it to his face, inhaling the sweet baby smell and sobbed.

Barbara fidgeted nervously in the living room, constantly checking the clock; walking to the window to look out; straightening cushions that were already straight; and picking off specks of fluff that were visible to no eye but her own. She thought about the last time Liv had stayed with them for any length of time, when she'd finished university and started her first job as a community reporter for the Gazette. The move back home hadn't lasted long, however. It was barely six months before they clashed mercilessly on too many occasions. Restless and ambitious, when Olivia managed to get a job as a junior researcher/reporter with the Evening Standard in London, they all breathed a sigh of relief. Was it really only six years ago? The passage of time often played tricks on Barbara and even though she was barely fifty-two, today she felt older than her years and wondered how they would all get on now.

The London job coincided with Arthur's diagnosis of heart problems; nothing too serious but enough to set Barbara into protection mode. She had been as much relieved as pleased when the London job came up. A quiet life was the best remedy for Arthur, despite what he said. Rest was what Barbara prescribed, rest and an endless supply of tea. And she was in no doubt that that was what would be needed for her daughter.

However, the broken figure who arrived on the Renfold doorstep that afternoon was not the daughter she knew. Barbara quickly realised that her Olivia's care would take up every reserve of patience, and careful handling. If she was ready to take on whatever was needed for her and the baby, she was not ready for what she saw. Nothing could have done that. Hollow-cheeked and rail thin, the past sixteen months were written in every ravaged line across Olivia's face.

Wordless, she was brought inside and led towards the sofa where she lay her head on Barbara's lap. Barbara gently stroked the hair of her child. As the baby slept Arthur looked helplessly on.

Chapter Eleven

1996

Following two years of slow and painful progress, Liv was persuaded that there might be a benefit to counselling. Two years of accepting what happened to Daniel, coping with the demands of a toddler and living with her parents, were taking their toll. Barbara and Arthur had willingly stepped up to the mark. They nursed their own broken child back to health even though taking on a severely troubled daughter and the daily demands of a grandchild, were not achieved without cost. Arthur's heart was being closely monitored on the understanding that he might need an operation if things got worse, a fact they went to great pains to keep from Olivia. However, one morning at breakfast, the questions they had avoided inevitably began.

'Mum, what are those tablets Dad's taking?'

'Oh nothing...nothing to worry about love, just precautionary.'

'Is it his heart again?

'Well...'

Liv fell silent; for a while, she'd known it was time.

'You can't keep doing what you do for me...I've got to make changes haven't I?'

'You been ill yourself love, we know that.'

'I'm so sorry...you shouldn't have to do all this for me...it feels wrong.'

'We do what has to be done that's all.'

'It feels as though I'm just coming out of a bad dream... even though I know it's not a dream. I have to face things now, don't I?'

'It's been two years...time to move forward love? That little girl needs her Mummy more as she gets older.'

'I'm so sorry...'

Liv shoulders shook with the tears she couldn't hold back.

'Don't, love...don't...we're getting through it.'

'Have you still got the name of that counsellor?'

'I have...but only if you're sure that's what you want.'

'I'm sure.'

Liv's third visit to Marion Fletcher saw her sitting in an empty waiting room with twenty minutes to spare. Having been ushered out by Barbara to catch an earlier bus than was necessary, and a 'You never know what that traffic's going to be like,' Liv acquiesced.

Like a child, she'd grown accustomed to accepting what was asked of her for over two years, but she wasn't a child and needed to make her own decisions, starting with a refusal to let Barbara go with her and asking the doctor to help her reduce the medication that left her in a stupefied state much of the time.

The decision to take up counselling had been long in gestation, but it was another hurdle to cross on the road to recovery. Barbara and Arthur watched with growing hope as small signs of progress appeared in their daughter.

'I think our Olivia's put on a bit of weight Arthur,'

'Aye, it's nice to see her start to get through a plate of food again.'

'She was singing to Bee this morning...'

'And she's starting to put a bit of lipstick on...make more of an effort.'

With that, they both took great pains to let Olivia shoulder more of the responsibilities of bringing up Bee and relaxed their control a little.

Liv's session with Marion that day saw her open up more than she had done during the previous two visits. A lifeline had been offered and she grasped it.

In the silence of the waiting room, she thought about Robert and his over-cautious nagging the week before. Was there really a time when they had been truly happy, when he allowed her to make her own decisions and show trust? They had been apart long enough to see the divorce go through without question and he had what he needed now to marry Marsha. Funny how it hadn't been urgent until recently and she wondered if Marsha was pregnant. She felt no jealousy, only relief that he might not make any more ridiculous demands about getting custody of Bee. They had both moved on and he needed to let go.

Those long minutes, waiting on a hard chair in a stark room devoid of embellishment, allowed Liv to give herself a counselling session without distraction. Another letter had arrived from Savannah who had not yet managed to come home and she planned to write a long overdue reply.

Deep in thought, Liv barely noticed someone else in the room until he made his presence felt by the clattering of a dropped pen. He'd already pinned a flyer to a noticeboard near the door. On a narrow table below, he spread out a pile of remaining flyers, moving aside the older, yellowing collection, to get maximum recognition for his own. Liv jolted from her thoughts and looked up.

'Sorry...didn't mean to startle you...you were miles away.'

'Don't worry.'

'Not the most stimulating of places to wait in, is it?'

'No...'

'Not too much in the line of reading matter.'

'No.'

The man, looking somewhere between fifty and sixty, paused, unsure whether to go on, but was intrigued by the sad young woman in the dark blue coat, faded jeans and scuffed brown boots. She straightened her back and turned her head towards the closed door marked 'Marion Fletcher' willing it to open. An impressive string of qualifications, none of which Liv knew the meaning, came after the name. It was time, but the appointment was running late.

'I won't disturb you, but if you think you might be interested in this, I'm starting a new group soon...just down the road...I take a room at top of the Flying Horse.'

He gave Liv one of his flyers: 'Write Yourself Well' it said in bold at the top, with a quill as a backdrop. She didn't read any further.

'Oh I'm not sure I...'

'You don't have to sign up now,' he said and gave her a broad smile, 'I'm not running a secret cult...really...you can ask Marion...she'll vouch for me...I hope so anyway.'

He had a pleasing smile, open and honest, with eyes that matched the gesture.

'Yes...I'm sure,' she replied and smiled in return.

'There's more info on the back...and my number if you want to...you know...or just turn up I don't mind, m'dear. The more the merrier...my name's Dom by the way...Dominic Raywell if you want my Sunday name'

'Thank you...Dominic Raywell.'

She put it into her pocket to show willing as the office door opened, and Dom left as quietly as he'd arrived.

There was no one else in Marion's room; Liv assumed that the previous patient had left by the side door that she had used herself that first time; it helped maintain privacy when it was needed, when her face had been blotched with tears.

'Liv...hi...hope you've not been waiting too long...afraid we ran over a little.'

Marion Fletcher looked all of her sixty-three years. With severe, short-cropped, grey hair that went beyond taming, it sat atop a face susceptible to deep lines that had already formed around her mouth and eyes. Her manner though belied her appearance and was warm and open.

Liv's reluctance was slowly melting over each session as she responded to the gentle coaxing of Marion's easy manner. By the end of that third session, she would start to tentatively approach the deep-rooted pain that still remained inside despite outward shows of moving on. She was pleased to see Marion.

'No that's ok...there was a man here just now putting up a poster...gave me one of his flyers.'

'Ah, that'll be Dom...lovely man. I've heard nothing but good things said about his writing groups. I know of a few people who've given him a try and been amazed with what they've done. It's great to see he's starting up again...he called me the other day...I thought we'd lost him for a while but I'm pleased to see he's back.'

'He seemed nice,'

'Think it might be something you would want to give a go? You told me last time about your writing, said you'd been a reporter...so you won't be new to it...not that that would make the slightest difference to Dom'.

'That was a long time ago...I'm not sure now...'

'You know, I went once out of curiosity and I was really impressed...'

'Mmm...maybe.'

'Anyway, let's continue shall we...come on in...sit down and make yourself comfortable.'

A glass of water and a box of tissues were the only items on a small table in front of her chair, both placed within easy reach. Marion sat opposite and commented on how well she was looking that day. Before long, they moved on to the reason she was there and Liv recounted her progress of the previous week. With Marion's encouragement, she also opened the door to her past just a little wider.

'How did it go today, love?'

Liv had barely set foot through the door before the kettle was on and Barbara began the first of many questions. Arthur had been working in the shed on another project for Bee, a wooden shop for which Barbara was already collecting little boxes and packets. The sound of hammering reached the kitchen until he was reminded that it was time to pick Bee up from nursery, something he always looked forward to.

They were into their third year of living together, still a time of adjusting their lives, finding the right words and gestures to fit in with each other, and as Arthur put it: a time of walking on eggshells so as not to upset Olivia and give Bee as happy a childhood as they could manage. It wasn't exactly the retirement they had planned together but they would always put Olivia and Beatrice first no matter what the circumstances, heart condition or no heart condition, which Arthur convinced them all was fully under control. Like Liv, he preferred going to the doctor's appointments on his own and felt it only necessary to give the briefest of information.

He already knew that an operation was inevitable but would tell Barbara in his own good time.

Barbara had taken to living a life vicariously through her daughter, adopting a leading role in childcare with all the organisation and routines that went with it. She felt it only right that she should be allowed to ask questions about Olivia's therapy, which she did quite frequently. Liv evaded most, usually by putting the kettle on herself and making the tea when she came home. Today was no different and she got away with the stock reply that seemed to placate her mother, but in reality, didn't.

'It was fine, Mum...same as last time and the time before... helping me to put some things into perspective...move on... you know.' It was followed by a smile and a hug, and the need for saying anything further was saved by the entrance of Bee and Arthur back from nursery.

'Mummy...look.'

'Wow, BeeBee that's a fantastic picture...we'll have a whole gallery of them soon...won't we Grandad?'

Grandad had promised to put it up on the wall and in a rash burst of enthusiasm he said he would make a new frame. Making Bee smile was a priority in his life.

Liv crouched down to Bee's level, holding the picture and looked at Arthur beaming with pride. The distraction of Bee never failed to save them from awkward conversations that were better left unsaid.

'I remember the last time you were let loose with a saw and a bag of nails...still got the scar, Dad?'

Arthur raised his head and turned away.

'Cheek...that was a little misjudgment on finger placement, nothing more. The next project's coming on just fine I'll have you know.'

'Mm.'

He went back to his Daily Mirror and rustled the newspaper page by page until he reached the sports section. Barbara sniffed and drank her tea; she'd tried to put him off the idea of more woodwork, but had actually warmed to this one when she'd seen what he'd started. Arthur's DIY skills were rudimentary at best, but he relished his frequent visits to Draper's, and even more the company of his friend Charlie, although he always came away with far more than he went in for.

Liv's return to what Barbara and Arthur considered a 'normal life' was a gradual work in progress; small milestones indicating that slowly but surely they were getting her back. Taking Bee to nursery and clawing back the little things of a previous life she'd given up on, was a light switching on in a darkened room.

Despite Robert's pleading, he soon knew that having Liv back in his life was never going to happen. When Marsha appeared on the scene the certainty of it brought relief and closure. Despite his early promises of change and protestations that Bee needed him around more, Liv remained steadfast in her resolve. There were no more mentions of returning to her former home and Bee accepted life with Grandma and Grandpa without question when she knew no other.

'All our Olivia needs now is a social life again...she needs to get out more...meet people...not be stuck here with us every night...what's happened to all the friends she used to have eh?'

'I don't know love, but all in good time.'

'I think we have to accept that she's never going back to Robert, not now there's another woman on the scene.'

On some things they did agree, and one was that filling books with half-finished tales in her spare time was not going to expand her shrinking group of friends or replace a dying marriage that was never going to be revived.

Chapter Twelve

Tea was prompt at five, as always, and by seven, Bee was asleep in bed. Arthur and Barbara sat in companionable silence and Liv was upstairs writing. An unexpected knock at the door breaking the routine was not welcome. Barbara answered after peering through the window to see who it was. She called upstairs to Liv.

'Robert's at the door love...you never said he was coming,'

'What? He never said he was coming round...tell him I'm not in.'

Barbara looked at Arthur, 'What does he want now, Dad?'

'Well you won't know until you talk to him, will you, love.'

'Tell him I'm not here...please.' Liv hissed down the stairs.

'If I do that he'll only come back later...you know what he's like.'

The door was opened to an anxious-looking Robert standing on the step.

'Hello Barbara...is Liv in?'

'She's not expecting you is she?'

'No...but I really do need to talk to her...sorry I didn't ring first.'

'All right I'll go fetch her...you'd better come on in.'

Robert was taken to the small sitting room at the front of the house, the one still used to store Liv's belongings that wouldn't fit into the box room she now had as a bedroom. It had been a dining room but hadn't been used for that purpose in many years, not since her grandfather's funeral.

When Liv was eventually coaxed down she found Robert sitting on one of only two chairs that were clear. He stood up when she appeared.

'What is it, Robert? What do you want?'

'How are you, Liv?'

He sat down again, hands clenched, twisting them as though washing under a tap, searching for the right words. Liv remained standing and said nothing.

Robert finally looked up, combing his fingers through his hair; shifting in the hard seat, also wishing he too could be elsewhere.

'Liv, I won't mess about...I've come to tell you something you ought to hear from me...I wanted to tell you in person so...so...'

Liv's face registered no emotion; she wasn't about to make it easy.

'I'm getting married and I want to get the divorce finalised as soon as we can.'

'Really...I asked you for that a long time ago if you remember.'

'I know you did but I always hoped that you might change your mind one day. I was wrong I know...and I'm sorry.'

Liv tried to read the expression on his face. Was he still hopeful despite what he had just said?

'Rob from the day Bee was born you've never stopped trying to control me, coerce me, make me into something I can't be for you. You left me a wreck. I'm not that same person.'

'Whatever you think, Liv I did love you. Still do. What we went through was…'

'Rob don't bring all that up again, please. What *we* went through? What you put me through more like.'

Robert winced at the words. That wasn't how he saw it all but he had enough about him to realise that now wasn't the time.

'Please get the papers ready and I'll sign. I presume this has something to do with your new girlfriend?'

'Partly.'

'Partly?'

'Yes…no…all right yes. We want to get married.'

'Finally, we're getting there. Congratulations Robert. I hope you'll both be very happy.'

Robert's face fell.

'Liv you know I wouldn't if…if you…you just have to say the word.'

'Oh Rob, we were over a long time ago.'

Liv softened slightly, perhaps remembering something of the time when they had loved each other; when life was full of promise and they were happy.

'I know.'

If there was part of him deep down that hoped against hope Liv would still relent and come back to him, he stopped pursuing it further. He knew better by now than to try to persuade her to come back with Bee. Besides, a new life with Marsha was already in progress and over the last three months she had lived more at his house than her own. The signs were there: the toothbrush in the bathroom, the hairbrush and nightie in the bedroom, food in the fridge and flowers on the table.

Liv had an inkling of what was going on long before

Robert even mentioned her name. She'd bumped into a colleague of his in town one day who'd let it slip that Robert and Marsha were getting close. Having thought that he might be in with a chance of dating Liv himself, he expressed the hope that she would want to go out for a drink with him sometime. The fact that he was still married was never mentioned but the response Liv gave made it perfectly clear where she stood on the offer. Robert and Liv had in the past laughed about the fantasy he'd held for her; it had been a joke at the time but he was persistent.

'Right I'll get it done then.'

'Absolutely...you should have started it when I moved out.'

'What...'

'Is there anything else?'

'No...yes...perhaps one more thing.'

Liv knew what was coming before he could say it and it wasn't the first time he'd broached the subject.

'The answer's no, Robert. Bee is perfectly happy here...this is her home now.'

'You know if I thought there was a chance that we could try again...'

'It's taken me a long time to piece my life together after all you put me through but I'm getting there...there really is no going back so please don't bring it up again.'

'No...I understand.'

'No you don't understand...that was always the problem... you never did.'

Robert let it rest. He might not be in a position just yet to argue about custody when childcare was readily available through Barbara and Arthur, but things were about to change.

Robert left quietly and Liv sat for a moment absorbing the news. She felt no bitterness, just intense agitation; there was nothing left to hold against him, but still a niggle as to how far he would go in his mission to take custody of Bee. 'I am not that same person Robert so don't even think about it.'

The calendar showed three cute kittens on September's page and had a ring around the ninth: Liv's thirtieth birthday. They would celebrate as they had for the previous three, with a family tea. Barbara made a cake that Bee helped ice and decorate with edible pink roses. In the morning, the usual gifts of chocolates and flowers were duly given before Liv took Bee to nursery and the day bore no difference to any other beyond a birthday card from Savannah and the usual lament that she couldn't spend it with her.

Arthur met Liv in the hall when she arrived back home:

'I'm taking you out this lunchtime.'

'What? Why?'

'We've nothing much planned before the big birthday tea and your Mother's out...and I just want to spend a bit o' time with my daughter.'

'Dad we spend every day together one way or another.'

'I know that. I just want to have you to meself for an hour or so...if that's all right with you?'

'Course it is. It would be lovely...just a surprise that's all... so Mum's not coming too?'

'She's out at Betty's...it's just me and you.'

Liv was puzzled but nonetheless pleased at the prospect. They'd always been close and it wasn't often they had time together; just the two of them.

'That's lovely Dad.'

The night before, Arthur had watched Olivia sitting in front of the television looking at nothing more challenging than a continuous loop of soaps and quiz shows with her Mother. He could never stand more than five minutes before he wandered back to the kitchen to pour over every word in the local evening paper. He would stay there until the news came on at nine o'clock then join them both in the living room bringing in a last tea before bed. Although he could see Olivia making progress in all she said, did, and ate, the sadness on her face lingered; not the sadness of depression, but the sadness of the loss of a life she would never get back again. It pained him to think of her spending day after day with no more than what they could offer.

The Dog and Duck was the nearest local and took a good fifteen minutes walk. Liv linked arms with her Dad as they set along at a slow pace, and she took care not to tire him too much.

'This is nice,' she said and squeezed his arm, 'now are you going to tell me the real reason for our little outing, or when we have a glass in front of us? I get the feeling it's not just because it's my birthday.'

'Cheeky beggar.'

Liv squeezed a little more tightly and they talked about Bee and past birthdays until they reached the pub. It was quiet inside and they had no problem finding a table free.

'You sit there Dad and I'll get the drinks and a menu. Pint of Tetley's?'

'Better make it a half,' he replied in concession to his promise to Barbara that he would have nothing more than a shandy.

Liv came back with a pint and a glass of white wine for herself.

'I won't say anything if you won't...it's my birthday and I've already ordered your favourite.'

'Cheers love...happy birthday.'

'Cheers, Dad', and they clinked glasses. Arthur took a long draft of the foam-headed pint,

'Aah, that's good.'

'So, what's on your mind then? I'm curious.'

'What, can't a Dad bring out his daughter without there being any other reason than he wants to? He took another sip of the beer, savouring the taste. Heart problems were one thing, but they were soon dismissed in the euphoria of the moment.

'You're only partly right...I worry about you, Olivia. I just want to know if you've any plans beyond watching Corrie with your Mum of a night.'

'Oh no! Am I turning into Mum already?'

'Get away wi' yer...you know what I mean.'

'I know, but you don't have to worry about me. I'm getting there...in fact, there is something I might give a go.'

'What's that then?'

Liv fished the crumpled flyer out of her pocket and showed it to Arthur,

'Write Yourself Well' eh. Is that what they give you nowadays instead o' tablets?'

'I met the guy who's running it when I was waiting to see Marion a while ago. She says he's good...and I want to get back into more writing. The next course starts soon. Might give it a go. And you're right; I can't go on as I am. I do know that. Counselling is ok as far as it goes but I want to do more for myself. I started writing something the other night and really got into it; the old feelings were coming back...tingling in the fingers and all that...it felt good.'

'I was going to say why don't you give me a hand in the garden, but ...'

'Dad you are joking. I'm worse than you.'

'Humph...no this sounds more up your street...you should sign up,'

'I think I will...I'll give him a call.'

'Good...good.'

They sat in comfortable silence before two plates of sausage and mash arrived.

'I just hope this doesn't spoil the birthday tea...Mother'll never forgive us.'

'We'll be fine.'

'It's been a long time since you and me came out together. I never get a word in edgeways when your Mother's about. It's nice to get you on your own for a bit...if that's all right.'

'Don't be daft...course it is.'

Liv put her head on his shoulder before eating.

'I know you worry about me but I will get back on track... I promise. Please don't think I don't want to change because I do...just not certain what to do yet work-wise...but this course is a start.'

Over lunch, they talked about her options for employment, how it could be managed and where she should start looking, and Arthur was content.

'Right, that's enough of the serious stuff...I can't pretend knowing where to start looking for a job for you...how about another round instead? We've earned it. All this talking makes your throat parched. Mother can wait a bit longer.'

'I love you, Dad. You always make me feel better.'

'Love you too Olivia...and I'll never stop worrying about you...you know that,'

'There's no need...I'll be fine...there's something out there waiting for me.'

'Talking about something out there...you all right about that wedding in December? You've been quiet on it since Robert told us'.

'Again Dad...I'll be fine. It'll be good for Robert...stop him probing into my life as much as he has...hopefully anyway.'

'Aye, there's that I suppose.'

Arthur reflected for a while before adding, 'Soon be Christmas!'

'Behave!'

.   .   .

Despite Liv's argument to the contrary, the wedding was never going to be an easy day to get through, but she coped with the mix of emotions better than she thought. Bee paraded through the house in a pretty dark blue velvet dress, trimmed with white lace, set off by shiny black shoes. December's page on the calendar, four puppies wearing red bobble hats, showed a circle around Saturday 7: Robert and Marsha's wedding.

'Bee you look beautiful!'

'Why aren't you coming Mummy?'

'I can't my darling...I'm going out to the shops with Grandma this afternoon.'

Bee, with no recollection of ever living with Robert, viewed the wedding with few feelings beyond wearing a pretty dress and going to a party.

'Let's get your coat on sweetie, Daddy will be here soon.'

Robert turned up promptly at two, already attired in his wedding suit and ready for the registry office at four. Marsha was dressing at a hotel nearby with her mother, newly arrived from Cornwall, and Debbie in attendance. He would drop Bee off and get back to his best man waiting at home. It had been a late night and his sore head was just starting to feel the welcome relief of two painkillers.

'Thanks for this Liv...are you ok?'

'I am...I'm happy for you Robert...really.'

They looked at each other and their faces conveyed all that neither could put into any more words.

'Ok Bee, try not to get too many stains on that gorgeous dress of yours will you?'

She took a deep breath as she watched Bee skip along with Robert to his car and felt a sharp tug inside when she turned and waved. There was no going back now. No matter how hard Robert had tried to get her to change her mind, at last, he was moving on. 'I don't love you, Robert,' she'd plainly told him when he persuaded her to go out for a drink one last time,

'Just to talk, Liv.' He'd cried in the car park of the pub when they parted and even though part of her wanted to hold him and tell him it would be all right, she'd walked away.

Thoughts briefly flew to their wedding day but hopes and dreams for a future together had long drifted away.

The door closed as Barbara emerged from the kitchen.

'Thought it best to leave you to it...everything all right?'

'Everything's fine Mum...just as it should be. Wrap up warm, it's cold out.'

Chapter Thirteen

1997

Liv's first visit to The Flying Horse was a tentative experience, not quite what she expected, although if asked beforehand she couldn't have said what that was either. Not as inviting as the Dog and Duck, it was dark inside as well as out, emitting a low hum of conversation from regulars who were already collecting at the bar. There was no music and no other entertainment beyond an electronic gaming machine with constantly flashing lights grabbing the attention of passing punters. The optics behind the bar were basic and few when demand rarely went beyond the brewery's standard beers and lager. And the food on offer was nothing more than crisps, nuts and pork scratchings hanging from cards on the wall.

Liv was almost tempted to walk back out, but a new strength of mind decided that she should at least give it one go and she approached the barman.

'Can you tell me where the writing group is please?'

'That I can love...top o' those stairs and on the right... and you can take a drink up if you want something.'

'No, it's ok thanks,' Liv replied before later realising that buying a drink might be expected when the room came free of charge. At the top of the stairs, she paused at a hand-printed notice that read, 'Yes, this is the Writing Group. Come on in!' before stepping into the unknown.

The door was open and the first person she saw was Dom with two men and a woman, each with a drink in hand. Dom stopped talking when he saw her, made his excuses, and came straight over, always pleased to welcome a new face.

'Lovely to see you...I wasn't sure if I'd put you off after you rang me but I'm glad I didn't...I can be a bit evangelistic sometimes.'

The expression on Dom's face was as welcoming as his voice. Liv smiled shyly and reassured him that no, he'd been fine. As they spoke three more joined the group and Dom nodded a greeting to each.

'Come to the table and I'll introduce you', he said extending an open arm.

'I'm glad you've come. When you told me you'd done some writing before, I was hoping to see you.'

'I wasn't sure what you'd expect...I...I...'

'I don't have expectations of literary grandeur if that's what you mean...I'm just here to help you help yourself by writing whatever comes to mind...it's a therapeutic process and it works...really. I will guide you and you take it from there. Nothing too prescriptive.'

There were ten of them in total when four more slipped in and Dom marked the names of those present on an officially printed sheet. It was a locally funded programme and records had to be completed to keep it going.

Liv smiled in response to the 'good evenings' of the four new entrants as they made their way to the table. It seemed that most of them knew each other already, but introductions were made at the start of the session for the benefit of Liv and the one other new person that night: a middle-aged man with an unfortunate stammer and a tendency to blush when asked anything. The kindness and patience shown to him was encouraging and by the end of the session, his hunched shoulders relaxed just a little.

Dom was very happy with ten attending; the minimum requirement was six, so four above that number was good. There should have been twelve but two didn't turn up: one had to take care of his sick mother; and the other changed his mind when he thought himself not a good enough writer, despite Dom's protestation that it didn't matter how much or how little he had written before. Dom wouldn't press him further, but left him with the option of changing his mind if he ever reconsidered. They were a good mix tonight and it boded well for future meetings.

Trevor and Richard, brothers, possibly between forty and fifty, had been coming for over a year now and always sat together. They struggled with issues the others could only guess at, but Dom understood that somewhere in their background lurked an abusive father. The trauma of their past was masked by a double act and quick-witted humour.

Amanda, grey, short and stocky, with a face saddened by the loss of her beloved husband of forty-two years, saw through the humour at times. She would comfort them in motherly fashion during the break when she'd glimpsed their pain breaking through. It deflected from her own and was how she coped with life: helping others cope with theirs.

Patrick was the serious writer of the group, and when he read out his poetry, the rapt attention of the others encouraged him to continue and overcome his fragile state of mind. With a backlog of shame and embarrassment in a life he'd had no control over, his writing stirred compassion inside those who listened.

Liv wasn't sure that she could ever bare her soul in that way, but after the first hour, she warmed to this little group of broken souls and to Dom's gentle reassuring ways. He helped them tease out words that the voice couldn't speak. It was a slow, cautious beginning, chipping piece by piece at the enormous whole, but over time, a sense of relief would burst through the dam and encourage her to go on.

There was no compulsion on what they should write. Dom saw and understood the struggles and with gentle encouragement, let them dictate their own pace. And as part of this welcoming group fixing plasters over a wounded past, Liv recognised herself. Memories too raw to share were buried so deep that the thought of exposing herself to scrutiny was unthinkable. But as time went by, and with Marion's encouragement too, committing the past to paper became a promising further step in the right direction.

On that first night, Liv listened to Dom's low, mellow voice that soothed like balm on a hurting wound. She tried her hand at writing poetry, something she'd never done before, and surprised herself when the words flowed from pen to page.

It was only much later when Liv could finally acknowledge, and write the words, 'it wasn't my fault,' that the story of Daniel began. Stilted, incomplete, the words gave her a voice.

Daniel.

On May 2nd, 1992 Daniel was born. He was our first baby and he was perfect. I adored every inch of him. He is still with me. Every day. If I close my eyes I can feel his soft baby skin and see those blue eyes that followed me around the room. His baby blonde hair, sprouting at funny angles made me smile. His round soft cheeks; the baby smell. I ache for him still as I write. I close my eyes and he's here. When he woke me up in the middle of the night, I never minded. I used to tell Rob not to worry. He was just checking up on us, that's all. I paced the nursery, cradling him after feeding until he fell back to sleep. Only one night he went back to sleep and never woke up.

On Wednesday, August 5th I woke up first, surprised at having slept through the night. The sun was bright and our curtains were thin, letting in the summer sun. I knew it was going to be a beautiful day. I was going to take Daniel to the Park. I was happy that morning. So happy. So grateful for that first unbroken night's sleep. Yes, I was grateful.

When the police came they told me 'It's standard procedure' and 'These things happen'. But no one told me why. Or what I could have done. Should have done. Even now I do not know. Only you can tell me that my beautiful baby boy, but you are not here.

1992

When Rob went back to work, Liv swallowed the prescribed tablets that should have eased the pain and numbed the grief and guilt. But they did neither. Christmas arrived but it meant nothing. To celebrate the gift of life when the most wanted gift had been taken away was not possible. Daniel wasn't there and Liv didn't want to be there either.

Decorations appeared and a tree was put up. They drank sherry when the lights were switched on and raised a glass, thinking but not saying the words 'last Christmas we...'

Last Christmas they were happy; last Christmas they made plans and chose names.

Chapter Fourteen

Draper's hardware store sat in the middle of a small commercial estate, nestled between 'Deb's Top to Toe Tanning' and 'Dave's Auto Repair Workshop'. Last year, during the latest expansion, Charles Draper, in a move to show that he wasn't completely out of touch with the modern world, embraced new technology and the age of the computer. Of course, he struggled when the theory did not match the reality of what he had done.

The newly arrived box took up a good part of his desk, and the thick volume of instructions that came with it bore witness to his total incomprehension about what to do next. Arthur was there when it was unpacked. They walked round it, stared at it as though it had landed from another planet, and looked again at the instructions. Arthur, sucking through his teeth, didn't know what to make of it,

'No good looking at me Charlie boy.'

'No...thought not.'

'Get someone in's my best advice.'

'I've been thinking that for a while now. I could do with a bit of help in the office. Helen's pestering me to work less...

take her out more she said...and Michael's too busy with the other side of the business.'

Arthur's ears pricked up,

'Take her out more?'

'Something about old houses...gardens...that kind of thing.'

Arthur looked again at the computer, and then back to Charlie, 'You're never too old to learn y'know'. He knew exactly what 'that kind of thing' meant. Charles made a brew. They talked about football and the upcoming match on Saturday and the computer sat in a state of solitary neglect.

The following week, an ad appeared in the local paper for a part-time worker in office administration 'with computer experience'. Arthur was pondering over it at the kitchen table when Olivia walked in and filled the kettle.

'Tea Dad?'

'No, I'm all right thanks.'

'Anything interesting?

'Usual rubbish...although this might be worth looking at,'

'What's that?'

He swivelled the newspaper around to Olivia with a smile across his face. She read it and gave him a quizzical look.

'You're retired Dad...and anyway you know you'd end up spending all your wages there'

'Not me lass...you. I don't know anything about computers but it could be right up your street. Didn't you do some computer learning at the library?'

'I did but it was just basic stuff.'

'Well, it's a sight more than me and Charlie have done. You'd stand as good a chance as anyone.'

'Mm...I'll take a look.'

Arthur didn't tell her about the conversation he'd already had with Charlie and the throwaway parting shot that 'it could be just the thing for our Olivia. She knows everything about computers.'

Liv took the newspaper upstairs with her tea and gave the ad full attention. The last job rejection, along with three others, had hit hard and her confidence was at a low ebb. Barbara and Arthur steadfastly maintained that there was no rush but Liv was desperate for change and in a rush of enthusiasm rang Draper's the next morning. The hours were flexible and few to start. With the thought of Bee already at nursery, and soon to be starting school, the door to more freedom was inching open just that little bit wider. The tedium of long days, with little to occupy her mind, was telling in the itch of restlessness that needed to be scratched.

Within a couple of weeks, old Mr Draper sat behind his office desk and interviewed the three applicants he deemed suitable from the fifteen applications received. He gave all a fair hearing but it was obvious that two of them knew as much as he did about computers.

It was soon concluded that Olivia Smithson was just the asset he needed to keep the office ticking over. With little fuss, a three-month trial was offered the same day and happily accepted, much to the delight and relief of the Renfold household, the only blip being the contents of a wardrobe that went little beyond jeans, tee shirts and trainers. First day nerves began even before she had set foot in the office door.

A day that began with coffee and introductions, soon morphed into a confrontation with a workload that put paid to the sensitivity of nerves. Overloaded filing cabinets, overdue invoices and a pristine copy of the computer manual were sufficient to fill the remaining hours and the working days that followed. It might not have been the job of choice but Liv thrived and the office gained the order it had cried out for after years of minimal attention.

Robert voiced approval for once; he couldn't fail to notice, and acknowledge, the changes it brought to Liv's appearance: eyes that grew brighter in a face that was filling out in response to a healthier appetite. If he felt any regrets of the past, he kept them to himself however and merely pointed out that Marsha had done exactly the same thing when she'd started at the Parks Department.

Chapter Fifteen

1997

With the passing of time, the more Liv wrote at Dom's group, the more she couldn't stop. Words crawled through the dark like a potholer through an unknown cavern, eventually emerging into the light with relief and a sense of freedom.

Liv admired the bravery of those who read out their work, bravery that took her a long time to summon up. After that first session, Dom came over and sat beside her,

'Was that all right for you...will you come again next week?'

'It was...you have a way with words and putting everyone at their ease.'

'Thank you...I'm pleased to hear you say that.'

Liv put on her coat and watched Dom go to the other newbies; one was crying. She saw through the sadness of their little group and understood the need to reconcile the past with the present.

As the meetings progressed, her writing began to go

beyond the brief of the course. Encouraged by Dom, who saw how talented she was, that tingle of inspiration returned. Occasionally, however, the stresses of life also made their presence felt.

'Is anything the matter, Liv? You've been very quiet tonight.'

'Oh, I'm fine...just a lot going round in my head right now.'

'Anything I can help with?'

'I doubt it...just been one of those days.'

Liv didn't tell him about the latest confrontation with Robert, or the growing strain of living at home with no end in sight.

'Look, I'm going for a pint downstairs...want to join me?'

She looked at her watch. Her bus would be here soon, but there would be another along in an hour. Tea and twenty questions at home could wait and Bee would be in bed soon anyway.

'Ok...I'd like that.'

When the others had gone, they went down to the bar. It was quiet; most of the locals had drifted away leaving only the hardened drinkers with no one to go home to.

'Go sit down and I'll get you a drink. Wine is it?'

'Thank you, yes...white.'

Liv had accustomed herself to getting a single glass at the start of each session, as expected, and a second was welcome that night. Dom came back with two glasses and a bag of peanuts.

'Rubbish wine but beggars can't be choosers...and I've not had tea yet.' He rustled the packet of nuts.

'I hope you'll be having more than that.'

'Don't you worry, there's a curry at home with my name on it in the fridge.'

Liv laughed, 'We don't get anything like that in our

house. My Mother won't contemplate anything beyond meat and two veg...even spaghetti's seen as 'that foreign food."

'Can't imagine life without a good curry and a decent red. I did a wine appreciation course with my wife some years ago and I've never looked back. French is my go-to usually. Not sure what this stuff is but you can bet your life it's not what the French would put on their table.'

He opened the peanuts for them to share and Liv took a couple.

'How come you got involved teaching this class? Is this your main job?'

'No...no not at all. I work at the college in town. I teach literature...adult ed up to degree level. Been doing that for fifteen years.'

'And you do this as well?'

'I love this more than anything...this is where I give something back.'

Liv looked puzzled and Dom frowned. He sensed that Liv might not want to talk about her troubles yet and obliged by filling in the gaps on his own

'To put it briefly, when my wife died, I fell apart. We had no children...couldn't...she was my life. But at some point, I was thrown a lifeline with a course just like this. It didn't stop the pain, but it did a lot to help me get through,...how can I put it...a difficult time.'

'I'm sorry Dom, I didn't mean to pry.'

'No don't be. I don't ask questions anyone in my class doesn't want to answer, but when they do open up...when they put that pen to paper, I can sense the release. I've been there. I've done it. We've all been there...broken, damaged and sad. Grief and pain have no limits it seems to me but...' Dom's voice trailed away and he took a drink from his glass and grimaced.

'I never thought that I would do something like this but I am glad I came.'

'Over the past few sessions, I've come to realise what a first-class writer you are Liv, which is another reason I wanted to talk to you on your own. I've worked with a good many students at college and your skill is every bit as good as...no beyond...most. Have you any plans to take it further?'

'I don't know. I have a degree...even started out as a junior reporter in London...in the early days...but it didn't work out. I've started writing more in my spare time...thanks to you and this course. In between caring for Bee, it's opening up a new world for me.

'For what it's worth, if you want to talk about your writing after the class I'm always happy to stay a bit longer.'

Liv looked uncertain and Dom quickly added, 'Please don't read anything into that...I mean it only as someone who would like to see you go further that's all. I promise!'

Dom flushed at the possibility that he might have come across with an ulterior motive but Liv smiled at his consternation.

'Understood.'

Dominic Raywell was in his mid-fifties, stocky rather than fat, with eyes that held attention when he spoke. What hair he had left was closely cropped and he was clean-shaven. Liv felt safe in his company and they became good friends. With Dom's encouragement, he let her believe that her writing could become more than a way to while away a couple of hours on the road to recovery, and it soon took on a life of its own.

'You have a real gift, Liv, it's a pleasure to read your work,' he would say more than once, and one week he gave her details of a competition he wanted her to enter.

'I don't know...'

'What have you got lose?'

'My dignity when I see how much better the other entries are?'

'Rubbish.'

'And time, now I'm a working girl again.'

The earlier problems of the day evaporated in an energetic discussion on her latest piece and Liv went home in a happier frame of mind than the one in which she'd arrived. Dom left for his curry and a decent bottle of wine, and Liv to twenty questions and tea.

Chapter Sixteen

1998

On days when the school run ended with a free couple of hours at home before work, Liv's mood soared at the thought of getting back to writing. Despite the dusty, still unpacked boxes that stared accusingly in the corner, and the washing up accumulated from the day before, she hung up her coat, made coffee and picked up a pen.

Words flowed fast and furious but after an hour without pause, her back and fingers began to complain. Stretching up her arms, she was satisfied with the progress; ideas that came out of the walk back hit home and she went to make a second coffee of the day.

Clutching her mug, Liv wandered into Bee's bedroom. 'Wow Bee-bee, how come your room is still so tidy?' She breathed in the smell of books, papers and paints and looked at her daughter's latest output; impressed by a talent so young.

The little chest of drawers, refreshed by a coat of white paint by Dom, had been randomly filled, but at least its contents weren't scattered across the floor; and the open door of her wardrobe revealed dresses and coats hung in a neat row.

'Wabbit' lay soldier-straight on top of the bed and Liv remembered their conversation that morning:

'You can't take Wabbit to school Bee...you know that.'

'Why can't I?'

'Because he needs to look after your room when you're not here.'

Bee had looked uncertain.

'Wabbit needs to stay in your room to tell those other families of spiders where to go, Bee. It's your room now and not to be shared with anyone, including spiders.'

Stories of spiders and their families had grown, especially when new ones put in an appearance. Liv gently kissed the battered toy, clutching it to her chest as she sat on the bed. The room was a place of calm and quiet, inducing emotions that should have been kept in check. Staring back into the abyss did not help.

'Enough of that Wabbit, we've moved on...both of us. We can do this! What do you think?' Her heart beat furiously as she shook the stuffed animal's head into a nod and placed him carefully back into the same position on the bed. She straightened the cover where she'd sat.

'I should really make a start on that kitchen before work,' she sighed and quietly closed the bedroom door behind.

By the time Liv left home, she was satisfied. The kitchen was pristine and the fridge full. At thirty-two years of age, she marvelled at still finding herself seeking her mother's approval, but she did anyway and the day felt better for it.

A couple of hours at Draper's, covering lunches, checking invoices and sorting next week's shifts, meant she would still be back in time for Bee leaving school. Timekeeping was a finely tuned work of art and mostly achieved when she was left to get on without interruption. But not today; old Mr Draper popped in as he sometimes did when he knew Olivia was around.

'Ah, Olivia, you're here,' Liv smiled and let the barely disguised surprise pass with a smile. Despite the thought of losing half an hour at least, she resigned herself to company.

'Come for your cuppa Mr Draper?'

'I wouldn't say no...if you can spare the time?'

'I always have time for you...you know that.'

He looked pleased and made himself comfortable in the chair opposite her desk. Of course, the work she'd intended to finish wouldn't quite get that far, but she didn't have the heart to say she was busy. The old man was lovely company despite the age difference and so much like her Dad.

Charles Draper had been semi-retired for two years, unable to make that final break despite the encouragement of his wife, but finally allowed his eldest son, Michael, to at least take the reins of the business. He still liked to think he had the greater input to the smooth running of the place and no one seemed to mind. Olivia was the last appointment he'd person-ally made; she was his 'breath of fresh air' as he liked to call her; as well as someone who could brew a decent cup of tea. Mr Draper was a gentleman of the old school and loved nothing more than to regale Olivia with tales of how the busi-ness began.

At seventy-eight, he was fourth in a line of Drapers who'd owned the store. Starting with his great grandfather, Edgar, it was conceived over a century earlier when D.I.Y. was more an essential in life than an option. It had been a small shack back then, as depicted in the old black and white photo with a young Edgar standing at the door. It had been discovered by Charles during a major clearout before their last expansion and now proudly hung behind the counter in the shop as a reminder of their humble origins.

Since the early days of his marriage to Barbara, Arthur had

come to know Charles well over the years despite the difference in age. He'd found out early in his marriage that life with Barbara would entail a long list of decorating projects and essential repairs, neither of which came naturally to him. Unlike Charles, Arthur learned the hard way and his frequent visits to Draper's, and equally frequent requests for help led to a lasting bond between the two men. It had also brought welcome employment for his daughter.

Quite simply, Liv loved her job, the people she worked with, and the home she returned to at the end of a working day. And when time allowed, promised herself she would get to know more about the old lady next door. She was sorry that she'd not yet had much time to get to know her better. Slowly, the pressures Robert threw in Liv's direction slipped in priority and pushing him aside became easier as life was more fulfilled.

Over the weeks, Frances Fenton watched the comings and goings of mother and daughter with a mix of pleasure and sadness. Delighting in the occasional doorstep hellos, smiles and waves as they came and went, she tended the roses, and would have liked to get to know them better. Maybe in the fullness of time, she mused, but time was something not on her side.

Chapter Seventeen

School broke up for the June half term and fifteen-year old Luke Monro's sullen face showed exactly what he thought of working yet more hours with his Dad at Draper's. Marcus's eight o'clock start had been the first battle, learning what the job entailed, the second.

'So we're there before anyone else just so I can open up the gates and put the kettle on?'

'Got it in one, my lad! I knew that education wasn't being wasted.'

'Very funny.'

'Come on Luke...this way I can keep an eye on you. After that last stint of yours, you've got a lot to learn. Your Mam and me are not made of money y'know.'

'That wasn't just me...and anyway it was derelict...'

'I don't give a stuff about who else was involved but I'm not having you vandalising anything anywhere, got it? You were lucky the police didn't get involved. Now give me hand getting this lot set up before the others get here.'

'Ryan didn't get forced into slave labour,' he muttered.

'I'm not Ryan's Dad but I do know that Adam he won't

let him off lightly either. That neighbour did you both a favour by ringing me up when he saw what you were up to'

Luke knew better than to thwart his Dad's plans and was making his own on what he would do with his next wage packet. He already worked Saturday mornings if rugby allowed, but working during the week on a holiday brought fresh resentment. At least he would do what he wanted with the money.

Mid morning saw Luke dispatched to the sandwich van in the car park when the smell of bacon had proved irresistible; it was one of the few pleasures of a working day. Marcus liked to think that his son's wilder inclinations were kept in check at Draper's and at least stopped his wife Gemma from worrying too much. His first foray into bringing Luke was soon after flunking the mocks,

'I'll give him a taste of the real world Gem and maybe then he'll pull his finger out and start concentrating at school.'

'Let's hope so. I just don't understand what happened to that lovely boy of ours. What did we do wrong?'

'Don't go down that road...we'll get him back if it's the last thing I do.'

After two bacon sandwiches, Luke was laboriously loading an order of pavers into a customer's van when Liv arrived for work.

'Morning Luke,' she called out and waved. His flushed face was unsmiling and he sweated profusely, loathing every minute. Receiving nothing more than a mumbled incoherent reply, Liv went into the office where Marcus had just deposited the morning's mail.

'Morning Marcus...is Luke ok? Looks a bit miserable.'

'Mornin' boss,' he grunted, still rattled by Luke's lack of enthusiasm. Marcus, if not a man of many words, was usually more upbeat. An indispensable presence at Drapers, he came with a wealth of experience as well as bodily strength. His physicality was hard to ignore. It amused Liv to watch the ease with which he managed jobs that would take two of the others. He was proud of his fitness, and as spring gave way to warmer summer days when tee shirts replaced the winter cocoon of hoodies and a thick fleece, his bulging arms rippled to unbelievable effect. Standing at just over six feet, he dominated any room in which he stood. He liked to go to the gym after work twice a week and catch up with the men he'd known since their rugby playing days. He wasn't vain; just proud of the way he looked after himself and was mostly, if not entirely, oblivious to the glances of a female customer waiting to be served.

Marcus liked Liv; 'I like a grafter who gets on with the job and doesn't complain', he replied to old Mr Draper when asked how they were getting on after her first week, and he agreed that yes, she was 'like a breath of fresh air.'

At Draper's anniversary celebration, Liv had been amused by the elfin figure of Gemma Monro at the side of this giant of a man. She stood over a foot shorter than her husband, but her manner clearly showed who had the upper hand in the relationship.

'Luke's fine...can't handle the booze...which he shouldn't be drinking anyway...been a bit of a handful recently...hard work for me and Gem.'

'Ah, the lads went off the pub afterwards I gather...weren't you there?'

'Nah...rest of the night in with the missus and a take-away...bits of sausage rolls and cheese don't go that far...I'm not sure I shouldn't have gone now, but Luke sees enough of his old man as it is.'

'But that was a few days ago. Has it given him a taste for drinking?'

'Who knows? He goes off when he should be doing school work and I can't keep track.'

'The joys of having a teen in the family...I'll come to you for advice when Bee gets there.'

'Nah, not that little cherub!'

Liv raised an eyebrow and Marcus looked at the photograph of Bee on her desk in her school uniform before changing the subject.

'Took a couple of calls for you this morning...a man... wouldn't leave a message. Said he'd call back later.'

'No name?'

'Sorry, forgot to ask...I only came in for a pencil.'

'Well you wouldn't make much of a receptionist'

Marcus smirked, 'Good thing we've got you then, boss'

'Get away Marcus before I sack you.'

Marcus knew very well who it was, but that was a conversation he didn't want to get involved in. It was none of his business, but all the same, he liked the thought of those two getting together. He knew a little of Liv's background, they all did. They knew she was on her own but nothing was openly said and Liv was grateful.

Marcus left for the more familiar territory of the workshop at the other side of the store, deep in thought once again about Luke. He didn't tell Liv the trouble the boy was causing at home between him and Gemma. Handling a fifteen-year-old, they had very different ideas on how to approach Luke's sullen moods and constant disregard for acceptable behaviour. At one time, he'd been top-grade material in school, but something changed and he was at a loss of how to handle it or to understand why. Marcus found it impossible to keep his temper under control. They'd both had great hopes for Luke's future up to that point and took pride in the fact that he might be the first in the family to go somewhere using his brain; they wanted to see him apply for university, a feat unachieved by anyone they knew, and that would be a welcome first. Now Luke wasn't even sure he wanted to do 'A' levels. Gemma's soft approach was not something Marcus understood, but he wasn't making any headway either.

At Luke's age, Marcus already knew that work of a physical nature would be his calling, just like his father, and his father before him. At one time, he couldn't hide the pride he'd felt in his son, even if he'd wanted to, and despite granddad, Frank's scoffing at Luke reading Dickens and Shakespeare. Liv had loaned Luke one or two books of critical essays on the works he was studying and he'd been grateful. She even thought that it might be good to introduce Luke to Dom if he had any difficulties and wanted someone to talk to, but obviously something had changed.

It was an uneventful afternoon and by the time it reached four o'clock, Liv had cleared much of what needed to be done that day. The newly set up afterschool club was proving a welcome blessing where Bee loved the chance to paint. The desk looked tidier than Liv had found it and the 'out' tray considerably smaller than the 'in'. She watered the geranium that had been wilting in the summer sun, recalling Robert correcting her on its correct name of pelargonium, and finally gathered the mail for posting. Before she could leave however, the phone rang,

'Hello, Draper's can I help you?'

There was a moment's silence before she repeated, 'Hello?'

'Oh hi, yes sorry...is that Liv? It's Adam...Adam Davies...I tried to ring earlier but they said you weren't in. Is this a good time? I can call back tomorrow...if you're busy...if it's late... just say.'

Liv knew exactly who it was and she was pleased that he couldn't see her blushing like a teenager who had caught the attention of the boy she secretly fancied.

'Adam, hi. Is it about your order? I did chase it up yesterday but...'

'No...no not that.'

'Oh, right...' she smiled at the sound of his voice and sat back down. There had been no man in her life for so long now, she wasn't even sure of the protocol of flirting and dating, not that she was sure he was going to ask for a date, but hoped he might.

'Ok, what can I do for you? Was the last delivery all right? Marcus checked it out and it was all there when it left the yard.'

Adam, thrown for a moment, 'No, nothing to do with deliveries and orders...something else.'

'All right...'

'I want to ask you something...completely different.'

He paused, hoping that she might take on his meaning. They had spoken quite a few times recently, broaching subjects beyond the stock at Draper's, and each taking a greater interest in the other when they discovered a mutual interest in a world beyond D.I.Y.

'Are you still there?'

'Yes...I'm still here...go on...ask away.'

'You don't have to answer now...tell me if you want me to stop...I won't be offended...but...'

He lost the words until Liv took over

'Yes, I'd love to.'

'What?'

Elation replaced despondence at the unexpected response.

Adam gave an audible sigh of relief and laughed out loud, 'You're amazing do you know that?'

'Just don't tell me now that you were going to ask about that new line of paint we got yesterday.'

'Funny you should say that but...'

The ice was broken and they both laughed.

'Right...that's great...well how are you fixed next Friday? Would you like to come out for a drink with me?'

'I think I've already answered.'

'So you have.'

When Liv put down the phone, she sat back in her chair to take in what had just happened, her head a maelstrom of intruding thoughts, most of which were not helpful.

'Was that really me? More to the point, have I done the right thing?' Shocked at the conversation she had steered Adam into, her brain immediately entered a maze in which the path was by no means clear. Going on a date would have been unthinkable even a year ago, but now a different Liv was emerging. 'Am I brave enough to do this?' She made a list of reasons to go on a scrap of paper; always back to the lists:

1. Easy to talk to. 2. When he appears at Draper's my day is brighter. 3. Not unattractive to look at. But is that really the most important consideration? 4. He's tall!!!, Fairly important when I am five foot nine; 5. What do we have in common?

She screwed up the piece of paper and threw it in the bin and the next day spoke to Marcus

'I got that call you mentioned yesterday.'

'Oh yeah...and who was it then?'

'I think you know very well who it was Marcus.'

They exchanged sly, knowing looks.

'It was Adam and you know him quite well I think.'

Marcus's face broke into a broad grin, 'That right?'

'You've known all along. Why didn't you tell me he was interested?'

'Well if it wasn't D.I.Y. related and he didn't want to talk to me about rugby...I've seen him watching you when he thought no one was looking...I'm no matchmaker, but it didn't take much.'

'You might have warned me.'

'Get away with yer. I've known Adam a good few years now...first through our lads. His Ryan's at the same school as our Luke...not the same class but both play rugby on a Saturday afternoon. Got talking to him one day after the match...DIY that kind of stuff and he started coming in...not a bad bloke.'

'That's praise from you...and I presume there's no wife...I don't know anything about him'

'If he is married he's sneaked that in since last Saturday... better not be if he's sniffing around you. We don't get on to the personal stuff much but there's no wife on the scene as far as I know.'

'You are unbelievable you know that...with your 'don't get on to the personal stuff'. But you like him?'

'He's ok yeah...and when I think about it I've never seen him with anyone at parents' night...or when the lads go to their awards night...so I would say he's on his own.'

'Thanks, Marcus...I guess I'll find out more next Friday.'

Marcus rubbed the back of his neck, itching to get back to the job in hand, safer ground, leaving Liv to sort out the rest for herself.

It was hard to concentrate after their chat. With very little back catalogue to go by, dating-wise, it was a new and strange territory. Robert had been her first and last serious relationship. At school, there were boys who were keen, but beyond dates at the cinema and the odd dances and concerts in town, didn't amount to much. Either they found her too bookish or she found them too keen to see how far they could go with wandering hands. University produced much the same result; odd dates, one that started out promising but fell flat as a duff firework when she found out they had far too little in common, including heavy metal. Coming out of the wilderness after illness and divorce left her feeling vulnerable, but perhaps not so much that she didn't want to give dating a try now.

She knew that Adam deliberately sought her out whenever he could, asking about an order, or just passing the time of day when she saw him in the yard. She'd even caught him staring up at the window of the office one day as he waited for something to be collected from the back. He must have been married at some point, but the adage that you don't know what goes on behind closed doors was a valid one.

'We haven't even had a first date yet. What am I doing?'

Liv groaned when thoughts of what to wear emerged.

Chapter Eighteen

Friday morning arrived early. It was six twenty and Liv was wide-awake after a restless night. Going back to sleep was not an option. She made coffee and brought it back to bed before another chaotic start to the school-morning rush. Robert would be picking Bee up from school for the weekend and her bag was already packed. Liv felt smug at being so well organised for once.

She pulled up the thin bed cover and propped herself up with pillows, cradling her drink. In the midst of sorting out the day in her head, a message flashed up on her phone. It was Adam: 'Looking forward to seeing you tonight'. She felt relief on two counts, one, he wasn't cancelling, and two, even more important, he hadn't forgotten.

One brief meeting at Draper's hadn't amounted to much when there had been little chance to talk beyond a 'See you Friday.' Liv mulled over her list of first impressions of Adam Davies and they were all promising: 1. Sense of humour. 2. Gentle manner. 3. Kind. But was he too good to be true? Why wasn't he with anyone? Was anything lurking behind those first impressions and that wonderful smile he gave whenever they met? The answers were no; don't know; please no. The repercussions of getting him so wrong didn't bear thinking about.

Marcus had already told her that Adam was one of the good guys and she trusted his judgment, allowing herself to bask in the promise of an evening to enjoy being her normal self and stop worrying.

She put down the empty cup and reached over for the pen and notebook sitting on top of the bedside clutter. To clear her mind, Liv re-read her last piece, a tale of drama, retribution and redemption that she now decided would have a happier ending than the one planned. Her pen flew across the page as fresh thoughts surfaced before Bee came strolling up to the bed.

'Hello Beebee'. Liv put down the pad and pen to a flushed and dishevelled Bee, whose eyes were half closed.

'Mmm.'

She crawled under the covers and snuggled in close to Liv who wrapped her arms around the warm sleepy body until the alarm signalled time to get up. Bee sat up and frowned,

'Do I have to go to Daddy's tonight? Can't I go tomorrow instead? Can we have another picnic in the garden...please like last time.'

Liv was already up.

'Sorry sweetie...maybe Daddy and Marsha will do a picnic if you ask them.'

Bee thought for a moment.

'I suppose...but you won't be there will you?'

'No, but you'll be back on Sunday...and I tell you what... we can have tea together on the sofa and watch Rosie and Jim before bed.'

Bee, placated by the idea of watching the same favourite again, smiled.

'And can we write another bit of Lulu's Adventures?'

'Why not…if you can remember where we got up to…I'm not sure what I did with Lulu when we moved.'

'She was going to fight the dragon…all on her own!'

'I'll see if I can find it for when you come home then.'

'Good.'

Despite the fine start to the day, a sudden summer downpour kept Liv indoors with lunch. Sitting at her desk, she fretted about the leak in the kitchen roof, which was definitely getting worse, and tried to remember if she'd replaced the bucket underneath.

The office door opened, disturbing her thoughts as well as loose papers that weren't held down. It was a long day and four thirty couldn't come around quickly enough. The men in the yard had cleared up and gone off to wives and girlfriends, or the promise of a pint at the pub if they were lucky enough. They all finished early on Fridays. Liv locked the doors and set the alarm, pleased to see that at least the rain had stopped.

Her date with Adam wasn't until seven thirty, plenty of time to get ready and focus on the night ahead. Impulsively, on the way home, she bought a bunch of spring flowers from the florist to take to Frances next door. They hadn't had much of a chance to chat and she felt guilty about not making the time. Bee was already at Robert's and tea was not an issue when Adam's last text was 'Don't eat. We'll get something out. Nice place I want to take you.'

Bags and umbrella were dumped inside the door at home and Liv went to check the kitchen ceiling. Mercifully. the bucket was under the leak, and having filled from the latest downpour was emptied and put back. She looked up to the roof. There was little doubt; it was getting worse, but nothing could be done right now. Liv put it out of her mind and went next door with the flowers.

The front garden at number fifty-two was small and pristine: no grass but pretty rose beds surrounding a small flowering cherry tree from which hung two bird feeders. A cluster of sparrows flapped noisily at her arrival and flew off. A fresh verdant scent filled the air after the rain and she thought how Robert would approve of this garden. Her own bore little comparison where a predominance of dandelions and daisies poked through the overgrown grass. Like the leaking roof, she ignored it in expectation of something much more pleasant, and Frances Fenton opened the door.

'Hello there, dear, how lovely to see you...sorry it took me so long to answer but my knee has been playing up a little recently.'

'Oh, no problem...I've just been admiring your beautiful rose garden...puts mine to shame.'

'You've had other things to keep you busy I'm sure...and I do have Geoff who comes regularly to keep it in shape.'

Liv held out the flowers, 'I just wanted to say hello and sorry for not coming round again sooner. I thought you might like these.'

'How very kind...it's been a long time since anyone bought me flowers...you are thoughtful. Please do come in...I was just about to have a drink if you want to join me? If you have the time that is.'

'I don't want to disturb you, I...'

'My dear, disturb away...it's been so long since I had visitors...at least someone who wasn't paid to be here.' The old lady had a beautiful smile set in a face that in no way betrayed her ninety-two years. Lightly made up, she wore a hint of lipstick and just a smear of rouge that emphasised the high-sculpted cheekbones. Her brows too were carefully coloured to complete a natural look. Seeing her up close for the first time, it was obvious to Liv that she must have been a real beauty in her younger days.

'Then thank you...I'd like that. I'm going out later but not for a couple of hours yet. I'm Liv by the way...Olivia Smithson...we've not properly introduced ourselves have we?' and she held out her hand.

'And I'm Frances...Frances Fenton...so happy to meet you, Olivia Smithson. Do come on in.' Her smile was warm and welcoming as she held the door open.

'No little girl with you?'

'Not this weekend, no.'

Frances thought it imprudent to ask anything more when Olivia didn't volunteer any other information.

Liv followed inside, taking in the outfit of this elegant and remarkably straight-backed woman. She was slim, wearing a pair of tailored cream trousers with a blue and pink striped shirt tucked inside. The collar was turned up around her neck where it met with a short grey bob. Her appearance, understated yet compelling, perfectly matched the diction and pronunciation with which she spoke.

The hallway was dim, lit only by two small wall lights, unlike the sitting room that opened up to a bright and airy space that was as immaculate as the person she followed inside. Liv took a sharp breath, trying, and failing, to take in the splendour of the surroundings. She cringed at the cheap bunch of flowers in Frances Fenton's hand. They should at least have been an elegant spray of lilies or a perfect bouquet of summer roses, but her neighbour merely reiterated her delight at receiving such a welcome gift.

'You are very kind to bring me these...they are lovely.' She laid them carefully on a sideboard, 'I will arrange them in a vase later...I have the perfect one somewhere that will complement their colours beautifully. Now, about that drink...I will confess that at this time I usually take a schooner of sherry.

You are welcome to join me, my dear, but if you prefer tea, it's no problem to put the kettle on.'

'No sherry sounds fine...thank you.' It might not have been Liv's first choice of drink, but she felt sure it would not be the supermarket's own brand Barbara drank at Christmas.

In the corner of the room stood a circular drinks trolley, a wrought metallic gold design with two shelves: one displaying a selection of crystal cut glasses, the other several bottles and a decanter. Alongside the trolley, a tall fig plant presided over this perfect display. Frances poured out two glasses from the decanter and passed one to Liv. She took a sip of the dry, pale liquid.

'Mmm, this is really nice' she said in surprise.

'Yes, it's a manzanilla...quite refreshing in the warmer weather. Not as heavy as some of the others...the Christmas sherries I call them. Please do take a seat...come here under the window where it's light and I can see you properly.'

'This is a beautiful room, Mrs Fenton...'

'Oh please do call me Frances. I got over the Mrs Fenton stage quite some time ago.'

'Frances,' and Liv raised her glass.

Everything, from the carpet she walked on to the ornately framed paintings that adorned the walls, were stunning; Liv was certain they must be original.

'I can see that you are wondering how come I live on a street like this, and in such a house.

'Not at all...no.'

'When I first moved here it was a very different prospect to what it is now. Please, I'm not putting down where we are but over the years, it has fallen on hard times. I cannot move now, even if I wanted to.'

'Please you don't have to explain anything to me...I'm here because the house was all I could afford...and even so...' Liv's words trailed off, unwilling to go into the detail of her life and financial straits to a stranger.

'We all have to start somewhere my dear...and it really doesn't deserve the reputation some people, including my son, choose to give it.'

Liv was about to respond with 'and my ex,' but thought better of that too. Again too soon, and instead allowed the warmth of the sherry to flow through her body. There was something about Frances Fenton she also warmed to and Liv relaxed enough to look more closely about the room. On the wall opposite, her eyes were drawn to a portrait of a woman's head and shoulders, beautiful in its simplicity with little background to detract from her face.

'Is that you,' she asked, trying to make out the signature at the bottom.

'Gracious no...' She paused in thought and a smile spread across her face, 'this one is just a print...but I did meet the artist once on a visit to Paris.'

'Really? It's stunning...not one I've ever seen before.'

'Perhaps I will tell you about it one day.'

They both looked at the sketch in silence but Frances did not elaborate further and Liv was too polite to ask anything more. It was Frances who eventually spoke,

'Now tell me about that beautiful daughter of yours. Such a pretty little one.'

'She's at her father's this weekend...we're divorced and he's remarried...'

'Oh please I didn't mean to pry, you don't have to tell me...'

'No that's all right...it's fine really...she's called Bee, Beatrice Rose to give you her full name.'

'It suits her...Beatrice,' and Frances pronounced the name with an Italian intonation.

'She loves to paint; as soon as she could hold a brush she's never stopped. Painting and reading are her two passions.'

'Then I'm sure we have much in common. You must bring her over soon. I have many paintings that she might like to see.'

'Then I will...she would love that...but for now, I have to go and get ready. Thank you for the sherry and we'll both come and see you very soon I promise.'

'I'm so glad you came across, you've made my day. I feel sure that we will get along very well you and I...and Beatrice Rose. Charming name. And now I will put those flowers in a vase. I hope you have a lovely evening Olivia.'

'So do I.'

Frances looked puzzled.

'I have a date...someone I've known for a little while, but this is our first actual date.'

'Then you'd better get off instead of listening to me chatter on. We'll meet again soon enough I'm sure...you are always welcome.'

Frances took Liv's hand and pressed it in her own warm gentle palms, 'I already feel like I know you, and I like what I see.'

'Bye for now Frances...please don't come to the door, I'm happy to see myself out.'

'I need all the exercise I can manage, Olivia...especially until this knee gets sorted.' As Liv left, she called to her, 'Please do come and see me again...I would like that.'

'So would I,' replied Liv, waving, and she meant every word.

Chapter Nineteen

Once again, Liv stood in front of her wardrobe in a state of despair at the mealy collection inside. 'Forty minutes to go. Come on Liv make a decision.' Time had run away with her at Frances Fenton's when a planned five-minute visit turned into thirty.

She pulled out a couple of dresses that hadn't been worn for some years and held them up to the light.

'Good grief...one extreme to the other.' One was far too short, and the other, a baggy postnatal affair that buttoned to the neck, rested two inches below knee level. 'Tart or nun?' She threw them on the bed with a 'No, no, no!'

There was now little time to spare. Liv finally decided upon a pair of fairly new, dark blue fitted jeans and a white blouse. Neither too dressy nor too relaxed, at least she would feel comfortable. Make up was a five-minute affair of liner, rouge and lipstick and perfume the last of the L'air du Temps given two Christmases ago. A quick brush of the hair, tucked behind her ears completed the look. She surveyed the image before a full-length mirror in the hall, tidying stray wisps of hair and pulling her shirt out slightly to give it what she thought could be a relaxed, thrown together look.

'What do you think, Sav? Will I do?'

Letters between the two friends, forwarded from home, had resumed once Savannah had sorted out her own complicated personal life in Africa and resorted back to support mode. Although she had yet to know about Adam, Liv knew exactly what she would say. Plus she should let Sav know her new address.

'I think you'll do perfectly well, Livvy. Get out there and get a life.'

Almost satisfied, Liv picked up her bag and coat and left for the bus .

The ride into town was in turns, too long and too short: too long in that it allowed a fragile state of mind to conjure up reasons why the date wasn't going to work; and too short to convince herself that it would. Banter over the phone and chatting at Draper's was one thing, but a proper planned date was a different prospect altogether.

Composing conversations in her head were interrupted only when trying to remember if the bowl, now accompanied by a bucket in the kitchen, had been put back in place.

Liv straightened her blouse and noticed with horror that one of the buttons in the middle was hanging on by a thread. On the plus side, however, she'd lost so much weight that it was loose enough not to tug apart.

Two stops to go and her heart pumped fast. What if he didn't turn up? What if he soon realised that she wasn't the happy-go-lucky woman she put out at Draper's and over the phone? What if he was disappointed? The what-ifs came fast and furious but it was too late to turn back now.

Adam was waiting, just as he said he would.

'Hello,'

'Hi.'

His smile was warm and genuine with perhaps just a hint of relief when the bus rolled in five minutes late. He leaned in and lightly kissed her cheek. 'I was beginning to think you might have changed your mind.'

'No, I would never do that,' she lied, cheeks flaming at the kiss and the thoughts she'd harboured earlier.

'You look amazing.'

'You don't look too bad yourself but then I'm sure you didn't spend half as much time as me deciding what to wear.'

The impulse to gabble was kept in check by the inner voice but at least the what-ifs had been banished at his first hello.

'I thought we'd go to the Black Bull first...unless you'd prefer somewhere else?'

'I'd not thought of anywhere in particular...that's fine with me.'

Liv did not tell him that she hadn't been into a pub in the centre of town for over six years and didn't mention the Flying Horse.

'I wouldn't know where to start...happy for you to lead the way.'

It was a relief not to make any more decisions. Deciding what to wear had been enough.

Walking side by side, their hands were close enough to touch but remained apart.

'Busy at work today?'

'Oh you know, normal stuff. Marcus still fretting about Luke and Luke with a face on telling us all exactly where he would rather be...but apart from that, all was well. Everyone's happy it's Friday...apart from those on the weekend shift that is. You?'

'Yeah, yeah a good day...two new jobs came in and I managed to fit in a quick run after work.'

'You run?'

'I do...not fast and no more than 5k but it helps clear my head.'

'Did you need it before coming out with me then?'

'Absolutely...you could be anyone behind that façade of the sweet woman who works in Draper's office. How do I know what I've let myself in for?'

Getting back to the banter put them both at ease during the short walk to the pub, and the balance was enough to set the tone for the evening.

The Black Bull was neatly tucked away down a side street and Adam found a small, quiet table away from the bar.

Liv took the opportunity to watch him as he went to get the drinks. He wore jeans well, fitting in the right places, and she blushed at noticing that from behind, they showed a runner's physique to advantage. A pale blue shirt completed his outfit and she blushed again as she visualised the body beneath when he returned with a glass in each hand. Unbidden thoughts of Robert only briefly spoiled the moment when she tried to remember the last time they had shared an intimate time together.

Adam set down the drinks.

'Thank you.'

'Hope it's ok?'

'I'm sure it's fine.'

'Busier than I thought back there...you all right? You look worried about something.'

'No...I'm fine...really...I like this place...good choice.'

Adam beamed, pleased to have got the venue right at least and took a mouthful of beer. He deliberately sat opposite Liv, the better to take in the face of the woman he had long wanted to ask out and had finally done so.

'Cheers...and thank you for being here.'

'Cheers...and thank you for asking me.'

'Oh...I thought that it was you who'd asked me...you know I was just playing hard to get, don't you.'

They both laughed; the ice well and truly broken as two glasses chinked together.

'You know I've never done so much DIY since I saw you at Drapers...Ryan can't understand what's come over me...my son that is.'

'Yes...Marcus told me you had a son...said that he and Luke play rugby together...go to the same school?'

'Ah, you've been asking about me then...'

Liv blushed for a third, and what she hoped would be the last time that evening and took a larger mouthful of wine than intended.

'Sorry...and I confess I did ask Marcus about you...nothing too personal...just...well...if...sorry.'

'No don't be...I could have been married with six kids for all you knew.'

'True...' Liv took another drink and the effect was as relaxing as she'd hoped,

'And have you? Don't tell me there's a wife and six kids at home. Is that one of the secrets you keep to yourself?'

Liv might not be ready to shed light on her own secrets just yet, but she was happy to relax in finding out more of Adam's life over a drink in a pleasant pub.

Robert and his demands, as well as a leaking roof and how she could afford an expensive repair bill, were successfully banished for one night at least. The roof was on the list of things to do when other, more pressing expenses, had been sorted.

Conversation flowed and as the evening progressed, Liv's shoulders dropped; she even forgot about the loose button, and her smile, fixed into place on seeing Adam at the bus stop, never left.

Outside was not so sunny, however; dark clouds gathered unnoticed and the first rain of the evening began to fall.

'Do you realise it's taken an hour to get through one drink? A record when I have a decent pint in front of me.'

'Then let me get you another,' and Liv rose to go to the bar. 'Have you seen it outside by the way?'

Rain was now beating heavily against the window and soaking coats of new arrivals dripped to the floor. 'I don't think these jackets are going to be much use against that...look you sit down and I'll go find us a menu. I don't fancy going anywhere else right now.'

'I'm happy to stay here if you are.'

At that moment, two plates of lasagne were carried past and an appetising smell trailed in their wake.

'The food doesn't look too bad...and we've got a good seat...wait there a minute.'

Adam went back to the bar for more drinks. Liv didn't object; she felt light-headed from the earlier schooner of sherry, the large glass of wine and nothing to eat since lunchtime. Food would be very welcome right now. Any doubts she'd harboured over the evening left completely as she again watched Adam go to the bar, liking very much what she saw, and what he said when he returned.

'I just want to say that this is the best evening I've had...by far...for a long time...thank you...and don't feel you have to say anything in reply...just let me bask in the moment. Your company is exactly what I've needed and whether or not you'll let me see you again; nothing will change how I feel right now.'

Liv nursed her glass and raised her eyebrows, staring at the man opposite, saying the words she could easily match.

'Thank you for that...whatever happens after tonight, for me it's just so good to feel...I don't know how to put it...

normal?...yes normal...I think that's the word I'm looking for...I think.'

'You are funny...here's to another 'normal' night out then...unless the food's so bad it puts you off for good.'

A tray laden with rustic bread and an antipasti board was deposited on the next table.

'If the food tastes as good as it looks and smells, we could be in for another night out.'

Sated with plates of pasta and a final round of drinks, Liv and Adam made a move to leave. It was time. The rain had stopped, leaving no more than glimmering puddles in the dying rays of the sun. Adam took Liv's hand this time and brought her fingers up to his lips, impulsively kissing their tips. She did not pull away and that simple action was enough to begin a sexual re-awakening that had been long absent in her life.

Unfortunately, the combination of flimsy footwear and a wet oily patch on the pavement intercepted the happy moment and Liv fell hard to the floor. She sat for a while in shock and disbelief but once they had ascertained that no real damage had been done beyond a loss of dignity, possibly a bruised backside, and the loose button giving up its thread, saw the funny side of it. Giggling like two schoolchildren, he pulled her up and brushed her down. Neither saw the man opposite snapping photographs in their direction.

'I'd better make sure you get home in one piece, Ms Smith-son...you are obviously in no fit state to manage on your own...if that's all right?'

It was; Liv made no objection and thought it rather touching that he would go with her on the bus despite the detour he would have to make. Yes, it was all right.

Their first kiss at her door unlocked emotions that took

them both by surprise. Soft and heartfelt, yet deep enough to register that the physical attraction between them was not just superficial, they parted and looked at each other to check that the feeling was mutual.

'I hope you didn't mind...I've been wanting to do that all night.'

'I'd have been disappointed if you hadn't...but...'

'I know...take things slowly.'

'Come in for a quick coffee before you go...just coffee. We can plan that next date.'

Liv took Adam to the living room where she put music on from the collection of CDs amassed over the years. None had been to Robert's, or Barbara and Arthur's taste so it was good to be able to resurrect the music that was an important part of life. She found Van Morrison's Astral Weeks and set it to play before going to the kitchen.

'Now here's a real test when you tell me what you think of my music,' she called out.

'Could be a deal breaker then?'

'Absolutely...I don't care how good a kisser you are...'

She left Adam singing along to the first track:

'If I ventured in the slipstream...' and pumped her fist in delight.

As he sang, Adam smiled at the lived-in clutter of the room. An eclectic array of unrelated objects brought colour, and the room, to life. A neon blue vase at the window was filled with pinks and ferns, and next to it sat a small wooden robin wearing a red hat. Several of Bee's paintings in various stages of completion were spread out to dry underneath.

Everything he saw prompted Adam to want to know more about this woman who had come into his life. She intrigued him as no other since his wife. He sat on the sofa as the melodic notes of Astral Weeks softly circled the room. Liv returned with coffee and Adam again sang the familiar words.

'Have I passed the music test?'

'You know the words...of course you've passed.'

The coffee sat untouched as the proximity of their bodies moved closer and his arm found its way across. As they talked, he kissed her hair and his free hand stroked the soft, silky waves and their eyes locked.

'I'm going to go now...much as I don't want to break the spell you've clearly put me under.'

Adam pulled his arm back.

'If you've enjoyed this evening just a fraction as much as me, I will be happy.'

'You don't have to ask...it's been perfect...thank you.'

'Just don't now tell me you've got a collection of heavy metal hidden away!'

'There's a lot you don't know about me..'

'True...but I'm sure there's nothing you can tell me I won't like. Already I know that you have a gorgeous little girl called Bee; you like to shut yourself away to write when you can...and I really would love to read your work if you'll let me...and of course, you work at Draper's...God bless Draper's for bringing us together. We all have a past life Liv, but the nice thing about the past is just that...it's past.'

Liv realised that she had revealed more than intended on a first date, but Adam had been so easy to talk to. Despite a pull to the contrary, they stood and parted. It was the right decision.

'Wise words...the past...but now it's goodnight. I'm doing a Saturday shift at Draper's tomorrow...they're a bit short on counter staff so I'm up early. But thank you for a really lovely evening...and for liking my music. Next time though it will be the Iron Maiden back catalogue...you know that?'

Adam rolled his eyes and left her on the doorstep with the taste of his kiss on her lips.

Chapter Twenty

Weather-wise the summer of '98 had not been impressive so far, but on this particular Saturday in July, the trend was bucked; the sun shone brightly, the sky was blue and Grantham Park was alive. Entwined couples sought solitude in its furthest corners and families spread out under the trees.

Beneath a large oak, Liv sat on a soft, cashmere rug with legs outstretched, head up and eyes closed, soaking up the warmth of the sun. Sated by more food that neither she, Bee nor Frances could possibly finish, she was sleepy from two glasses of chilled Chablis enjoyed with the food. Frances' hamper basket, bought from Harrods when her husband George was still alive, was as pristine as the day it had been delivered. Replete with crystal glasses, cutlery that wouldn't break the first time it was used, and china cups that didn't distort the taste of the tea, it was a luxury profoundly appreciated.

Frances relaxed on a picnic chair in the shade, reading her book. The pain of arthritic hips had eased as she too appreciated the warmth that enveloped them. Her long white linen skirt hung in folds about her legs, topped by a pink blouse, belying her age with elegance and style, and the ensemble was topped with a large straw hat. Her back was as straight as the chair would allow and her fine ash-grey hair blew gently in the breeze. Before long, the words on the page began to blur and the soporific effect of sun, food and wine took effect.

Frances, too tired to read any longer, lay the book face down upon her lap and beneath half-closed eyes looked across to Liv. She smiled at the changes she'd noticed in her young friend's face. Lines of anxiety and dark shadows, evident at their first meeting, had receded; she was, to her eyes, relaxed and content. Liv's golden hair trailed down her back as she tilted her head, and she rested on arms stretched out behind. Frances liked what she saw, having quickly built up a fondness for her new neighbour who struggled to maintain an independent life with a lively daughter.

Liv caught her look.

'What are you smiling about?'

'I'm smiling because I'm loving every minute of this outing my dear...thank you so much for asking me... persuading me...and it was a great excuse to use the picnic hamper. I never thought it would see the light of day again.'

'Did you go on many picnics with your husband?'

'George?' Frances scoffed, 'George could no more sit still under a tree than...well, I don't know what, but picnics were not his thing shall we say...what about you and Robert?'

On this day they were comfortable enough with each other to bring up respective past husbands, although so far it had been more in passing than anything deep and personal. Frances was not the only one affected by the wine and the sun, and despite the difference in age, there was a mutual fondness growing between them.

'Robert liked picnics, yes...although he took more interest in the state of the grounds we were in, and what he would do if he was in charge, rather than sit back and appreciate the beauty...he could never close his eyes to the sun.'

'What a pair we married then...but here we are.'

'Here we are indeed...and we will do this again...if we get another nice day.'

Frances winced with pain on straightening her back, placing hands on both sides of her hips.

'Are you ok?'

'Oh don't mind me Olivia...aches and pains of old age that's all.'

Liv turned to look at the families around them; laughing, crying, playing, eating; normal family life, some with Dads, others not, but what constituted a 'normal family life' anyway? To anyone from the outside, they were a contented, happy little group with a classy hamper, drinking wine from crystal goblets, and enjoying each other's company whilst eating a picnic from china plates.

A comfortable silence fell between them as they watched Bee at play, running around blowing bubbles from a tub they'd bought from the kiosk nearby. She squealed with delight, chasing rainbow orbs in the breeze that rose until they popped and dispersed tiny droplets into the warm air.

The mention of Robert no longer caused the agitation of old, nor any feelings of guilt; and this morning she marvelled at the one-year anniversary of the day she'd completely stopped taking tablets that had been prescribed during the darkest times. She no longer began each day with a feeling of dread. Instead, she daydreamed of Adam and what it would be like to be with him here, perhaps just the two of them, lying on the grass in the Park, beneath a secluded tree, like the young couple she spotted, kissing and stroking one another, oblivious of anyone else.

Liv had seen Adam on three dates now, each one shoring up trust and a longing for more of his company, bringing a yearning not felt for years. They'd not gone further than a kiss on each occasion, and passionate though they were, they were still hesitant. After years in a wilderness of denial and rejection, it was strange to feel that hunger once again. Today she felt confident that their relationship would go further. The more she thought about Adam, the more the intensity of her feelings grew.

'Penny for them?'

Liv was brought back into the present.

'Mm...where do I start?

'My dear, by the look on your face, they are pleasant thoughts.'

'Well read Frances...all right I'll tell you. I've met someone...someone that I like very much. Someone I've only seen three times...on a date that is...but I think it looks promising.'

'I see...is he the gentleman you told me about when you brought me those flowers? And does Bee know this someone... have they met?'

'Yes, the very same, and no I've not told Bee just yet... maybe soon if all goes well.'

'If it's meant to be it will be...you are too young to spend the rest of your life on your own. Remind me again, what is his name?'

'It's Adam...Adam Davies. I met him at Draper's...he's a customer so not exactly a stranger. It's funny but when I first met him he seemed quite ordinary but the more I get to know him, the more I see that he's anything but...oh and he's taller than me...a definite plus!'

'I take it Robert wasn't?'

'Put it this way, I could never wear heels...not that I particularly wanted to...goodness, I sound superficial...please don't take it the wrong way. Robert...'

'No more mentions of Robert, please...you don't have to justify yourself to me you know.'

'I know...I'd like you to meet Adam though if things work out between us.'

'I would like that very much.'

Unbidden, Liv recalled Adam's last kiss and flushed at the memory.

'And you met Adam at Draper's...a customer you say? Oh that could be useful, my dear. George wouldn't have known one end of a screwdriver from the other. Anything of a practical nature and he would get someone in to do the job.'

'Frances...what are you saying here?'

'Oh don't mind me...but a little practicality can go a long way in this world...especially in those old houses like ours.'

'That may be so but I don't even know if he's any good at the D.I.Y. stuff...he could have a house of wonky shelving and collapsing cupboards for all I know.'

They both laughed.

'And what do you know?'

'I know that he is good company, he makes me laugh, and after a date, I look forward to the next...although he's not been in touch for a while so I won't be lining up the jobs just yet.'

'Oh I am sure there will be another date...lovely girl like you...he'll be back. You seem to know your own mind...and what you want.'

Liv gave her last words some thought before answering.

'You know what, Frances? You're absolutely right...I do know what I want...but what's more to the point...what I don't want.'

The conversation was brought to an abrupt end by a panic-stricken Bee, being chased by a wasp. After much flapping, shrieking and several swipes, the emergency was over, but then so was their day out. A picnic that had begun as a quick and makeshift affair could not have been more perfectly planned. Liv was grateful for the basket, and for the luxurious rug laid out on the warm grass. The taxi Frances had insisted on booking for the short trip was due in thirty minutes.

'How about an ice cream to finish off the day and cool us down?'

'Yes please, Mummy!'

Despite the amount of food consumed, Liv went over to the van and bought three soft ice creams with flakes. The afternoon sun still shone, unmolested by cloud, and the cones were already dripping down her hand by the time she reached Bee and Frances. The old and young pair had their heads together, deep in conversation, making a touching scene.

'What are you two plotting?'

'Mummy, Mrs Fenton is going to help me paint...did you know she could paint?'

Liv handed out the ice creams and three tongues licked at the cool, creamy mounds before Bee continued

'We're going to paint together one day after school.'

'That'll be nice Bee...although I'm not sure Mrs Fenton knows what she's letting herself in for when there'll be as much paint on you and the table as the paper'.

'It would be my pleasure, Olivia. This little one is like a sponge, so keen to learn...what are a few splodges between friends? I could never get Simon interested at any age...even then he was more interested in the value of a painting on the wall than having a go himself...too much of his Father in him.'

Soon enough, the ice creams brought a close to a perfect day in the Park.

'It's almost five...we should think about getting back home.'

Dark clouds had started to appear on the horizon and contrary to the forecast, it looked like rain again.

'We don't want to get caught in a downpour, do we? The taxi's due soon so we'd better get a move on.'

The basket was packed, the chair collapsed and the blanket

folded. Bee collected books, bubbles and toys she'd been allowed to bring for the day and they set off for the main entrance.

'You might as well keep the basket...and the rug Olivia...I don't think I will have much use for them now.'

Chapter Twenty One

The rain held off until they'd arrived back home after the picnic, but by mid morning on Sunday dark clouds engulfed the sky and a relentless downpour followed. Bee solemnly looked out of the living room window wishing it was yesterday again and that they were back in the Park. She breathed on to the window and in the mist drew a stick figure with an umbrella before getting back to her piles of paper and crayons.

'When am I going to Mrs. Fenton's to do some painting? Can I go today?'

'No sweetie I think she might want to have a rest today... you can occupy yourself perfectly well until Grandma and Grandpa get here.

Liv had just returned from the kitchen, dragging and emptying a large bowl from underneath the dripping ceiling and replacing it with a large bucket brought back from Draper's the previous week. Repairs really couldn't wait much longer, but where to get the money fuelled inactivity and she just prayed that the rain would soon stop. In between times, when the leak would become no more than a brown stain, it would more easily be forgotten once again.

Bee lay on the floor, engrossed in drawing a tree.

'That's a fine big tree,'

'It's the one Mrs Fenton sat under yesterday.'

'It was such a lovely day, wasn't it?'

Liv's train of thought shifted back to the picnic, and then moved on to Adam, and the inevitable 'if only'. At that same moment a message from him flashed up on her phone and hopes of a fourth date surged. Nothing had yet been arranged but the following Friday Bee would be staying at Robert's and the weekend was free. However, hope was short-lived and the text perfunctory. 'Something's come up. Sorry. Will call soon I promise.' Was that it? She stared at the phone and waited in expectation of something more, but no, no explanation, no kisses, nothing more. Disappointment weighed heavily and did nothing to brighten the gloom of the day.

'When are grandma and grandpa coming…I want to give them my picture and tell them about our picnic at the Park?'

Liv would love to have felt some of Bee's excitement; it was usually infectious and enough to get her through the day, but the niggle of doubt over Adam's text and what it meant suppressed everything else. She went back into the kitchen to clear their breakfast things into the sink, then realised that they were out of milk again.

'Come on BeeBee, I'll take you over to Mrs. Fenton's just for half an hour. I need to go to the Co-op…can't offer Grandma and Granddad a cup of black tea and an empty biscuit tin, can I?'

The rain had thankfully stopped, the sky was clear and the bucket under the leak stored back in its cupboard. It was better out of sight, but the stain on the ceiling had expanded twice in size since yesterday.

The return of the sun made for a pleasant walk to the Co-op where Liv was pleased to see that it was Debbie at the checkout.

'No Bee today?'

'Not today...left her with my neighbour. Mum and Dad are coming soon and I need milk.'

'Say hi to that little one for me and tell her that picture she did for me is up on the fridge.'

Liv and Debbie were getting to know each other better with each visit. They chatted easily, were on first-name terms and discovered a mutual liking for the cinema. She knew that Debbie lived on her own, that she had a best friend on the other side of town, but that the friend couldn't always get away easily and now had a baby to consider. The next time a good film came out they'd agreed to go together. Tentative plans were made for the following week when both shifts allowed and Liv's mood was lifted another notch by the prospect of a visit to the cinema and making another friend. She went home happy.

''Bye Liv...have a nice afternoon with your parents.'

'Thank you...I'm sure I will...'bye...you have my number. I'll look forward to the cinema soon.'

'What on earth are you putting into that bag Barbara?'

'Just a few bits and bobs...you know what she's like Arthur. There'll be nothing to have with the tea...and I just thought they might appreciate something for later, when we've gone.'

'And who's going to eat that duster and can of polish then, eh?'

'Never mind about that...I just like to help out.'

'I thought we were going to let her get on with things herself? So how's she going to do that when you turn up every time like Mrs Mop on a mission?'

'I know but she has her head in the clouds half the time...

always has. You know what it was like when they were here with us.'

Arthur knew exactly what it was like: he put it down as a lived-in muddle, not minding the toys and books; empty cups and the drying clothes strewn around. That was life; a bit like the one he'd lived in before marrying Barbara. But Barbara's sensibilities were put into turmoil until she could restore their house to the order she needed once Bee was tucked up in bed and Liv had settled down with her writing.

'I just don't want her going down that black hole again...I couldn't bear it.'

'I know love...I know...but it won't get that bad again... she's in a much better place now...getting stronger by the day as far as I can see... enjoying her job and the house.'

She knew Arthur was right, but rarely admitted to the fact, and in the car, on the short journey to their daughter's house, recalled the dark days when Liv struggled to even get out of bed; days when the weight of Daniel's death, and the repercussions of the investigations, had consumed them all. Headlines in the local Press and TV reports hadn't helped

'How did we ever get through it?'

'Same as always love...we stuck together.'

Barbara pondered on the past until they turned into the road to Liv's house. She stepped out onto wet pavements steaming in a dazzling sun and the welcoming sight of her granddaughter waiting on the doorstep.

'Grandma! Grandad!'

Barbara thrilled at the tightness of her hug 'Beatrice Rose...goodness I can't breathe in that big bear hug,'

'I've missed you Grandma...I've been waiting to show you all the pictures I've done for you and Grandad.'

Grandad trailed behind with the coats as they all trooped inside. Barbara found Liv in the kitchen unpacking the milk.

'Hello love...we're here.'

Their embrace was longer than it took for the usual peck on the cheek. Liv held on to Barbara's shoulders and looked into her face when she detected tears about to fall.

'What's all this? Is everything all right? Is Dad ok?'

'It's fine...I'm fine...Dad's fine...it's nothing...I just miss you both that's all', and she swiftly dried her eyes.

'It doesn't look that way...tell me.'

Seeing Arthur occupied with Bee, Barbara moved close and lowered her voice,

'All right...your Dad's been called back to the consultant next week...but don't worry...doctor said that it was just a precaution...you know what I'm like...I worry if any of you sneeze'.

'That's true but this is different...'

'I can't say anything to your Dad...goes off the deep end so I don't.'

Liv was thwarted on asking anything further when Arthur came in.

'What are you two whispering about?'

He shot Barbara a warning look.

'I'm just telling our Olivia about your new project...planning a new colour for the living room...he's been pouring over four colour charts for a week and still can't decide but I've told him we get someone in this time. Took me an age to get those splatters out of the carpet...not to mention his hair...after last time.'

'Get awa' with yer woman...that was nothin'...can't rush these jobs. Nine-tenths prep and one-tenth doin'...now where's that tea?'

They sat at the kitchen table where Barbara presided over the general chit-chat and Liv listened with feigned interest to the comings and goings of their neighbours and friends, as well as people she barely knew or was ever likely to meet.

Arthur had long gone off with Bee to play with her new doctor's kit.

When Barbara ran out of steam for gossip, she finally asked the questions she really wanted answers to,

'And how are you doing, Olivia? We don't see enough of you nowadays...'

'I'm ok Mum...really...getting there...life's good right now'

'You know I still worry after all that you've been through... what we've all been through...I can't help it.'

'Then stop it, Mum...you concentrate on yourselves...on Dad. I'm fine...I love my little house...I'm getting to know my neighbour, Frances. She might be in her nineties but goodness she is amazing...an inspiration to us all...you've got to meet her...and I'm getting to know a few other people...Debbie at the Co-op...we might go to a movie one afternoon if we can plan it right...and...well...there's someone I met through work...'

'Oh...who's that then?'

Barbara was quick off the mark; the way Liv had said 'someone through work' piqued her interest as soon as Liv's cheeks turned pink.

'His name's Adam...we've been out a few times that's all... when Bee's been at Rob's...nothing serious.'

'Adam...that's a nice name...Adam who? What does he do? Does he live round here?'

'Mum it's early days...I haven't grilled him on his full life story just yet...but he's a chartered surveyor, and we get on well.'

'And has Bee met him?'

'You sound just like Frances. That's what she said...anyway no not yet but maybe soon.'

Barbara wasn't sure what she thought about a new man. It would give her something else to worry about, and she had enough on her plate right now but was prevented from saying more when Bee came in to drag her away to her room. Arthur followed behind with a bandaged arm and a plaster on his cheek.

'Grandad's much better now,' Bee proudly announced.

'I can see that, love...is it my turn now?'

'No silly you're not poorly...I want to show you my pictures.'

Barbara went off holding Bee's hand. Arthur was happy to sit and rest when a fit of coughing brought on a pain in his chest. Liv gave him a glass of water.

'Come and sit down Dad...drink this.'

'If you start fussing like your Mother I'm off.'

'Don't worry...I'll never get to that stage I promise, but don't keep anything from me will you?'

'So how are you managing the house? I see that shelf's still up that I put in Bee's room. Not fallen down yet.'

'Dad...'

'Seriously, we should make a start on that garden, love...it's a jungle out there.'

'Don't worry it's on my list.'

'You and your lists...I'm still finding them at home...tell you what, I'll pop over one afternoon and give it a mow.'

'You'll do no such thing! I'll get round to it...next time you come it'll have stripes and a neat edge just like yours.'

'No wonder you're good at writing stories...the things you make up. How's that going anyway...have you got time, what with work and Bee and everything?'

'I've just sent another piece off for a competition...fingers crossed, Dad'.

'That's good.'

Arthur always took an interest, but his reading matter rarely went beyond the local paper. He was rescued by Barbara's questioning voice reaching them from Bee's room, and they both smiled when they knew what that would be about.

'Goodness me...little Bee...so much...I can't see the wall-paper for all those pictures...or much of the carpet come to that.'

Barbara trod carefully around a half constructed Lego house, two board games started but not finished, and the doctor's kit.

'But what about my pictures...don't you like them? I drew this one specially for you...it's the tree at the picnic we went on with Mrs Fenton next door.'

Bee produced a small sheet of paper from under the bed.

'Oh...a picnic? That's nice.'

If there was a twinge of envy that Barbara had not been included in the outing, she didn't show it.

'This is for me? It's lovely thank you. I'll put it up at home.'

Her eyes went from the picture to the overflowing wash basket in the corner and scuffed school shoes that were badly in need of a polish. 'Must get Arthur on to that, although I doubt there's a tin of polish in the house,' she thought to herself.

'Grandma! You're not looking.'

'I am dear...'

Barbara turned back to Bee and took the picture from her granddaughter. She was truly amazed at the detail when she finally gave it her full attention, surprised at such talent in a child so young.

'Oh my, this is beautiful Bee...I'm sure I don't know where you get it from...not from me...or Grandad...you and your Mum...writing and painting'

'Mummy says I was born with it,' she beamed proudly.

'There's something in that I suppose...now come on little

miss, let's get this lot sorted shall we then I'll go get my duster?'

Barbara set to, collecting clothing from the floor and filling the basket before straightening Bee's bed where they'd been sitting. She placed Wabbit gently back on the top, in the middle, his usual place, just as she had always done, and Bee stuck her head in the toy box.

Dusted and tidied to Barbara's satisfaction, they went back to the kitchen to find Liv and Arthur, heads together, deep in conversation. It stopped as soon she walked in. She couldn't be certain, but thought she heard Robert's name, although she didn't delve any further when it usually meant something to get upset about and Arthur would avoid that at all costs.

'Time for another cuppa I think. Get that kettle on. I've brought something to go with it in one of these bags...you have a search Bee.'

'I drink more tea in an hour with you two than I drink all week on my own.'

'Nothing wrong with tea...now try this cake and tell me what you think.'

She cut generous slices for Liv and Bee and they were back on familiar territory; drinking tea and eating cake.

'This is so good Mum...I've missed your baking.'

'I brought two so you can put the other in your freezer.'

It was comforting sitting around the kitchen table together, drinking tea and eating cake; embracing the company and the love that couldn't always be said in words.

When they'd finished, Barbara insisted on washing up. She gathered the cups and plates, along with crockery already in the sink from the night before, and anything else she could find lying around. Ignoring Liv's protests, she spent the next half hour wiping down cooker, work surfaces and strange splatters that had dripped on the cupboard doors. Arthur knew better than to object and Bee, oblivious to anything else, chatted about the picnic.

The visit saw her parents in a satisfied frame of mind; Barbara that she had left the house in better shape than she'd found it; and Arthur to have reassured Liv that Robert would only be allowed to take Bee into full custody over his dead body. Another visit was promised very soon with plans for another picnic, including Barbara and Arthur.

The visit that had all the markings of supportive parents had also unlocked the beginnings of a role reversal between them. Arthur's illness was manifest in newly formed lines across his forehead and Barbara, trailing after him even more than was customary, looked tired and drawn.

Arthur had always been the strong one, the one who'd sat with his daughter in the middle of the night when she couldn't sleep; the one who held her tight when she couldn't escape the visceral pain that engulfed her. Sometimes on those nights, they didn't even talk; he instinctively knew when the time for words had passed and would simply hold her until she had calmed enough to get back to bed and sleep in what was left of the night.

Barbara's tack was different, but still effective; she was the no nonsense one, the mother who saw to the daily tasks that 'wouldn't do themselves' and was mistress in the art of practicality. She understood the essence of keeping the wheels of the household well oiled. But this afternoon saw the beginnings of a shift.

Chapter Twenty Two

After tea, a makeshift affair of cheesy beans on toast, Liv's phone buzzed, and for a moment her heart beat just a little quicker at the thought that it might be Adam. It had been a month since their last date and communication had been sporadic as well as spare.

'Oh it's you Dom...hi'

'Knife to the heart Liv...you expecting someone else?'

'No...no sorry...I was expecting a call...but you know I always love to hear from you...'

'Stop it right there. I know my place.'

'Behave Dominic Raywell. To what do I owe the pleasure?'

'That's better. Apart from waiting for an upgraded offer on calls, how are you? Not heard from you for a couple of weeks...everything ok?'

'Yes all's fine here...just had Mum and Dad over.'

'Ah...the house has been given a once over then...sweet smell of polish in every room?'

'Something like that.'

'What are you up to now?

'Nothing much...just given Bee her tea.'

'I'm just on my way back from town and wondered if you fancied some company for an hour.'

Liv smiled at the prospect.

'Your company is always welcome, you know it is...that would be lovely...you're my perfect antidote to a clean and tidy house.'

'Not sure how to take that but I'll be with you in about fifteen minutes...I'll bring a bottle shall I...must be about the right time?'

'Sounds good to me...see you soon'

Dom arrived, and as promised, was not empty-handed.

'It's good to see you,' Liv said mid-hug, 'but you don't have to bring something every time you come over...'

'Well in that case...' He made to put the wine back in the bag.

'No you don't...I've even bought a decent cork screw after last time...you're the only person I know that doesn't buy screw caps.'

'It's always my pleasure to buy a decent bottle...us writers need something to look forward to at the end of the day.'

'It is the end of the day,' Liv pronounced and took the bag to the kitchen, followed closely by Dom.

'Is the visit something special? Or just the pleasure of my company?'

'Well you and Bee are the little rays of sunshine in my life... you know that...and after catching up on a backlog of college work, I needed to get out...preferably somewhere that didn't involve a supermarket...so I thought of you and Bee.'

'And?'

'And there's something I...'

Dom didn't manage to finish. At the sound of his voice, Bee came running out of her room.

'Uncle Dom!' she squealed and ran to him.

'BeeBee I've missed you honey bunch...' He rummaged inside a second bag and produced a book, 'I saw this little witch and thought of you!'

Bee's face lit up; witches were her new obsession. The book was second hand but remarkably clean and in good condition.

'Thank you, I love witches...and so does Wabbit'

Clutching the latest acquisition, Bee ran off again to her room when adult conversation proved nowhere near as interesting as her new book. Liv had produced two glasses and a corkscrew, calling out, 'Ten minutes before bed BeeBee,' which fell on deaf ears.

'Oo...what gorgeous wine is this then?'

'A lovely Bordeaux I tried the other week...not too warm and not too chilled...just as it should be.'

Dom had been teaching Liv about the essence of a good wine; she raised her glass to inspect the colour and sniffed its before taking a sip.

'Mm lovely, cheeky little number with a most seductive bouquet...'

'Ok...ok.'

'Now tell me what you have really come for...you're like my Mum, you say one thing but your face tells me something else.'

'As long as you don't expect me to pick up a duster...'

'Dom...I'm taking your glass until you tell me what's on your mind.'

'Harsh woman Liv...but you are a perceptive soul.'

'Well?

Dom looked at Liv and smiled.

'What happened to that timid young woman who first

joined my writing group? You know the one who barely opened her mouth let alone voiced an opinion?'

'I'm trying to lose her.'

'Then you're doing really well...I'm proud of you Olivia Smithson...give me that wine and I'll make a toast to this new Liv.'

The wine, expensive as it was, was reassuringly good. Relaxing on the sofa, he went on:

'You know I had no real expectation when you came to me, but you shone with your creative flair and that wonderful imagination of yours. It was always a pleasure for me to read your work. I saw something in it that I knew was lacking in my own.

'What? I...'

'No let me go on... you've come a long way from the young woman I first met. I love how you've blossomed, taken on this place, shown the world, including Robert, that you can make it on your own...you and Bee have a wonderful life here and I feel very privileged to have been part of it. I...'

'Stop right there...what do you mean to have *been* part of it? You are part of it. You're scaring me...are you ill?'

'Sorry, sorry...no...I didn't put that very well. I'm not ill I promise...and I always want to be part of your lives...*will* always be part...but I am going away for a while.'

'What? When?...Where are you going?'

'Go pour us both another glass and I'll tell you all about it...it's all good...and it's not permanent...I just wanted you to be the first to know now it's settled.'

Dom watched Liv's tall, still-too-skinny frame reach for the bottle but was pleased to recognise that she was at least starting to fit the clothes that had until so very recently hung from her bones. Her face too had gained a healthy glow, and whereas at one time any conversation about the future would have been stilted and unsure, she now showed an optimism that lifted his spirits. He could never explain exactly why Liv had appealed to him so much, but every time he saw her it reignited the old longing he'd had with his wife, for a child in his life, someone who he felt sure would have grown up to be just like Liv.

A re-filled glass was handed over.

'This really is fabulous...nothing like the cheap plonk I usually resort to. Thank you Dom and cheers...now tell me you're not going too far from us...please'.

'Cheers m'dear...to you...to us all.'

They took another drink and Liv waited impatiently for Dom to go on.

'Well?'

'It's nothing too drastic...I've been offered a two-year work exchange in Iowa...at the university there...it really is just too good an opportunity to pass up on...and at my time of life, it might not come up again.'

'You've never mentioned this before...why didn't you tell me?

'It seems to have been under discussion forever...and when nothing was certain...I began to think it would never actually happen...but all of a sudden it did happen...and now it's here and it's mine if I want it.'

'You can't...I need you...what will I do without you here?'

'You'll do perfectly well...you know you will...you're a much stronger person now'

'I'm sorry...that was selfish...I shouldn't have said that...I don't blame you Dom...it's just a bit of a shock.'

'Imagine what it's like for me. It's taking a bit of getting used to, but I'm ready for one last challenge before I get pensioned off and spend my days playing bingo at the Sunnyside Rest Home.'

'Pfft...you're a long way off that...at least for another two years.'

'Thanks Liv.'

'Seriously though, you deserve it...is it all arranged?'

'Just about...we've exchanged resumes...they know about the work I do outside of college, working with people going through trauma and the like, and it seems that was the clinching part in getting me over.'

'Dom that's fantastic...they're lucky to get you...but I'll miss you so much.'

Dom put his glass down and took Liv's hands.

'Anyway, moving on...did you put in for that competition I told you about?'

'Yes I did, but stop changing the subject'

'Don't you dare cry...I can't have that...no sadness...it's two years Liv and you've so much that you need to concentrate on...I want to come back and find that your writing has finally taken off. You are one talented lady.'

'It's only because of you that I started writing again.'

'And now you don't need me to tell you to keep on going.'

A reluctant Bee was finally coaxed to bed by seven thirty following Dom's second reading of 'The Worst Witch' and he left for home.

Back on her own, Liv sprawled full length along the sofa with thoughts of the day swirling in her head and back upon her Dad. Out of earshot of Barbara, Arthur had confided he knew there would be a heart operation soon and was waiting for the call. He promised it wasn't major surgery and a stent would make a big difference to his life; Liv chose to believe him when anything else was untenable.

Barbara and Arthur were still as protective over her as ever, but no longer treated her like a helpless child. Despite the untidiness and messy garden, they saw how she'd blossomed into her new life and praised how well she was managing on her own with Bee. In turn, Liv began to see them through different eyes and considered the day when their needs would overtake her own. Deep in her heart, she knew that they could be on their deathbeds and still want to make sure that she was all right. 'Mum, despite your fretting over Dad, you still have to make sure my house is clean and tidy before you leave,' she mused, looking around the room.

Liv put some music on and turned the volume up as far as she dare to drown out the unwanted chatter that threatened to spill into darker corners. Astral Weeks caught her eye, bringing to mind the last evening spent with Adam and a happier place.

Dancing close to 'Beside You', they became so much more than good friends that night. He'd held her tightly, face closing into her hair and neck, hands stroking her back. But was that it? Where was he now?

'This won't do' she mumbled and turned it off, afraid to go back there. What was the point if it was all going to come to nothing? The internal chatter would not be turned off so easily, however. How could it have been nothing after all he'd said? She considered calling him, to put her mind at ease about whether or not there would be another time, another date to look forward to; or whether he had decided that she wasn't the 'someone' he wanted after all. But musings were brought to an abrupt end by a noise outside.

A car with throaty exhaust had pulled up next door. Liv checked the clock; it was gone nine and late for Frances, but light enough for her to see how very expensive the car looked. Intrigued, she looked across as discreetly as possible.

A man, possibly in his fifties, or early sixties and smartly dressed, got out. The car door closed with an expensive clunk and he walked in a confident gait to Frances' front door. 'Odd time to be visiting,' she thought, but on further consideration, presumed it could very well be Simon, her son. Frances had told her that he liked to drop in unexpectedly.

Liv turned away and ignoring the wine, and the activity next door, decided to make the most of what was left of the evening and took out her notebook and pen. A new story was demanding to be written and the next sixty minutes passed like five until the sound of footsteps outside caught her attention. She went to the window again to see the boot of the car open and Simon, if indeed it was her son, carefully loading two large, flat, wrapped objects. Closing the lid, he looked back at the front door that was already shut. Behind it, the hallway was in darkness. He sat behind the wheel and within seconds gave two loud revs of the engine and sped away.

Chapter Twenty Three

A couple of weeks passed before Liv had an opportunity to pay Frances another visit, by which time she'd forgotten about the nighttime visitor next door. She called round on her afternoon off work to take bread and milk.

Frances answered the door with a pale face and dark shadows under her eyes. It might have been a lack of sleep, but something told Liv it was more than that judging by the wavering in her voice.

'Ah, Olivia...come in my dear...very kind of you to bring me these.'

'Is everything all right Frances? You don't look well.'

'I'm fine...just need a little more sleep I think.'

Frances' usually straight back stooped slightly and she walked more slowly than usual, as she led the way inside.

'Let me make the tea this time. You go and sit down.'

'I can still make a cup of tea my dear...it's you who are the guest.'

'Never mind that...I'll bring it through.'

Frances was beyond arguing and went to the living room as told. She gratefully took the offered tea, but her hands trembled spilling it into her saucer and the plate of biscuits was left untouched.

'Are you sure you're feeling all right? You look ever so pale...is it just lack of sleep?'

'Mostly...it comes with age I'm afraid and some nights you have no choice but to make friends with the very early hours.'

Frances' face assumed a little more colour as she drank the tea and they talked of Bee, the weather and life in general, but Liv could still see that there was something else behind the chitchat.

'Frances, tell me to mind my own business but if there is something bothering you, please let me help...you know I will if I can.'

Frances put down the tea and thought for a moment before answering.

'I don't want to burden you my dear...you have enough worries of your own.'

'Really it's no burden. I mean it when I say if there's anything I can do, I will.'

There's nothing you can do but it would be nice to have someone to talk to. There's no one else left now you see.'

'Then you have me.'

'He came again the other night...Simon...usually at night... sometimes he lets himself in with his own key. I should never have let him take the spare but he insisted, 'I need to keep it just in case Mother. You never know.' But I do know...I know more than he thinks.'

Liv remembered the car.

'So that was who I heard pulling up outside. I did wonder if it was Simon.'

'It was Simon, yes...come to take more paintings...he sells them for me and when I have very little pension, it helps...but he takes me for a fool. I know the value of the objects he sells... and those he has his eye on. I knew the value of the vase that went last month and the paintings he took two weeks ago...I know the difference between the money he transferred to me and the money he kept back for himself. My Sherrin watercolour was exquisite and I will miss it...'

On the wall behind Frances' chair, a dark rectangle was shadowed by age and dust. Liv's eyes followed her gaze but she kept quiet, to let Frances talk without interruption.

'I may be in my nineties now and my body in decline, but I'm not stupid. It upsets me more that he should treat me this way when I have never refused him anything in his life. He's just like his father...they both knew...know...the price of everything and the value of nothing. Simon might be my only son, my only remaining child after...after...well he's all that's left... but we are not close. We never really talk...he never gives me his time...I'm just an old woman who gets in the way of what he wants...him and Sarah. Of course he will get everything soon enough.'

Liv interjected, 'I'm sure he must love you too...and you are not going any time soon...you always look so well...you've got years before you.'

'Thank you my dear, but I've stopped counting the time I have left in years...'

Frances fell silent, summoned by thoughts that usually came unbidden in the middle of the night. After finishing her tea, she felt strong enough to continue, to confide in Olivia.

'If Hermione had lived, I'm sure things would have been very different...I think of her still, even after all these years... probably more now, and especially when I look at your beautiful little girl. Bee reminds me of her. The other day when I watched her playing in the garden, chasing a butterfly in that long grass...it took me right back to her.'

'To Hermione?'

'Yes...my daughter...I haven't spoken of her to you have I? She loved to dance you know...so full of life until one day the boundless energy began to leave. At first we couldn't understand why she was so tired all the time. I thought she was just doing too much and would pack her off to bed early...but no amount of sleep could put it right. Nothing put it right...the doctors were helpless....

Frances' eyes misted.

'She died at five years old...it was leukaemia that took her and in those days not much could be done. I often wonder what she would have become had she lived. Each year on the anniversary of her death, I would try to picture her...how she might look...but it became too painful...it's all in the past and I can do nothing about it. If I was a religious person, I might think about being reunited with Hermione in the next world, but I have been left with little faith.'

'I'm so sorry Frances...'

The words struck deep and personal, and unlike Frances, Liv couldn't control her tears when it brought back painful memories of her own.

'Does the pain ever go away?'

'It's not so biting as the years go by, but it doesn't disappear altogether...you just learn to live with it...get on with your life. Make friends...try to be happy with what you have got... and I did have a healthy son...he was such a lovely...loving child.'

'I'm sure he must love you still...' she said, but soon realised that repetition of the words would never make them true.

'Love? He doesn't know the meaning of the word any more'.

Frances sounded so unlike the woman Liv had got to know over the past three months, she wondered what it had taken to make her feel that way. How sad it was to own such antipathy towards a child you had given birth to; someone you'd nurtured and guided into adulthood.

'When was Hermione born?'

'March 16th 1933 at 8:45...so long ago but still fresh in my memory...she was a very special child. It was very windy that day and rained heavily...but my heart bathed in the sunshine of my baby's face.'

'I'm so sorry Frances...'

'You know George wanted to call her Fay...a film, King Kong had come out that year, and that was the name of an actress, but I was adamant that she would not be called Fay. It was to be Hermione, after an aunt I had been particularly fond of. I had my daughter for five beautiful years...the happiest years of my life. When she died, I died a little too...a special part of my life had gone forever.'

Frances was like an old chest lain dormant in an attic, full to the brim, each item revealing something new about its owner. She had a daughter who died in 1938, in childhood, but the way Frances spoke of her, it could have happened last week, not sixty years ago. Daniel had been gone for only six.

'Do you ever see friends...go out?'

'Not any more...I did at one time and we were all very close...me, Marjorie and Mary...and Delphine; our little group, but they've all gone now. We had such good times together... but everything must pass as they say...and so did they...one by one, until there was only me left. Inevitable I suppose when you reach my age.'

'That must be hard...have you not made any new friends since then?'

'I was introduced to the day centre in town last year...my cleaner put me on to it...she thought it might be good for me to meet other people. It was fine at first...they all told me how marvellous I was doing for my age...made me very welcome... but what's so marvellous when there is no one you have anything in common with? We all need to share things we experience, things we have known, our interests, but no one understood what I was talking about...and I certainly didn't understand them. They spend a great deal of time watching television and looked at me as if I were quite mad when I told them I didn't even own one. I only went twice...I knew very quickly that it wasn't for me when I could not find the kind of conversation I crave, the conversations I have with you, my dear Olivia...' She gave a short laugh, 'Even the conversations I have with Bee.'

Frances saw Bee in her mind's eye; the little girl always made her smile even if the happiness she engendered was always tinged with sadness at the loss of her own.

Frances' mind drifted back to the centre and she laughed again as she pictured some of the people she'd struck up a conversation with. Her face began to lose the pallor of an hour earlier and took on a pink glow, her eyes finding their glint once again.

'Over a cup of tea and a biscuit from a plate of 'variety mix', the conversations went from complaints about the weather and the effect on their joints, to what had happened in the soaps the night before...my dear at first I dare not admit to not watching them or not knowing who on earth they were talking about until I had no choice but to confess about my lack of a television. Don't get me wrong...I wasn't entirely ungrateful...it was all gentle banter and sometimes even humorous...but perhaps not for me, my dear.'

'No, you've never come across as a fan of Coronation Street...but don't you get lonely sometimes?'

'Not so much...one gets used to ones own company...one person I really do not miss is George. It was hard at first when he went...we had been together for over sixty years, but life without a husband who had not considered my thoughts and opinions of any value, had become a strain for most of those years...I didn't realise how much of a strain until he died. I'm sorry to say it, but it was a relief. For many years afterwards, I experienced some of my happiest days...apart from Paris of course, and Hermione. Socialising with friends was wonderful, and oh those lovely holidays we had...sadly, I can't do it now even if I had the friends to do it with. The most life I see now, apart from the cleaner and occasional visit from Simon, is through this front window...and of course you my dear... you have done wonders for me since you moved in and I can't thank you enough. Goodness, listen to me...I hope I don't sound needy...I really don't mean to.'

'Never needy...I love your company. Don't ever think that.'

Frances went on with her reminiscence as Liv felt guilty over not paying Frances more attention.

'This street though...this street may not be quite what it once was...aging and crumbling...a bit like me really...but it is intriguing nevertheless...and far more interesting than watching those soaps on television. I did try watching once and actually bought a small set, but it really wasn't for me... that's it over there.'

Liv could just about make out the television beneath a lace-edged cloth. On top sat a small figurine of a girl with flowers.

'That's a Meissen. Simon has been eyeing it up for some time and I'm sure he has already established its value.'

Frances paused a while and finally looked up at Liv as if suddenly remembering that she was there.

'I'm sorry...going on a bit am I not?'

'No you're not...not at all...please don't stop...I'm listening.'

Frances took another sip of tea, tepid now but refreshing enough for a parched throat. She'd not talked so much for such a long time, not since the days of Marjorie, Mary and Delphine, and of course the picnic; it was a relief to have someone like Liv to listen.

'When I first saw you and little Bee arrive next door, something told me that you would be good neighbours, and I've not been wrong. I appreciate your taking time to come and see me...all the little things you've done for me...and do. And Bee...Bee is such an unexpected delight in my life...I can't tell you how much...and that picnic was the highlight of my week...my year!'

She pulled out a freshly laundered handkerchief and blew her nose. Frances was not sentimental; showing emotion was not in her upbringing. Old values, along with parental admonition, were too deeply ingrained to change her now.

'I'm always here for you Frances...any time.'

'I know that my dear...and I'm grateful...let that little girl of yours know that she is welcome to come and paint here any time won't you?'

'Course I will...she loved it last time...even told me about Picasso and Turner...the one who painted ballet dancers?'

'Ah yes...I was amazed at how interested she was...for one so young.'

'She makes up stories about meeting them too...she has a wonderful imagination.'

'Indeed...and now tell me your news...how is your Father. I'm so sorry, I should have asked earlier. You must think I am very self absorbed.'

'I think nothing of the sort.'

Shortly after her visit to Frances, in the stultifying heat of a hospital waiting room, Liv tightly held on to Barbara's hand. Both were still taking in the reassurances given two minutes earlier on the success of Arthur's operation. But despite all she had been told of its routine nature and chances of complete recovery, Barbara's anguish would never dispel until she could see him for herself. At that moment, she didn't know whether to laugh or cry, but managed both within a very short space of time.

'He's going to be all right.'

'Of course he is Mum...I never doubted it for one minute.'

'I don't know what I would do if anything happened to your Dad.'

'And you won't find out will you...not for a long time yet.'

Barbara's eyes welled up again. It was Liv's turn to be the strong one now and she rose to the occasion.

'You heard what the doctor said...he'll be back to normal in no time at all. Just a short while taking it easy until he heals then he'll be back in his shed looking for a paintbrush.'

'I'm glad you're here with me Olivia...I feel a lot easier now. Are you sure Bee's all right staying with Robert?'

'She's fine Mum don't worry about her too. It's the summer holiday and Robert was due to have her over for a week anyway.'

'Just you make sure he brings her back that's all. Cheeky beggar with his 'She'd be better off living with me' nonsense.'

Once the reassurances over Arthur's recovery hit home, Liv had to smile as Barbara's relief manifest in getting back to the other worries in her life, and she soon reverted to her usual self.

Chapter Twenty Four

With an hour left before collecting Bee from school, and after calling home for confirmation that her father was still on the road to recovery, Liv's instinct was to write. The collection of short stories was growing in pace with an imagination that started them, but most still needed tweaking before she would be anywhere near satisfied. In reality, she never thought that they were good enough. However, a full hour with no interruption was taken when offered and Liv lost herself in other worlds, other lives and other places far from her own. Dom still pushed competitions her way and berated her for not entering and Liv was becoming confident enough in her own ability to know when the time was right. She took place of runner up in a competition entered the previous month, and it provided the impetus needed. Writing was a luxury fitted around essentials of the day, but it was always at the top of the list when the opportunity presented itself.

Another piece was finished that day, 'There, not bad, I do believe I actually like that.' She put down her pen and stretched back in the chair. Ten minutes to go.

Calling Adam was an impulse that came out of the feeling

of euphoria. She pressed call but almost immediately regretted it. Too late now; he would already know it was her. 'Why couldn't you have called me Adam? Let me know one way or another if you want to see me or not. Is it so hard?' she muttered to herself. All she had received over the last few weeks was a string of noncommittal texts and excuses. Her heart beat fast as she waited for the call to be answered. She almost wished that it would go to answerphone and hovered over cancelling. Too late to stop now and Adam picked up.

'Liv...you've read my mind...I was just about to call you.'

'Really?' She tried to sound other than nervous, flustered and annoyed, and hoped he wouldn't notice.

'Really!'

Liv tucked the phone under her chin as she put on her coat.

'Then what stopped you?'

I'm too old to play dating games was what she wanted to say.

'I should have called sooner and I am so sorry but there've been things I had to do first...please let me see you again...let me explain.'

'Are you sure? Please don't mess me about Adam...I...'

'I would never do that Liv...we've only know each other a short time but I know already what I think I feel for you... what I *know* I feel for you...and I promise with all my heart that I would never mess you about...come out with me... please? Let me explain?'

He sounded genuine despite her annoyance.

'All right we could arrange something I suppose.'

A date was finalised for the next weekend when Bee would be at Robert's, a date when Ryan was planning to stay over at Luke's.

Liv's next impulse was a surprise to herself.

'Would you like to come over for dinner? I'm not the

world's best cook but I can read a recipe...and Bee can vouch for me.'

'I'd love that...perfect...I'll bring the wine'

There was no hesitation in his voice.

'Great...around seven? I've got to go now to collect Bee'

'I can't tell you how lovely it is just to hear your voice again Liv...really...I've missed you.'

The walk to school was full of plans for the evening, not least what to cook and the perennial decision of what to wear.

Adam hung up and sat with folded arms, grinning and looking very pleased with himself when Ryan walked in.

'Hey...what's up? What you smiling about?'

'Can't I smile without it being about something? I could just be happy to see my son.'

'Nah...doesn't work like that.'

'Ok it was Liv'. Today was not the time to hide anything from Ryan, especially not now.

'So you *are* going to see her again?'

Cynical disapproval was written across his face.

'Yes...I am seeing Liv again...we've arranged another date'

'I just hope she's an improvement on the other losers'

'You'll like her Ryan...and she's nothing like the others.'

He wasn't sure how far to go in pleading his case but desperately needed Ryan on side. Life was hard enough without another battle with his son.

'I don't know what to say...but please just go along with me...I really do like her you know.'

'Your life.'

'Don't be like that...your opinion matters to me.'

Ryan shrugged and looked at his phone when it started bleeping.

Further conversation was at an end.

'Gotta go.'

'You finished your homework?'

'Yeah...won't be late.'

'Where are you going?'

'Just out with a few of the lads.'

'Where with the lads?'

'Around.'

'Where to Ryan...I need to know?'

'What's with the fifty questions? We'll start at Luke's and then...who knows. I won't be late back...stop fussing...you got your life, I've got mine, ok?'

'Just don't be late...it's school tomorrow.'

'I won't!'

The door slammed; Ryan was gone leaving Adam in a state of flux. 'Was I ever like that? Can I really bring Liv into all this? And can I really expect Ryan to understand that she's not like all the others.

The dates Adam had been on since Sally died were few. It had taken two years following the funeral before he found the courage, or even the inclination, to set foot into what he considered a minefield as opposed to a pleasurable event.

The first tentative foray came when the Diane stepped into his life. Beautiful Diane, set up by well-meaning friends, couples who wanted his company but didn't want him to be the odd one out. They sat side by side at the dinner table and Adam dusted off a limited repartee that was anything but natural. It didn't put Diane off but in truth, it wasn't the relaxing evening he'd been looking forward to. A mutual liking for decent coffee and a café they both enjoyed paved the way for a meeting the next week and Diane lasted one further date before he realised that they really had too little in common, apart from the coffee.

Six months later, came Caroline. They met at a pub when he was out with friends from work one Friday night. He was unsure who had caught whose eye first but they struck up a conversation at the bar whilst waiting to be served. As the evening wore on, their chairs moved closer and a date was arranged two nights later. He soon discovered that she had recently been left by her partner of six years when wedding jitters overwhelmed him. She lasted for three further dates but it was obvious she was searching for a husband, wanting babies before she got too old, and not necessarily in that order. The last thing Adam wanted was another child, especially when he could barely cope with the one he had.

Finally came Davina; lovely, quiet, unassuming, they met at the regional office Christmas party when they were the last two sitting at the dinner table. Neither had planned to dance, Adam out of embarrassment and Davina for lack of a partner. They talked instead and a tentative relationship began that lasted almost two months. For a while he was happy to enjoy female company that made so few demands of him; she was content to let him suggest where they went and what they should do, but before long, Davina's undemanding nature ignited no spark and it was over.

It was Liv who brought the spark and lit the flame, although the timing was unfortunate. Ryan's sweet and biddable nature had morphed into truculence and trouble. He'd made it perfectly clear what he'd thought of the other women who appeared on the scene and there was no doubt that Liv was in line for the same treatment.

Adam studied the framed photograph he picked up from the sideboard, a happy family group taken at a friend's barbecue, only two weeks before Sally's diagnosis of the cancer that couldn't be cured, two weeks before the decline of a life taken away just days short of her thirty-sixth birthday. Three smiling faces looked out on a summer's day when the sky was blue, the grass was green and all was well in their world. Ryan was eleven, about to start high school and showing promise at junior rugby. Adam had got the promotion he'd been after and they'd celebrated with a bottle of champagne. Sally, working three days a week in a solicitors' office, was keen to study for the LLB now that Ryan was older and in theory there were not quite so many demands on her time.

Ryan and Adam clung to the memories and shreds of Sally that were left behind. They forged a new life together as the gaping hole slowly shrank over the years. This wasn't the first time Adam addressed the photograph for advice.

'Sally...what do I do? The other women didn't matter...I really didn't care whether I saw them or not...but this time it's different...I've tried not to get too involved but I want more and I think she feels the same.'

He put the photograph back; he knew exactly what Sally would tell him; she'd told him in the days she lay dying at the hospice, in the time and space they were given to speak of all that was left between them.

'Find someone else Adam...promise me...don't be on your own...Ryan will need a female figure to put him straight on a few things...he might resent it a first...but I know you'll make the right choice. You chose me, so I know you have good taste.'

'How can I do that...how can I replace...?'

'She won't replace...she won't...just promise me you will try?'

She gripped his hand as much as she could manage until sleep and the drugs took over. It was the last conversation they had.

Adam walked to the bottom of the garden where he and Ryan had planted a pretty sorbus tree in Sally's memory. It had gone beyond the spindly stage; the trunk had thickened and it grew strong and healthy. The spring blossom had fallen but in autumn vivid red leaves and yellow berries would present a different beauty. No one would take Sally's place; but Liv was the closest any woman had come to fulfilling the promise he'd made to his late wife.

It was half ten by the time he heard Ryan's key in the door. A grunt that passed as greeting came with a whiff of alcohol on his son's breath, although he wasn't drunk. Now wasn't the time to get into an argument Adam told himself; he had neither the energy nor the inclination to get into anything that night. Relieved not to get the third degree, Ryan slumped up to his room.

'Night.'

'Night...I'll see you in the morning...you got training tomorrow?

'Yeah, straight after school...big match Saturday.'

'Ok I'll pick you up after work'

It was a difficult path to navigate and Ryan's mood swings were unpredictable. Timekeeping, schoolwork, homework, laziness; they were nothing new in the scheme of things, but new to Adam and he struggled on his own. The only person who understood was Marcus when Luke was going through the same thing, although Marcus suspected that it wasn't just alcohol with Luke. He hoped he was wrong.

Adam fought with the idea that it wasn't right to embroil Liv in his life right now. He understood at least part of the struggles she'd battled with and the strength she was just finding to get her through. It was a fight he was happy to lose when she made him feel something of how life used to be. She was different from Sally, but in that difference began a longing for something new and unexplored. He was prepared to face the consequences and hoped that Liv would too.

Chapter Twenty Five

Marsha was clearing the kitchen when Robert arrived home with Bee. They were later than expected. In between icing the cupcakes especially made for his daughter, and testing the one that looked a bit out of shape, for the past hour she'd periodically looked out of the window on to the drive.

The garden was immaculate with its freshly cut striped lawn, neatly trimmed edges and weed-free flowerbeds. Marsha had sighed in resignation when she caught Robert going over the work she'd done earlier when Eddie was having his nap. It wasn't easy living up to Robert's standards. Still, their garden always drew admiring glances and comments from neighbours and passers-by, and it pleased her.

Robert arrived an hour later than usual, which was not like him, but the look on his face as he walked up the path with Bee, told her all she needed to know about the mood he was in. Bee didn't look too happy either, which saddened Marsha, as she was usually so excited, especially since the arrival of the baby.

Bee was good with Eddie; she liked to help with his feeding now he was on solids and he could sit in a high chair. Marsha would prepare their tea as Bee read him his favourite books and she would help with bath time when they'd finished eating. It made her feel grown up; she was no longer the baby in the family, loving the fact that she went to bed much later than Eddie.

Marsha embraced their new routine with Bee and Eddie, and was pleased at the lack of jealousy on Bee's part. It was quite the opposite; right from the start, there had been nothing but love shown towards the new arrival. And Marsha, in turn, always made an extra effort when Bee was coming to stay. Today it was cupcakes. She wiped her floury hands on a tea cloth and went to the door.

'Hello, Bee...it's lovely to see you again.' She opened her arms for the usual hug before noticing the state of her uniform.

'Oh dear, what's happened to you? Had a fall? Everything all right Rob?' Marsha looked up at Rob's scowling face.

'Far from it,' he answered, evading the proffered kiss from his wife. He bustled Bee inside but still managed to notice the mess in the kitchen.

Bee's face lit up at the sight of the buns, 'Are these for our tea?'

'They are...made especially for you.'

'Thank you...can I have one now please, I'm starving!'

Marsha looked to Robert who had just come back into the kitchen from taking Bee's bag to her room. He was normally strict about snacks before tea but this time said, 'Just one.'

A pot of tea was made and as Bee sat at the table pushing her tongue delightedly into the luscious cream and jam filling, Marsha wanted to know what was going on.

'We'll talk later,' was Robert's terse reply and the only one she was going to get.

'Ok'.

The muddy gingham dress was included into that night's

laundry and she would work on the repair tomorrow. On closer inspection, it wasn't even as bad as she thought. Bee appeared unfazed by the events of the day and Marsha was convinced that Rob, being Rob, was probably fussing over something or nothing. By the time they'd had tea and Robert had taken Bee to play in the park for half an hour, Marsha continued with her usual Eddie routine and put Rob's foul mood out of her mind. She'd long ago learned not to rise to it and for now was happy to bathe Eddie on her own; it was much more fun when no one minded how wet the floor got. Eddie delighted in splashing and chortling at his attempts to pour water from one container to another and Marsha sat in pleasure beside the bath. Normality had returned.

But later that night, when Bee and Eddie were asleep, Robert launched into a full account of the incident of the torn, muddy dress. All that had been simmering in his head since picking Bee up from school was given vent.

'Bee can't stay at that school...it's not fit.'

'Oh Rob, we've been through all that...Liv's not going to let her go back to her old school...you know that. It's too far from where she lives and the new school is in walking distance...she...'

'She's being bullied.'

'What?'

'Her teacher, Miss Farley called me in...tried to make out that it had been sorted and wasn't as bad as it looked but you saw the state of her...and she wasn't the only one...there was a new boy, Aadi, moved up from London...apparently he was being mocked over his accent and it all got way out of hand.'

'What did that have to do with Bee?'

'Well, Bee being Bee took him under her wing and defended him; then there was a scuffle and this bully pushed her over...and worst of all it wasn't the first time. She assumed I knew all about it.'

'Who did?'

'Miss Farley of course!'

'Oh dear...so what are they doing about it?'

'Not enough as far as I can see...Miss Farley said that next week they would do an assembly about bullying...an assembly for god's sake...that's really going to help. I asked for the bully's name and if he was going to be suspended but she didn't think that was 'an appropriate move' right now...they'd seen his mother...she said she was shocked but in agreement about what they wanted to do and really hoped that I might be too. I made no comment on that one.'

'If they think they can sort it without doing anything drastic, surely that would be better?'

'Good grief, Marsha, you're just as bad as they are...that school is a dump...a breeding ground for bullies considering where it is and the problem kids that come out of it.'

'Does Liv know what happened today?'

'No...but believe me she will soon enough...I told her to leave it to me. I'm going to have it out with her...I want to know why she hasn't told me about this before.'

Marsha was about to say more but then reconsidered. In disagreeing with Robert she chose her battles carefully and this was one best left alone for now.

'That's up to you Rob...I'm off to bed...you coming?'

'I'll be up in a minute...still thinking things through.'

Marsha kissed the top of his head and left him to it. Her mind was on Eddie and whether or not she would get an unbroken night's sleep.

The next day began without incident. There was no further mention of the school or the school bully. Marsha saw it as a wasps' nest best not poked. Bee was her usual chatty self and delighted that the repair Marsha had made on her freshly laundered dress could hardly be noticed. Best of all, Robert was more upbeat than Marsha had seen him for some time. He took them all to Stanton Farm, a few miles down the road, where they could feed and pet the animals, before having lunch in the café.

Eddie sat in a high chair playing with finger sandwiches that partly reached his mouth but mostly found the floor; and Bee focused on a plate of lasagne in between helping her little brother. It crossed Marsha's mind how nice it might be to have another baby, hopefully a girl, to make their family even more complete. She pictured Eddie doing the same for a baby sister. She looked across at Robert who was whispering something to Bee; a worried look crossed his daughter's face and she shook her head.

'This is lovely, isn't it?' Marsha was anxious not to lose the upbeat nature of the outing.

Tears had ballooned in Bee's eyes and Robert looked at his wife, putting fingers to his lips and shook his head. Marsha said nothing and forced a smile.

'If we've all finished shall we get back out into the sunshine and give the goats those carrots we bought?'

There was no response.

'Right then, let's get ready.'

They asked for the bill and Robert felt for his wallet.

Eddie, much happier playing with the remains of his food than being wiped down and plucked from the chair, yelled loudly, attracting attention, and Bee gave a sullen nod. The waitress came over with the bill and insisted Marsha shouldn't worry about the mess when she'd apologised profusely; the waitress was used to it and would clear it. As they left the café behind, any thought of another child left with it.

Chapter Twenty Six

It was Saturday morning and Liv woke early. Despite the opportunity of a lie in, she got up. The room was bathed in light and her mind was already on the evening. There would be no more sleep.

The curtains were drawn back and despite the light of the room, it was dull outside. At least the forecast predicted a later sun and definitely no rain. Sitting at the kitchen table with coffee, Liv ruminated on the day ahead.

Her first thoughts, as always, were for Bee, but they were closely followed by thoughts of Adam. Tonight's date had come round quickly and she'd still not decided what to wear or what to cook. Reliving their last parting kiss brought on a flutter of nerves: would he still feel the same; would he have second thoughts? Was that why he'd not been in touch much? Things could so easily have gone much further last time, but he held back.

Nerves turned to panic when she reached her wardrobe, a perennial minefield of despair, but it was too late to do anything about the abysmal collection. She also remembered her promise of calling in on Frances this morning with items from the small shopping list.

A pale lemon summer dress, hidden at the back was hauled out for inspection. It turned into an unexpected blessing; a dress that fell at calf length; neither too short nor too long; and fitted rather better than it had last summer, filling out in all the right places. She hung it over the door to let out the creases and was pleased that at least one decision had been made that morning.

Food was easy; salad and quiche followed by strawberries and cream. That should do it she reckoned. It was hardly worth even writing a list. He could sample her cooking another day. Liv started to relax, but having made those crucial decisions so early in the day meant there was room for anxiety to build up around plans for the evening and what would, could, happen.

The bedside clock showed still only eight thirty. Throwing on shorts and a tee shirt, she made another coffee and a slice of toast. Writing was always a good escape from reality, so she sat for a couple of hours at the kitchen table where the words flowed easily and took her away from a fluttering, anxious heartbeat.

The rest of the morning was spent bringing order to chaos in the house. The living room floor was cleared of detritus built up during the time when no one was visiting. Every available space and corner was awash with books, toys and games. Bee's room had slowly morphed from the orderly, contained space of their first days to something expanding into whatever room she chose to play in. Liv never complained but occasionally scooped up the paraphernalia and put it in an approximation of where it might fit best, as she did today.

Eventually, she reached her own bedroom. Again, the flurry of nerves came on as bedding was changed and clothing strewn over the chair and floor, some found the laundry basket. Whether in hope or anticipation, she could not say, or wouldn't care to admit, but satisfied with this unaccustomed order, she left for the shops.

Debbie was at the checkout. She gave her a broad smile and beckoned her over the moment she'd stepped through the door.

'Hi, I'm pleased you're here...if you still want to go to the cinema there's a film starting next week and I wondered if you fancied it...'When Harry Met Sally'...it's on at the Odeon... good cast...Meg Ryan and Billy Crystal...what do you think?'

'Yes...I'd love to...I read a review the other day...right up my street.'

'Ok, just let me know when you're free. Give me a call...I can do most evenings next week...but daytime only Tuesday and Wednesday.'

Debbie hastily scribbled her number on a scrap of paper as a queue started to build up behind Liv.

'Ok, leave it with me and I'll call you...sounds great.'

Further conversation was cut short by the trail of impatient shoppers and tutting from an old man behind. Liv found all she needed, paid and left, pleased not to be held up more than necessary when Debbie had gone on her break, but happy at the thought of going to the cinema with her new friend.

Butter and milk were duly delivered to a grateful Frances and apologies were given that she couldn't stay longer.

'Another day will do my dear.'

Frances hid her disappointment well but Liv was sorry not to be able to stay, sensing that the look went beyond loneliness and a need for company.

'Absolutely...I'll see you very soon.'

'Enjoy your evening.'

By six-thirty, the bottle of white in the fridge had been opened and a glass poured, but before the first sip could be taken, her phone rang. Her first thoughts were that Adam was cancelling and for once, she felt relief when she saw Robert's name. Annoyance and a mouthful of wine preceded answering. Her inclination was to reject his call but as Bee was staying she answered, just in case of an emergency.

'Liv...hi...I need to talk to you.'

'Robert, I'm busy right now, can't it wait until Sunday?'

'This is serious...I want to know what's been going on at Bee's school.'

'What do you mean what's been going on? Has something happened?'

'Oh come on, I think you know...don't play the innocent.'

'For goodness sake just tell me what's happened...you're worrying me.'

'Then let's start with the bullying shall we?'

'Bullying.'

Liv's heart sank that he should have caught up with an incident that did not need his input; did not need a mountain made of a molehill.

'Robert there's nothing to get worked up about. They're children. They say things they don't understand and the school is sorting it.'

Robert snorted at her last remark and Liv took a second mouthful of wine.

Incensed at her easy dismissal of the incident only increased his determination to let her know his view of the matter. But it was almost seven o'clock and she refused to be drawn into a long conversation that would incite agitation and increase his anger. They had been there many times before and it would get them nowhere.

'We'll talk on Sunday Robert...not now...not over the phone.'

'Just know I'm not happy with the school's attitude...or yours. This is serious.'

Robert hung up, seething. Liv picked up her glass and took a third and longer drink. It was gone seven now and Adam was late. By ten past, as Liv considered a second glass, the doorbell rang.

Straightening the silky yellow dress, last worn too long ago to remember, she tucked her hair behind her ears, checked herself in the hall mirror and answered the door.

Adam stood with a broad grin, clutching wine in one hand and a bunch of flowers in the other. They'd been carefully selected at the florist's near his home, with assurance from the assistant that they were a perfect selection for a girlfriend and that she would be thrilled if someone were to choose them for her. She was just eighteen, still learning the trade, but enthusiastic, and the romantic in her was touched that he asked her opinion; the men who usually came in simply went by price and size of the bunch.

'Hope I'm not late?'

'No perfect timing...come on in.'

The wine had helped to calm her.

'You smell nice,' he said and leaned in to kiss her cheek. The flowers and wine got in the way and they both flushed.

'They're beautiful...thank you...I'll put them in some water.'

She took them through to the kitchen with Adam following close by.

'Please...just put them down a minute'

He took them out of her hands and sat them next to the wine.

'I need to do something first...if you don't mind...something I've wanted to do ever since I last saw you. He pulled Liv close, and when no resistance was shown kissed her long and hard on the mouth.

'I can't tell you how often I've thought of doing that...I hope you don't mind,' he asked when they eventually parted.

Liv said nothing; her response was a second kiss, longer than the first, during which their arms encircled and moved in a passionate response.

He looked into Liv's eyes when they eventually parted.

'I just needed your answer that's all...before anything else'.

'And did you get it?'

'Oh yes.'

Liv laughed; Robert's call was completely forgotten and Adam was all she wanted to see and hear.

'Are you ready for dinner?' she asked, 'Are you hungry?'

'No...not yet...not for food anyway. Let's have a glass first.'

Liv was the first to wake on Sunday morning. Her eyes opened slowly to see and hear Adam gently snoring beside her. Memories of Saturday night rolled in, in waves, as she turned and closed into his warm body, savouring the moment, until the urgency of a pee took over. Slipping carefully out of bed and rummaging for something to put on, Adam's shirt came to hand from the tangle of clothes hurriedly discarded the night before. She brought it close to her face and inhaled his smell, before slipping it on and going to the bathroom.

Adam rolled onto his side, still sleeping, but quieter now. Liv looked at him and wondered what it would be like to live with a man again, to live with Adam, to have him in her bed every night, close and content after making love.

She filled the sink with cold water and splashed it over her face before Adam came up behind. She felt his body move in close as he kissed her neck. Warm hands slid round to join hers in the water where their fingers mingled before finding their way inside the shirt. He held her breasts and Liv murmured in pleasure before turning and putting her arms around his neck.

'Good morning, beautiful,' he whispered.

'Good morning to you' she smiled back.

'I missed you back there...it was getting lonely in that bed.'

'Really?'

'Really.'

She stroked his unruly slept-in hair,

'I knew it was a mistake to evict that family of spiders... they could have kept you company while I was gone...'

'What?'

'Oh, nothing...I'll let Bee tell you that story.'

Back on the bed, morning lovemaking held none of the tentative, questioning moves of the night before; it was sure and certain; demanding and giving, without restraint or restriction.

They fell to the floor, breathing hard and exhausted, duvet and pillows in a tangle. Adam's body glistened with sweat and Liv's legs encircled his own.

'Wow, I don't know where that came from, but you are amazing Olivia Smithson, simply amazing.'

'You're not too bad yourself, Adam Davies', she whispered back.

'Thank you kindly...See what happens when you mention spiders?'

'I'll bear that in mind.'

Before Adam could say anything further, his stomach gave a long, low growl of complaint. Neither had eaten since lunch the day before.

'Food! We've not eaten yet.'

'Food,' she agreed.

Ignoring the quiche and salad in the fridge, Liv produced bread, butter and eggs and set to making a pot of fresh coffee. Adam made a decent job of scrambling the eggs, which they ate with toast and enthusiasm.

'It's good to know you can cook.'

'I wouldn't go that far but I've not poisoned my offspring

either, although it's fair to say that he eats pretty much anything.'

They took the rest of the coffee to the living room where Adam wandered to the large bookcase, mug in hand. He tilted his head and read the spines, curious to know what interested this fascinating woman.

'You do a lot of reading then?'

'Yes...are you a reader...you have books in your house?'

'I do...not this many...but I do enjoy a good book...mostly crime I must admit...I see from this collection I need to broaden my horizon.'

He continued perusing the shelves until he reached the bottom two.

'What are the blank-covered books? Don't tell me...your secret stash of porn?'

'Behave...they're mine...that's my writing...'

'Ah...yours...do you write much?'

'I do...always have...I'm sure I told you?'

'Sorry, I didn't realise you were so prolific.'

Liv nursed her coffee on the sofa; it had been a long time since she'd talked about her writing to anyone other than Dom.

'I'd love to read your work...if I may?'

'Maybe...when I'm ready...I'm finishing a short story to send off for a competition...I might let you read that when it's done.'

'You write fiction then?'

'Mostly fiction now...yes...'

She wasn't ready yet to share the intensely personal volumes when Adam wasn't aware of the full backstory of her life. This wasn't the time or the place, but maybe soon, maybe in time. Adam didn't push further and changed the subject.

'What time are you kicking me out then?'

'Well, Bee usually gets back from Robert's around four thirty, so...'

'Mm...so that means we still have another...'

Adam looked at the clock.

'Let's see...another six hours and fifteen minutes to fill...or thereabouts...'

Chapter Twenty Seven

Just after four, Liv switched off the radio and wandered over to the window. Bee was due home soon and she needed distraction. Adam had been gone for over an hour, leaving her head in a riot of thoughts. She went back to the writing table to re-read the last output but concentration was nowhere to be found amidst flashbacks of the past twenty-four hours.

There was no escape from the lingering memory of Adam naked in her bed, their legs entwined as he kissed her long and soft after making love, whispering as he took in every inch of her body. Adam reawakened a passion not felt for so long, if indeed, ever. She closed the writing.

This was normally the day and hour she felt most agitated, but for other reasons than a beautiful evening spent the night before. She and Robert would go through the same doorstep performance, dancing around what she had done, or failed to do, but not today. Today saw a different Olivia Smithson.

She began a half-hearted attempt to empty the last of the packing cases, but lost interest when she couldn't even remember why most of the contents had been kept in the first place.

At four seventeen the doorbell rang and for once she felt calm and prepared for anything that Robert might care to throw at her. It was time to stop his ridiculous intimidation. It was pathetic. She went to the door expecting Robert to say his piece and leave shortly after, as usual. But today he stood resolutely on the step.

'Can I come in for a minute? I need to talk to you.'

He put his foot inside and blocked the door. He would take no rejection. Liv's heart sank along with the earlier resolve and her state of happiness sank with it. This was another level of intimidation. Bee rushed in, needing the bathroom.

'What's wrong now Robert?'

'I want to talk to you about a couple of things that need to be sorted.'

'What things...you're not still going on about the so-called bullying are you?'

'Please Liv let me just come in just for a few minutes...it won't take long.'

'If you must.'

Bee ran downstairs and saw this saw this as a great opportunity to get Daddy to come to her room and show off her latest work. She pulled at his sleeve.

'I'll come in a minute sweetheart...why don't you take your bag upstairs to unpack and I'll see you when I've talked to Mummy?'

'Promise? You won't forget like last time?'

'I promise.'

Liv led Robert through to the living room where the contents of the packing box were still strewn across floor and table. There was no clear seat and she made no effort to move anything. They stood face to face; Liv waiting to hear what he wanted and Robert itching to say all he'd prepared on the way. There were no pleasantries from either side and he had no option but to get to the point.

'On Friday when I went to pick up Bee, her teacher Miss Farley called me in. Why didn't you tell me there had been problems with bullying at school?'

'Because there really was nothing to it...because I knew exactly what your reaction would be...because I knew it would all blow over.'

'But it hadn't blown over. I had to find out when I picked Bee up on Friday with a ripped dress covered in mud. And before you say anything, this was no slip. That Farley teacher tried to make light of it, telling me that the boy who pushed her was getting counselling to control his aggression, that he had a difficult home life.'

Robert spat the words out.

'She wanted to reassure me it had been sorted, they were 'friends' now but I'm not happy at all with that, Liv. I presume you know about it...but what I want to know is why wasn't I told? Why am I the last to know?'

'Oh for goodness sake, Robert, please don't get it all out of proportion...there was one instance that's all. Bee was defending her friend Aadi and got caught up in the middle...it was nothing...it was sorted. Aadi's a new boy and got picked on... the bully, Brad, has been hauled out before but this is not usual. He's a troubled boy and it's sad more than anything... Bee understands...we've talked about it.'

'I told you what that school was like and you wouldn't listen, would you? You drag her to this god-forsaken area and Bee pays the price. If she was living with me she'd still be at her old school and none of this would be happening.'

'Ok, now stop right there...I'll tell you exactly what I know and what happened.'

Liv cleared a couple of chairs and Robert reluctantly sat. She surprised herself with how calm she felt and a newfound confidence encouraged her to go on.

'Bee came home one-day last week very quiet...I knew

there was something wrong...she's usually full of what she's done that day and can't wait to tell me all about it. So I made a special picnic of tea that night, on the living room floor... something she loves...I thought it might help...and it did. Eventually, she opened up to me about what was happening to her new friend at school.'

Robert's face was set in stone but he listened without interrupting, waiting for Liv to dig a bigger hole into which he would watch her fall.

'She's made friends with this new boy...Aadi...he's from down south so of course he talks differently and Brad picked up on this. He thought it fun to mock him and one day took it too far. It's not the first time he's done something like this but the school is aware and they are trying hard to work with the boy and his parents. He's fostered Robert, and the poor boy has had a troubled start in life. We have to cut him some slack and hope that he will understand given time...and with the right support. Bee was just standing up for Aadi and got caught in the crossfire...but I'm sure it will be sorted. These things happen in the best of schools...and I agree with how they are handling it.'

Liv's appeal to Robert's better nature fell on deaf ears, but Liv continued anyway.

'I've told Bee she can invite Aadi for tea this week and she was really happy with that...you know how caring she is...she collects lame ducks like others collect stuffed toys.'

Robert scoffed, having none of it.

'Nothing like this ever happened at her other school...and obviously, it hasn't stopped has it? Or she wouldn't have come back in the state she was in.'

'Oh for goodness sake Robert...it happens everywhere! What planet are you living on to think that schools in so-called 'nice' areas know nothing of bullying?'

'And what makes you so sure that you know what is best

for our daughter? You've only just managed to stand on your own two feet and look after yourself...if you can call it that. Just look at this place...it's a tip. You're too used to your Mother doing everything for you.'

The blood drained from Liv's face and with it her earlier calm. She was in danger of falling into the old default response of agitation and uncertainty. But this time, she fought back.

'Stop it! I'm not going through all that again...if that's all you've got to say then I'd like you to go...unless there's anything else you'd like to pull me up for?'

Robert, seething, wanted to say more. He stood at the front door and turned back,

'There is something else...'

'There's always something else...'

'I found out from a good friend of mine that he saw you rolling out of the Black Bull in town...apparently, you fell over drunk, shirt ripped open, with a man he didn't recognise. Is that how you pass your time nowadays? Is that what you get up to now when Bee's with me?'

'Get out Robert...I don't know who you've been talking to, but I have never in my life fallen over drunk...and who I go out with is none of your business...or your spying friends!'

'It is if you introduce him to Bee...it's very much my business,' he shouted back.

Liv pushed Robert out of the door and slammed it behind. Bee came running down the stairs, upset at the noise.

'Mummy, why are you shouting? Where's Daddy? He was going to come up to my bedroom...he promised.'

Liv's whole body shook with anger; and Bee was on the verge of tears.

'It's all right Bee...it's nothing...really...Daddy had to rush off but he'll see the pictures next time...why don't you tell me what you've been up to this weekend while I get your tea ready? I'm doing your favourite...boiled egg and soldiers.'

Bee wouldn't be placated and followed her mother into the kitchen, still demanding to know why they were shouting, but all Liv could hear were the old noises in her head. Accusations of old raked up with the new,

'Don't you ever notice what goes on under your nose? Maybe that's why our son died. You never notice anything wrong, Liv.'

Her heart beat hard as she stood over the boiling eggs.

'Mummy...Mummy the toast's burning.'

'What? Oh no...sorry.'

Plumes of smoke floated to the ceiling. Liv coughed and opened a window.

'Sorry BeeBee, Mummy was miles away...I'll make you some more.'

'Shall I do it? I can you know.'

'No...no I'll do it...I'm fine darling...and I'll definitely concentrate this time...naughty Mummy!'

Her hands shook as she put more bread into the toaster.

Bee ate the egg and soldiers in silence and didn't complain about the hard yolk; she had sensibilities way beyond her tender years. Liv tried to put into practice the advice of old starting with deep breaths and the mantra, 'None of it was my fault. I did nothing wrong.'

Slowly, slowly she came round to the present, and slowly, slowly her heartbeat came down too. With supreme effort, she focused on Bee and listened to the childish chatter about the reading she needed to do for the next day. Liv looked intently at the face of her daughter who, despite the earlier fracas with Robert, had thankfully moved on to the more pressing subject of schoolwork.

That night, Robert's accusations came back to taunt her with the full force he'd intended. She took out the emergency bottle of pills from the medicine chest in the bathroom and even got as far as opening the bottle. It was a struggle, but with a supreme effort of will, understood that she hadn't come this far to face defeat now. She would not let Robert win this battle. The top was screwed firmly back on and the cabinet door shut and locked.

Chapter Twenty Eight

Marsha's whole body relaxed when Robert finally left for work on Monday morning, and the soothing balm of silence washed over her. On the kitchen table a plate of two slices of toast thickly coated with butter and the last of the strawberry jam she'd made last summer, sat waiting. A mug of tea, made by Robert without sugar remained untouched until emptied and a fresh one made with two large spoonfuls.

Marsha's eyes closed in pleasure at the first bite of toast and a small rivulet of butter dribbled down her chin. Eddie was asleep and she relished the time on her own before he awoke.

She'd had no problem adapting to the new routine in her life with a baby, but Robert invoked so much stress it was difficult to see where simple caution ended and over caution began. He was too keen to pick the baby up on the slightest pretext, setting an unnecessary precedence of unwarranted attention, which of course Eddie loved.

The early morning sun shone through the kitchen window showcasing the mess on the table. Marsha sighed when she'd finished eating and her immediate instinct was to wash up. Robert had already set that response in stone when he hated mess of any kind.

She switched on the radio, re-tuning from Radio Four to Two, and turned up the volume when David Bowie was belting out 'Let's Dance'. Eddie slept on as Marsha's hips swayed at the sink, and she sang to a long-time favourite. Once done with the clearing and cleaning, she decided that it was too nice a day to stay home; when Eddie's howls of protest announced he was awake, she changed his soaking nappy, fed him and got them both ready for a walk. It was too early for Debbie's, but the call of the Park made for a pleasant detour on the way.

'Hey, baby...just me and you for a couple of hours. Daddy won't be back from work until six and Bee is at her Mummy's house.' She kissed his face repeatedly as he squealed in delight.

Grantham Park wasn't far and always an enjoyable stroll to while away the time. Marsha was starting to see familiar faces en route; she took pleasure in people asking after the baby and cooing over the pushchair. Eddie loved it too. She sat at her usual bench, looking out, over the pond. Ducks and swans swam over in hope of bread but soon got bored when nothing arrived.

'Oops forgot again Eddie...this is so nice...out in the park looking at the ducks. Five minutes peace.' Marsha took a deep breath, ran her fingers through the mess of overgrown blonde curls and pulled in her stomach as far as it would go. Her hair had grown out of its usual style, but it nicely framed her pretty round face. 'Desperately need to get this mop of mine to a hairdresser.' Blessed with a happy disposition, she attracted second glances from the men who passed by and smiles from the many old people out for their daily walk. She took in another deep breath,

'Thought this baby flab would have shifted a bit more by now...all this walking we do...oh well, all in good time. Want to come out little one?' She unbuckled Eddie and lifted out the smiling baby.

'You are such a good little boy' she said as she smothered his uplifted face with more kisses.'

'Good morning, Mr. Richmond.'

The old man stopped.

'Morning my dear and it's all the better for seeing you two...and how are you today?'

'I'm well thank you...we're on our way to lunch with a friend.'

The old man smiled at them both, doffing his hat in a gentlemanly fashion and went slowly on his way; his heart was full today; saddened by an anniversary he dreaded each year. He would never get used to taking the walk on his own. Marsha provided a bright moment in an otherwise lonely day and momentarily he forgot his wife.

'Poor old man, all on his own after his wife died; I do miss seeing them both together.'

When it was time to go, Eddie was strapped back in the pushchair despite the protests, 'No more nonsense young man it's time we set off...don't want to be late for Debbie do we?'

Debbie's flat was thankfully on the ground floor and the pushchair could be wheeled straight in. It was only another fifteen minutes walk from the park, but she would tell Robert she had covered more than her daily goal of a long brisk walk.

It was Debbie's day off from the Co-op and they made the most of the opportunity to meet up. Marsha arrived pink-cheeked and slightly out of breath from the uphill climb of the street.

'Marsha come in! It's so good to see you. You look a bit flushed...where have you been? Not had a secret assignation in the Park again with Mr Richmond?'

The door was flung open and before Marsha had even stepped through the door, a volley of questions was fired. Debbie's face at seeing her old friend and baby was evident. Eddie, wide awake now, smiled in delight at the attention when they were all ensconced in the small sitting room. He was more than happy to be passed between the two of them.

'Love you to bits young man but you have a lot to answer for...ruining our get-togethers and nights out. I don't see your Mummy half as much as I used to.'

Marsha and Debbie had been friends since school, accepting the single life as part of their lot when Mr Right had never put in an appearance for either of them; that is until Robert appeared on the scene. Their closeness had not diminished with the change in circumstances and both slipped comfortably into each other's company whenever they got the chance, but opportunities were harder to find when Marsha struggled to manage time away from home and the many demands of Robert.

Marsha loved Debbie's flat in its showcase of glorious colour. The wooden floor and worn rugs were magnificently offset by an exuberance of primary shades on the walls. In turn, they were embellished by bold prints, each reflecting her love of animals and woodland scenes.

'What on earth have you been buying now, Debs?' An overlarge print of bluebells sat proudly above the fireplace.

'Oh you know me...can't resist a bargain in the market... but never mind about that...I want to know about you. Have things improved in the Smithson household? You never get back to my texts.'

'What do you mean, improved? Everything's fine.'

'You know perfectly well...has he stopped peering over your shoulder every time you so much as burp that baby?'

'It's not that bad Debs...I shouldn't have said anything...

it's fine...he just worries that's all...you know...after what happened.'

Debbie bit her lip at reminding her that that was over eight years and two children ago but knew when to let things drop.

'Right then...let's have some lunch.'

Lunch was already made and always a welcome distraction. Back on safe ground, they ate ham, sausage rolls and cheese, accompanied by a green salad that they barely touched. Afters were two chocolate éclairs, eaten with relish.

Conversation never stopped in between mouthfuls of food, two mugs of tea and the feeding/pacifying/playing with Eddie. There was no censorship at Debbie's table when it came to leaving salad and devouring cake. By the close of lunch, Marsha had brought Debbie up to speed on what was worrying her.

'So let me get this straight Marsh...Robert wants you to look after Bee as well as Eddie...take her away from Liv...where she's perfectly happy...because he thinks Liv is incapable now she's on her own...because Bee is having a few little problems at school...all perfectly normal by the way...and she had a bit of mud on her dress when he picked her up. Have I got that right?'

'Mm...it's not quite...you make it sound worse than it is... he's not like that to spite Liv...he...he...'

'He what? Marsh, you've got to lay down a few ground rules here. One, you have a new baby of your own; two, Bee is perfectly happy with her Mother; and three, if there was a problem surely her parents would be the first on call?'

'I know, I know...he just worries...after all they've been through...Liv has been through...the breakdown...he just wants Bee to be safe and happy.'

'But what he is suggesting is crazy...you have to see that.'

'Let's leave it for now shall we? I've had such a lovely time with you...it'll get sorted one way or another. Anyway, I can't see Liv handing Bee over because Robert thinks she should... and Bee...well Bee loves her Mummy...I know that.'

'Ok...I'm sorry, Marsh. You are my best friend of all time... I'm just looking out for you...and you know you can talk to me about anything.'

'I know you are and that's why I love you so much. Life might not exactly be living up to the dream I was promised but who is? We'll work it out. Bee lives with her Mum and comes to stay with us every other weekend...and part of the holidays...that was the arrangement...and that won't change, not if I can help it. I really don't know Liv that well but I do know she is a good Mother to Bee...I would know if there really was something wrong.'

Marsha scooped Eddie up from the sofa where he'd soundly slept after his feed and put him back in the pushchair.

'When I first met Robert, he was a different person...actually listened to me and asked my advice. He'd been through a rough time...but I know what a lovely caring, kind and funny man he was...still is...deep down. The break with Liv was always going to happen and I did feel for her. The baby dying and the anguish over Bee when she reached the same age...then Eddie...it was never going to be easy but who knew it would hit her so hard for so long. It's not as if I presented myself to him on a plate...or took him away from her...I kept my distance for three years. Don't forget she had to cope with all that too.'

Debbie saw Marsha and Eddie to the door after plonking a kiss on the baby's head and hugging her friend tightly.

'You take care, Marsh...I'm always here for you.'

'I know that...thank you for being such a lovely friend... and giving me cream cake when I need it...even though I shouldn't!'

She patted the bulging stomach.

'Get away with you...what's life without cake?'

They parted, each steeped in thought, Marsha wondering if she'd said too much, and Debbie if she'd said too little.

Marsha relaxed on the walk home; it was good to talk to Debbie who always understood even when she couldn't find the right words, but by the time she was close to home, she tensed again. There was always a twinge of guilt on the horizon over Robert. Had she said too much?

Eddie recognised no such issues, however, and ten minutes from the front door all thoughts were banished when there was no mistaking why Eddie was loudly protesting. It would soon be his teatime. He liked to be fed on a very regular basis, and judging by the smell that came from the pushchair his nappy was due for a change. At least he was taking more solid food now and slept better for it.

Robert had persuaded her to stick with feeding him herself long after she wanted to try out the baby rice, until after five months she put her foot down at the howls of complaint. She didn't care what the book said. Bottles, formula and rice were bought and Eddie was happy once again. The Parks Department had agreed that Marsha could go back to work part-time and a date was set for the autumn.

Marsha pushed on faster when the promised rain fell in earnest. There was no time to stop and work out the rain hood that always baffled her, and by the time they reached home both were soaked, leaving Marsha giggling and Eddie confused.

A relentless rain continued off and on into the next two weeks, whipped up by a strong north wind. Liv listened to it howling, rattling a loose windowpane in her bedroom. She pulled the duvet tightly close but couldn't get back to sleep. September had slipped into October and again seeing Adam was sporadic. When she called she either got through to his answerphone or was given a quick reply that he would ring back soon. It was all too confusing yet again and confusion held sway over emotion. At four am, the storm still raged.

Liv was about to get out of bed to check the buckets in the kitchen when a thunderous crash came from downstairs. She sat upright, hoping against hope that it wasn't what she feared. Maybe it was something outside. She switched on the lamp and reached for her dressing gown before making her way downstairs. An intrusive wind blowing from the open kitchen door gave little doubt to what had happened and the answer to all she'd been dreading.

A gaping, jagged hole was laid bare to the night as rain and debris mocked the few remaining tiles surrounding it. Liv stood helpless in the face of the enormity of what had happened. She quickly checked the ceilings of the other rooms; all thankfully intact, and went back to inspect the damage. There was little to be done beyond switching off the electrics and closing the door. Liv's mind raced as to who to call first for help.

Chapter Twenty Nine

The storm that night was the least of Adam's worries. When Ryan finally came home after midnight, the smell of alcohol on his breath and the slurring of his voice gave rise to Adam's increasing frustration in losing control of his son.

'Ryan you're fifteen! What are you thinking of?'

'I've been out with a few friends...cut me some slack will you...it's nothing.'

Before anything else could be said, he rushed upstairs where the sound of retching behind the bathroom door put paid to any further discussion that night, or any time before noon the next day.

Ryan put an appearance in the kitchen, went to the fridge and drank what was left from the bottle of milk in one go.

'What's going on Ryan? Last night wasn't the first time, was it? We've talked about this.'

'Not now Dad...'

'Yes now.'

'Where do you get the drink from? What are you drinking? Who's with you? Luke?'

'What's with all the questions? I was with a few mates... having fun...not much of that round here.'

'Ryan you're under age...I worry about what you get up to...it's got to stop.'

'Just back off will you...it's no big deal.'

'Yes it is a big deal...you're grounded until I say so.'

Ryan laughed, 'Christ I'm not ten,' and he went back upstairs, ignoring Adam's protests. Loud music thumped from behind his door and Ryan emerged only to satisfy a growing hunger when he heard the sound of the front door closing and Adam leaving to do the weekly shop.

Any thought of inviting Liv over for a meal with them both evaporated. He couldn't bring her into this mess no matter how much he missed seeing her. He loved his son but was completely at a loss at what to do next. This was all new and for the first time since the death of Sally, he felt completely out of control; everything else paled in comparison. What he wouldn't give for the lovely young boy who looked up to him for all the answers and wanted nothing more than to chat to Dad about his day and school and rugby. Even the rugby was hit and miss; training sessions cancelled when there was always something more important, then being dropped from the first team. Adam was bitterly disappointed for his son but Ryan merely shrugged and told him he didn't care one way or another.

The final straw came soon enough. Just when Adam thought he was making headway, when Ryan settled at home each night without protest, he sneaked out on Saturday night. They'd managed civilised meals together, watched the rugby on television, and he'd even talked about getting back into playing, but all the while alternative plans were being made, plans that Adam knew nothing about.

It was two in the morning on Sunday when the police called. Adam hadn't even realised that Ryan was out. Failing to understand what he was being told, he went into Ryan's room with the phone in hand to see an empty un-slept-in bed.

'I'll be there as soon as I can...yes...thank you.'

He sank onto the bed and threw the phone down beside him. With head in hands, he searched for a reason, or some sign that he'd missed, but came up with nothing. The police had mentioned that drugs had been involved, and once he heard the word that he never thought to associate with his son, he lost the rest of what was being said. Drink was one thing, but drugs struck terror into his heart. How could he have let this happen? What had he done wrong? Was there something in Ryan's life that he had no knowledge of? Was it because Sally died, or because he was seriously seeing someone?

'I'm so sorry Sally...I promised you I would look after our son...always be there...and I've failed.'

Adam quickly dressed and headed for the police station with dread in his head and heart.

After a busy night, it was now quiet at the station and the sergeant at the enquiry desk gestured to empty seats along the wall.

'Sit and wait...someone will be out to see you soon.'

Across the room sat a man who could be any age from forty to sixty beneath the dirt and cracked exterior. Bleeding from a cut above his eye, it was obvious he hadn't a clue where he was. Every few minutes he went up to the desk demanding to see someone in charge before being abruptly told to sit and wait. Near him, a woman with a torn skirt, quietly sobbed on the shoulder of another trying to comfort her. They all had to sit and wait.

This wasn't his world, and it wasn't Ryan's. He should be asleep at home; safe. When did the boy turn away from everything he had known, from the comfort of home? Adam not only struggled with guilt, but struggled to even understand what he was guilty of.

All thoughts of Liv had been dismissed; nothing in his head could get beyond how he was going to sort out this mess Ryan was in; how bad the situation was; and how far the police would take it. His mind was on a loop of worry and despair; thinking the worst but hoping for the best; hoping it was all a big mistake.

Fifteen minutes waiting seemed like hours until the outside door opened and Marcus walked in. His face was white, but whether in anger or shock, Adam wasn't sure.

'Marcus...'

'Mate...'

'What's going on? Do you know anything about this?'

'About as much as you...I was just asked to get down here...something about Luke being found with drugs...my god I could swing for that lad. How many times have I said to him, whatever you get up to don't do the drugs.'

The anger in Marcus' voice rose as he spat out the word 'drugs'. He'd come across enough youngsters hanging around the estate where he worked to see the damage close up. They were so young but so far gone they didn't even care when the police turned up; hardly bothering to run off, but probably couldn't even if they wanted to. The thought that Luke could become one of them brought on a rage he could barely contain.

'So you'd no idea about any of this?'

'You're jokin'...Luke came home worse for wear the other night but I was so sure that was just alcohol. I remember doin' the same at his age...we've all done it...been there...but this is different...'

'Gemma must be worried sick.'

'She wanted to come but our Claire's only ten...at least she didn't wake up when the phone rang. But how do I explain this to my ten-year-old?'

The two men sat in miserable silence lost in thought.

It was another thirty minutes before Sergeant Andy Draper called them through to a side room where Draper's third coffee of the night had gone cold. He wasn't happy. His back tooth stabbed with pain where a filling had fallen out, and his wife had issued warnings that morning over the long hours and overtime that meant she was virtually living the life of a single mother. He was weary in mind and body. He'd been through this same scenario so many times he'd lost count. Youngsters caught in the act of taking drugs for the first time, full of remorse; parents shocked at how a child of theirs could get into that scene; and total disbelief when they ended up at a police station. Basically, good kids from good family homes. Some would be pulled back from the brink, others not so lucky. It was a lottery where the odds of winning seemed to get lower and lower.

Adam and Marcus followed him to find their sons already seated in an equally stark room, devoid of comfort or reassurance. This was a police station, not the headmaster's office. The consequences of their actions would not be constituted as a misdemeanour, but a crime, and not so easily punished with detention.

Sergeant Draper looked into the faces of Adam and Luke as they turned towards the door; he had already made up his mind what the outcome of the confrontation would be but let the conversation take its due course.

All four sat across from each other at a table that held the sergeant's paperwork, his cold coffee and two glasses of untouched water. He wanted to get home and salvage what was left of the night with sleep and hopefully a welcoming wife. Ryan's face was blotched and his head turned back to the floor. Luke sat dry-eyed and looked away.

Sergeant Draper spoke, his booming voice demanding attention, and all eyes looked in his direction, but what went on behind the eyes of the boys varied wildly. Ryan was full of remorse and shame, but Luke felt nothing beyond defiance and anger. They were given a full account of what they were getting into and what the consequences would be if they were ever caught again.

'You boys are lucky...you need to know that...you're young and you got caught early...but you need to listen carefully to what I'm telling you and learn from it.'

The words were slowly spoken and the enunciation was precise. Sergeant Draper already knew the older boys who'd been with Ryan and Luke. Like Fagin's recruiters, they groomed the young, the willing and the gullible, starting them off on alcohol before moving on to soft drugs, and then working their way up to something more addictive until they couldn't say no to what was asked of them. Then they were hooked. They knew the score; Fagin had escaped of course.

'You're not the first to get mixed up with that lot and you won't be the last, but if you've any sense, you'll keep well clear from now on. You come from good families...I can see that... don't let them, or, most importantly, yourselves, down.'

He paused to let the words sink in, before addressing Adam and Marcus on exactly what he expected to be done and said. The boys remained silent and by the early hours of the morning, formalities were completed.

Adam and Marcus, still in shock at what they'd heard, were immensely grateful when they realised that that night would go no further. They would be let go with a caution.

'So what's it to be lads?' Sergeant Draper addressed them eye to eye, 'I suggest you finish it now before you get caught up in something you, or your families, can't dig you out of...a place that would put you somewhere where you have no control...and believe me, you wouldn't want that.'

'Yes sir,' answered Ryan quietly, looking back down towards his feet. Luke remained impassive.

'Don't worry...he'll be back here again over my dead body,' put in Marcus, with eyes fixed firmly on his son.

'Let's hope it doesn't come to that...now get out of here and as I said earlier...count yourselves lucky.'

Sergeant Draper was happy to see them go and hoped never to see them again, but would not put any bets on it, not as far as Luke was concerned anyway. He'd seen it too many times before, becoming a good judge of character over the years, but he never stopped being hopeful of being wrong.

Adam and Marcus escorted Luke and Ryan to their respective cars. All trace of defiance was erased from Luke at the sight of his father's angry face and he knew better than to say anything more on the subject. No giving voice to how it wasn't that serious, only a bit of weed and how he knew plenty who'd done the same without getting caught.

Conversation between Adam and Ryan was kept to a minimum,

'You'll get through this Ryan...it's a hard lesson but it could have been worse...have you any idea what I was going through when I took that call.'

'I know...I'm so sorry Dad'

Nothing more was to be said that night. Ryan's slumped body and face wet with tears told Adam all he needed to know. When they arrived home, he went up to his room, and in shame and embarrassment stayed there with his headphones on for most of the following day.

Adam checked his phone where he found two missed calls and a message from Liv asking where he was. He wrote a brief text back to apologise and explain he was under pressure at work and needed a couple of days to focus on a problem that had cropped up. It was pathetic and he knew it, but he wasn't ready yet to expose his problems over Ryan. Now knowing something of Liv's history, he considered she had enough on her plate and he wouldn't add to it. Instead, he mulled over the events of the past few couple of days trying to work out how and why things had got so out of hand, and more importantly, where it should go from here. He desperately wanted to see Liv but not yet. Instead, he poured a scotch and pressed 'send' after his message.

Chapter Thirty

Liv's first call the next morning was to leave a message for a roofer whose number she found in the yellow pages. It was Sunday and no one was available on a Sunday. On Monday she called again and he reluctantly agreed to come round to take a quick look, but emphasised he already had a long list of jobs to get through, all equally urgent and had no idea when the job could be done.

The second call was to Robert. It was half term and she knew that Bee would be better off staying with him and Marsha rather than with her in a cold draughty house with no kitchen. Of course, he jumped at the chance of a full week.

Barbara and Arthur would be a last resort only if all else failed. They had been through enough and to land them with a roof collapse was not an option.

With unaccustomed clarity, she made all necessary arrangements, amazing herself at the calm she felt during such a time of crisis. The worst had happened and she would deal with it. Her next move was to go next door with Bee for a cup of tea if nothing else, let her neighbour know what had happened and make plans. Frances too rose to the occasion, providing breakfast for them both, a listening ear and a practical suggestion.

'Oh my dear I did not realise the roof was that bad. I truly thought that the last people had fixed it...I am so sorry. What will you do until it's put right?'

'Good question...I've called Robert...he's on his way later to collect Bee. It's half term so that's one good thing, she won't miss any school...not yet anyway.'

'And what about you?'

'Oh, I'll manage somehow.'

Frances did not hesitate before replying,

'My dear, you must come and stay with me until this is sorted...you can't possibly live there...I've plenty of room...for you both if you wish.'

'That's so kind but Robert at least has a room already for Bee.'

'Then there's no more to be said...you must stay here with me.'

Liv was standing at the living room window when she received Adam's apologetic, 'sorry work pressing' text. She snapped the phone shut, put it back into her pocket and continued looking out for Robert's car. It wasn't Robert she wanted right now but there was little choice in the matter. Liv still didn't want to put unnecessary strain on her Mum and Dad and made the decision not to call them just yet, not until she'd thought out what to do. Of course Robert jumped at the chance to have Bee. As far as he was concerned, this was his winning lottery ticket. He arrived at three o'clock sharp. He would have come earlier but Liv told him that she needed time to get Bee's things ready. After receiving Liv's call, he could hardly contain the feeling of vindication of everything he'd said from the start; the house wasn't fit for purpose and its upkeep was way beyond Liv's capability. But when he arrived, and saw her face at the door, he relented a little; he didn't have the heart to voice the opinions that were ready to fall from his lips.

Liv's top was damp from starting the mopping and clearing, and her hair, roughly tied up, sprang from beneath a scarf tied at the back of her neck. Her face was flushed from exertion and without a trace of makeup. Bee had thought it all a wonderful game, helping Mummy, until she was asked to get her things ready for her stay with Daddy.

There was no 'I told you so' from Robert, not today anyway.

'I'm really sorry Liv...how bad is it?'

'Bad enough.'

He walked in uninvited and went to see for himself the hole in the roof and the damage below. The storm had made its presence known and the rain took full advantage.

'As you can see, bad enough to put the kitchen out of action for a while...but...c'est la vie!'

She shrugged and tried to make light of it, but it was a hard knock-back. Robert gave a low whistle as he inspected the damage.

'Doesn't bear thinking about what might have happened if Bee...or you...had been in the kitchen at the time.'

Liv waited for words of condemnation, but Robert still refrained and said nothing more.

'It was in the middle of the night...Bee never even woke up unbelievably.'

'Yeah, I heard a lot of people suffered with damage...roof tiles, trees uprooted and the like...'

'And I'm one of them...lucky me.'

'It'll cost a bit to put right I would think...but the insurance should cover it...'

Liv didn't answer.

'You've got insurance I hope?'

'Of course', Liv lied. She had no intention of telling Robert that insurance had been intended, as she'd promised her Dad. It was on the list but was just something else she hadn't got around to. In fact, she had no idea at all where the money would come from at that moment.

'Haven't you got anyone to help...your Mum and Dad...friends?'

'Dad had his heart op a couple of months ago...Mum still frets over him despite the all-clear...which is why I couldn't let Bee go there...I'll tell them later...I've just told Frances next door.'

'I'm sorry...I didn't realise he'd already had his op...how's he doing?'

'It went well and he should lead a normal life but you know Mum, overprotective so I don't want to say anything just yet.'

'I'm glad you called me...Marsha's getting Bee's room ready and...'

Robert was cut off by the sound of Bee clattering down the stairs,

'Daddy Daddy! We've got a big hole in the kitchen...there was a huge crash and the ceiling fell in...Mummy can't cook in there 'cause everything is all soggy but I've been helping.'

'I know Bee, that's why you're coming to stay with me for a while...with me and Marsha and Eddie until Mummy gets it sorted,'

Liv stood silently waiting for the inevitable.

Bee frowned, 'But I want to stay with Mrs Fenton...she said she was going to do some more painting with me in the holiday...why can't I go with Mummy?'

'Bee I did tell you this morning why you can't...and it won't be long sweetie I promise.'

Bee clung to Liv, still believing that she might be allowed

to stay and take the packed bags next door. Robert knelt beside her.

'Don't you want to come back with me...Eddie can't wait to see you...he loves playing with you...and Marsha's looking forward to you staying...she's got your room all ready.'

Liv winced at the happy family scene his words conjured up. Marsha and Eddie, Bee and Robert. How cosy they would all be. She was eaten with resentment and jealousy at the unfairness of her situation and what it was forcing her to do. She stood up straight, and against all odds, mustered whatever strength and resolve she could find. It wasn't a time to show weakness; if she did, Robert would find the chink and prize it apart with the accustomed ease of old.

'Come on BeeBee...I'll see you when I can...and Mrs Fenton will still paint with you when you get back. You can practice at Daddy's and I'll ask Mrs Fenton if you can go later.'

Bee wasn't sure but let go of Liv and allowed herself to be poured into her coat, scarf and gloves. There was a bitter wind blowing, as testament to the cold kitchen. Robert ignored the unhappiness emanating from both of them and for once, he was the cheery one.

'I'll do some painting with you, Bee'

'But you're not as good as Mrs Fenton...you can't do what she does.'

'Then I promise I'll try to get better.'

Liv left them both chatting about painting as she went to collect Bee's bag. This was more of a wrench than usual. In truth, she had no idea how long it would take to put the problem right, or if she could afford to stay in the house at all considering the work that needed to be done.

Bee's bag stretched at the seams, filled as much with books and toys that were 'really needed', as with clothes. Liv's stomach was in knots, and a sickly taste rose to the back of her throat. Nothing boded well: letting Bee go, Robert's irritating, cheery acceptance of the situation, and her imminent isolation colluded against her. The calm waters of earlier began to ripple.

The small battered Wabbit was the last to be packed and Liv went back downstairs with a smile to cover a heavy heart.

'Right then...you be good for Daddy and Marsha, BeeBee, and I'll see you very soon'.

She handed the bag to Robert and saw them both out to the car where Bee waved frantically through the back window until they disappeared down the road.

It was time to pack her own bag now and take it next door. There was too much to do to wallow in self-pity. She had to be around when she'd persuaded the roofer he could fit in a quick inspection the next morning, hopefully providing a temporary cover. There had been much emphasis on the maybe and temporary. At least no more rain was due but how to manage a full repair was a problem and not so easily fixed.

Frances had watched Bee and Robert leave and went out to Liv:

'Come and have a cup of tea with me before you do anything more...let me make you something to eat...I presume you've not eaten much have you?'

Frances' kindness was the last straw. Overwhelmed, Liv covered her face with her hands and her shoulders shook. Frances reached out,

'It will get sorted, my dear...I know it's hard right now but you'll get there...come in here...you need food to restore that fighting spirit I know you have in you.'

Liv wiped her eyes and managed a smile as she followed Frances inside.

'You're right...I'm not going to cave into this...'

'No dear...it was the roof that did that.'

They looked at each other and laughed, and over a bowl of

homemade soup and fresh bread, managing to find some small humour amongst the disaster.

'What would I do without you, Frances?'

'You would do whatever was necessary darling girl.'

'You're right...I've not come this far to give in at the first sign of trouble.'

Marsha stood at the open door with Eddie in her arms as soon as she heard Robert's car pull into the driveway. At six months old, he had firmly established that this was the place he wanted to be most and chortled with delight when Robert and Bee appeared.

'Hi, Bee...I'm so sorry your house got damaged in that awful storm but really happy you're coming to stay with us for a bit...look Eddie's smiling too...he's so pleased to see you.'

Marsha reached out to stroke Bee's hair and cheek.

Robert gave Marsha and Eddie a brief kiss before ushering his daughter inside and dropping her bag in the hall.

'I think it'll be for more than 'a bit' judging by the state of that kitchen roof...I had a look and it's not good...I would...'

'Not now Robert...let's look on the bright side...eh Bee?'

Marsha gave Robert a glance that left no doubt about her meaning when she saw Bee's crestfallen face. She knew exactly what Robert had in mind but wasn't happy about going along with any of it. Liv had had one child taken from her and Marsha would make sure that she would not lose a second, no matter what line of reasoning Robert gave. Bee was attempting to lift her bag, oblivious to the conversation and the exchange of looks.

'Let Daddy bring that heavy bag, sweetheart...what on earth have you brought with you?'

'Not much.'

Robert said no more on the subject; it could wait, as could

the fact that he'd called Bee's old school to see about the possibility of her returning. A meeting had already been arranged with the head after half term. Marsha would need to come too of course, there had to be a united front, but he'd taken the first step and he would work on Marsha later, once she could see how right it was that Bee lived with them.

'Right then Bee let's get you settled in your room.'

Chapter Thirty One

Having taken three days off work when her Dad was in hospital, Liv had no more than a couple left to deal with the roof disaster. Her saving grace was that Monday's temporary cover was doing its job until she could sort out something more permanent. The roofer had left in a hurry saying that it might be a month at least before he could come back to finish the job. It wasn't ideal but would give time to sort out a loan. The weather was one problem, but more urgent than that was the problem of finding money with which to pay him. The estimate was eye watering.

Liv missed her Dad; the rock who gave good advice and knew what to do. He had always been there in times of crisis, but now it was time to stand on her own two feet and get on with it.

These were lonely thoughts, but out of them came a fresh determination to deal with whatever was thrown her way. Last year she would have sunk beneath the waves; this year she would swim. Or at least that was the theory. Arthur's operation had been successful with odds all in his favour. The stent was doing its job and when she spoke to him last, he was raring to go, held back only by Barbara's caution. She clung to that thought as she swam to the next life raft: the bank.

There was no point in calling Adam again. He'd made it perfectly clear he was too busy. Hurt by the lack of communication she dare not even think about what that might mean.

The first night with Frances was surprisingly restful and gave her strength to face up to the reality of what she had to do. For the second night, Liv prepared a casserole comprising what had been left in her fridge to go with the beef Frances had in hers. The process of clearing was painful and slow but at six o'clock, following a warm, luxurious bath, saw Liv and Frances, sitting with a sherry in hand, contemplating the day.

'Please try not to do too much in one go my dear. It will get sorted and you know you may stay here as long as you need. You should let your parents know though...they would want to know and support you.'

'I know that but just for once, I want to show them that I can stand on my own two feet...I can sort out my own mess.'

'I understand that but nevertheless, this is a big problem for you to shoulder.'

'I know...and thank you for your help...hopefully the bank will give me the loan I need...and when that's in place, I'll tell them. Right now I would love to switch off for five minutes... think about anything but that roof...and enjoy this sherry.'

'You need a little distraction, my dear.'

'I do...any suggestions...before my head explodes?'

Frances tilted her head to one side and studied Liv's face.

'Perhaps there is something you might like to hear...something I have shared with no other person... something very dear to me that recently has left me unsettled too.'

Liv's eyes lifted from the sherry glass to the curious expression on Frances' face.

'Sounds intriguing.'

'I've never told a soul before now but perhaps you may be the right person...if you care to hear my story of course?'

'You have me hooked already...let me refill your glass.'

Frances acquiesced and sat back in her chair.

'This is a day I spent in Paris...one day when I was a little younger than you are now...a very long time ago.'

She paused.

'You have my full attention... I would love to hear it very much... it would be an honour to hear your story, Frances... take me to Paris... please...away from my collapsing kitchen roof.'

The old lady's mouth and eyes smiled. Her face, although lined, did not betray the beautiful features beneath. At ninety-five, friends and family were few, but Olivia Smithson had already filled an empty space in her life that no one else had for a very long time. She closed her eyes and allowed the past to draw close. For a few moments, the only sound was the slow, tick, tick, tick of the Grand Sonnerie clock on the wall, part of a testament to another life Frances had known.

'The year was nineteen thirty-two...so very long now ago but I remember every second of that visit to Paris. I was twenty-eight years of age and had been married to George for almost six of them. We were not blessed with children as yet but that did not bother me as much as it did my husband. By that time I was under no illusion as to why he had married me. I was a pretty young woman on his arm, from a good family, and on his part, I was hopefully someone who would help continue the Fenton line. Early in our marriage, I knew that he'd never really loved me...most of the time I felt like one of the precious objects in his collection...but that's by the by...I only mention it because it was a factor in what happened in Paris that year.'

Frances paused to take a sip of her sherry Her cheeks were flushed but the drink also gave her the courage to continue.

'As I said, I have never spoken of this to another person but tonight I sense that you might appreciate hearing it...I don't know why...perhaps it's that you have given me a glimpse of the relationship I might have had with Hermione had she lived...someone close...someone to talk to...someone who would understand.'

'I'm glad you see me that way, Frances.'

'George wasn't well at the time and the journey by boat didn't help either...but I rather enjoyed it. After all, I was going to Paris for the first time; I was excited despite George's foul mood, and happy we were going at all. I knew for a fact that if it wasn't for the painting so urgently needed for the exhibition, he would have cancelled...we wouldn't have gone and I wouldn't have met *him*...and that would have been a tragedy when I was about to experience the most memorable day of my life.'

Liv's attention piqued at those last words, 'the most memorable day of my life,' words whispered more to herself than out loud. Frances paused again and took a moment to replace a wisp of hair that had worked loose and lifted her head just a little higher, caught in a time and place far from the room in which they sat.

Liv said nothing more, unwilling to break the spell.

'The boat journey was a delight...to me anyway...very comfortable, and the crew couldn't have been more charming and helpful when they saw the predicament I was in. Of course, it helped that I was rather pretty in those days, and we obviously had money to tip them handsomely; I was nothing like the old lady you see before you today.'

'Frances, you are still beautiful.'

'You are kind but I am under no illusion...what I am or

what I have been and what I have done...there is no one left to judge any more.'

Frances looked into the distance and continued, her words were slow and certain.

'At the other end of the crossing, and with much-needed assistance, we took the train to Paris and eventually reached the Palais d'Orsay, our hotel. It was like stepping into a fairy-tale, although George immediately took to his bed upon arrival with strict instructions not to be disturbed. Fortunately, we had our own sitting room and I was able to order some tea and take in the delightful views beyond the window. I was desperate to go out but being rather timid in those days, dare not go on my own. We were fortunate to have money to spend on such lavish accommodation so I appreciated just that. However, staying in a beautiful hotel was rather poor consolation for marrying a man...a man thoroughly approved of by my parents may I add...who turned out to be quite the obnoxious boor. As I said, we had been together just over five years, four of them as man and wife, but long enough for me to discover many things I did not know when we first met, including the fact that he liked to gamble and that he was not a kind man. He took huge risks on works of art he was certain would increase in value once the artists achieved recognition. Some did, I grant you, but in later years, one too many didn't, hence my moving here when I discovered what a perilous financial state he had left me in when he died.'

Frances gestured acknowledgement of the room, but there was no self-pity amongst the simple statement of facts.

'As you can see, I couldn't bear to part with some beautiful objects...whether they were valuable or not...but this is just a fraction of what was left when I had to sell so many to pay off the not insubstantial debt he left me with.

Frances turned towards several blank spaces where paintings had once hung.

'Of course, many pieces had to be sold when George died, but that was no matter, I survived and even rather enjoyed life once I was free of him.'

She spoke without rancour and sighed, eyes half closed in remembrance of another life; one she might have led had things been different.

'Are you tired, Frances? Would you stop now? Dinner's almost ready. You can tell me the rest later.'

'Just a few minutes more my dear. I would rather enjoy being back in Paris...where was I?'

'You were at the hotel in Paris enjoying tea and George was ill in bed.'

'Ah yes... the Palais d'Orsay...we were only to be there two nights and in the morning we were to take the painting to the exhibition. I don't think I've mentioned that yet have I?'

'No...what was it? Must have been pretty important to go all that way, especially when it took so much longer than the few hours it would today.'

'Oh yes...it was a very special painting...one of George's better investments ...and it was a very special exhibition. I'm not sure the seller George bought the painting from believed for one minute that it was genuine...and George didn't let on, either then or when the authentication came through. Mind you George always said that Picasso was not so well regarded at that time, not in England anyway, and that was his excuse. I wasn't convinced my dear, but that was his business and I never interfered.'

Liv's eyes opened wide in disbelief.

'You actually travelled to Paris with a Picasso in your luggage?'

'George would not let it out of his sight...it was small you see but easy to keep with our hand luggage and very much needed for the exhibition apparently. The next day George spent more time in the bathroom and his bed than anywhere else, too weak to move further afield, and it was left to me to take it to the Georges Petit Gallery.

George's father, Edmond, had known Petit himself, a fellow art dealer...they were just as ruthless as each other as I found out. They got on well and when George was learning the trade, Petit was a major influence. It was a different world then, Olivia.

By the time I arrived at the Gallery, Petit had been dead some ten years earlier and I was rather glad not to be dealing with him. Ambition ran through his veins and George was no different. I learned that he'd made a great deal of money out of the impressionists' market. I didn't know when I visited that day, that the Gallery would close the very next year, so I was rather fortunate to be able to visit for myself and see where the likes of Renoir, Rodin and now Picasso himself had been displayed.'

Liv sat in awe, mesmerised at the words tripping so easily from Frances' tongue. She dropped names as if reciting a roll call of the art world at the turn of the century.

'Edmond Fenton had met some of them on his many journeys to Paris, and when he started out in the business, George would go along too. And now here I was. The problems that beset me at the start of the day evaporated in my wonder at a world I could only imagine and read about the day before.'

Frances was lost in that other world, oblivious of Liv leaning forward in her seat.

'I was a little nervous to say the least when it was time to leave for the Gallery, but a driver had been arranged to take me that morning. I'd slept little the night before and after a breakfast I could barely touch, we left just after ten o'clock. I have re-lived that day so many times since...just to myself.'

'It sounds exciting...I would be nervous too...just thinking about what you had to do is mind-blowing.'

'Oh, that's only the beginning of the tale my dear...I will

tell you the rest if you would like to hear it...but perhaps we should eat now. You must be hungry...not listen to me prattle for hours on end.'

'No, you can't stop there...I do want to hear the rest...but we won't let the food spoil...and you need to eat too.'

Chapter Thirty Two

On Tuesday morning Barbara rang her daughter, knowing it was half term, asking if she could visit. Temporarily it threw Liv, but facing up to the inevitable she related an edited version of the calamity that would hopefully not engender too much panic in her Mother. Of course, she was wrong, despite assurances that everything was in hand and they weren't to worry. It was the fact that she was staying at Frances Fenton's that stirred more unease than the state of the roof, but she let the matter pass.

Following her call, Barbara and Arthur did what came naturally after many years of practice, they fretted about their daughter. Sitting with their tea, the line of conversation was as predictable as the rising of the sun.

'We should be there helping, Barb...how's she going to manage all that clearing on her own?

'I've been thinking about that...obviously you're still in no fit state to go anywhere yet, not so soon after your operation, so I'm going to get the bus...I've checked the times...it's doable and there's one in an hour and half...now there's plenty in the fridge to keep you going till I get back...stick to the salad and don't you dare fry that bacon.'

'Don't go on...and I can still drive you know, love. It's time you stopped watching over me so much.'

'Just a bit longer Arthur...until you've been properly signed off. I know you...we'd get there and you'd insist on coming in and then there'd be no stopping you...no...I've made up my mind...I'll call our Olivia and tell her to expect me.'

Arthur knew there would be no arguing with his wife; many times he'd called her his own 'Iron Lady' who wouldn't be turned when she was set on something. Right or wrong he knew better than to stand in her way.

'Mebbe you're right...once I've got the all-clear after the check-up next week I'll be more use.'

Right now Arthur planned to use his time working out whether or not they could afford to replace their old Ford Escort with the new Focus about to come out.

'We'll see.'

'You try and stop me...I'm not going anywhere just yet.'

With another hour to spare Barbara had already gathered what she could pack into her shopping trolley and the door-bell rang.

'Now who's that? Not expecting anyone are we?'

'Well we won't find out sitting here...want me to go?'

'No you sit there, I'll go.'

Barbara disappeared to the front door where Arthur could just make out a cry of surprise and an animated conversation. It sounded like a woman, but not one of Barbara's friends; sounded too young, and anyway, they all knew better than to turn up unannounced.

Arthur opened to the motoring pages of the paper in full and certain knowledge that he would get every last detail of who it was when she'd finished, especially when it looked like they weren't coming in.

He was glad to have at least gotten through the whole page without interruption before Barbara came back fifteen minutes later. Her face glowed pink with pleasure. In readiness, Arthur neatly folded his newspaper, put it down on the coffee table beside him and then looked up at his wife.

'You'll never in a million years guess who that was.'

'If it would take that long Barbs, you'd better just tell me... who was it and what did they want?'

'Very funny...it was Savannah Richmond...you remember...Olivia's best friend from school.'

'Blimey...Sav...yes...couldn't really forget a name like that... it's going back a bit...didn't she clear off abroad...wanted Olivia to go with her as I remember. Why didn't you bring her in to say hello?'

'She was in a bit of a rush...had to get to her Dad before it got late...said she'll be back when she's got more time... desperate to see our Olivia though. They do write sometimes, I know that, but they've not seen each other in years. Well, she's come back...sorting out her Mum and Dad's affairs apparently. Sandra died six weeks ago...I didn't realise...had a stroke and never recovered properly...she was in the infirmary for a month...I could have gone to see her, poor love...we used to get on quite well when the girls were little...pity we lost touch...and now Harry's going into a home...dementia she thinks...well, I said I could cope with anything physical, but dementia...you don't know what they'll get up to...Ethel Grainger down the road was always wandering off...'

At that point, Arthur switched off and his eyes wandered off too, back to the paper. Experience told him that once Barbara was in full flow there would be no stopping her. She could easily go on for another hour and it was all bound to be repeated several times over before the subject was exhausted, but following one of Arthur's 'looks', she got back on track.

'All right I'm getting there...Savannah was abroad...in Africa somewhere. She did tell me but I can't remember the name...working with poorly children she was. Anyway, the project was finishing and she had to come back when the money ran out. No funding left.'

Barbara prodded him on the arm,

'Are you listening to me, Arthur? I said she wants to get in touch with our Olivia'

'That'll be nice...wonder if she's any good at fixing a roof?'

'Trust you to make a joke of it...'

'You did tell her that now might not be a good time, what with the roof and everything...and our Olivia staying next door? You did tell her that?'

'Of course I did, but she said that she had urgent papers to sort first anyway before she'd be able to call round. I gave her Olivia's new address and number though...said she should always ring first.'

A second pot of tea was called for after all the talking, and a 'Goodness, I'm parched' preceded a quick brew before the bus. Arthur managed to finish reading his paper when Barbara disappeared to the kitchen, but when she came back it was obvious she wanted to continue where she'd left off. A new topic of conversation was always welcome and this new topic moved seamlessly to the girls when they were at school. Arthur, a captive audience, returned to familiar resignation.

'Don't suppose there's any chance of another biscuit?'

Barbara ignored him until he moved on to a topic more acceptable:

'I do remember she was good for our Olivia...brought her out of her shyness when they started high school. They both loved their music and when they were older went to all the concerts together...playing those tapes in her room upstairs at all hours....'

'Too loud as I remember...she could be a bit forward sometimes.'

'She was spirited that's all Barbs...anyway how did she come across when you talked to her?'

'Glad to be back I think...it took a minute or two to realise who it was...she was well tanned...hippy clothes...long hair...a bit like Olivia I suppose...apart from the tan. She was sad obviously...her brother's not been much use, leaving it all to her to sort. He'll be the kind to turn up for the funeral wondering about his inheritance I shouldn't wonder.'

'Bit harsh that.'

'Mebbe...said he'd done it all when their Mother died and she was nowhere to be seen, but he would help when he could...anyway, enough of that or I'll miss my bus.'

She thought Arthur looked tired and despite his protests was glad to be going on her own.

'Why don't you have a nap, love?'

'Ay, mebbe I will...you get off and give Olivia a hug from me...tell 'er I'll be there soon.'

'I will...won't be too long.'

Barbara's journey gave her time to think, but not enough to ease the strain of the past few months. The bus was almost empty, giving room and space to contemplate events of the past year, but also time to allow the 'what ifs' to intrude.

It was an unusually quiet Barbara Liv met from the bus.

'Hello Mum, what on earth have you brought with you?

'Just a few bits and bobs love.'

Liv took the two heavy bags noticing that her Mother's smile didn't quite reach the rest of her face.

'Everything all right? Dad ok? You shouldn't have to come if it's too much you know.'

'Oh...he's fine...I've left him reading that blessed paper... reads the print off it.'

When they reached the house, Barbara's first port of call was the kitchen.

'Good grief, that's a sorry state of affairs. You didn't tell me it was this bad?'

Shocked to see it worse than she'd been led to believe, she stared at the rubble, broken tiles and dust; here was another disaster to confront. She fell quiet, not a usual reaction to any situation, let alone one on the scale of a gaping hole in the roof. Liv came up behind and put her hand on her Mother's arm.

'Don't worry about this...I'll get it sorted soon.'

Barbara trembled at the gentle touch; that was all it took. The pressure cooker of strain and worry over Arthur's illness finally found its release in tears.

'Your Dad...'

Liv took her Mother in her arms and the two women stood for a moment until Liv could guide her to the living room. She hadn't seen her cry many times beyond the day she'd married Robert; when they'd buried Daniel, and when she and Bee left home. Barbara wasn't one for showing emotion; what she felt was usually displayed in more practical terms. She liked to be useful.

'The cleaning can wait, Mum...tell me what's going on.'

'I thought he was going to die, love...at one point the pains were so bad...you've no idea. I couldn't do anything. Talk to him now of course and he just shrugs it off...but when I saw him like that it was hard.'

Barbara wiped away the tears, but the strain of Arthur's illness was plain to see.

'What would I do without him? How would I cope on my

own? We've been together since we were at school. He's the only man I've ever known.'

'I know Mum...but he's fine now...the doctor said that he could live a normal life...he just has to go in for the checkups... and you need to let him get on with life.'

'Oh, I know that. It's just...well it makes you think. We're not getting any younger.'

'You really didn't have to come here, Mum...I could have managed on my own.'

'No, I couldn't do that love...I've left him with food on hand...and strict instructions.'

'I bet you have...'

'And?'

'And what?'

'I know what you both think of me...I fuss too much...I take charge...but sometimes Olivia it's not easy for me when I see what's going on. I love your Dad...of course I do, but if I hadn't taken charge, made him go to the doctor...and he didn't want to go you know...things would have been a lot worse...and when you came back...well, let's just leave it there. But at least you're doing fine...apart from the roof.'

They laughed at the absurdity of what she'd just said as they looked at the damage, but there were traces of a different Barbara. Liv, for the first time, saw her Mother in a different light. She was right, of course, what would they have done without her practicality, her organising, her getting things done when everything else was falling apart?

'I just need to pull meself together...and I needed to get out for a bit.'

'I'm glad you told me Mum...I'm here for you as much as you are for me you know. It works both ways.'

'I know that love,' and Barbara's smile spread in the relief of opening up.

'Come on, let's get cracking...there's a lot to do I can see.'

Barbara went back to the kitchen, back to her usual self, in her element, and rolled up her sleeves, searching for a brush, bucket and cloths. She liked nothing more than a cleaning job where 'you can see where you've been.' She missed the days of Bee and Liv at home; the busyness of it all and the constant demands on her time. Liv's breakdown after Daniel had been a hard cross to bear, but they'd all come out the other side of grief and learned to live with it, each in their own way.

'Let's hope the cover on that roof holds up before it rains next and you can get it fixed,' she said more to herself than her daughter although she wasn't convinced.

By the time Barbara left, however, a great amount of mess and debris had been cleared and Liv too was in a more buoyant mood. Halfway through they ate packed sandwiches and drank tea from a thermos. The radio played and they sang to the music of a decade earlier as Barbara turned chaos into order.

Both in a happier place when it was time to say goodbye, Liv let her mother believe that the money would be there to pay for repairs, and Barbara was content. They even managed half an hour with Frances before she left, bonding over tea and cake in an orderly kitchen that Barbara thoroughly approved of.

It was only after she'd gone Liv thought about her mother's words when she'd arrived. It was true; they weren't getting any younger; illnesses would crop up as time went on, she accepted that, and she would be there for them, but now it was more of a reality than a passing thought. It pulled her up sharp and made her realise just what her parents meant to her, the love and care they had shown for her and Bee during the good times and the bad. They were always there no matter what, and in future years she would need to be there for them. It put a new perspective on all of their lives.

. . .

An evening with Frances was welcome after the long arduous day. Frances had made a simple supper of baked potatoes with butter and cheese, and the two women recounted their day until heavy eyes necessitated an early night.

'You go on up... and get a good night's sleep...I can see that you need it my dear.'

'I will if you don't mind...I'm so grateful to you for letting me stay here.'

'It's a pleasure to have you, Olivia, I'm just sorry that the circumstances are not pleasant for you. You know I envy your mother...having a daughter like you.'

'And I was looking forward to part two of your story.'

'Oh, that will keep for another day.'

Chapter Thirty Three

By Wednesday, Liv had no choice but to go back to Draper's. Already, a mountain of paperwork had grown in her absence. It gave her little time in which to worry about her father, or Bee, or the roof, although each cropped up in between ploughing through invoices, schedules and orders. Marcus was kindness itself, bringing coffee on a regular basis and doing the sandwich run at lunchtime. At one o'clock, he came through to the office with food.

'Come on and sit down love...you need a break from this lot'

'I need a break from everything right now'

Liv looked up with tired eyes.

'I thought something was up...you've been quiet...what's the matter...if you don't mind me askin'?'

'Where do I start?'

'From the beginning?'

'You don't want to know my problems, Marcus.'

'Believe me, I'd rather hear about yours than worry about mine.'

'What have you got to worry about? Lovely wife, lovely children...and you are an expert in DIY!'

'Eh?'

'My kitchen roof fell in at the weekend.'

'What?'

'It's been leaking for a while but I didn't realise how bad it was until the bucket underneath wasn't enough all of a sudden...after that storm we had and endless rain, the roof came crashing through.'

'Gawd...sorry to hear that...you're getting it fixed though... told the insurance people?'

Liv's wince gave him the answer.

'I managed to get someone to put up a temporary cover and I'm trying to sort out a loan to pay for repairs before the weather breaks again.'

They both looked up from their sandwiches to the sky outside the office window; there were a couple of grey clouds but nothing that looked too serious. Not today anyway.

'Long may this continue then.'

'I've been on to the bank, so hopefully, something will be arranged money-wise...but the roofer's really busy right now... looks like I'm not the only one needing his services...and I might need to find someone else, he's so busy. Either way, it's not cheap.'

'Pressure's on then...Arthur been over to take a look?'

Liv fell quiet.

'He's doin' ok now?'

'Dad had his op last month as you know...and it's gone really well...he's already up and about...but my mother's now fretting he's doing too much too soon.'

'Of course she is.'

'So Bee's staying at Robert's instead of Grandma and Granddad's, although neither of us are too happy about that... I'm with Frances next door.'

'The old lady you were telling me about...Picasso's friend?'

'Get away...that's a story for Bee...anyway that's my problems listed...I've told you mine...now you tell me yours.'

Marcus made a noise somewhere between a snort and a grunt.

'Oh, just teenage boys stuff...Luke and Ryan getting into a bit of bother...but it's getting sorted.'

'Teens...difficult years...I remember them well...we're not always nice people at that age are we?'

'You can say that again.'

Marcus was a man of few words when it came to himself and left it at that.

'Right...thirty minutes is up...problems sorted Marcus... back to work'

'You seen Adam recently?'

'He's called a couple of times but since the roof and Dad, we've not arranged anything more just yet...unfortunately. Said he was busy with something at work so I thought best to leave him to it.'

'Oh...right...work eh?'

'Why?'

'Nothing...just wondered that's all. Can't see how that should stop him seeing a beautiful girl in between.'

'Get away.'

Liv was due to finish at four, and at fifteen minutes past as she collected her coat, the phone rang. She considered letting it go to answerphone but relented and picked up.

'Hello, Draper's can I help you?'

'You certainly can...'

'Adam?... Is that you?'

'It is...I want to apologise for not calling before now...I'm glad I've caught you in...I did try your mobile but you didn't answer.'

'No, I switch it off at work. Avoids nuisance calls.'

'Ouch...I deserve that.'

'Not you silly...the 'other one.''

'Right...so you're still talking to me? Thank you...can I see you soon...I want to explain what's been going on...and I will make it up to you I promise. Life's been miserable without you in it.'

'Really? I'd better let you make up for it hadn't I? Did you get the work done?'

'Work?'

'Isn't that what you've been doing all this time?'

'Oh right...yeah...I mean yes that's all done.'

'Good.'

'How about dinner this Saturday? Can you make it then?'

'I'll have to get back to you on that...you know I'd love to but...too much on right now. Bee's at Robert's...'

'At Robert's for half term?'

'No...yes...actually she's living there for now...but I'm not sure how long it'll be.'

'What? Why? Has something happened?'

'Well...when your roof falls in and you've no kitchen...not much choice I'm afraid.'

'Liv? Why didn't you tell me? How bad is it?'

'Bad...very bad...and I didn't tell you because I knew you had a lot on.'

'But this is serious Liv. You should have called...are you there on your own? Can I come and help?'

'No, it's ok...like I said I'm staying with Frances next door until I can get it fixed and Mum came over yesterday.'

'I had no idea...I wish you'd called me...work could have waited. I could have done something.'

'Adam you might be good at DIY but you're no roofer... I've got a temporary cover as a stopgap. I just have to wait until

I can find someone to fit the job in...and find the money of course. I'm seeing bank number two tomorrow about a loan... the first wasn't too receptive...and once that's sort, it's just a waiting game...and hoping there'll be no rain in the meantime...or at least no storms.'

'Let me come over tomorrow...after work...I feel bad about not being there for you.'

'No, you don't have to really...I'm fine honestly. Anyway, I'm going to Mum and Dad's straight from work. He's getting restless according to Mum so I'm off round to see them...bring them up to date.'

'Oh wow, you've really been through it. Look why don't I collect you from your parents tomorrow...I'll take you back home...next door...wherever...I know what the buses are like at that time...or we could have a drive somewhere...find a nice pub?

Liv thought for a moment. Adam hadn't met Arthur and Barbara yet. Was it a good idea; the right time? Would it suggest something more serious between them? Her mother would make assumptions if a man came to pick her up, and that was a certainty. But there again, the buses weren't that frequent at night.

'Ok...let's do that...and you can tell me about your work.'

'Forget that...I want to hear about you...I've missed you Liv.'

There was a short pause before she answered.

'I've missed you too Adam...see you tomorrow.'

Liv called her mother when she got home, mentioning Adam without really meaning to when Barbara queried the hassle of catching the bus both ways.

'I'm getting a lift back so no problem.'

'A lift? Who with?'

'Just a friend...he lives nearby and offered.'

'He? Do I know him?'

Liv took a deep breath, filled in the missing information and the subject of Adam was broached at last. Barbara at the other end of the phone bridled with interest and was ready to launch a hundred questions. The floodgate had opened. Liv tried to cut her short but her Mother would have none of it. A man in Olivia's life was someone she needed to meet.

As the conversation progressed, Barbara wheedled out the information she wanted until Liv admitted that Adam had started to become something more than a passing interest in her life.

'Mum, I've got to go...lots to do... I'll see you tomorrow.'

Before she had time to hang up, Barbara insisted he come for tea with Liv. And before any objection could be given, she interjected with 'I'm sure that Dad could do with a bit of male company as well.'

'You really don't want to be bothering with tea Mum...I can...'

'I can cope with a simple tea Olivia; Your Dad and me would love to meet this Adam'.

The decision was made and left to Liv to issue the invitation, for which there could be no refusal. Liv was left in a state of bemusement at what she'd agree to, but secretly pleased with developments. Arriving at Frances' house, she felt a little more optimism than of late.

Chapter Thirty Four

On Thursday morning, Liv woke early after a sleepless night, and before setting off for work, called home to check the current state of the roof. There had been a slight drizzle during the night but the temporary cover still held up, it did its job, and the floor looked dry. A meeting at the second bank had been arranged for Friday and she held hope over expectation that a loan would come through this time. But how much could she raise? And the bigger question was, would it be enough?

Amongst yesterday's post of one circular and two flyers for local takeaways, she spotted a cream envelope with her name and address neatly typed up but no clue as to where it was from. Liv ripped it open, prepared for nothing more than a sales proposition, but it was far from that. The letter inside could not have come as a greater surprise.

The sender was proud to announce that Olivia Smithson had won first prize in their short story competition. It had been so long ago, she had even forgotten entering. Her instinct, after the third read through ensured that it was definitely her story, her name, and her prize, was to pick up the phone.

'Dom...it's me...you'll never guess what I have just got in the post.'

Dom yawned 'You're an early riser...'

'Sorry...you still asleep?'

'No, but it's ok...time I was up anyway.'

The happy news opened his eyes more than the cup of strong coffee he was about to make would have done.

'Always knew you had it in you...my well done my lovely. My only surprise is that it's not happened sooner...but there again you do have to enter these things, Olivia Smithson.'

'I know I know...you are good for me Dom...it's you who keeps me going sometimes.'

'You don't need me anywhere near as much as you think. My little caterpillar turned into a butterfly a long time ago.'

'Thanks for that! Anyway someone's at the door Dom, I'd better go...see you soon I hope...before you leave for America... don't forget you promised?'

'You will don't worry...you and Bee are top of my list...'bye for now.'

Liv checked her watch; surprised that anyone should call this early and went to answer. For the second time that day, she could not have been more wrong in her presumptions when she opened the door to a smiling, sun-bleached Savannah.

'What on earth!'

There was no room for any other words amongst the amazement she felt at the welcome sight of her long-absent friend standing at the door.

'Savannah? Is that you?'

'Aren't you going to ask me in?'

'What...yes...come in...wow this is a surprise!'

They fell into each other's arms in a long, overdue and emotional embrace.

'What...why...why didn't you tell me you were coming? When did you get here? I thought you were still in Africa.'

'I wanted to surprise you...I went to your Mum and Dad's...found out you'd moved on and Barbara gave me your address...I know it's early but...'

'Mum and Dad knew? She managed to keep it a secret from me!'

'Yup...and here I am.'

Then you know I'm not actually staying here right now?'

'Oh yes...I was just about to go next door...I heard all about the roof...every last detail...just wondered if you'd moved back in yet.'

'Not yet...but never mind about that...I want to know about you...how long have you been back?'

They faced each other and held hands, both not knowing where to start first in the pleasure of reconciliation.

'So much to catch up on Sav...so much.'

'You are right there Liv although the bulk of it will have to wait...I haven't got that much time today, hence the early morning call, but I'm not going far I promise...I just had to come and say hello...I really thought you were still at your parents with Bee.'

'I couldn't let you know...when you told me you were moving on to Africa you didn't give me your new address.'

'I know and I'm so sorry...it really was a crazy time.'

'As you can see, this is my home sweet home...usually... mine and Bee's that is'.

She gestured around with outspread arms and led Savannah to the kitchen.

'Oh dear, bit of a mess...will it get fixed soon do you think?'

'Hopefully...we really love it here, me and Bee...perhaps

not as sweet a home as it should be right now, but we are happy...I'm just gutted I can't put you up...where are you staying?'

Savannah's smile faded into a long sigh.

'I'm at Mum and Dad's old place...well Dad's. When Mum died I really was sorry not to be there with her at the end but it was so sudden you know...work was a nightmare...plus I was ill at the time and could barely move. Peter, my ever-delightful brother, wasn't impressed...didn't make it any easier for me. It was a really bad time Liv.'

'I'm so sorry... I had no idea but why didn't *you* tell me?'

'Liv with all the problems you've been through I couldn't foist mine on you as well...we're both pathetic really aren't we?'

'No...no...you should have told me...Mum always got on well with Sandra.'

'Sorting out our rebellious days yeah...I remember when they attempted to do that one...it's all past now...we're grown ups Livvy...I've got Dad to sort out...Alzheimer's...and if that's not enough stage four bowel cancer...and that's just for starters...the house is a nightmare.'

'Oh Sav, you make my problems here look like a walk in the park in comparison.'

Savannah no longer tried to keep up the pretence that all was under control and the weight of what she was facing showed.

'That's horrible...but where's Peter in all this?

'As ever, my younger brother is nowhere to be seen at the sniff of a problem if he thinks he can avoid it...told me he had to cope with Mum's funeral and now it was my turn, can't take any more time off work...blah, blah blah.'

Savannah's younger brother had been a surprise addition to the family when Sandra was forty-three. He had been a delightful baby and toddler, but the constant attention produced a young man with overinflated expectations of entitlement.

'Dad's in hospital now but I doubt he'll come out...and even if he does, he can't come home. I'm spending all my time shunting between hospital and house...sorting out paperwork...god everything is in such a mess...I had no idea what was happening...Pete's been over twice...brief visits...duty calls and his 'Now you're back sis, you can cope...you've more time than me.'

'Poor Harry...and poor you...what a state to come back to...how on earth are you managing.'

'At the moment it's good days and bad days...but I can't leave Dad on his own too long...when he does remember me I need to be there...so I'm sorry it's a short visit to you today... but I just needed to see a friendly face.'

'Oh Sav, any time...you know that...let me come and see him sometime soon?'

'That would be nice...but you've got enough on your plate from what I can see...get yourself sorted first. I know I've not been good at keeping in touch recently but I really have thought of you so often...how I would love to go back to those teenage days...maybe I would appreciate them more now. How did that song go?... 'Everybody's Gotta Learn Sometimes'...can't remember who sang it but seems about right'.

'Oh me too Sav...me too...come here...let me give you a hug.'

'I'll give you a call in a couple of days, yeah?'

'Yes...you'd better! I'm always here for you...and get something to eat, you're too skinny!'

'It's funny, I was always jealous of you, you know...you were always the skinny one.'

'What? You are joking...you were the one that turned heads.'

'Never happy are we?'

Savannah had always been plump, but it sat well on her; she had a shapeliness that suited the jeans and loose tops; the long scarves and colourful hats she loved to wear, but today she was very different. Her face had lost its plumpness and there were lines around her eyes. Liv could see how much her friend would need someone to help her through her own dark days ahead and vowed to be there.

Before leaving for work, she went back next door to find Frances at her usual place in the sitting room.

'Hello, I wondered where you were.'

'Sorry...I sneaked out early to check on the roof situation. Took a bit longer than I thought...I had an unexpected visitor.'

'That's all right...we have no timetable here my darling girl...was your visitor the roofer offering to make a start?'

'Not quite...that's still a way off...it was an old friend from my schooldays...back from her travels and working abroad.'

Liv filled her in on the backstory of her friendship with Savannah and the troubles she had come home to.

'Oh my dear, you must bring her over when you can...a situation like that needs a good friend for support and I should know...have you time for a quick cup of tea before you leave for work?

'Just a quick one. Let me get it.'

'No no my dear...I need to move a bit more than I do before I fossilise myself to this chair.'

They went to the kitchen where Liv allowed herself to be waited on.

'Oh, before I forget...I'm celebrating today...I've just received a letter telling me that I've won a writing competition...it was for a short story I sent in months ago...completely forgot about it...nearly threw it in the bin would you believe?'

'Marvellous...then here's to you for winning and for getting your friend back...always a silver lining somewhere Olivia.'

Cups were raised to better days ahead, and despite the troubled times, they found comfort over tea in each other's presence.

'You know, I would love to read your prize-winning story Olivia...if I may that is?'

'If you'd really like to then yes...I think I might have a copy here with some other pieces I brought with me. Want me to take a look?'

'Please, that would be lovely.'

Liv knew that if she had any ambition of taking her writing more seriously, there had to be a much wider audience than Dom, and Frances was as good a person to start with as any. She handed the story over.

'"Traces'...I like the title...can you leave me with it so I can read without distraction?'

'Yes...no problem...I need to get to work now anyway.'

'Of course...don't be late...and thank you, Olivia.'

Chapter Thirty Five

Frances settled on the sofa and waited until the front door closed, wanting to concentrate in quiet seclusion on the six neatly typed sheets in her hands. Past hopes that she might one day write her own story had long ago faded, but another solution had crossed her mind. Time was running short. Her last check-up at the hospital had raised concerns but further tests were not what she had in mind: 'I will take my chances thank you, I feel quite well and when my time comes I would rather not protract the end in a hospital bed' and she came home without telling a soul.

Today Frances was in good spirits. She made herself comfortable and read the story, not once but twice, the second time to take in the subtlety of the text and the nuance between the lines. She was satisfied that it proved every bit as good as she'd hoped it would be and made plans of her own.

That evening, when the pleasantries of the day had been sufficiently aired, and Liv had put a chicken casserole in the oven, they talked about the story.

'My dear, this captivated me in a most unexpected way. You have a particular style that I like and I could see myself in parts of the telling...the traces of a past life that stay with us always...I can relate to that. Your main character is intriguing and I wanted to know more about her by the end.'

'I want to write more, in fact, I've already started a longer piece...I'm halfway through in fact, but with everything going on right now, I've had to shelve it.'

'I know but you must find time...a talent like this needs to be allowed to grow and flourish.'

'I like your optimism and faith in me Frances but it's not that easy. There are so many other writers out there just as talented...more talented.'

'That may be so but it makes no difference...there is still you...and you have such a lovely way with words.

'It's all I was ever really good at...words.'

'We will talk more about this when that roof is done.'

'The roof is all I can think about.'

'Moving on to practical matters, how are you progressing with it? Before you arrived next door, I remember thinking I hope that the next people realise the problems the last inhabitants had with the leaky roof...George and Martha didn't last long because of it. Shame in some ways as I had hoped we would get on as neighbours...but we didn't quite get beyond 'hello' and 'nice day isn't it?' and they only lasted a few months. But I truly thought the roof had been sorted. Now I am so happy to have you, my dear...and shame on them if the roof problem wasn't pointed out to you before you bought it.'

She reached out and gently touched Liv's hand.

'My fault I guess. I should have had a better survey done, and I should have done something about it sooner. It's a hard lesson to learn but...well, I've learned the hard way. Anyway enough of the roof...are you hungry?'

'Just a little my dear...and the chicken smells delicious... you really are a wonder, Olivia.'

'As I said, I'm learning...in so many ways...I just wish I'd taken more notice of Mum in the kitchen.'

'Never too late to learn.'

'True...the roof is proof of that...certainly pulled me up short. Another bank tomorrow, my last hope because otherwise, I don't know how I can keep the house going'

'Oh Olivia, I'm sure that something will turn up...banks love you to be in their debt...you'll be fine.'

It was a sombre evening, despite best efforts on both sides and dinner was eaten with minimum conversation. Frances realised that Liv had much on her mind and held back on her own. When they'd eaten, and the dishes had been washed and cleared, Liv was about to make her excuses and go to her room when they both heard the sound of a key in the front door.

'Did you hear that? Are you expecting anyone?'

Liv's reaction was to search for her phone, ready to call the police but Frances showed more resignation than surprise.

'Don't be alarmed Olivia, I believe I know who it is.'

'You do?'

'There is only one person who calls unannounced at this time of night and doesn't always bother to knock on the door.'

With that, a tall, striking man appeared in the doorway, with thick grey hair and sporting an expensive camel coat.

'Mother...how are you?'

He hadn't noticed Liv standing in the shadows, clutching her phone, but spun around at the sound of movement.

'And who are you?'

'Simon, this is my next-door neighbour Olivia; Olivia this is my son, Simon.'

Unsmiling, they looked at each other, Simon with suspicion and Liv with surprise.

'Olivia is staying with me for a few days until her roof can be repaired.'

'Is she indeed?'

With a quick flick of the eyes, Simon checked Liv from top to toe, taking in all he needed to know. Without further enquiry, he made assumptions: a penniless neighbour staying with his mother, very likely hoping to benefit from the arrangement.

'I'm sorry to hear that...much damage?'

'Enough to keep me out of the kitchen until it's fixed...but work is starting soon.'

'Good...we're due more rain next week and I wouldn't like to think of you homeless.'

'Oh Olivia won't be homeless...not when I can be of help.'

Simon's only response was a raised eyebrow. He sat and looked straight at Liv. It was time to get down to business and she was in the way.

'Olivia...would you mind very much if I had a word with my Mother on her own? I'm sorry I didn't realise that she had company before I came.'

'No of course not.'

She was glad of the opportunity to leave them alone,

'It's been a long, tiring day so I think I'll have an early night, Frances.'

'It has my dear...you sleep well and I'll see you in the morning.'

'Good night...you too Simon...it was nice to meet you.'

'Likewise...good night'

Simon said nothing more until the door closed behind her. He went up to his Mother and gave her his usual kiss on the cheek.

'To what do I owe the pleasure of this visit, Simon? I presume it's not just a social call.'

'It's always a social call...you know that.'

Simon went over to the drinks table and poured himself a whisky.

'Anything for you?'

'No thank you I've had my sherry.'

'Of course, you have...thirty minutes before dinner...I remember it well...and have you introduced...Lara?...'

Simon raised his hand as he searched the name.

'Olivia'

'Olivia...yes...have you introduced Olivia to your nightly ritual?'

Frances watched him get comfortable on the sofa, his long legs outstretched as though testing for future ownership. She thought how remarkably like his father he had become; even more so as the years rolled by; confident with an arrogant air of entitlement. It saddened her. Duty calls were made but none came out of the pleasure of her company and as the years passed were fewer and fewer. Simon hadn't counted on her living to such an advanced age.

He'd confessed at his last visit that recent investments had not paid the dividends expected and, in the 'short term' as he put it, he was struggling. That was when the last two paintings had been liberated from the wall.

Frances had often wondered when it was that the loving little boy turned into the cold, hard man before her. Boarding school elitism and George introducing him to the cutthroat circle he moved in were certainly contributing factors. Holding on to the child he'd once been was a battle she was always going to lose. Simon soon learned what his father required of him and cut the apron strings he was accused of being attached to. Unfortunately, Simon did not have the savvy, or yet the contacts in the higher circle, who would trust him as they had George.

'So how did the last sale go...any better than last time?'

Simon stroked his chin and finished the whiskey, 'Not quite as much as I expected...but I think you'll find a nice return in your bank account.'

'And a tidy sum deposited in yours I expect to cover other losses.'

'I do put in the time Mother, you know that...and there are expenses to be covered...'

'Ah yes...expenses...and how is Sarah?'

Simon gave half a smile at the mention of his wife's name. The two women had never seen eye to eye after the wedding, and since that day had barely come into contact with one another. During the course of the marriage there had been no children; Sarah had made it perfectly clear to Frances on the eve of the wedding that she never wanted 'any brat to tie her down' and lived up to her promise. The vehemence of her words never left Frances, nor did the unanswered question of whether or not Simon felt the same. Sarah and Simon were well matched in most respects, however, and lived a lifestyle that suited them both. They loved to travel; had a fine house in a fashionable area of the city, furnished with the latest and the best; and they liked to entertain. Sarah had money of her own, of which Simon felt the full benefit and he would not muddy the waters of their relationship by insisting on regular contact with his Mother. Sarah knew how much he relied on her and took full advantage. In turn, Frances rarely received an invite to Portman Avenue and visits to her house were by Simon alone.

'She's fine...apart from a strained back...sends her best of course.'

'Ah the strained back...a long-standing complaint...she should have it seen to. But please give her my regards...it is sad that I never get to see your wife.'

'You know what she's like...always busy...but I'm sure we'll all get together soon.'

Probably at my funeral, Frances thought to herself but let the subject drop.

'So what is it you have come for this time?'

Chapter Thirty Six

The bank official was nothing if not meticulous. He had all facts and figures ready, neither of which fell into Liv's favour. It turned out that more was needed than Frances Fenton's optimism, in borrowing enough money. Weighing up Liv's income against outgoings, the offer would not bridge the gap between the hole in the roof and a replacement. Despite Liv's pleading otherwise, it was hard to argue; the tight budget she already had in place could hardly be stretched further and the unsmiling face at the other side of the desk could only suggest asking family if they could help.

Catching an early bus back, the alternatives were not good. She could sell the house, but where to rent that would not cost more than she currently paid in a mortgage was not easy. Memories of the dubious digs in London arose. Moving back with her parents would be an option, but losing an independent life that had been so hard fought for would be worse. Neither had a happy outcome.

. . .

Adam left work early on Friday afternoon, closing the door on two new clients and a substantial portfolio of others who were more than satisfied with the work he had completed. Confident, with an exceptional record, his opinion was sought in many an uncertain scenario and his reputation was growing. However, this confident professional was not the same man who arrived home.

Coping with an unaccustomed attack of nerves, he was inclined to cancel the invite to tea. The struggle with a rebellious Ryan had left him unsure of his ability to handle situations for which he was ill prepared and as a consequence, his relationship with Liv hung in the balance. He sat and weighed up the alternative, and the alternative was not attractive either. To not see Liv would mean throwing away an opportunity to find the joy missing in his life since Sally.

Borne out of the desperation to see Liv again, and wanting their relationship to survive any objections from Ryan, he determined to go and meet Arthur and Barbara and take the consequences. If they were to survive, it had to happen sooner or later. 'You're forty-two years old for goodness sake. Stop behaving like Ryan's age. You want to see Liv so get a grip.'

Ryan caught him in the kitchen, smartly dressed and ready to leave.

'What's happening?'

'Ah...glad you're back...I was going to leave you a note.'

Ryan filled a bowl with post-school stopgap cornflakes, poured in milk until it almost overflowed and topped the mountainous pile with a heaped spoon of sugar, a good deal of which scattered on the table. The remaining milk he drank straight from the carton before putting the empty back into the fridge. Adam, too preoccupied to notice, didn't comment.

'I'm out for tea tonight but I've left enough money for you to get a pizza for yours...I won't be late back though.'

Ryan grunted through a mouthful of cereal.

'You're not going out are you?' was said more as a statement than a question.

Ryan put down his spoon and chose his words carefully:

'No pater, I shall be completing the project set in history for next Monday and will be in studious solitude whilst you are gone.'

'Right...playing one of those war games then?'

'You know me so well Father...so who are you going out with, where are you going and exactly what time are you back?'

'Ok...ok...if you must know I'm going with Liv to have tea at her parents.'

'No biggie then.'

'No...no biggie...I'll see you later...and it won't be late so don't go sneaking out without my say so.'

'Absolutely.'

Adam smiled to himself, relieved to have got their relationship back on firmer ground after the drama at the police station. He even believed it had been the wake-up call Ryan needed. He was still feeling his way through uncertain times but had to accept that Ryan was a good lad at heart. His school grades might not be as high as they should be, but they weren't languishing at the lower end either. He went across to the table and put his arm around Ryan's shoulder

'What's that for?'

'Nothing just wanted to...see you tonight.'

Ryan shrugged him off.

At teatime, Luke rang Ryan. They'd not seen much of each other at school when Ryan had managed to avoid any contact. He knew what Luke wanted.

'All right?'

'Yeah ok'

'All set for tonight? Banksy, Riggs and the rest are meeting at the Park at seven...usual place...I'll see you there...

Ryan didn't answer as swiftly, or as enthusiastically as Luke expected.

'All Right? Tell your Dad we're off to the Odeon if you need to.'

'Yeah...ok...see you there.'

'We won't get caught this time...got plans...and not in the Park.'

Ryan had no intention of going but to tell that to Luke would mean him coming over and dragging him out. It was easier this way. He'd get the message sooner or later.

Adam collected Liv at five as promised and met her at Frances' house. All doubts left him when she opened the door and the sight of Liv prompted a fresh surge of longing.

'Hello...it's good to see you Liv... '

'Hello, you.'

Their kiss was brief when time was short and with a quick 'bye to Frances, she grabbed her coat. Wearing a blue shirt, bought from the sale rack at River Island the week before, it did her justice, and none of the buttons were loose this time. The black denim may have seen better days, but the shirt lifted the outfit from drab and old to fresh and flattering. Her outfit suited her slim frame and blonde hair that hung loosely about her shoulders. Her face, as ever, was only lightly made up, but she had been practising more since seeing Adam after years in the wilderness of wearing none at all.

Adam noticed little beyond a smiling, welcoming face that improved his day beyond measure.

Liv's cheery explanation of why she was staying with Frances had been good enough to not raise undue suspicion.

The roof issue was no big deal, soon to be sorted, and they didn't want to be late for tea.

'Shall we go?'

Adam fought the recollections of their last of their last time together and put them on hold in light of a more conservative evening. But 'You look beautiful' didn't cover anywhere near all he felt inside.

'You don't look bad yourself.'

'Will I do?'

'You'll do fine.'

Liv forgave the lapses in communication and felt a surge of warmth and affection at seeing Adam again. For the first time that day, she forgot about the bank and the disappointment over the loan. This evening was enough to contend with.

Adam kissed her on the cheek.

'I have missed you...you have to believe me when I say it wasn't intentional that I haven't been knocking on your door every single day since that amazing night.'

'I know...you've had a lot on...we both have...I still have...I didn't quite give you the full extent of my collapsing roof.'

'What? You never said anything about collapsing! That's bad...is it being sorted? Insurers on to it?'

'Not quite sorted...yet...getting there. Anyway let's not talk about that now...are you ready for tea with Barbara and Arthur?'

'Yes but...'

'No buts...I need a break from it...please?'

'For now ok, but I want to help you where I can. No arguing.'

'Later maybe. Now back to this tea. I need to warn you...'

'Sounds ominous,'

'Listen to me carefully, my Mum only has to have the sniff of a man in my life and she's on to it. She likes lots of detail too so get ready for an interrogation. It has to be done so we might as well get it out of the way...plus she's desperate to put a face to your name.'

'So, I'm the man in your life, am I? I like that.'

'Don't say I didn't warn you.'

He leaned towards her when they were in his car and before she could pull away, he gave her the kiss he'd wanted to earlier, leaving them both in no doubt of how they felt.

'Barbara, how much food are you putting on that table? There's only four of us love'

'I know that but what I don't know is what he likes and what he doesn't...he could be one of those veggies for all I know or that other one...you know...when they won't eat anything coming from an animal...not even an egg.'

'So that quiche there...the veggie one...you know that's got egg in it so if he's one of them others, he can't eat it.'

'Oh...I never thought of that...mebbe he won't notice.'

'Daft bugger...we'll just have to hope he's not one of them and just a veggie then...if he is a veggie that is.'

'Ay...we'll just have to wait and see.'

'Goodness there's the door...we'll soon find out Arthur'

Liv walked through the door to the living room where two pairs of eyes were already looking towards the man walking behind.

'Hello love...that's good timing...everything's ready.'

Liv could see through the open door to the kitchen,

'Wow, there's a lot of food on that table.'

Everything was laid out in readiness, cling film covering much of it. Barbara thought the dining room was too formal for a first introduction but if they were still courting by Christmas she would give it a rethink.

'This is Adam...Adam this is Barbara and Arthur, Mum and Dad.'

'Pleased to meet you both.'

Arthur made to stand in greeting and held out his hand.

'Mr Renfold please don't get up, I...'

'I'm not that decrepit lad',

Arthur stood and shook Adam's hand with a firm grip, 'I've been given the all clear although to listen to Barbs you'd think I was still on death's door...not that I was in the first place mind.'

'There's a difference between takin' it easy and overdoin' it though Arthur.'

'All right...'

Arthur turned to Adam to whisper 'I'm givin' 'er a couple more days then I'm back in charge...' then a louder 'Nice to meet you lad.'

Adam's tension evaporated in the warmth of the welcome. He gave Barbara a bunch of flowers put together by the same young girl at the florist shop who'd made up the bunch for Liv. 'You're meeting the parents now,' she'd said 'Mm...must be getting serious...we need to get this right.' She gave him a knowing smile and put together a collection of anemone, aster and carnation, carefully wrapped and tied with pink ribbon. 'There...you can't go wrong with this.' 'Wish me luck,' he'd said. 'Nah you'll be fine.'

Adam was fine; Barbara went as pink as the carnations, thrilled at getting a bouquet of flowers for no particular reason other than he'd come for tea.

'Oh, Adam they're beautiful...I only usually get flowers like this on my birthday.'

'What about our anniversary then?' Arthur gave a look of feigned indignation.

'Oh yes, I forgot about that...that too'

'And this is for you Mr Renfold...that is if you're allowed?' Adam looked to Barbara as he handed over a bottle of red that Liv said he was particularly fond of.

'Just the one glass I suppose will be all right,' Barbara conceded.

'Very generous I'm sure...and none of that Mr. and Mrs. stuff Adam...it's Arthur and Barbara.'

Glasses were poured and they sat around the table, Barbara itching to ask the questions that had been on her mind all morning, and Arthur happy to listen. Satisfied that Adam was neither vegetarian nor vegan, she relaxed, and a couple of mouthfuls of wine emboldened her.

'So your first wife died I hear...I am sorry about that.'

Liv paused eating and gave her mother a withering look. Barbara's hunched shoulders and raised eyebrows gave a reply of 'only asking'.

'Yes, she died just over four years ago now. Ryan was eleven at the time...'

'Can't have been easy for you lad, losing someone you're close to,' Arthur put in, thinking of Liv and the loss that they had all faced.

'We've managed, just. I've even learned to cook...sort of anyway.'

Arthur steered the conversation around to a less contentious subject when they all fell silent and focused on the food in front of them.

'Liv tells me you're a chartered surveyor...how's that line of business going? We could have done with you when our Olivia took on that house of hers'

'Generally speaking, they're sound little properties on that road...it's just unfortunate she didn't know about the leaking roof.'

'You can say that again...a few years ago I'd have been up there takin' a look at it meself.'

Barbara snorted at the thought but let it pass.

'You do much D.I.Y. Adam?'

'A bit...but not that...not roofing...too specialist for me...I can tell you if it needs doing but someone else would have to fix it.'

'It's just Liv said you met at Drapers...I go there regularly... I like to do a spot of D.I.Y.'

'We did meet there...she caught my eye over a bag of pea gravel'

'Did she now?'

'Ryan, my son, plays rugby with Luke, Marcus's son...he's really helpful on the D.I.Y. front.

'I saw Marcus the other day, he popped over to see me, nice fella. That Luke's a bit of a rum 'un though...been in a bit of bother I hear.'

Now it was Adam's turn to flush. He said nothing about the incident; he didn't want Arthur getting the wrong idea about Ryan. There would be plenty of time for them all to get to know each other better at a later date. First impressions were far more important.

'You're quiet, love?' Arthur said looking across at Liv.

'Oh, I'm happy to let you two get the questions in that I know you've been dying to ask since I first mentioned Adam.

''Well I for one am pleased we've met you at last...cheers Adam...here's to seeing you again soon.'

'As long as you've not put him off.'

They raised their glasses before ending the meal with a coffee and a packet of petit fours Barbara thought would be a nice finishing touch. Arthur wasn't allowed one when Barbara reminded him that he still needed to watch his waistline, but he took one anyway when she turned her back for more milk.

Chapter Thirty Seven

Friday teatime saw Marsha, Robert, Bee and Eddie sitting around the kitchen table. The remains of a fish pie had been cleared away and Eddie was happily picking peas out of the spill tray around his neck; his chubby cheeks and a good appetite were an eternal delight to Marsha. Dessert was apple pie she'd made that morning as Eddie slept, and Robert had brought in a tub of ice cream on the way home.

Marsha was relaxed; relieved to notice that for once, Robert's mood was buoyant. The past few days had been unnerving when she'd watch him disappear after tea with a determined look to 'clear some paperwork.'

'Have you finished that 'paperwork' now Rob? No more tonight?'

'Getting there...almost done'. He smiled, but that too was unnerving.

'What on earth is it? Must be serious the way you looked last night...is there something I need to know about?'

'I'll tell you later,' he said, still smiling.

Marsha was not appeased but got on with dishing out dessert.

'Right then...who's for apple pie and ice cream?'

'Me please.'

Bee had been quieter than usual, as though she too was in on something Marsha knew nothing about. Marsha felt like a schoolgirl who hadn't been invited to the party with the more popular classmates, but chatted on and dished out the pie. Bee ate slowly then paused halfway through.

'When's Mummy coming again? Am I going home soon?'

'Darling she's just been...it's a bit difficult right now when she's working and trying to sort out that roof...anyway you like staying here don't you? You're happy to be with me and Marsha and Eddie? You know how much Eddie loves you.'

Robert tried to make light of the situation and assuage any uncomfortable feelings Bee might have about wanting to get back to her mother. He'd even asked her what colour she would like her bedroom painted and offered to put up another bookshelf. They made several visits to the bookshop in town during half term, much to Bee's delight, and her collection was rapidly growing. They also chose books for Eddie together and he encouraged her to read to the baby even though he preferred to chew them with newly emerging teeth.

'But it's school again on Monday...how am I going to get there?'

'Don't worry, I'll take you.'

Robert paused a while before adding, 'I think it's such a pity you're not at your old school...don't you...only round the corner?'

Bee frowned and considered the question.

'I think I like my new school better now...I like my teacher, Miss Farley, and I like my friends.'

'But your other friends are still at the old school and you liked them.'

'Yes...but it's not easy to see them any more.'

Marsha had an inkling of where all this was leading but

was confused when she'd already assumed that Robert had dropped the subject. Hadn't she made it perfectly that clear she didn't agree with what he was planning? Did her opinion count for nothing?

'Right, time to wash up and then it's Eddie's bath...just look at the time...do you want to help me wash the pots Bee?'

Bee liked nothing more than to stand on a stool at the sink with a bowl of water overflowing with suds. Marsha was patient with her and accepted that some plates would need to be re-washed, but felt for the child who obviously missed her Mummy and wanted to get back home.

It was gone eight before Marsha and Robert sat together after the bedtime routines were done. Eddie now slept through until at least seven and Bee was happy in bed once she'd been read a couple of stories.

'What's going on Rob? You've been acting very strangely these past few days.'

'Marsha please, just listen to what I've got to say.'

'All right...I'm listening.'

'Bee has settled in really well here with us. This past week has been amazing, I've loved it and so has Eddie...and I think you have too.'

It was obvious that Robert had prepared his little speech, got all his facts lined up and was ready to present his case.

'It's looking likely that Liv is going to have to sell the house...after the roof caved in, she tried to get money from the bank and they've refused to give her what she needs. She just can't afford it...and this means that she will most likely move back in with Barbara and Arthur...no choice. I spoke to her this afternoon...she still thinks she can raise the money but I don't see how unless Arthur can come up with more...hardly likely when I know that all their savings went into giving her a deposit in the first place.'

Marsha sat in silence, waiting for him to finish so she could have her turn.'

'When Liv took Bee to that god-awful place, she took her out of one of the best schools in this area...and look what happened...dumped where there's bullying...kids with problems...social services involved with half of them.'

Robert, convinced that Marsha had to come round to his line of thought, failed to take in her impassive response, and went on regardless.

'As you know, I've spoken to Bee's old school and they are more than happy to have her back...they do have a spare place luckily. I think Bee should come here and live with us on a more permanent basis...it wouldn't be good for her to be shunted around...apart from which Arthur's just had serious heart surgery and a six-year-old running around won't give him the peace and quiet he needs will it?'

Marsha still kept silent.

'I've been getting some legal advice and I'm applying for custody...it doesn't mean that Liv won't see her on a regular basis...let's face it, I've been doing that for most of her life...but I think it's time for a change. Stability, better school, better area...what's so wrong with me wanting the best for her, eh?'

Robert had finally closed his argument in full confidence of a watertight case.

'Wow, you've really gone through this thoroughly, haven't you? Hardly a word said to me...especially when I thought I'd made it clear what my opinion was...but you've not listened to anything I've said have you?'

'What do you mean? Of course I listen to you...but you have to listen to me. I'm Bee's Father and have her best interest at heart. And I don't see what's so wrong about her living here with us...you love having her...I can see that...in fact, you're great with her...make her welcome...and she's good with

Eddie. She's a real sister to him and can get to know him even better as they both grow up.'

'Rob this is serious...what you're suggesting is a massive disruption of all our lives.'

'Not as much as you think...just look at us now...Bee living here is not as big a disruption as you think...we're ready for her.'

Marsha turned towards him, outwardly calm, looking accepting, but inside formulating plans of her own now that she knew the extent to which Robert had gone. It would broker her case no further to argue tonight and she made no other comment. Robert, satisfied, moved closer and put his arm around her before switching on the television.

'I'll talk to Liv soon...we need to show her this can work in all our best interests.'

It was getting late and Marsha had no desire to get into a full-blown argument, but her mind was not on the television.

Chapter Thirty Eight

On Saturday morning, Liv woke up to loud pop music blaring from outside. When it didn't stop after ten minutes, she went to investigate and dragged herself out of bed. A man's voice was shouting instructions and a heavy thud followed ribald joking and laughter. From her bedroom, Liv could hear perfectly well but saw little beyond a parked truck below.

There was a tap at her bedroom door.

'Olivia?...Olivia, are you awake?'

'Yes...I'm up...come in.'

Frances came in, already dressed and ready for the day ahead.

'Have you seen what's going on outside? Did you know they were going to make a start on repairs today...you never said?'

'Start what?' Liv was confused.

'The roof of course.'

'I don't understand...I told the roofer the other day that I hadn't got all the money together yet...and there was no way I could ask him to start the job if I couldn't pay.'

'Well someone didn't get the message, my dear.'

Frances had watched from the doorway, bemused by the fast-paced activity next door, and was pleased to see something happening at last.

'They do seem to know what they're doing.'

Liv threw on yesterday's clothes and rushed out to find herself confronted by a building site of tiles, beams and machinery around her house. Workmen milled about as Magic FM blasted out from a paint-splattered radio, and voices sang in gusto to Mary Wells' 'My Guy'. It took several moments of incredulity before she realised who the men were. She spotted the radio and turned the volume down, the only way to get attention. A voice on the roof shouted down,

'Oi, I was enjoying that...turn it back up!'

It wasn't the roofer who had put up the temporary cover with his workmates; it was Marcus and Adam, Luke and Ryan, and a man she didn't recognise at all. He was astride the roof, releasing the temporary sheeting and throwing it to the ground.

'Who are you? Marcus?...Adam?... What's going on?'

The roofer looked down.

'Keep clear love...can't stop now...you explain Adam, would ya?...and put that radio back on!'

'Ok just give me five minutes and I'll be right back.'

'You'd better be mate or I'll be docking ya wages'

Adam turned the radio back up, waved and bowed his head in acknowledgement to Brian the roofer.

At that moment, a very different Dom came into sight, resplendent in overalls, boots and heavy-duty gloves. She'd barely seen him since he broke the news about America and accepted that he'd had much to do and organise before the move. They'd spoken on the phone but that was all, and now here he was getting stuck into a roof repair.

Liv's eyes widened in disbelief as he went to the back of the truck when ordered.

'Come on...make me a quick cuppa and I'll fill you in... you heard the boss...I've got five minutes,' and Adam shunted her away from the worksite.

Adam's face was flushed from the banter, the singing and the challenge in hand. They went into Frances' house where quick introductions were made and the kettle put on. Frances revelled in the pleasure of being useful. She had already decided that she liked the look and sound of Adam. 'I always get the measure of a man by the tone of his voice...a true give-away,' she would later tell Liv. It was Frances who made the tea as Liv stood with Adam by the kitchen table waiting for an explanation.

'Do you think the others would like a drink too?'

Adam turned,

'I'm sure they would in a while Mrs Fenton...that would be very kind of you, just not right this minute.'

Liv was getting impatient.

'So what's this all about? How come you're all here working on my roof?'

'In a nutshell...remember when you told Marcus about the roof? Old Mr Draper called in after you'd left and between them, they decided they wanted to help. Mr Draper agreed to provide the materials at cost...Marcus has a roofer mate who owes him a favour for a couple of building jobs he'd helped out with and he miraculously had a couple of days between jobs...then Marcus told me about it when I called in early this morning and I said count me in as a labourer. Mr Draper had told them he thought Arthur might have a spare key to your place...they did, and oh was he over the moon when he knew what was planned. You hadn't told them how serious it was either, had you?'

'No...I just...I don't know what to say...you are all so...'

'Thank us all later...and I'm sorry but tonight's dinner might be off...could be a long day.'

'And what about Dom...how did he get roped in?'

'Ah...top man...we've just met but I like him. It was Arthur who told him what was going on when he paid your Dad a visit after we left last night and apparently he said there was no way he was going to be left out of this...said he'd served time at the house when you moved in and was glad of something to fill the days before going off to America.'

'Wow...you are all so...so brilliant...marvellous...wonderful...but you have to know I didn't get the whole of the amount I asked the bank for...I can try other banks but...'

'If it's enough for the materials...and a regular supply of tea...you'll be fine Liv...don't worry'.

Adam's face beamed with pleasure,

'I honestly never thought I'd get past this.'

'You will...we'll get there Liv, I promise'

'I will never forget today as long as I live.'

'Get away...right...time's up...need to get cracking on with the job.'

He drank half of his tea, gave her a firm kiss on the cheek and left Liv in a state of shock at how fortunes can change in a moment.

Frances came back into the kitchen when she heard the back door close.

'What lovely friends you have Olivia...to do this for you.'

'And I hadn't a clue. Yesterday, I was sure that I'd have to sell up and today...'

'You are so lucky...you treasure them, my dear. I had friends like that once and I miss them every single day, although I now have you...and Bee...and perhaps that lovely young man of yours too.'

Yes, he was a lovely young man, she thought, and then pondered on the vagaries of life that had just swung in her favour. It felt good and her mood soared after the disappointments of earlier in the week.

In the garden, Luke and Ryan had been dispatched to clear weeds and cut the grass having been given a quick lesson in what was weed and what was flower by Adam. With little choice in the matter, following the fracas with the police, it wasn't too great a hardship even though the work was challenging when briars and nettles were knee-high. They were given gauntlets for the job and both got stuck into the daunting task. Luke in particular was determined to get the job finished as soon as possible.

'I reckon we got away light enough...how was your Dad after?'

'He was pretty good all things considered...we've not talked about it too much...yours?'

'Bit of a ball-ache but he's happy when I don't interrupt... just a 'yes Dad, no Dad' when it's called for...he shouts a lot but he's ok.'

'So that's it then...tell me you're not going back to that crowd?'

'What? It'll be fine...this work puts us in credit...they think we're doing great. Look, there's not much else in this crap town to get excited about. We can't leave so might as well have a bit of fun where we can, anyway how come you didn't turn up the other night?'

'I don't know...I'm not cut out for it.'

'You'll be fine I promise...Riggs' Dad has a lock-up he never uses...and you won't believe what's planned. We're gonna set it up... Come on Ryan it's no biggie...a bit of weed never hurt anyone...that's as far as it goes. Johno's in now and Si, he's always a laugh'

'I'll think about it.'

Ryan had never taken to Johno; his lairy ways and the language he used about the girls left him too uncomfortable. They were nice girls mostly and didn't deserve that. He'd never really wanted to be part of the crowd that Luke was drawn into and regretted letting himself be dragged into it in the first place. They'd hit a crossroads in their friendship and Ryan increasingly knew that this was where they would part company. He was sorry for that; they'd been best friends since Thurston primary and later bonded over rugby, but Luke had even talked about giving that up recently. He hardly ever turned up for training and on the days he did, might as well not have bothered. Marcus keenly felt the disappointment and the shame of his son's lack of enthusiasm and despite all efforts had to admit defeat. It had been his greatest wish that Luke could have gone even further than he had and harboured secret thoughts of his son playing at county level. He saw the ability but not the mental attitude needed to go with it.

Luke refused to be shaken off by Ryan's lack of enthusiasm:

'What's there to think about? It's a no-brainer...supply's good...lock-up's nicely tucked away...few cans...mebbe get the girls in later...pimp it up a bit...you know what they like.'

'Maybe.'

Luke wouldn't give up but Ryan left it alone for now.

'Come on...let's get this lot bagged up...build up that credit.'

The first day of work was carried out efficiently and at a pace. Liv and Frances, as promised, provided a regular supply of tea and food, all gratefully received, and by the time it was getting dark, they were well on the way to achieving a good repair. Liv was overwhelmed by the way they'd volunteered their time and whatever gratitude she tried to show, it was dismissed in a few words: 'happy to help out.'

'No problem.'

'Can't see you stuck with a hole in the roof.'

They made it sound like it was no big deal, but to her, it really was a very big deal; this meant she and Bee could stay after all when the money released by the bank would at least cover materials. Flushed with happiness, she began to make plans for their return home.

Adam was the last to leave and he and Ryan joined Liv and Frances for a last drink.

'It really is our pleasure to help you out you know. Hopefully, one more day should do the major structural part, then all that's left is tiling and making good the damage in the kitchen...and decorating. I'm sure that between us we can get that done. What do you think Ryan?'

Without meaning to, Ryan was getting caught up in the project; he was quietly proud of what they'd achieved in the garden and decided that he wouldn't mind helping out some more. 'Yeah' was enough of an answer to let Adam know he was on board with it.

'I can't believe what you managed to get done in the garden...it can be called a garden now and not 'the jungle' as Bee named it when we moved in. Goodness, I'll be learning the names of plants next...Dad will be impressed when he sees it.'

Ryan flushed. Liv was very pretty and maybe she was ok too.

Liv looked from Ryan to Adam and to Frances, beaming with delight.

'I don't know what to say. You've all been so amazing!'

'Olivia, that's what friends do, help you out in times of need.'

'Yes, but there's helping out, and there's major building repair work. Not exactly the same thing is it and you kindly putting up with my company?'

'Perhaps not, but there may be a day when someone needs your help too.'

'Can't see me straddling a roof though...'

'On that note, I will love you and leave you...early start tomorrow.'

Adam and Ryan made their move before the conversation became too sentimental. Liv went out to the car with them and Ryan quickly jumped into the passenger seat. Adam held Liv close, not caring whether Ryan was watching or not, and kissed her firmly on the mouth. The words he wanted to say would have to wait, but the kiss was a good start, and he drove off waving from an open window.

The saddest part of the day had been saying a final goodbye to Dom, and Liv finally had the chance to dwell upon their conversation. Whilst he tried to make light of his going, Liv knew how much she would miss him. She'd watched the ease with which Dom and all the men got on; listened to the ping pong of banter and loud laughter as they worked, and she envied the camaraderie considering some of them had barely met.

'I won't see you again after this will I?'

'Not for a while, my lovely, no…but I'll be in touch don't you worry. I'll keep you updated…call you up when I've found my American drawl.'

'You better.'

'You're doing ok Liv…keep on as you are…you'll get there. And keep on writing. Don't you stop now…not after that win. Maybe the next story could be on the lines of 'Three Men and a Roof!''

'I'll bear that in mind when I can fit it in.'

'Oh, you'll fit it in all right. Too important not to, love'

They hugged tightly before he drove away and Liv felt the space he left with a mix of sadness and happiness at what he had helped her achieve.

Chapter Thirty Nine

Frances was waiting in the sitting room, enlivened by the day's activity and relieved that Liv's biggest problem seemed to have found a perfect solution.

'Are you all right my dear? Are you crying?'

'Oh don't mind me. It's been a long, strange day. I'm so happy with what's going on next door, but I've just said goodbye to Dom. I won't see him now for at least two years.'

'Oh my dear, that's a blink of an eye when you've lived as long as I have. Trust me, it will fly by...and from what you've told me it's a wonderful opportunity for him...one that he must take otherwise he will never know what he's missed.'

'I agree...I know all that...I'm just being selfish. I've got so used to him being there. He's played a big part in my life recently and I'll miss him that's all...Bee will miss him too.'

'Of course you will, but that young man of yours is a real charmer. I like him, he has a great presence about him.'

'I like him too, perhaps more than like him. And after today what can I say?'

'You keep hold of that one Olivia...I think a little celebratory drink is called for, don't you? If you look in that cupboard there's a rather nice port if you'd care for a glass with me. I do believe we've finished the sherry' There was a twinkle in Frances' eye as she spoke.

'Aren't you tired Frances? You're usually ready for your bed at this time.'

'Not tonight...it's funny but when you were seeing Adam off I was thinking about the moments in my life that overwhelmed me with emotion...obviously getting married and the birth of my darling girl Hermione, and then Simon, stand out, but beyond that, there were other times that have never left me. In fact most days they pass through my mind however briefly...'

Frances' thoughts were drifting away from Liv, the room and the port until she suddenly sprang back into the present.

'I don't suppose you would care to hear the next part of my story... whilst I'm still able to tell it?

Liv thought it a strange thing to offer and would rather have liked an early night to think about the day's events, but she could sense that Frances wanted her company for a while longer, wanted to talk and she would not deny her.

'I would love to hear it as long as you're sure you are not too tired.'

'I've been so anxious to tell you my dear...it should have been Hermione but...I need someone to tell and you are the only person Olivia...the nearest person to my other darling girl.'

'In that case, Frances I can't wait to hear it.'

Frances sat back and collected her thoughts before resuming her day in Paris. They made themselves comfortable, drank the port and the story continued.

'Where was I up to?

'Driving to the Gallery I think.'

'Ah yes...I was driven to the Gallery by a chauffeur from the hotel. It did not take too long; in fact, I would have loved it to take longer. It was such a beautiful June day. The air was warm; the sun showed much promise and the sky was the clearest blue. The sights and sounds and smells of Paris floated through my open window and beckoned me like nothing before. It was a heady mix that sent my head spinning. Gerard, my driver, explained the sights we drove slowly past and I do think he went a little out of his way to make sure I saw the Eiffel Tower and Notre Dame, at least from the outside. He knew I'd never been to Paris and wanted to show off the city he was so rightly proud of. I made up my mind that he should take me on a guided tour if George was still indisposed the next day. I did not want to miss out on this wonderful city that beckoned me with every minute that went by.

I was so pleased that I had bought new dresses for the trip when I saw how elegant and beautifully turned out the ladies were on taking their promenade. I still have the dress I wore that day; it was green silk with white flowers and short sleeves, and a green leather belt at the waist...such a tiny waist I had then...'

Frances was no longer in the sitting room, but back in her beloved Paris of 1932, no longer an elderly woman in her nineties. Sixty-two years melted away. Her face revived at the memory and at that moment she was back in time.

'We arrived a little before eleven o'clock and Gerard dropped me off at the door. He was to park the car and would enquire later when he would be needed for the return journey. Of course, I was a little nervous at first; the main door was firmly shut and there was no response to my knock; it was to keep out prying eyes before the grand opening, as I was later to discover. I looked down the side of the building where a smaller door showed life coming and going, and I cautiously made my way there and went inside. There wasn't as much activity as I had thought there might be, even though the exhibition was due to open the next day; but I found out soon enough that the bulk of the work had already been done. Really George should have got the painting there much earlier but he insisted it couldn't be done due to other commitments and would not trust it in the hands of anyone else.

A tall, thin man noticed me immediately as someone who should not be there and came across to where this young woman, me, was standing in awe and amazement. He demanded to know what I wanted, but when I explained who I was and what I had in my possession, his whole demeanour underwent a dramatic change. He became civility itself and led me to the back of the building where several chairs were set around a small table. He bade me sit and wait even though I would have much preferred to look around at the wonderful works on display. From the poor position of my chair, I could only strain my eyes to take it in; but after half an hour, when no one came to see me, I could contain my curiosity no longer and stepped out into the main gallery. The few people still left inside took no notice, which encouraged me to be bold.

The works on display took me by great surprise. Some were very sensual, but enigmatic too. I found myself not so much shocked as intrigued. I walked over to one particular painting that drew my attention: it was entitled 'Reclining Nude'. I tried to make sense of a work that was so far from my field of knowledge, I couldn't quite take it all in. I must have been standing there for at least ten minutes, completely lost in my examination before I had the feeling that someone was standing behind me. The person made no noise and the proximity to me was sensed rather than heard. When I turned there was barely a foot between us. Of course, I stepped back in utter embarrassment when I realised who it was.

'I am sorry I startled you but you were so engrossed I did not want to disturb.'

He spoke only French, his voice low and gruff. I was grateful that my command of the language had never left me and replied in kind as best I could.

'No...no I am the one to be sorry...I didn't mean...I only came...I mean I am waiting...'

'Don't worry young lady...I know why you are here. I heard and I wanted to see for myself the beautiful woman who was making such an important delivery to me.

I blushed of course. I was at a loss of what to say. My throat was dry, my tongue was tied and my head was in a whirl. I looked around for the man who had told me to wait, but there seemed to be no one left in the room now but us two. The throng of activity had ceased and the people around earlier...well they had all disappeared. I gave my apology and I would have gone back to my seat had he not laughed and told me to stay.

'What do you think of the painting, at least give me your opinion.'

'I...I would not dare to presume.'

I was still reeling over the realisation that this was Picasso himself. There could be no mistake. I had seen photographs of him of course but in person, he commanded much more than a cursory glance. We were standing so close I could reach out and touch him. I could smell him; I could describe in detail the paint stains on his shirt; the colour of his eyes; the lines across his face.

George had rarely asked my opinion on anything let alone a painting. It was all too much. My head was swimming and I felt faint...the room began to spin.

Seeing my distress he led me back to the chairs and sat me down. He even brought a glass of water, which I gratefully took even though my hand was shaking dreadfully. I was so embarrassed. The Gallery was completely empty now, eerily so after the earlier commotion. I realised that it must be lunchtime and I also remembered that I had not eaten since dinner the night before. I hastily explained to him why I was there and produced the painting I had kept with me. George had impressed upon me many times that it should never be left out of sight. He raised his hand saying not to worry and repeated that he knew exactly who I was. He took the painting over to a window to examine it in the light. Obviously pleased with what he saw, he told me that the formality of the paper-work was complete and ready for me to take in exchange. Refreshed by the seat and the water, I managed to thank him at least. I expected to be shown out when I was given the documents, but no, he made no move to leave the office I now found myself in.'

Frances fell silent as weariness crept upon her and the exertion that went with the memory proved too much.

'Shall we call it a day now Frances? I do want to hear more but it can keep for now. What you have told me is incredible... the whole day has been incredible but we both need sleep.'

'I think I will retire for the night Olivia if you don't mind.'

She didn't want Liv to know about the pain in her chest and fought the compulsion to rub at it.

'That's all right... can I get you anything first?'

'Just a glass of water if you please.'

'I'll take one up for you.'

It was gone eleven by the time Liv climbed into her own bed. Too late and too tired, the day's events, and the fantastical story, swirled and merged until sleep took over.

Within days, the end of the roof repair was in sight and a final visit to see Bee was made to reassure her that she could come home very soon.

Marsha was busy at the sink and turned, wiping dripping hands, to welcome her.

'Tell me how everything's going. Sit down and I'll make some tea.'

'That would be lovely thank you...and yes, the roof and kitchen are just about finished now. I can't believe how well it's all gone...you heard about what happened?'

'I did...so kind of Mr Draper...and so nice to have such good friends...I'm really pleased for you Liv.'

'Great friends and a kind boss...I am lucky...Bee can come home now but thank you so much for looking after her so well.'

Robert came into the room. His body stiffened at Liv's words.

'You want Bee to go back with you?'

His anger was ready to pour like molten lava. The case he'd built up would not be laid to rest.

Marsha diplomatically took Bee and Eddie out of the room with promises of stories upstairs.

'But I want Mummy.'

'We'll come back down in a few minutes Bee...Mummy and Daddy just need to talk about something first.'

Marsha glared at Robert as they left for Bee's bedroom.

'Please Robert don't do this now.'

She touched his arm and Robert stiffened in response.

The room upstairs was as perfect as it could be with everything a little girl could possibly want; space to play and books to read, it was a child's dream. A beanbag sat in the corner next to the bookcase and a colourful picture book lay open on the floor next to it. The curtains and duvet sported matching animal prints and on the wall, an array of Bee's paintings had been hung and framed by Robert. It was a room filled with attention to every detail.

Downstairs, Liv's calm served only to fuel Robert's ire.

'I'm moving back home tomorrow morning and in a couple of days Bee can come back too.'

Robert's face paled, his jaw tight.

'This past week has been really settling for Bee. I don't think she should go back with you...she needs stability...a decent school and a proper home life. I, we think...we know that we can give her that.'

'What are you talking about? This was only ever going to be temporary...she's lost a couple of days at school, but I've spoken to Miss Farley and they understand what's happened.'

'And I've spoken to Bee's old school who are happy to take her back.'

'You've what? How dare you go behind my back?'

Liv formed her words carefully, emphasising every last syllable even though Robert barely listened and continued with his own well-prepared speech.

'I've taken legal advice Liv...and like I said, I've been in touch with her old school, who still have a place free for her, and I've...'

Liv determined to stay calm but beneath the façade, her heart hammered and her fists clenched in anger. She resisted the urge to hit him.

'Just think about it for one minute...it makes perfect sense...she could have started today.'

'I don't need one minute Robert...I don't need one second... My daughter is coming back home in a couple of days and that's the end of it. Dad will come with me in the car so please get her things packed for when we get here.'

'We'll see about that...Farrow thinks I've got a good case for custody...and he...'

'Farrow! That shark...Robert, I don't know what's got into you but this is not going to happen...have you for one minute thought of Bee in all this? About what she wants?'

'That's exactly what I am doing...Bee is happy here. She has her own room...everything she could possibly need or want and...'

'Good, I'm glad she's happy here but you saw her, she's even more happy to know that she's coming home...you're not thinking of her at all...this is your guilty conscience coming out all over again over what happened to Daniel...you couldn't handle that and you can't handle this!'

'Don't you dare throw that back at me...I had nothing to do with losing Daniel!'

'And neither did I...even though you made damn sure that I wasn't to be left with Bee for one minute...I know you blamed me but it was no one's fault. Not me. Not you. No one! Do you hear me? It took me years to believe that but it's about time you believed it too. Bee is safe and happy and there's nothing you can give her that would make up for what we lost. You have a baby, Robert. Be satisfied.'

Tears flowed down Liv's face. Would he never give up? Robert sat in silence.

'I want to see Bee now before I go...but next time I come I expect to see her bags packed and ready to go.'

Their eyes locked, each afraid of disturbing a past that threatened to rip them wide open yet again. In that momentary silence, Marsha came back into the room with Eddie in her arms.

'Go sit with Bee for a while Liv...she misses her Mummy...Rob, it's Eddie's bath time now,' and she handed over the yawning little boy.

'Think about it Liv,' he said as he took Eddie from Marsha's arms. The baby startled by the unceremonious interruption wailed loudly.

Liv roughly wiped away her tears on the tissue offered by Marsha and left them to join Bee, now sitting in front of a video.

'Mummy, why are you crying?'

'I'm not Beebee...I think I'm getting a cold that's all.'

287

The immediacy of acceptance was gratefully received; unlike the next question she had difficulty in explaining away.

'Why were you and Daddy shouting?'

'It's nothing sweetie...just a little disagreement...now, what part are we up to in this film...what have I missed?'

Bee was still young enough to accept that a cuddle from Mummy was enough to solve most problems in life and for that, Liv was grateful. They sat close with arms entwined, giving rise to the promise that all was well before she left. Unfortunately, it did little to alleviate Robert's threats. A crack had appeared threatening to blow apart her resolve and the nagging inside that he could succeed.

Bee snuggled in closer.

'I should look after you Mummy if you're poorly. Can I come home with you now?'

'Just give me another day or two...Grandad will come with the car and we'll bring you home I promise.'

'Promise?'

'Promise'

She had to believe it would happen when the alternative was unthinkable.

Chapter Forty

Liv returned to Frances' house with the intention of packing her belongings to take home. She had to be busy and stay positive, but also needed the time on her own. Adam was working late and catching up on what he'd missed; Barbara and Arthur, content that the worst was over, wouldn't be back for a few days; and she wasn't sure when Savannah would be over next.

Pushing Robert's threats of custody to one aside; hoping for the best whilst preparing for the worst was the only option. She did wonder if legal advice was needed, but then, where would the money come for that?

'Hi Frances, it's only me.'

Liv had knocked lightly and let herself in with the key given to her. There was no answer; it was too quiet. Then she found out why. Frances was on the floor half sitting, half propped up by the sofa, pale and shaking, hands clasped at her chest and wincing with pain.

'Frances! What's happened?'

'I'm all right...just a dizzy turn...they happen...stupidly fell over.'

'I'm going to call an ambulance.'

'No, I'm fine. Give me a minute...get my breath back...'

'No arguments. I'm calling now.'

Frances appealed with her eyes, but the call was made.

'Help me up to the sofa...I can't seem to manage...'

'Don't talk...please...I'll help.'

She managed to get Frances' slight frame more comfortable on the sofa, placing a cushion behind her head and tucking a cover around her shaking body.

'How long have you been like this Frances? Why didn't you tell me about these dizzy spells?'

Frances recovered her composure a little,

'You have enough on your plate my dear...and I know that you are looking forward to getting back home with Bee. This will pass...it always does.'

The pain spoke otherwise. She'd rallied long enough to respond but her voice reduced to a whisper. Liv stroked the translucent skin of her hand and pushed back strands of hair that had fallen over her face, praying that this was not how Frances would end her days. The clock on the wall ticked loud and slow and minutes passed in hours.

When the paramedics arrived, it did not take long for the decision to be made that she should go to the hospital immediately; they suspected a heart attack and Liv went with her. It gave Frances comfort to know she was not on her own as she drifted in and out of consciousness in the ambulance.

Whilst the assessment was underway, she called Simon, but it was Sarah who answered. His wife was fully prepared as ever to let the caller know that it wasn't convenient for Simon to come to the phone and that if they left a number he would call back when it was. She did not take kindly to their evening meal being disturbed but when the words hospital and Frances were uttered in the same sentence, she relented.

'Simon, you need to take this...your Mother has been taken to hospital. Looks like a heart attack. Not good.'

His first reaction too had been irritation at being disturbed in the middle of dinner but underwent a dramatic change when he understood it was about his mother.

'It sounds serious...I need to go.'

'Of course, you should go darling...we don't want that neighbour mistaken for next of kin, do we? But do finish your dinner first. You never know when you might get anything else to eat and you know what hospital food's like.'

'This is my Mother we're talking about. I need to go now.'

He left Sarah alone at the table and the meal half-finished.

'I know...I'm sorry darling and I would go with you but you know my back's playing up again.'

'Don't worry...I wouldn't dream of asking.'

Simon looked at his wife and wondered if she would be the same when his time came, 'I'm sorry I can't come to my husband's death bed but my back's playing up again.' She would manage the funeral if only for the wake afterwards and the opportunity to be the grieving widow who had inherited another tidy sum, as she had when her own parents died. He gave a swift peck on a cool cheek before leaving with a hastily packed bag just in case.

'I'll ring you later.'

'Do that...and do tell her I'm thinking of her, she called as he left.

Simon didn't reply but grabbed his coat and car keys from the hall. Sarah finished eating, resenting the time she'd spent cooking dinner when most of it would end up in the bin.

The frigid nature of Simon's relationship with his Mother in no way prepared him for the emotion that arose when he arrived at the hospital. Liv sat beside the bed watching over the still figure. She stood to let Simon get close.

'I found her on the floor this evening...she's been having dizzy spells apparently but didn't tell anyone.'

'What?'

Simon looked quizzically from Liv to Frances until a doctor came over, and explained the situation.

'I have to tell you that her heart is very weak. Considering her age and the advanced stage of the illness, there is little we can do now apart from keeping her comfortable. I should also let you know that she has declined any intervention from us too. She has requested not to be resuscitated.'

'Can she do that? Don't I have a say? I'm her son.'

'I'm sorry.'

He left Simon alone with Liv. Mental turmoil took over. Years of preparation counted for nothing at that moment. Yes, she was almost ninety-six years old; of course, it had to happen sooner rather than later, but he wasn't ready for this quite as much as he thought he was. With no Sarah beside him to dispense cold facts of inevitability, he only had Liv's gentle support and kindness.

'Simon...I am so sorry.' She put her hand on his arm,

'The nurse told me that she would probably sleep now until morning...'

'Yes...yes...I...'

Liv was not prepared for his reaction. This was not the same man she had met earlier.

'I'll leave you alone but let me know if there's any change... please? Or if there's anything I can do...Frances means a lot to me...I've grown very fond of your Mother.'

Simon looked as if he couldn't quite make up his mind about the truth of what she said when Sarah's words still rang in his ears.

'I will.'

.   .   .

The last time Simon had felt any love or bond with his Mother, had been many years ago but sitting at her bedside, alone now Liv had left them together, he recalled times in his childhood when it had just been the two of them: a day by the sea, sitting on a windy beach eating sandwiches and ice creams; laughing as they ran to catch an empty bag drifting on a swoop of warm air. Memories came unbidden but they were vivid, one after another. Visits to the zoo were planned to get him over his fear of strange, wild animals. He had been a timid boy, berated by a father who only saw weakness, but the reassuring hand, and calm, soothing voice of his Mother told him he would always be safe with her. In the quiet times, before bed, she would read his favourite stories until he fell asleep. It was always just the two of them. Where did these thoughts come from, these memories that had lain buried for decades?

Simon couldn't say when or why the changes in their relationship happened but it wasn't sudden. A slow insidious development crept up as his Father's influence took precedence. When Simon started working with him, the harsh realities of a cut-throat business and the ruthless deals made by George overtook sentiment. And when Sarah came into his life, the transformation was sealed.

He looked at his Mother quietly sleeping and wondered when exactly the day arrived when he saw her as no more than an old lady who'd outlived her expected years.

The prominence of George grew and the grooming of Simon sealed his fate. The arrival of Sarah Chester, a wealthy and eminently suitable wife played no small part. He had been willingly led, grateful for the attention of the long-absent Father, and ready for the opportunity of making money to show his Father he was worthy of attention. He embraced the excitement of a calculated risk and chose the life that came with it, but it came at a price.

His Mother could only watch in helpless resignation. She

knew that he did not have the ruthlessness of his father; he did not have his gift, if 'gift' was the right word for the business, but he was caught up in the excitement of the chase and the wins. George and Sarah had the 'gift' and he allowed them to use it at the cost of his relationship with his Mother.

Sarah drew in investors, like a black widow spider. She notched up successes where he could only watch in amazement. He let George and Sarah run his life as he looked on and learned.

The nurse came back to check on Frances. Simon was advised to go home and come back in the morning. There was nothing more to be done that night. He kissed his Mother lightly on the cheek and left for her house. In the hospital car park, he sat with uncomfortable thoughts until he could better compose himself to face the drive. What was the use in regretting the past? It was too late to change it now, but at least he could be with her. It was a bitter pill to swallow but he was prepared to stay as long as it took and the thought of what might have been was pushed to one side.

Chapter Forty One

Liv welcomed Savannah's arrival for a few days; her shifts were mercifully short that week and having a friend close by would come with the comfort and reassurance she desperately needed. No one else knew as much about her situation as Sav, and the need for support was mutual.

Sav had taken Liv's call from the hospital and the friendship antennae immediately picked up on the despondent tone. Frances' illness; Robert's plans for taking custody of Bee; the aftermath of a collapsing roof; and worries over Arthur had all clearly taken their toll.

Savannah had her own issues but she was a tougher breed. She travelled light and had lived with drama and crisis long enough to learn to cope. Years of necessity taught her much and her arrival at Liv's found her friend sinking beneath the waves of worry.

'Come on Liv...it's not that bad. I might not be Adam but you can get through this.'

'But you've got worries of your own. I don't want to...'

'Stuff that! Where's the glasses?'

Liv smiled in spite of herself,

'You never change, do you?'

'Nope and don't intend to.'

'I'm sorry, I'll pull myself together and...'

'And we'll put the world to rights...the Robert bit anyway...speaking of which, how is the shit-for-brains?'

'Not given up yet but neither will I... not without a fight.'

'That's ma girl!'

'And how's Frances doing? Can't be easy having heart problems at her age.'

'It's not looking good. Simon, her son...he's with her so I left. It's funny you know, but I actually don't think of her as being that old...it's all been a bit of a shock. I've not known her that long but we've grown close, you know.'

'You need more friends your own age...and me! And where's that knight-in-shining armour of yours?'

Liv thought of Adam and his last parting words.

'He's got a few things of his own to sort...work's been piling up. After helping me with the roof and kitchen...taking time off...he's a bit behind so I'm leaving him to it.'

'I hope he realises what a little treasure you are.'

'I think he's the treasure in this...him and Dom and Marcus and his roofer friend who owed him a favour. How can I ever pay them all back?'

'We'll think of something don't worry...maybe a party? Oh, we love a good party...we *need* a good party.'

'Can't remember the last time I went to a 'good party'. More important than that, though, how's your Dad? How's he doing with the Alzheimer's and cancer? How are you coping?'

'To be honest, there's not much I can do for him now... physically anyway. He's being well looked after but mentally...he doesn't even know me. My job right now is to sort out the house. The house! It's an unbelievable mess, which is why I'm looking forward to spending a couple of days here with you...I'd rather sort out you...much less complicated!'

'You're the tonic I need. I really thought I was getting my life back Sav...but there's always something.'

'You'll get it back with interest...don't worry so much... believe me, I've been through worse in Africa.'

'I know, I'm sorry...thought I'd stopped being so pathetic.'

'You are not pathetic...enough of that. You've had a rough few years...I know Robert's not been much help but you're not on your own.'

They sat at the kitchen table over the remains of a bolognese and a half-empty bottle of the cheap red Sav had brought with her.

'Now this is pathetic. We can't even get through a full bottle of wine without blubbing into our glasses.'

The two friends smiled across the table, the glasses were refilled and clinked.

'God this is truly awful stuff.'

Sav looked at the label and sniffed, 'Tomorrow I will find us something decent,' and she threw the empty in the bin, 'Come on, let's get comfy on the sofa.

'Remember Glastonbury?'

'What's brought that up?'

'Oh you know, happier times and all that. We need to think about other stuff to cheer us up.'

'And how could I ever forget Glastonbury...Richard and all that mud?'

'Oh god, that was a weekend...Big Rich...and the mud!'

'The Pogues.'

'And the mud!'

'Echo and the Bunnymen...'

'And the mud! And Big Rich was our saviour!'

'Glastonbury 1985... possibly the wettest mudfest ever?'

Savannah dug deep into the bank of memories.

'I managed to fall on a mudslide and couldn't stop until Big Rich caught me!'

Richard Hastings, soon to be known as Big Rich, through an alcohol and spliff-fuelled weekend, stood like a doorstop as she ground to a halt. He held her aloft, claiming ownership, as a gust of wind blew up her skirt. Shock. Exhilaration. Whatever it was, it created such hilarity between all three they immediately became inseparable for the rest of the weekend. Big Rich proudly escorted them both, one on each arm, to anchor them down amidst the strong winds and relentless rain, ploughing through otherwise impenetrable fields. He took them to their bands of choice, buying the beers to boot. He'd never in his life had so much fun before, or probably since. The beer, the bands, dancing in the mud and endless laughter stayed with them throughout the weekend.

'As I recall you'd wanted to go home by Saturday afternoon.'

'Not until Rich,'

'Not until Rich...wonder what happened to him?'

'No idea but I don't think I have ever experienced anything like it since. How old were we back then?'

'Seventeen? Eighteen? Was it our last year in school? I remember we bunked off on the Friday. No exams that day. We just packed up a two-man tent borrowed from your Dad... it was an ex-WW2 army and a bugger to put up, two sleeping bags and a few measly pounds between us, nothing else...well maybe a couple of tee shirts and a pair of spare pants, and off we went.'

'And by Sunday night we'd lost the lot.'

They never did find the tent they'd tried to put up on the Friday. Richard shared his, which was remarkably roomy and quite stable considering the foul conditions. In their stupor, they slept side by side. 'We were Babes in the Woods...'

They travelled down memory lane until the laughter

turned to tears and they both agreed that no matter what life threw at them they always had Glastonbury.

'Let's do it again.'

'How can I with Bee?'

'We'll take her. There are thousands of kids there every year. You know that.'

'I know but...'

'But nothing.'

'Maybe...'

'We need more fun in our lives my darling.'

'I need you in my life Sav. We were always good for each other weren't we?'

'You said it.'

'I've missed you so much.'

Liv bathed in the memories and the comfort Savannah brought with wine and her company, and for two days put aside the troubles that could wait. Together they sorted the kitchen and cleaned the house. Frances was stable and Simon at least kept her updated. Liv sent flowers and her love and promised to visit when Frances was up to it.

By Wednesday, Savannah went back to her Dad's house to finish what she'd started before leaving for her new job in London, at Plan International. Liv would collect Bee on Thursday with her Dad after work and was cheered on by the thought that they would be back together. It had been a very long week.

Chapter Forty Two

Marsha thought long and hard before making the decision on Wednesday morning. After tea, she told Robert that Debbie was feeling down and needed to talk about something. She did not tell him about the detour she would make first.

'She's not ill, is she? I don't want you bringing anything back to pass on to Bee and Eddie.'

'No, she's not ill Robert. Do you really think I would risk anything like that?'

'Just, be careful.'

Marsha wasn't about to take the conversation further but it was enough to cement her resolve as she picked up her bag and coat.

'I'll take the car if that's ok...won't be too long.'

Robert was left holding the baby and watching over Bee.

On the drive across town, Marsha had not even considered that Liv wouldn't be home, or that she might not be on her own. Neither had she thought much about what she would say until she stood on the doorstep and knocked.

There was no car outside and a single light shone from the

living room. So far so good. She took a deep breath and knocked again, music reached her ears, but no voices.

Liv answered the door in lounge trousers and a hoodie. Her hair was tied back and there was a biro mark on her cheek. Savannah had already gone back to her Dad's house leaving Liv in a slightly less anxious frame of mind, although still greatly worried about Frances. She hadn't called Adam when she understood how much work he had to get through. The hospital had given out the usual stock answer that she was 'as well as could be expected'. That could mean anything, but Liv wasn't a relative and would get no more. Simon's contact was now perfunctory.

Marsha was the last person she expected to see on her doorstep.

'Hello, Liv...I hope you don't mind me coming like this...I would have called but, well it wasn't possible so I've come on the off-chance you were home...which you are, it's not a bad time is it? I can come back another day if it is...really. I'm on my way to see a friend close by and it just seemed like the best opportunity...and I wanted to see you on my own'

Marsha's voice was soft and low, nervous, so unlike Robert's abrasive tone.

'You're on your own? No Robert with you?' Liv looked behind in confirmation.

'No, he's looking after Eddie and Bee.'

Liv wanted to ask if he'd done Bee's packing but that could wait.

'Can I come in for a few minutes? It won't take long I promise.'

'Yes...come in...it's getting cold out there.'

'Thank you.'

Liv lead Marsha to the living room where she was greeted by the chaotic aftermath of the kitchen repairs. In truth, it was an improvement from two days earlier. Marsha marvelled at how Liv and Rob had ever lived together in the same house. Her second thought was one of envy. On the floor, amidst the detritus of daily living, surrounding the space where Liv had been sitting, were sheets of typed pages. Neat sentences disfigured with coloured marks in red and blue, and black pen notes scribbled in the margins. On a low table sat a coffee, long gone cold.

The sofa was a mess of cushions and throws, and a pile of what looked like Bee's books stacked on one side. It thrilled Marsha that it was possible to live like this without disapproval or guilt.

'You're busy...I'm sorry.'

'No, if I'm honest I'm at an impasse and need a break. Have a seat, would you like a coffee?'

Liv pointed to the cold mug.

'No, thank you I won't...'

'Tea?'

'No really, I'm meeting a friend and just wanted to come to tell you something you might want to hear.'

Marsha sat amongst the cushions and colourful throws like a bird in a nest. It was surprisingly comfortable. Liv watched her closely. What could she possibly have to say? Surely it wasn't to do Robert's dirty work and tell her that Bee should be living with them. Marsha had never been involved with that conversation; she'd always left the room when it came up. She'd been tactful, careful; sensitive to the effect their arguments were having on Bee, and kept quiet.

'Is Bee all right? Nothing's happened has it?'

'She's fine honestly. Wrapping Robert around her little finger I should imagine. She wanted to do some baking but I'm not sure his skills go that far...I did promise one day but what with Eddie and...well you know how it is.'

'I know...I also know that my baking skills are dreadfully

wanting. I miss her Marsha. Mum and Dad were asking after her.'

'I know that...and she misses you...all of you...how is your Dad now?'

'He's fine...they're both doing ok...but that's not the reason why you've come to see me is it?'

'No, although I am pleased he's back on his feet.'

'So...what is it? What can I do for you?'

Marsha took a deep breath and looking directly at Liv, prepared to say her piece.

'It's not so much what you can do for me but something I want to do, or rather something I've already done...for you.'

'I presume this involves Bee...'

Liv's tone of voice changed, her words were clipped, her brow turning into a questioning frown.

'It is...but please let me finish...it's nothing bad...not from your point of view anyway. I've done something that might give me grief but it's something I feel strongly about.'

'I'm all ears...tell me what you've done.'

'On Friday I went into town...with Eddie...no choice...and arranged to see Mr Farrow.'

'Farrow? The shark Robert's been seeing?'

'Yes him. He was actually very nice with me, especially when I explained to him how I felt about Robert's plans...'

'Which is?'

'Which is I don't agree with any of it, I never have. Oh, I wavered a bit at one point...Robert can be very forceful...and very persuasive when he wants his own way but...'

'Tell me about it...so what is your view on the custody he's demanding because all it's doing is giving me a lot of grief and upsetting Bee.'

'I know...I do know that Liv and I'm sorry for it. I've seen Bee's little face when Rob's suggested that she might like to live with us. She wants...she needs...her Mummy. I told Mr. Farrow just that.'

'Just what? What exactly did you say to him?'

Liv, warming to the subject that had been giving her sleepless nights and stressful headaches, looked up at Marsha from her position on the floor, straightened her back and folded her arms

'I told Mr Farrow that I wouldn't go along with Robert's plan. It wouldn't happen because I wouldn't let it.'

'That's a lot of wouldn'ts...and what did Robert have to say when you told him?'

'I've been telling him all along that Bee belongs with you... that she's happy in her new home...that she actually likes her new school and doesn't want to go back to her old one. I've spent quite a bit of time with Bee over this past week and she talks to me in a way she can't with her Dad. When she came to stay at the beginning of the half term the poor mite thought she might not be allowed to come back home if the roof couldn't be fixed. She was so upset. Robert refused to see how she felt about it, but I saw it. She was very quiet...not like Bee at all. But he wouldn't listen to me and then when the business of the bullying kicked in he went into overdrive with his plans.'

'Marsha, I don't know what to say.'

'You don't have to say anything...and please don't worry about this. I will sort it. I'll be telling Robert what I've done when I get back later tonight and he'll just have to get over it. But that's my problem, not yours.'

Liv hadn't seen this side of Marsha before and wouldn't have believed she had such a rod of steel running through her. It was impressive and she could see that Marsha might just be more than a match for Robert. Was this what motherhood had done to her? She was certainly more than an ample bosom and maker of cakes and buns.

'Wow, I wasn't expecting this. You had me worried there for a minute. I thought you were going to say...well, I don't know what you were going to say but not this.'

'I'd better get off now...Debbie's going to wonder where I am...she'll be home after her shift. I know I should get back and face Robert, but Debbie's so good for me at times like this, I need to see her first.'

'Debbie? She lives near here?'

'Literally round the corner...Ivy Street...works at the Co-op'

'Debbie?... I know her. The first person I met when we moved here, made us feel very welcome. She's lovely. You go and enjoy the rest of your evening... as much as you can anyway. We all need our friends. Say hi to Debbie for me'

'Small world,' Marsha said but didn't press further. Her mind was still on what she had to do when she got home. She knew it was right but it didn't stop the churning inside at the thought of it. She had agreed with Liv that tomorrow afternoon would be a good time to collect Bee, ready for school on Monday, and promised to have everything ready.

Liv felt a surge of happiness and gratitude for what Marsha had already done and was about to do. Was this really Little-Mousy-Marsha, Marsha-the-Magnificent? How unkind she'd been. How hurtful to someone who had never shown her any harm. Her own relationship with Robert had long been over before Marsha stepped in. And now, here was a woman who should never have been underestimated. Liv decided to have a glass of wine from the half bottle sitting in the fridge and raised it in salute to Marsha. She put on a CD and listened to Astral Weeks, which had never been returned to its case and thought of Adam, and getting Bee back home.

As if on cue, her phone rang. It was Adam again. He missed her. She smiled and made herself comfortable amongst the cushions Marsha had so recently vacated, and gave him the good news.

'And that's exactly as it should be...not that I think there's any way he would get custody at this stage, but I'm pleased you won't have to go through any legal wrangling. It's never cheap, and I'm not just talking money, never nice...for anyone. Bee is a lucky little girl having you as her Mummy.'

'Talking of which...I've been thinking...would you like to meet her? It's time I think. I've told her something about Mummy's new friend, and she really wants to meet you...if you're ok with that if you don't think it's too soon or anything?'

Adam went quiet and Liv rushed back in:

'You don't have to, not yet if you think it can wait...I...'

'No...no I want to really, just thinking about it from Bee's point of view, you know...Robert being her Daddy...then seeing me with her Mummy. Will she find it strange, too much?'

'We won't know until you two meet, will we? And she got used to Marsha well enough'

'Guess that's true...ok then...let's do it. When were you thinking?'

'How about Saturday? Come for tea...with Ryan too. Let's do it.'

'If you're really sure, that's a great idea.'

Chapter Forty Three

Friday was a half-day at work and Liv took the opportunity of visiting Frances before collecting Bee with Arthur. It wasn't easy to hide the shock she experienced by the change in such a short space of time. For the first time since they met, Frances looked all of her ninety-six years. Conversation was slow and stilted although her eyes lit up when she realised it was Liv now sitting at her bedside.

'Oh it's so good to see you Olivia...thank you for coming.'

'My pleasure...Simon not here?'

'Not right now...he'll be back later but...'

Frances struggled for the words.

'But?'

'I don't understand him...he's different.'

'Is Simon bothering you about anything?'

'No...no...the opposite.'

Frances gave up to a fit of coughing making further talk difficult. When it passed, she rested her head back on the pillow and closed her eyes. Liv sat without speaking, holding Frances' hand until she was sure she was asleep, then slipped away.

'You rest now...I'll come back soon I promise'

Liv arrived at Robert's to collect Bee, as planned with Marsha, at the allotted time. Following a lengthy debate, Barbara had agreed that only Arthur should make the journey with her. For once, Arthur had stood firm and Barbara stepped back. Driving up to the house, he couldn't help but experience déjà vu and remembered clearly the cold February morning of four years earlier.

'Was it really only four, Olivia? Seems a whole lifetime ago to me'. Arthur spoke more to himself than his daughter but she knew what he meant.

'It's not the same Dad...we're ok now...come on...Bee will be waiting for us.'

The house was silent. No television, no radio, no noise of domestic activity. Not usual at all. Marsha came to the door carrying a sleepy Eddie. Bee was in her bedroom and there was no sign of Robert. If he heard the knock on the door, he chose to ignore it.

'Come on in both of you...Bee's almost ready. She's just collecting the last of the toys that need to go back home.'

Liv warmed at the words 'back home'. Yes, Bee was coming home, where she belonged. Within seconds, she came running down the stairs in delight at the arrival of Mummy and Grandpa.

'I've been waiting hours and hours...where have you been?'

'BeeBee it's only six o'clock...you've just finished tea and we've come as soon as we can.'

'Grandpa, I've missed you so much.'

Grandpa's face lit up at the reception and the previous memories were soon erased.

'Eh not half as much as I've missed you honey bunch.' and he picked her up for a hug.

Marsha offered tea, which was politely declined and Arthur looked around,

'No Robert?'

'He's in the other room...I'm not sure he's coping too well with all this...I don't know what to say to him any more.'

She turned to Liv.

'He knows I came to see you and I don't think he's forgiven me for that either.'

'I'm so sorry Marsha.'

'I thought we were getting there but he's hardly said a word since he got back from work. Bee's not noticed thank goodness...too busy packing. And she's so excited.'

Liv didn't want to stay any longer than necessary. It wasn't easy. They'd all had the chance to air their views one way or another but the fact remained that Bee was coming home and nothing would change that.

'Why don't you take Bee out to the car, love...I'll bring her things,' Arthur offered.

Liv didn't argue, sensing the unease and Marsha gave Bee a tight hug.

'It's been really lovely having you here Bee...I know it won't be too long before I see you again for a weekend, but I've got something for you to take back.'

Marsha produced a chocolate cake, thick with cream, that she'd baked that morning. Arthur's eyes widened.

'Oo I hope I get a slice of that young Bee.' He was jealous; such delights had been banned for a long time at home.

'I'll save you a piece, Grandad.'

'Right then, let's get this show on the road shall we?'

Liv turned to Marsha before leaving

'Thank you for everything, Marsha...I really mean that.' and held open her arms. She wasn't sure whether the absence of Robert was a good thing or not but was grateful that there would be no confrontation today.

'He'll come round you know...tell him...tell him everything will be fine...'

There was nothing left to say. Liv took the car keys from Arthur and went out to wait with Bee.

'I won't be a minute love.' Arthur stayed with Marsha.

'D'you think it would be all right if I had a quick word with him?' he asked as he nodded towards the room where Robert's silence disturbed him more than any objections. He'd done this before and the thought wasn't lost on him.

'If you think it would help.'

'I'll not be long.'

Arthur tapped on the door and walked in to find Robert slumped in a chair.

'Now then, lad.'

Robert looked up. His eyes were dry but red; he said nothing and looked back outside.

'I had to come and say a few words...don't think I don't understand what you're goin' through. I can tell lad...but it's not the same as last time. We've all moved on...an' you need to move with us. Bee needs to be with our Olivia...you know that. No matter what you think...it's for the best. Don't punish her any more with your plans to keep her here.' Our Olivia's doin' fine too...you've got to see that.'

Robert turned and looked as though he was about to say something, but kept quiet.

'The roof and kitchen's fixed now...and little Bee wants to stay at her new school...she...'

'I only wanted to keep her safe...I wanted to keep her close where I could see her,' he said in a voice broken with emotion.

'I know that Robert...and I do know what this is all about. I might not say much but I've got eyes in me 'ead. I can see what's goin' on...Bee isn't Daniel...she's not a baby any more.

She's a little girl who's as safe as we can make her...all of us...and she needs to be back home. '

Now the tears flowed, 'But I didn't keep Daniel safe did I?'

'Robert...Robert...you've got to stop all this. Daniel dying like that was no one's fault. Not yours and not our Olivia's. You can't be with Bee every second of every day even if she did come and live with you...and forcing her back to her old school changes nothing...all that does is make one unhappy little girl.'

Robert broke down under the weight of all his fears. He knew deep inside how ridiculous he sounded, but it didn't take away the pain of how he felt and what he'd tried to do.

'I'm sorry,' he sobbed.

Marsha came through. The sound of Robert crying was unbearable but in some ways a relief. It had to come.

'I'll leave him with you lass...let him get it all out...you're the one to talk to him now. None of it's easy but he's got a lovely wife like you...I can see that...and a smashing little lad to care for...that's what's important now. I'll see meself out...you stay put with Robert. He's going to need you now but I think...I hope anyway...he'll come to terms with it all.'

'Thank you, Arthur, you talk good sense.'

Arthur snorted,

'Don't know about that...try telling Barbs and she'd have other things to say on the subject.'

'I'm pleased you came though.'

'Right...well...I'll be off...you take care.'

Arthur found Liv and Bee belted up in the car, anxious to be going.

'I hope it wasn't too much for you today Dad but I was glad you came with me. I couldn't face it on my own...didn't know how Robert was going to react even though Marsha said it would be ok, but then when he wouldn't come out I didn't know what to think.'

'That's all right love...brought back some painful memories though and I think that was running through his head.'

'You saw Robert? What did you say to him?'

'Well...he was in a bit of a state...been crying I could see that. All his plans for Bee coming to nothing...but I knew there was something else at the bottom of it.'

'He blames me for what happened to Daniel and he's never got over it. He doesn't think I'm fit to look after Bee and wanted her...'

'No...no love you're wrong there. He blames himself. That's the problem. Thinks the only way to keep her safe is if she's close to him...wants to protect her the way he couldn't protect Daniel.'

'What? But he's always made me feel the guilty one...I thought that...'

'Oh love...it's time you both put the guilt thing to bed...'

'Daniel's never far from my thoughts.'

'And ours love. I think you've come to terms with it but Robert's not there yet. He's let it fester inside him...it's been eatin' at him all these years. Poor Marsha's got her work cut out but she's a strong lass that one. She'll work it out with him...hope so anyway for all their sakes. Mebbe today's the day he'll start to let go.'

'Why are you whispering Mummy? Who's Daniel?'

Barbara was waiting impatiently at Liv's and as soon as she saw the car pull up, was at the front door to greet three happy, smiling faces coming up the path.

Bee fell into Grandma's open arms.

'I'm back grandma!'

'I can see that love...welcome home...did you have a good time at your Dad and Marsha's?'

'Eddie poked me in the eye...I know he didn't mean it but it hurt.'

'The little monkey.'

It didn't take Bee long to rush up to her bedroom, dragging a bag behind her. Wabbit was the first to be unpacked, lovingly placed on top of the bed, in exactly the same spot he usually lived.

'She's happy enough. Everything all right love?'

'Everything's fine Mum...we have Bee back home.'

Arthur brought in the rest of Bee's things, nodding and smiling at Barbara.

'That's all I need to know...we won't stay long Arthur...and you must be tired Olivia after all that running around...what with Frances in hospital on top of all this. How is she by the way?'

'Not brilliant, she's looking very frail and desperate to go home but I can't see that happening. Surprisingly Simon's still around. I missed him today thankfully. No Sarah though.'

'There's not much to be done now I should imagine...it's all very sad...and what are you up to tomorrow?'

Liv came clean and said that she'd invited Adam and Ryan over for Saturday tea to meet Bee.

'Oh...that's a good idea...and what are you doing for tea then?'

'Thought I'd give roast beef a go.'

'Roast beef? You do remember the last time you cooked a roast?'

Barbara remembered it very well and it hadn't been a success.

Saturday afternoon arrived and with it a rich, tempting aroma of roasting beef snaked its way to the living room every time the oven door opened. It was more than enough to ensure a pause in conversation when four faces lifted simultaneously in expectation. Arthur and Adam sat on the sofa clutching bottles of beer, talking as though they'd known each other for years, and Bee and Ryan were laid on the floor finishing a jigsaw. Ryan had also promised to show her how to play the old Gameboy he'd brought over in readiness of utter boredom. Liv came through after setting the table and being shooed out of the way by her Mother who'd taken complete charge of the kitchen. It took another fifteen minutes before the flushed, ruddy face of Barbara put in an appearance.

'That smells grand Barbs...we're all starving.'

'You're always starving...it won't be long now.'

'Have we got Yorkshires?'

'With three hungry men to feed, I had to do something with a bit of substance, so what do you think?'

There was a general assent and high expectation of Barbara's famous Yorkshire puddings. She liked nothing more than to feed a hungry family who would do justice to her cooking and beamed at the three men looking up at her.

'There's raspberry pie and ice cream for afters.'

'Blimey, that's a rare treat nowadays.'

'Don't think you'll be getting it too often, doctor said we had to watch your waistline remember?'

'How can I forget with you breathing down me neck.'

The arrival of Adam and Ryan had been welcomed by all of them and Barbara glowed at the sight of yet more flowers and wine.

'You don't have to do this every time I cook you a meal you know...I've still got some left from last time.'

'It's my pleasure Mrs...

'Barbara, love...it's Barbara.'

'Barbara.'

. . .

Sated and content, Adam and Ryan were the last to leave after doing the roast dinner the justice Barbara welcomed.

'That was amazing...a real family roast dinner. I've not had a meal like that in a long time...and your parents are the best. I wish mine were still around. What did you think of that beef Ryan?'

Ryan grunted his thanks; second helpings of the pie had given Barbara everything she needed to know on how satisfied he was, 'Such a nice young man.'

'I'm glad you came, Ryan...I think Bee enjoyed you teaching her how to play on the Gameboy...not sure how much she took it in but I appreciated it anyway...I haven't a clue.'

Ryan flushed and the colour in his face deepened when she and Bee gave him a hug before they left. The door closed once they'd been waved off, leaving Liv and Bee alone in a quiet house.

'Come here you...Mummy needs a cuddle.'

They sat together on the sofa, Liv trying to bring Adam into the conversation and Bee trying to work out if she could have a Game Boy for Christmas, as it was too long to wait for her next birthday in September. The clock showed seven pm:

'Right, then Bee...your bath time I think.'

'Aw Mummy!'

Chapter Forty Four

After several days in hospital, Frances rallied enough to be coherent and profess that she never felt better, and she was reluctantly discharged. Despite the diagnosis, the prognosis for the future and the recommendation of the doctor, she chose to make her own decisions. Even if she looked and felt much better than when she'd arrived, they all knew that her condition was not likely to improve. Simon prepared to take her home on the understanding that a community nurse would come every day to check her medication and that he would ensure that she was never left alone. So far, Liv had only been able to speak to her on the phone when the needs of Bee had taken over her days, but promised to help out when she could.

'Please don't tell me I'm wrong Olivia. I simply cannot stay here...I get no sleep...no rest at all...the noise...you wouldn't believe it,' and with as much of a laugh as she could muster, '...and no sherry!' even though that was the very last thing she craved.

'I do understand Frances...and I'll be able to see you more

at home...I'm there for you whenever you need me...I promise...with sherry too!'

'That is where I want to end my days Olivia...at home...in my own bed. I know I don't have long but I can't stay in here a minute longer...and I will try not to be too much of a burden. Help is being arranged for me...Simon is taking care of that.'

'Frances you'll never be a burden.'

Simon had other burdens to contend with and guilt has already set in when the needs of his Mother overtook the demands of his wife. Pulled between Sarah's insistence that he return to deal with the work that was piling up and this new found, unaccustomed responsibility, he had already made up his mind.

'Simon, your Mother will outlive us all...she could easily go on for months...may be years knowing her...she's strong as an ox.'

Sarah was not happy with the situation and over repeated telephone calls, pushed for other solutions,

'Your Mother simply has to go into a home...you know that...she needs 24-hour care and I don't think you can do that when you can hardly look after yourself darling.'

Simon said little but knew that would never happen despite the list of residences she had already made enquiries about. He returned to the hospital on Tuesday afternoon and brought his Mother back to the comfort and familiarity of home.

The relief it brought to Frances reflected in her whole demeanour, from the sparkle in her eyes to the relaxation of her shoulders. The move tired her body, but the spirit was revived and Liv arranged to visit the next morning when Bee was at school.

The flowers she took with her brightened up a bedside

table that was otherwise taken up by an array of drugs with unpronounceable names. A beautiful pink boudoir chair with a deep-buttoned back was placed next to the bed, where Liv could sit in comfort and keep Frances company for as long as needed, or until it was time to collect Bee. Simon had gone back home to collect a few more clothes and placate an irritated Sarah, but said he would be back after tea.

'Olivia it's so good to see you here darling girl...I think tomorrow, after a good night's, rest I may even be able to get up for a little while...I feel so much better being home.'

'Frances, you look better.'

And it was true; the euphoria of leaving hospital and coming home had worked wonders, but in reality, the exertion had taken it out of Frances. Her flushed face merely masked the lie that she was improving.

'Promise me you'll do no such thing when you're on your own,' Liv was horrified at the thought of another fall.

'Don't worry about me...this won't be for long...now tell me how are things progressing next door? Tell me all.'

'It's all going well...really well...Bee's home, and Adam and his son Ryan came over for a roast dinner on Saturday, cooked by my mother...'

'Oh, how lovely for you my dear. All there together.'

'I wish you could have joined us.'

'Maybe one day...but for now I'm so glad that you are here...tell me are you in a hurry or can you spare a little time?'

'I'm in no hurry this afternoon, it's my day off today and Bee is at school...so I'm all yours...tell me what you need.'

'Oh no...I don't need anything, I just wanted to finish the last part of my story, while I can. I never did get the chance earlier. Let's have some tea and we'll both get comfortable.'

'No sherry?'

'A little early...even for us! And not a good mix with the medication apparently.'

'Tea it is then.'

It was good to see Frances more alert, more the old self she had been before her collapse, but her face was showing the ravages of illness and age. Lines had deepened and her hair looked thinner, hanging loose about her shoulders and not pinned up as usual. The neatness had gone. With no trace of make up her pale lips and cheeks reflected the trauma of the past few days and her body looked lost in the large bed.

Liv brought tea.

'Ah just as I like it...thank you...I'm not sure what they gave us in that hospital but...well never mind...the nurses were very kind...are you comfortable on that chair?'

'Perfectly, but you have to tell me when you start to feel tired.'

Frances laid her head back on the plumped pillows and closed her eyes.

'I do want to finish my story Olivia...while there is still time...'

'I'm listening...there's no rush.'

'Thank you Olivia, but you know why I must do it don't you...why you must be the one to hear it?'

'I know it was very special to you and you've not told anyone else...'

'Partly yes, but also I want you to write it...I would like to leave something behind that was just me...the part of me that wasn't simply an addition to someone else's life...I don't want to be the old lady who just happened to live for ninety-six years with nothing left to show for it... you can understand that can't you? That day in Paris was the one that defined the rest of my life...'

Her voice lowered to barely a whisper,

'...and the tragedy of it still lives with me...I want to put it to rest before I go.'

Liv sat perplexed at the strength of the emotion and

waited as Frances composed herself to continue, helped by a cocktail of drugs that masked the pain.

'Now, where was I?'

'You'd realised who it was standing behind you at the exhibition.'

Frances took a little while to transport herself to the moment and the impact it made.

'Yes...I'd realised very quickly that we were alone...it was as if by some prior signal, the remaining organisers had vanished...perhaps for lunch... I don't know. He had taken me into the office and brought a glass of water. Of course, I had no idea of what to say to him; how to behave in such circumstances...I had no great wit or superior knowledge to fall back on...I was just a young woman delivering a painting. He was so far removed from my world that I sat there in a state of immobility...apart from shaking dreadfully.

I felt sure that he would want rid of me quickly...but no... this great man...Picasso...was kindness itself to the shy young woman who struggled to utter a single word. I remember exactly what he spoke of and how he put me at my ease. My tongue did eventually loosen; I found my voice and my French returned sufficiently to speak. He asked about my life and where I was from and was genuinely interested, or at least he seemed to be. He then gestured to another small table at the back of the office where several plates of food had been set. Bread...cheese...fruits...it was his lunch and he invited me to share it when I confessed that I hadn't yet eaten and had no other plans.

'Then we will share this. Together. You will eat,' he said.

He walked past me, close, and I could smell him as clearly as I could see; a heady mix of cigarettes and paint, and it washed over me in waves. It wasn't unpleasant. It emphasised the man and his overwhelming presence in this small room. We sat close and I *was* overwhelmed...I was a little girl again... shy, nervous, trying to make intelligent conversation, but losing the words between my head and my mouth. He was so kind to me though. I have gone over that afternoon so often since, what I could have done or said differently, but...'

Liv was as absorbed in the listening as Frances was in the telling. Time stood still in that small bedroom and the outside world disappeared.

'His features were strong...commanding my attention, with dark eyes that compelled me to look. I see him still...it doesn't leave.'

Frances paused, her voice weak from the strain of talking. Her words faltered.

'You really should rest now.'

'No...I'm all right...let me catch my breath...a few moments more and I will finish.'

Liv poured Frances a glass of water. It refreshed her enough to go on but Liv had to strain to hear.

'The invitation to eat wasn't so much an offer as an order. So I ate what I could. How could I refuse him, or the growing demands from my stomach?

He ate like a labourer in the field...one for whom the crops had been gathered and now there was a great hunger to satisfy. I was but a field mouse picking at the grain and the crumbs that fell below. He finished with a large red apple, which he cut in two, presenting the bigger piece to me. It was not peeled and the contrast between the creamy flesh and the skin was pronounced. 'Try this,' he said, and so I did. His half was demolished in two or three bites after which he wiped the juice from his mouth with the back of his hand. The apple was crisp and sweet, the most delicious apple that I have ever tasted.

When we had finished, he pushed the remains of food and the plates to one side and instructed me to sit still. A sheet of paper and pencils were brought out from a drawer in the table. I dare not breathe, let alone move, but I still trembled and hoped he would not notice.

'Be still...look outside,' he instructed, so I turned my head to the window where I could see birds flying in and out of the trees beyond. His strong hands took hold of my face, moving it up and at an angle. Without looking at him, his eyes burned into my face.

'I want the light to catch you...there...perfect.'

He sat back down. 'Don't talk...sit and look outside.'

Keeping silent was the easy part. In the stillness of that room, and from the corner of my eye, I caught the remains of our lunch and a rumpled bed in the corner. A faint scratch of pencil on paper and the pounding of my heart were the only sounds. My memory eludes me now, although I do recall the perfume of the strawberries left on my plate. It mingled with the smoke from a cigarette hanging from the corner of his mouth; gently blowing on a draft of warm air.

He had closed the door against intrusion. 'We will not be disturbed in here.' Time had stopped and this world was all I wanted; the scratch of a pencil; and his undivided attention; I lost myself in that room; my life stopped... it was Paris, Picasso and me.'

Frances' eyes closed. Liv was mesmerised.

'Frances...that was...is...incredible...'

Her eyes re-opened.

'Of course, we were eventually disturbed when the Gallery staff returned and there were repeated knocks on the door... voices telling him he was urgently wanted elsewhere.

And so he took his leave of me...gently touching my cheek and thanking me for such a beautiful afternoon. I sat there for some time, unable to move. The bed was hard. I hadn't noticed until that moment. In the distance, someone was calling my name. My driver was looking for me. He was discrete enough to let me ready myself sufficiently to leave and I was guided to the car, back to the hotel…back to George.

'And the sketch?'

'Oh, he gave that to me…I didn't realise it at the time but he'd put it in between the documents I was to take with me.'

'And George? You showed it to George?'

'Oh no…George never knew…when I was back at the d'Orsay, I took the loan documents out of the envelope to show him, by then George was getting back to his usual demanding self, and I found it. It was only a small sketch and I managed to hide it amongst my personal effects…somewhere I knew George would not look. If George had known about it, he would have sold it I imagine…and I wasn't going to take that risk.'

'I don't know what to say Frances…you've lived with that day for how many years…and told no other person… no one apart from me?'

'I don't have long Olivia…it is my gift to you. I had hoped to tell Hermione…it would have been important to her but…'

Chapter Forty Five

The timetable of care arranged for Frances was short lived. Whatever strength she had left in her body drained following the afternoon with Liv. There was no more left. Her breathing was shallow and she slept more than she was awake.

Simon had managed to extricate himself from work commitments, and Sarah's demands, and moved into the bedroom so recently vacated by Liv. Day by day the Frances Fenton Liv had come to know and love faded until communication became no more than a bare acknowledgement of her presence.

Simon took on the role of dutiful son and was even grateful for the time spent alone with his Mother. Although he couldn't be certain she could hear, he made a peace of sorts, tried to assuage the guilt of years gone by. But when Simon lay in bed at night it came back at him with unbearable intensity. He was the last one left in the long line of Fentons and when his Mother died, he would stand alone.

Liv came daily, snatching moments when time allowed. Simon could not mistake the look of delight in his mother's eyes, in times of lucidity, a look never shown to him. 'And who can blame you, Mother?' Whatever regrets he might have felt were kept within the confines of the confessional of his Mother's bedroom.

Liv, aware of a transformation that she chose to accept as genuine, had the good grace to remain apart. Maybe it was too little too late, but this was his Mother and whatever small effort of atonement he made deserved to be heard. It showed in his unshaven face; in the dark circles beneath his eyes; his uncombed hair and the creased clothing that was unchanged from the day before.

On the evening of Thursday 5th November, Frances Fenton quietly slipped away at two minutes after nine.

To the crack and whizz of fireworks in an illuminated sky, Simon held her hand. He sat without moving for an hour, motionless and numb. He wouldn't cry and only moved when stiffness and tiredness took over. He called the hospital and then Liv, insisting that there was nothing she could do that night.

Savannah had returned from London and sat with Liv talking until the small hours.

'Should I cancel the bonfire party on Saturday Sav? I'm not sure I feel up to it.'

'No way, we'll celebrate the old lady's life...and I'm pretty sure she would want you to go ahead with it. Bee is so excited...show the little one that we celebrate the lives of the ones we've loved not mourn them.'

'You're right I know...I'm just not certain my heart will be in it.'

'Trust me it will...and think of all that food your mother's planning to bring! The butcher's planning a week in the Barbados on the profit.'

'Sav, what would I do without you?'

Liv reached out for Savannah's hand and gave it a squeeze before calling Adam. She told him she was fine and not to come over; there was no more to be done and she wasn't on her own.

'Sav persuaded me that we should go ahead with the bonfire party, use it as a time to celebrate Frances' life.'

'Frances was a beautiful lady who deserves to be remembered, Liv.'

'Oh, she will be...'

Liv was persuaded to go to bed, although there was little sleep to be had that night. But tomorrow was still a working day for her, and a school day for Bee, and Sav would make herself useful.

The next morning before work, Adam called round. Sav had already left with Bee for school, both chatting and giggling as they went.

'Have a coffee with me and I'll drive you to work'

'Thank you...although I should go and see Simon first... ask if there's anything I can do to help...he said not but I want to offer.'

'That's ok, I'm in no hurry today.'

'I really will miss her you know...'

'I know...I guess the next big hurdle is to get through the funeral.'

'It'll be hard...I keep thinking about the last time I saw her...we'd grown so close...she was almost like a second mother to me...although I'm not sure that I fancy Simon as a brother... or even worse sister-in-law to that wife of his.'

Liv remembered the first time she'd met Simon, but it was tempered with a different man she'd seen lately.

'It's hard to believe that I've only known Frances for what...six months? She was a special person...I feel as though she'd always been there, waiting for me. Strange that.'

'When I watched you both together, I could see the connection...I can imagine her looking over you right now.'

'I'd like to think so...and I will keep her memory alive one way or another'.

'Right...you go see Simon and I'll be with you in a few minutes.'

Sarah had not demurred when Simon told her it would take some time to sort the paperwork, make arrangements for the funeral and prepare the house to sell. Her sympathy was at best perfunctory, but her response to the practical side of proceedings rose above sentiment.

She did not trust Simon to handle the practicalities and turned up that night, a striking figure in a rich woollen coat, fur-trimmed hat and long leather boots. Easing her way out of the car, she carried no more than a handbag and document case into the house. Sarah arrived with instructions, neatly typed, on all that Simon would need to do, from reporting the death; to informing the bank and utilities; to organising visits from three estate agents. The instructions had been prepared well in advance of the need to use them.

Straight-backed and tall, she could have walked straight from a window display in Harrods. A long forefinger extended from a fine leather-clad hand and rang the doorbell. Her black cashmere scarf was pulled closely around her neck in the chill of the autumn air.

Sarah entered the house that Frances had bought after turning down Simon's offer of her moving in with him when George died. He knew his proposal of marriage would have been turned down too if it had meant Sarah moving in with his Mother.

'What on earth possessed your Mother to move here?' she asked, not for the first time.

'Father left her with debts. She had little choice. He backed the wrong horses and Mother paid the price. '

Frances had snorted with derision at the thought of living with Simon; she had no intention of living with the son who was a constant reminder of the husband she'd lost.

A half-drunk scotch with melting ice sat on a table in the living room; it wasn't Simon's first and wouldn't be his last that night. He greeted Sarah with a barely-there kiss on the cheek and after a few words went to her car to retrieve the Louis Vuitton suitcase and black dress carrier.

'Can you hang that somewhere darling before you make me one of those please...it's been a nightmare day...nearly didn't make it...but here I am. Couldn't leave you to sort this on your own now could I?'

Her first words as he'd walked back into the warmth of the house left him in no doubt as to who would be in charge from now on. Divested of coat, scarf, hat and gloves, all of which lay in a heap upon the sofa, she sat back in his mother's chair and crossed silk-encased legs to wait for her drink.

Whilst he was out of the room, Sarah's eyes darted around the walls and floor, taking in the remaining paintings; the fine furniture; and a very appealing rug that had caught her attention. Age and provenance were quickly assessed. Sarah had picked up something of the business during the years spent with George and Simon. She was a quick learner and a good judge; in many ways better than her husband; and certainly better than Simon when it came to working around client sensibilities, or rather their susceptibilities.

Simon returned to find Sarah standing by the window.

'I've hung your dress in our room'.

'Thank you, darling.'

She took an approving sip of the scotch and gave a nod towards the rug.

'Looks Afghan...beautiful'.

Inwardly, she pictured the rug in their own house. It was a particular shade of red that would perfectly complement the new sofa she'd bought the previous month.

'My Mother always had excellent taste'.

'I'm sure she did, darling...I'm sure she did...and how are you getting on with preparations here...you have a date in mind for the funeral I presume?'

'The funeral people can do Wednesday 11th at 2 o'clock.'

'That soon...good...and what about the will?'

'I found a copy here, done through Jarrett's...most of it comes to me of course...just a few items and small bequests to see to.'

'Of course...so that woman next door hasn't managed to queer the pitch for you?'

'Olivia...she's called Olivia, Olivia Smithson. She's actually really nice...not what I, not what we...thought. She was genuinely upset when Mother died...was really good with her during her illness. She's offered to help if we need anything.'

'I bet she did...and you told her thank you, but no thank you...you hear about people like her, befriending an old dear who obviously has a bit of money and they hope to inveigle their way into a new will.'

'I don't think she's like that.'

'They're all like that Simon, don't be so naïve!'

Chapter Forty Six

The day of the fireworks and barbecue arrived with a promising forecast. While Savannah was occupying Bee, Barbara took control of the kitchen. Liv, once surplus to need, took a few minutes out of the way of the crowd of helpers. Grateful that the weather was no longer a dominating factor in her life, that the roof was sound and dry, and the kitchen fully restored, her mind was occupied with Frances. She was still trying to process her loss.

Support had come from all quarters when family and friends understood what she had meant; even Debbie at the Co-op reached out, bringing sympathy along with the crisps and nuts at her invite to the barbecue. Liv looked out of the window and marvelled at her change of fortune, but the force of grief would not relent.

'Hey, what are you doing on your own?'

'Adam...just needed a few minutes.'

Words of comfort had all been said and he hoped his arms around her was enough. They stood alone and still until it was time to get back to the guests.

'Come on...this party is supposed to be a time of celebration so let's do it. Celebrate the new roof, good friends and the life of Frances Fenton. Guy Fawkes has nothing to do with this bonfire night.'

'I know.'

'Barbara's got the kitchen under control...what that Mary Poppins bag of hers does not contain wouldn't be worth having...and Arthur's trying to sneak another beer.'

'No change there then.'

'Come on, let's get it started...everyone's here now...can't have the amazing hostess without a glass in her hand.'

At the bottom of the garden, Ryan poked at the bonfire Adam had assembled the day before. The collection of planks and broken wood was old but thankfully tinder-dry. Marcus had also brought wood from his own yard, stockpiled over several years in the belief that it might come in useful one day. 'Well now it can be put to good use,' Gemma informed him the day they'd received their invite, 'and you can put up that bigger washing line you've been promising me in its place.'

The bonfire stood well apart from the fireworks and food, which suited Ryan. At his vantage point he could admire the work he and Luke had put in on the garden, even though weeds were growing back at an alarming rate. Who knew they would come back so quickly? Gardening was a perplexing business compared to handling a bonfire.

He stood deep in thought as sparks rose and flew into the darkening sky, disappearing like miniature shooting stars. As the fire caught, his face burned in the fierce heat, but he was reluctant to move when he felt the cold at his back. It was a still night, good for fires and fireworks.

'Thank you for helping out Ryan.'

Liv, wrapped in a thick coat and sheepskin gloves was surprised to see him on his own and offered a can of coke.

'No Luke with you?'

Ryan shifted from foot to foot and poked at the fire.

'Nah...Johno's got a new game on his Play Station and Luke reckons he's in with a chance of beating his score tonight.'

'Not for you then?'

'Not for me...didn't want to miss fireworks and a barbecue.'

Liv wasn't entirely convinced and sure that Adam might have had something to do with it, but Ryan didn't seem to have an issue with being there.

'Good for you...food'll be ready soon if you're hungry'

He threw a fresh piece of wood on to the fire and sparks flew in all directions making them both jump back.

'Watch yourself with that wood, it's like a bag of fireworks all on its own.'

'I will... and thanks for the drink'

Ryan wiggled the can in her direction.

At the other side of town, Luke was enjoying a different celebration, but it had nothing to do with a Play Station or bonfire. 'You don't know what you're missin' Ry...can't believe you actually prefer goin' to a poxy bonfire with your Dad...you're crazy man' he'd spat out in contempt.

As Ryan stood over the fire with his coke, Luke lay on the floor of the lock up with an inane grin and his fifth lager. Music thumped from a ghetto blaster one of the boys had brought in and three young girls moved provocatively to the loud beat of 'Rockafeller Skank'. The following hours would see them all high on the contents of the little packets Johno had procured from his supplier at the Park. 'Hey this is good stuff...time to party.' The volume grew with the numbers who turned up, until ten past twelve when the police, alerted by neighbours weary of the same scene that played out night after night, loaded them into a waiting van. Sergeant Andy Draper was on duty and would not finish when he should. His wife was not happy and by the night's end she would be another step closer to giving him the promised ultimatum.

Marcus had accepted Luke's excuses for not coming to the party; he tried to understand the pull of friends over family, but puzzled over why Ryan wasn't with him. He was disappointed but tried not to let it get to him when to argue would rake up all the usual resentments; and he'd promised Gemma he would step back and give Luke space to work things out for himself. Marcus wasn't sure about how that would succeed but in this instance gave her the benefit of the doubt. Gemma and Rachael were having fun, so he would too and caught Liv coming back from the bonfire.

'Great party Liv...Rachael's having a ball...thought she'd missed out this year.'

'It's my thank you but don't expect it every year will you?'

'Oh I don't know...you do it so well.'

'Come and get another beer'

'Might just do that...Gem's driving tonight.'

Adam was in charge of drinks keeping everyone topped up, and Barbara and Arthur presided over the food:

'Them sausages are burning Arthur...they want turning... is it time to put the burgers on...is that chicken properly cooked? I don't want food poisoning on our hands.'

'Barbs you just see to the buns and the salad. I've done enough barbecues in my time to know what I'm doin' and we're all still living to tell the tale.'

'Mm...there's always a first.'

With a wink and a tap on the nose, Adam swapped Arthur's empty bottle with a full one when Barbara's back was turned. Satisfied that the food was cooked to her liking, she accepted the offer of a drink, 'just a small glass of white please Adam,' and Adam left them to it before going back to Liv.

'I love your Mum and Dad...we should hire them out as a double act.'

Liv looked across at her parents, relieved that the health crisis had passed and all was well once again in the Renfold household.

'Not a bad idea...then maybe I could afford a permanent gardener.'

'You mean you don't trust me and Ryan?'

'You're not here enough...and besides I'm not sure I could afford your rates.'

'That's easily remedied.'

'What is? You not being here enough or your rates?'

'I'm sure we could work something out...'

Adam pulled her towards him and kissed her full on the mouth, prompting a response she'd not quite intended.

'Hey...you don't have any brothers do you?' Savannah appeared from the house. Adam winked, 'None that I know of...sorry Sav.'

He went back to Ryan leaving a flushed Liv and Savannah with a wide grin. Savannah had connected with Adam in a way never managed with Robert.

'He brings out the best in you Liv...you're a different person from the one who married Rob.'

'I know...but it's still scary...making a commitment after all this time...I...'

'Woa...let me stop you there...life is scary. We both know that but we're here and right now it's good...and we have a party!'

'I wish you didn't have to go back to London'

'Don't worry I'll be back soon enough...checking up on Dad...and you...but I see my work here is done...for now anyway,' and she promptly downed the glass of decent red she'd brought earlier.

They sauntered over to the barbecue arm in arm.

'What's got into your Dad?'

Arthur was waving his arms in the air, eyes streaming from the acrid smoke of a sausage that had slipped through the grill before Patrick could retrieve it. Barbara was removing cling wrap from plates and fussing about whether there would be enough bread.

The sky had darkened sufficiently to do the fireworks justice and by an unspoken agreement, Robert took charge of the small display. With due safety and distance requirements, the fifteen-minute event passed without incident. Firecrackers and rockets lit the sky with a brief but dazzling blaze, prompting a collective cry of amazement until the pungent aroma of sausages, chicken and burgers beckoned.

A pasting table, laden with salads and bread, pickles and coleslaw, sat next to a second where Barbara's sherry trifle was displayed alongside a pile of muffins baked by Marsha.

'Come on Liv, let's eat.'

'Won't be a minute Sav.'

She went over to Robert and Marsha, where Eddie sat contentedly in his pushchair. They stood away from the rest of the group.

'Thanks for doing the fireworks Robert but come and get some food you two...there's a lot to get through...Mum's feeding the five thousand again.'

Her words reached only Marsha; Robert was keeping a hawkish eye on Bee waving a sparkler. Liv glanced in the same direction.

'Don't worry Robert, she's quite safe...she's having a great time with Rachael.'

'It doesn't hurt to keep a close watch' he replied tersely.

'There's plenty of us around for that...'

Marsha cut in before anything could escalate further,

'Thank you for inviting us Liv...it's a great night for it.'

Liv took the cue and turned her back on Robert.

'My pleasure...and I was really pleased Debbie could come after her shift finished. I can't believe that she's your best friend from school. How amazing is that?'

They both looked across at Debbie chatting animatedly to Patrick in the queue for food.

'I'm glad you've met her...we grew up together...friends since we were five.'

Liv smiled, warmed by having drunk three glasses of wine and she raised a re-filled glass to Marsha.

'To good friends.'

'To good friends.'

'Now come and eat...please?'

Touched with a twinge of envy when his own friends had slipped away over the years, Robert started pushing the now crying Eddie across the lawn.

'I know what Eddie needs...a sausage!'

Robert looked at Marsha like she was speaking a foreign language but she was becoming adept at steering away from the triggers of depression when she saw them appear. A look; the distant gaze; incomprehensible demands frequently washed over in waves. The ever-present strain of anxiety and anger were clouds that still needed to be cleared. But they wouldn't clear until he faced up to what happened to Daniel.

On a good day, he would marvel at the strength his wife had shown when Bee left the house to go back home, refusing to let him go under. In his heart, he wanted to change, be a better person for all their sakes, but today wasn't a good day; he wasn't in a party mood and struggled. When Debbie returned, Marsha smiled with relief and they steered Robert towards the food.

Adam and Ryan stood at the blazing fire finishing plates of sausage and chicken while Bee and Rachael squealed around them in delight with yet more sparklers.

'Right, come on, let's get some more food Ryan...the fire's fine on its own.'

Adam chose to ignore the can of beer that had replaced the coke at his son's feet and didn't ask who'd given it. He was hardly going to drink much when his Dad was around and it was preferable to him being wherever Luke was that night. It had given Adam as much pleasure as a surprise when Ryan said that he would come to the bonfire party rather than go with Luke to a Play Station gathering at Si's house. He'd never been keen on Si; whenever he was involved in anything, trouble always followed. Adam naively liked to believe that there was still something of the boy in Ryan amongst the teenage angst and anger, and was happy to have him in sight. What Adam didn't know yet was the appearance of Davina in Ryan's world; the skinny girl in his class who had started to develop attributes that caught Ryan's eye and who made it obvious that she noticed him too.

'Come on then old man, let's eat.'

'Less of the old if you don't mind.'

For tonight, with not much else on offer, Ryan made the most of the evening. Enjoying it might be a stretch, but he wasn't miserable about it either. It made his Dad happy. He even held a conversation or two when it was called for and complimented Arthur when he asked if the barbecue was to his liking, 'Fine thanks Mr Renfold, I like my sausages dark.' Arthur gave him a faux clip around the ear, artfully dodged, while Barbara offered more potato salad. 'What a nice boy your lad is Adam' she would say once again. Ryan thought Barbara and Arthur ok; they made him laugh, although he made sure that he took charge of toasting the marshmallows later.

Sausages, burgers and chicken legs were piled up on platters in various stages of incineration, but in the collective of waiting hunger, most were eaten, and Ryan tucked in with relish.

As the evening drew to a close, the wind changed direction and the air was thick with smoke. A lingering odour of sulphur mingled with burnt sausage caused an exodus towards the house. Marshmallows on singed wooden skewers were distributed and soon the dying embers of the fire signalled time to leave.

Liv took the opportunity to thank everyone for the help they'd given her over the past few weeks and again raised a glass in salute.

'I would also like to remember my beautiful friend and neighbour, Frances Fenton, who died recently...may she never be forgotten.'

Adam put his arm around her waist and gently squeezed amidst general agreement.

Robert and Marsha were the first to leave, with Eddie now fast asleep,

'It's way past his bedtime Marsh, we should get going'.

Liv went with them to the gate.

'Good to see you...take care.'

'You too', Marsha answered and gave her a hug, whispering, 'We're getting there...and thank you for inviting Debbie.'

'Bless her, she's helping Mum now with the clearing.'

'I know...I've said 'bye.'

Liv kissed her on the cheek and Robert, hanging back gave thanks of sorts, 'It was a good night...Bee was happy.'

Barbara took charge outside; producing rubbish bags and

cloths to wipe down the tables, while Liv, Adam and Savannah set to on the washing up. Arthur was dispatched to the living room after putting Bee to bed and reading her a story, 'You'll only get in the way Arthur, go sit down till I'm ready to go.'

At the end of the evening, Liv and Adam sat enjoying a few quiet moments alone. Savannah had gone for a shower and an early night, and Ryan persuaded Marcus to give him a lift home with a promise from his Dad that he wouldn't be too far behind.

'Just one other person missing today...apart from Frances...the one who first pulled me out of that black hole I'd dug for myself.'

'Here's to Dom...wherever he is at this moment and whatever he's doing.'

'To Dom.'

Adam sniffed and screwed up his nose.

'Do I smell as bad as you?'

'Mm, it's not Chanel No. 5 that's coming over.'

'We could take a shower...what do you think?'

'I think there's nothing I would like more but you have a son waiting for you and I have a guest sleeping next door to the bathroom'

'Pity...I could have washed your hair and scrubbed your back.'

'Is that all you had in mind?'

'And now you'll never know now, will you?'

Adam moved in closer and turned his body to hers. The kiss was long and his tongue met Liv's with an urgency and longing built up over the evening. They rolled to the floor where he met with little resistance.

Giggling until the heat of their bodies cooled in the nighttime air, Liv shivered

'Heating's gone off.'

Adam pulled the throw from the sofa and wrapped it around them both, rubbing her arms as he held her close.

'I wish I was staying tonight,'

'I know...my bed will be cold,'

'I could come and warm it first.'

She laughed, 'And then you would never leave...come on before I let you.'

Chapter Forty Seven

Liv, Adam, Barbara and Arthur sat two rows behind Simon and Sarah in the church; all had agreed that Bee would be better left with Robert and Marsha rather than come to the funeral.

The church was cold and the little heating it offered was ineffectual. It had long outlived a full attendance and today was no different; Frances' funeral was sparsely attended and took up very few pews. Most of her friends, family and acquaintances had long since died, and of those left, the majority were too infirm to make the journey. Of the few relatives that made up the other dozen figures present, Liv had never seen or heard of them apart from Simon and Sarah. What should have been an intimate and moving occasion moved into the realm of merely sad.

Liv had only spoken to Simon a couple of times since Frances had died, the last time on the Sunday following the barbecue. Sarah had been with him, keeping her at arms length and doing most of the talking. She was polite enough, but the message was clear, 'No we don't need any help, Olivia, but thank you so much for asking.'

Within no time at all, the process of dismantling Frances' life was swiftly put into action. A large white van appeared outside the house and over the space of two hours, pieces of carefully selected furniture, and meticulously wrapped items of value, were loaded, ready to be transported to the auction house where Simon and Sarah had dealings. Items to be kept were fitted neatly into Simon's car, and the rest of the contents of the house were boxed up for charity.

A 'for Sale' board was nailed to the fence when all signs of life had been sucked out of the building until nothing remained but an empty, dusty shell.

The eulogy of Frances Adelia Alice Fenton, nee Gerard, bore little resemblance to the woman Liv had come to know and love. When it came to the part of 'loving wife and Mother' she looked at the priest reading from a script provided by Simon in full knowledge that the man had never even heard of Frances until after her death. Yet here he was extolling a life presented to him on a piece of paper. Of course, it was devoid of that most momentous event in her life; of course, he had no knowledge, and neither did her son. And had it not been for a simple twist of fate, Olivia Smithson would never have known either. It would have gone with her, buried in the grave beside which they all later stood. Ashes to ashes; dust to dust.

Liv watched Simon brush a handkerchief across his eyes and blow his nose, it was a brief return to the man who had revealed a different aspect than the cold exterior.

'I did love her you know...when I was young she was every-thing to me...when it was just the two of us...Father was often away and we were close...she loved me then.'

'So why did things change?'

Simon couldn't answer, couldn't put words to the dark thoughts of the actions he could barely acknowledge. Sitting beside his Mother's bed as she slept, his mind had been in turmoil, trying in vain to formulate the conversations they should have had long before then. And then after her death, Sarah arrived. Liv had glimpsed another Simon at the hospital, but like a clam, his shell snapped shut upon the arrival of his wife.

Following the funeral, the small group of mourners gathered in a private room at the local pub. A table had been laid with a simple spread of sandwiches, quiche, crisps and cakes. Barbara looked it over with a raised eyebrow as she filled a plate for Arthur from the savouries and salad, deftly passing over the cakes and biscuits. Arthur sat at one of the small tables dotted around, as instructed, and waited for his allotted fare.

'Nothing homemade on there that I could see' she whispered, 'That daughter-in-law doesn't look as though her hands have ever been stuck in a bowl of fat and flour...not with those nails' She presented Arthur with his food and nodded towards Sarah who was in conversation with an elderly colleague of Simon's, someone who had known his mother in the past. In recent years they had only exchanged Christmas cards.

Arthur picked out a leaf of limp lettuce from his sandwich, inspecting it before laying it to one side of the plate.

Sarah was working the room. She had on a black woollen dress, fittingly worn with a sad and sympathetic demeanour. She would make a point of personally thanking all who had come and ensure that they all had a drink from the bar to raise a toast to her Mother-in-Law. Sarah was nothing if not as meticulous, and as gracious, as the occasion demanded. Simon hung back, eating little and speaking only when approached; counting off the minutes until they could all leave.

Liv was the last to talk to him.

'I really miss Frances...your Mother was an incredible

lady...an inspiration to me. It's hard to think of her not being next door any more. I've not known her long but we had grown close you know.'

Simon shifted uncomfortably, looking from left to right, checking where Sarah was. She had her back to them and was now in conversation with Mrs Gilles from the daycare centre. She spoke from the script of feigned interest and asked the right questions, but barely listened to any response before moving on. Simon admired and despised his wife in equal measure that day but knew how much he needed her too.

'I know she told me...and I'm glad. She spoke highly of you. I should thank you for what you did for her. Most of her friends have long gone so yes...thank you for that.'

'It was my pleasure...and thank you for the box of scarves she left me.'

'She loved her scarves...it was quite a collection.'

'I've not had chance to look through them properly yet... didn't Sarah want any?'

Simon gave a smirk, knowing exactly what Sarah thought.

'I'm not sure that she would think they go with her style...and anyway, the box was meant for you...Olivia Smithson was clearly marked on the label.'

'Well...thank you anyway...you take care. Looks like we're going now...Mum's fretting about Dad, and Adam's driving us all to collect my daughter.'

'Right...you take care too.'

Liv took the proffered hand; it was the first time they had made any physical contact; it felt clammy; limp and uncomfortable. He pulled away quickly when he saw Sarah approach.

Liv was about to make her excuses to leave but as she prepared to say goodbye to his wife, Sarah turned away and faced Simon,

'Darling, people are starting to leave...you should say your goodbyes...come with me to the door.'

Only then did she acknowledge Liv.

'Goodbye Olivia...so nice to meet you.'

She did not wait for a reply.

Adam took Arthur and Barbara to Robert's with Liv. Arthur sat in the front, content nowadays to let someone else do the driving and happy for the male company to discuss the finer points of the United match coming up on Saturday. Adam had let him assume he was interested in their plight and even began to read up on the team's progress in the league so he could contribute to the conversation. Liv ribbed him mercilessly and would question him on the previous match before they went over, which they were doing on a regular basis now. Liv and Barbara sat at the back of the car comparing notes on the guests at the funeral and looking forward to having Bee join them.

'Simon's an odd one...not sure what to make of him but I did *not* take to that Sarah...hardly gave me two words and when she did, she might as well have not bothered.'

'I know...I don't know what to make of him...one minute I think he cares, the next he's a cold fish and I can't get anything out of him...I just know that Simon and his Mother weren't that close.'

'What was in that box he gave you anyway... apart from those old scarves...nothing else in there?'

'Just scarves I think.'

Barbara sniffed and moved on to other more important matters like what they were having for tea when the buffet they'd had 'barely touched the sides'.

Returning from school the next day with Bee, Liv looked up at the windows next door. For just a moment, she could see Frances' face peering from behind the curtain, smiling. A breeze from an open window was blowing nets that otherwise hung as lifeless as the house itself. She felt the loss in her life, but at the same time was grateful for what they'd had, and the legacy Frances left behind. Frances Fenton would not be erased as easily as the contents of a house.

Chapter Forty Eight

Two weeks after the funeral, when Bee had gone to bed, and Liv was musing over the rollercoaster of the past month, she brought out the box of scarves from the bottom of her wardrobe and tipped the contents on to the floor. She ran her fingers through silks so fine and delicate, they barely weighed anything at all. The colours were as vibrant as the day they had been packed and Liv wondered why they had come to her, and why she had never seen Frances wearing any of them.

Simon had come across the box during the house clearance. It had sat hidden underneath his Mother's bed until the furniture had been removed. The name Olivia Smithson was clearly marked on the lid. He looked inside of course but found nothing more than an assortment of silk squares. He recognised names on some of the labels and thought perhaps they might have some value, but Sarah assured him that there was nothing to warrant not giving them to the intended recipient. She merely shrugged her shoulders at the collection and told him to pass them on. She was feeling generous after the greater haul they had both acquired.

Simon could just about recalled the glamorous figure of

his Mother wearing one of them around her neck when going out to dinner with his Father. She'd kissed him goodnight and he reached out to touch the bold animal print. The smell of her perfume lingered long after she left the room but he remembered it still.

Simon took the box next door on the morning he and Sarah were due to leave, before the funeral, and wished her well. He had begun to like Olivia but knew it was unlikely that they would ever meet again once his Mother was buried. He briefly wondered what life would have been like with someone like her in his life, a woman who was the opposite to Sarah in every way.

That evening was the first opportunity Liv had had to properly examine the contents of the box. She delighted in handling items of such exquisite beauty. Even if they were something she would not wear herself, she would treasure them, perhaps even put them to some other use. She puzzled over the choice of gift but even so appreciated the gesture. The box was beautiful too. The warm, smooth patina of the wood demanded to be touched and the lid was inlaid with an intricate fleur-de-lis.

She laughed to herself when she realised that the scarf at the bottom was a Picasso design, a seated woman dressed in varying shades of cerise, blue and green. She took it out and, and with it came several layers of thin tissue. The base came up too and beneath there was more. Within more tissue nestled a small packet, marked only by a date: 16th June 1932. She turned it over and around before carefully opening the top.

Inside Liv discovered a small sketch: a drawing of the head and shoulders of a young woman. The portrait reflected a sure and steady hand where firm sweeping strokes and lines brought clarity, beauty and simplicity. Liv was overawed. This carefully preserved work of art was almost as fresh as the day it had been drawn sixty years earlier.

The sketch wasn't signed, and on further inspection, gave nothing away on the back either. But the style was unmistakable. Liv was in no doubt about the treasure she held in her hands and it excited her. Her heart beat fast when she brought to mind the artist and his young sitter. 'Oh Frances, is this what you told me about. Is this part of your story?

The treasure didn't stop there. Two photographs had fallen to the floor, released captives from years of incarceration. The first, despite age and natural fading through the passage of time, also showed the head and shoulders of a young woman. The similarity to the drawing was astounding. Liv lay them side by side for closer inspection. This certainly wasn't some anonymous young woman.

Luminous eyes, gazing out into the far distance, were set in a face whose features spoke only of Frances. The dark hair, parted on one side, hung in loose waves about the shoulders, setting off a delicate necklace fitting close into her neck. Her head was tilted away, as though unaware of the photographer, mirroring to perfection the portrait.

She picked up the second photograph. It caught her breath. Here was a young girl, possibly four or five years of age, posing in a white dance dress in a studio. She held out her skirt with both hands and her left knee was slightly bent as if about to make a curtsy. A small white headband held back her hair and ever so slightly, she was biting her bottom lip. It was a tender moment beautifully captured. The back of the photograph gave all the information she needed:

'Hermione Florence Fenton, 12th March 1933 – 15th October 1938.'

Liv stared long and hard before placing it alongside the other two likenesses. Her eyes misted at the realisation of what she had before her. 'So this was your daughter. Your Hermione.'

Sadness engulfed her heart at the thought of what Frances

had lost. The dates and age suggested that Hermione couldn't have lived much longer after the photograph had been taken. Liv studied the dates once again and her eyes grew wide at the implication of what they could mean.

'Is this is the final chapter? Is this what you wanted me to know Frances? You couldn't put it in words so you gave me the these.'

Liv propped the photographs on her desk. Picking up a pen, and recalling Frances' own words when she'd told her story, she wrote across the top of a blank sheet of paper, 'Paris, Picasso and Me'.

Also By S.F. Taylor

SHADOW CHILD

1969

Yorkshire

Julia lay in her small cramped bed crushed against the wall of her bedroom. She felt like Lewis Carroll's Alice, found down a hole in to a room she had long outgrown.

She'd woken up unusually early this particular morning for three reasons: first, was the vivid violence of the dream she'd had for two nights in a row; the second was her uncontained excitement for the day ahead; and lastly the sultry heat of a room that had not cooled down from the day before. One leg flicked aside the thin sheet covering her body. Her foot found its way to the floor where it came across a school tie, trailing from the rest of the uniform stuffed under the bed. None would be needed for the sixth form and would not be missed.

She caught the tie between her toes and brought it up to her outstretched hand. The fraying blue and white fabric still held the badges of 'Prefect' and 'Constable House', both of which should have been handed in at the end of the summer term. She threw it back on the floor where it snaked across a well-read copy of Wuthering Heights, flattened open at Mr Lockwood's grip of Cathy's arm when she demanded to be let in.

What Julie lacked in life, she made up with a vivid imagination and the passage never failed to give a shiver of excitement. She became Cathy, wanting her own Heathcliff.

Julie yawned and stretched her legs, pushing aside the memory of the nightmare. The woman in the long brown, blood-stained dress was no more than a dress of her own hanging from the door.

It wasn't the first time sleep had been disturbed by bad dreams. They usually came after reading torrid passages of books that gripped her. She looked at the dress and remembered that it was too tight. 'Nothing fits anymore! Everything is too frumpy, too small; clothes, shoes, this awful house ...I want to scream!'

The clock in the downstairs hall chimed eight, Julia curled up in the bed ready to feign sleep before her parents left for work for the day. She heard her mother downstairs in the kitchen; the aroma of toast making its way up through the walls and hollow staircase.

Audrey Cavaner was at the sink; hands plunged deep into hot foaming water, washing up with regimental efficiency. Tightly permed hair framed a ruddy complexion and her mouth was pursed and set firm. She wasn't happy., as she often was nowadays when facing another battle of will with her daughter. The loss of the compliant little girl grieved her with its intensity and the lack of control brought a seismic shift in their relationship. Friday night's argument still unresolved made her tense.

Tom was no use with his 'Let it go, Audrey, she's growing up. You'll only make yourself ill fretting smooch.' He was never any use preferring quiet life, and let things go easily, but it would come to no good, of that she was sure.

Getting home so late, and where was she anyway until that time?

Audrey dried her hands on the tea towel undraped stover the oven handle to dry. The flush of the toilet upstairs signalled that they would be ready to leave. Audrey looked up at the ceiling as if she could see through to Julia's bedroom but remained seated at the kitchen table waiting with her bag and cardigan. Tom started early at the docks and Audrey was always first in for the early shift at the grocery shop in town.

Julia too read the signal of departure and turned onto her back, relieved that her mother had chosen not to come in. She looked around her room. Maybe it wasn't all that bad and at least it was a space she could claim as her own. It was some consolation for having to live under the same roof as a mother who understood absolutely nothing.

The walls of the bedroom, or what could be seen beneath the posters, prints and photos were 'French Grey' according to the colour chart she had eventually been allowed to choose from. Audrey hated it of course. Julia had picked out the colour not because she liked it but because it was French and sounded sophisticated. She had been reading Madame Bovary at the time and was introduced to Rimbaud at the beginning of the last term by the new young English teacher, Miss Hamilton, who was evidently pleased that one of her pupils took such an interest outside the curriculum. And there were only so many times she could re-read Wuthering Heights. 'Julia', she would say, 'you are a star pupil...' and would bring in works that Julia had never even heard of, including poetry, Rimbaud's 'Voyells' caught her imagination and she loved the words long before discovering the translation. It was not written out in a neat sans serif script and pinned up on the French grey wall above the single bed: "Je dirai quelque jour sous naissances latentes" The secret birth... it sounded so deliciously mysterious. Not something Maggie or Billy and the others would take an interest in. Maggie would want every detail of the nightmare though; she would love that.

Rays of sunlight shone knife-like into the room revealing piles of clothes around the floor, all tried on and discarded the day before. The dressing table displayed a fabulous rainbow of colours spilling out from tubs and tubes of cheap makeup bought from the market in town. After hours of practice, the remains waited for today's effort, 'Why can't I look like the models? How do they do it? Easy to achieve 'look of the season', yeah right.'

Magazine photographs were taped to the mirror. Beautiful girls, beautifully made-up, shone out from the covers of 'Jackie' and 'Teen', pictures of perfection and endlessly happy lives.

Julia's reverie was broken by footsteps on the stairs. She held her breath in the hope she would be left in peace, but it was short-lived when a tap on the bedroom door preceded her mother's face appearing in the room, 'Julia,' she said. 'Julia, we're going now.' Audrey waited for an answer, hoping to end the feud between them, but Julia's response was toter and face the wall and pull up the covers over her head. 'Don't like that love, you know it was wrong. We were worried sick.'

After Friday's confrontation, Julia was still smarting from its repercussions and had no intention of giving way. Arriving home from the school dance two hours later than promised hadn't gone down well and she might have apologised but for the prolonged and relentless arguments that followed. The result was her mother demanding an apology that never came and, promises that would not be given. She strode into the room, opening the curtains with a flourish, 'Stop it, it's too bright!'

'It's gone eight Julia, and I've left you a list downstairs of jobs to do from; it's time you got up anyway. Think about what I said last night and we'll talk about it when your dad and get home.'

'No,' she groaned, 'not again, I've told you, we just...'

'I was worried sick.'

Audrey looked down at her daughter, at a loss to what more she could say or do. With arms folded tight across her chest, she sighed, lingering in the hope of a response but none was given.

'We'll be back at six. Don't stay in bed all day, will you?

Julia lay still until the sound of car tyres crunching over the gravel drive reached her ears. She stretched over to the little radio behind the clock, turned it on and Fleetwood Mac echoed through its tinny little speakers as she lay back down remembering every minute of Friday night.

About the Author

 facebook.com/sftaylorauthor

twitter.com/suefrasertaylo1

instagram.com/soofraser